The Dark Night of the Soul

The DARK NIGHT *of the* SOUL

DANIEL HRYHORCZUK

Golden Bough, LLC
850 W. Jackson Blvd.
Suite 330
Chicago, IL 60607
goldenboughpress@gmail.com

This is a work of fiction. All of the characters, organizations, and events portrayed in this novel are either productions of the author's imagination or are used fictionally.

ISBN: 978-1-7352400-3-9
LCCN: 2024918550

To my granddaughter, Maria Zoriana

My previous novels – *Caught in the Current, Myth and Madness,* and *Amerikana* – explored the trials of youth: coming of age, individuation, and the search for belonging. Now, in the winter of my life, I wonder what awaits us when we die: Divine Light or the Abyss of Unknown Nothingness? Most of us are afraid to seek the answer for ourselves and put our faith in the doctrines of the great religions. Several years ago, I set out on a spiritual journey to search for an answer, or at least, to ask the right questions. I read thousands of pages that covered the spectrum from religion, mysticism and metaphysics to quantum reality. As a Ukrainian Byzantine-rite Catholic, my journey began and ended with the mystery of faith. In my novel, Lev Veles, an aging Ukrainian writer living in Venice, undertakes a spiritual journey in the hope of reconciling with his Russian daughter, Sophia, and making his life cohere. Father Stephan, a Basilian monk, advises him that "there are many paths to the Great Liberation, and the way of Christ works best for me." I too believe that there are many paths to achieving union with the Absolute. As I was grappling with metaphysics, Russia invaded Ukraine with the intent of destroying her as a nation. I realized that my own quest for coherence was taking place in a world that I had ceased to understand, where as George Orwell foresaw, "War is peace. Freedom is slavery. Ignorance is strength." I decided to tell the story of Lev Veles's spiritual journey against the background of the pandemic and Russia's war on Ukraine.

—Daniel Hryhorczuk

CHAPTER 1

Carnival

Lost souls wandered the streets of Venice. Lev Veles spied them through the eyes of his Plague Doctor mask as he strode through the maze of Sestiere San Marco on his way to Palazzo Rivelli. The souls seemed to linger near the bridges as if they were afraid to cross. Lev had been haunted by visions since the pandemic began. At first they were just shadows in the corners of his eyes, lurking and emerging as the sun arced over the dying city and the water ebbed and flowed with the tides. But at sunset the shadows assumed human form. He thought he recognized some of the faces: a priest who had heard his confession, a widow who had shared her dark secret, a courtesan who had given him some solace. Lev tried to avert their gaze, but they clung to him like beggars. He waved them away with his cane.

A Dead Bride chased him up the steps of the Rialto Bridge.

"Lev, is that you?"

Lev turned around to see a skull with red lipstick and yellow hair in a wedding veil. He raised his cane.

The Dead Bride laughed and lifted her mask. "Did I give you a fright? Look, it's me, Angela. I thought it was you behind that hideous beak."

"You startled me." Lev lowered his cane.

"Am I really that scary in this costume?"

"No. It's just that I've been seeing things of late."

"What kinds of things?"

"Apparitions . . . ghosts of those who have recently passed. In our Byzantine Christian faith, we Ukrainians believe that the souls of the departed wander the earth for forty days after they die."

Angela Rose climbed the few steps that separated them and tucked her arm into his. "What on earth do they do?"

"They try to reconcile with their life before undergoing final judgement. At first, they visit the people and places that are familiar to them. Then evil spirits confront them, accuse them of their sins, and try to drag them into hell."

"What an imagination!" Angela declared. "You must include these superstitions in your next novel. But for now, it's Carnival! Life is for the living. What do you think of my Dead Bride costume? Authentic to the last detail!" She lifted the hem of her lace wedding dress to reveal a long, lithe leg sheathed in a white stocking held up by a garter. The only mar to her beauty was her Dead Bride mask with its skull sockets, red sardonic grin, and yellow ribbons for hair.

"You're as seductive as ever," Lev replied, "even in death."

Angela Rose was an American heiress who had moved into her family's palazzo before the pandemic began. She was a stunning beauty who flaunted her promiscuity. She had several well-publicized affairs with actors, politicians, and royals. By the age of forty-five, she had divorced two husbands and was separated from a third. Lev wondered whether he was next on her list. He was an attractive man for his years, and his reputation as a licentious expat writer had captured the imagination of women who were tempted to take a bite of the apple. When Contessa Rivelli first introduced him to Angela at the Teatro La Fenice in December, she warned her: "Don't be beguiled by our esteemed author. The gossip from Paris is that he's a bit like our Lord

Byron: 'mad, bad, and dangerous to know.'"

Lev and Angela stopped at the top of the Rialto Bridge to savor the remains of the day. A lone *vaporetto* ferried costumed passengers along the Grand Canal. *Charon crossing the River Styx*, Lev thought. They watched as the water darkened and the colors of the stone banks and buildings faded from orange and red to violet and blue. The lights of the Rialto Bridge overtook the fleeting rays of the sun.

"Venice never ceases to amaze me with her beauty," Angela said.

"*La Serenissima*," Lev replied. "A good place to die."

* * *

The invitation to Contessa Rivelli's masquerade ball was handwritten on Venetian marbleized paper, personally addressed, and sealed in red wax with the family crest. The theme of the ball, "Remember the Future," celebrated the reopening of Carnival after a two-year hiatus. Though the Covid case count continued to climb, the pandemic restrictions were easing. The invitees included the crème de la crème of Venetian society and a handful of ex-pats who, like Lev and Angela, had made the guest list through fame or fortune. Lev's latest novel, *The Storyteller*, about Ukraine's Revolution of Dignity, had just won the European Book Prize. Angela's recent donation to the "Save Venice" foundation was the largest in its history. The Rivelli dynasty had been hosting a Carnival ball for Venice's high society for centuries. The ball was as much a Venetian tradition as the Flight of the Angel and the silent regatta. A novel virus was not going to stop it. The contessa had insisted that the invitees wear masks since it was, after all, a masquerade.

The Gothic façade of Palazzo Rivelli, with its three-foiled arches and inlays of red, blue, and gold marble, had graced the right bank of the Grand Canal since the 15th century. The dignitaries arrived to the *porta d'acqua* in launches and gondolas. Less illustrious guests were politely asked to enter through the pedestrian gate in the rear of the palazzo. A servant in a Harlequin costume stood watch at the medieval gates and allowed only those with invitations to enter. The wrought-iron gates opened into a moonlit courtyard surrounded by an exotic garden of palms, fruit trees, and rue. In the center of the courtyard, a spring nymph fountain trickled rivulets of water into a green pool. A worn flagstone path led to a raised bed with dormant plants and a wooden sign that read: HORTUS SANITATIS. Mandrake roots were crawling out of the earth like the dead rising from their graves. One of the roots had an uncanny resemblance to a human face.

"Stop staring at that creepy garden and let's join the fun," Angela said.

"Yes, of course," he replied. "I just find it curious that a family as wealthy as the Rivellis would grow their own medicinal plants."

He led her up an exterior marble staircase with vine-covered balustrades that climbed up from the garden to the *piano nobile*. The sound of music and laughter emanated from within. At the top of the stairs, they entered an antechamber adorned with frescoes of Artemis and Apollo. A maid in a *La Moretta* – black, velvet mask – offered flutes of prosecco and *fritelle* – sweet fritters filled with zabaglione – before the guests passed through the *portego* into the majestic rooms of the *piano nobile*. The *portego* was a grand hallway illuminated with Murano glass chandeliers and adorned with floor to ceiling oil paintings that depicted the major events in the rise of the Rivelli dynasty. Conte Rivelli, who had made his fortune in age-defying cosmetics, had restored the main floor of the palazzo to its original grandeur.

Contessa Rivelli, dressed as the Black Widow, greeted the dignitaries who arrived to the *porta d'acqua* by boat. She paid little attention to the guests who came in through the pedestrian gate. Her face was hidden behind a lacquered mask with pitch-black eyes and lips. Her figure was shrouded in a black lace dress, cape, and gloves. Her only adornments were dangling, black pearl earrings and a black lace fan. She looked like she had just buried her husband.

The contessa portrays the Black Widow to respect those who perished in the pandemic, Lev surmised, *as do I with my Plague Doctor mask.* For a moment he considered coming up to her to announce their arrival, but decided against it. He would find an opportunity later in the evening when the contessa was less engaged. The captivating music of George Shearing's "Lullaby of Birdland" drew him into the ballroom. With Angela in hand, they entered the palatial ballroom with its arched windows and balconies that overlooked the Grand Canal. The swing-era band with its celebrity torch singer had been flown in from New York specifically for the occasion. Costumed guests were mingling in small groups, but given the pandemic and the contessa's mournful garb, none had yet had the nerve to dance.

Angela tried to pull Lev onto the dance floor. "Dance with me. I feel really sexy in this wedding dress. I feel absolutely horny."

Lev pulled her back. "It's crass to dance when so many around us are dying. For now, let's just enjoy the music and appreciate the splendor of this place."

"Don't be such a downer," she replied. "You could dance on my grave, and I'd welcome it. We need to enjoy life while we still have it."

Lev marveled at the architectural grandeur of the ballroom as it soared from the inlaid marble floor up the majestic windows and ornate pilasters to a fresco of the Holy Trinity on the ceiling. *The celestial fresco must have taken years to complete*, he thought. God the Father and Son sat on thrones of billowy clouds with the Holy Spirit above Them. Dominions surrounded the Trinity followed, in a heavenly hierarchy, by the Cherubin, Seraphim, and lesser angels. The lowest circle included notable Venetians who had earned their place in heaven. Below the lower circle were the domes and rooftops of Venice. With his ingenious concentric design, the artist made it appear that the view of the Trinity was the same from wherever one stood in the ballroom. The observers looking up from the floor seemed trapped in the mortal realm unless they could atone for their sins and ascend to heaven above.

"Fascinating, isn't it?" a voice said behind them. "Wherever you stand, you have the illusion that God is looking down at you."

Lev and Angela turned to see Conte Rivelli standing behind them. Their host was wearing a simple *Bauta* – ghost mask – with a white wig, dark coat, and a tricorn hat. The simplicity of his garb belied his elegance.

"Conte Rivelli," Lev began, "allow me to introduce . . ."

"Signora Rose," the conte interrupted. "Your bride and I are intimately acquainted. You are, my dear, as ravishing as a Maenad."

"A Maenad? I don't know whether to be flattered or offended."

"A follower of Dionysus," Lev explained. "The conte, I believe, was calling you a free spirit."

"Lascivious nonetheless," the conte said and kissed her hand. "If not for our masks, I would have kissed you on the lips."

Lev put his arm around Angela's waist. "Our host is playing his role of Casanova to perfection," he said. "Perhaps he can tell us more about the fresco overhead."

The Plague Doctor, Dead Bride, and Ghost raised their eyes to heaven.

"A masterpiece. It took years and a small fortune to restore. It was painted by Amico D'Albo, a student of Veronese, and completed in 1577, the year of the plague. He succumbed to the Black Death shortly after completing it. He included himself among the Venetians." He put his hand on Angela's shoulder. "Perhaps our lovely Bride can guess which one he is."

Angela studied the faces of the departed with their hands clasped and eyes raised to heaven. "I think he's the one closest to the angels."

"And your guess, signor Veles?"

"I think he's the one closest to Venice. You see the young man just over the Basilica? Though his hands are clasped in prayer, his eyes do not look up to God. They look at us instead."

"Very perceptive," the conte said. "But why?"

"I think that he sees his immortality in his art and not in heaven above. As long as we see and appreciate his painting, he is, in a way, alive."

"Bravo!" The conte replied. "And the man with his head above the rest?"

"I would guess that he's the man who commissioned the fresco."

"Exactly. Antonio Rivelli, my great ancestor and the founder of the Rivelli dynasty. He was a soldier of fortune who earned his title during the Ottoman Wars. He was infamous for his bloodlust, but, with the grace of God, he became a benefactor of the church and a patron of the arts."

"So, he bought his way to heaven," Angela said.

"Perhaps," the conte winked as he stroked the yellow ribbons of her Dead Bride hair. "We are all sinners, are we not?"

The band struck up the "King Porter Stomp." A few intrepid guests stepped onto the dance floor and, uncertain of the moves, began stomping, shuffling, and cakewalking as if they were skipping on hot coals.

"I'm dying for a dance with signora Angela," Conte Rivelli said. "I've requested that the band play something a bit more romantic once they finish this St. Vitus dance. In the meantime, let me introduce you to two of our other English-speaking guests. I think that you, signor Veles, will find them most interesting."

Angela whispered in Lev's ear: "Save me."

Conte Rivelli led them across the ballroom to one of the balconies that overlooked the Grand Canal where an *Il Dottore* – Doctor – and an Alchemist were locked in a heated argument. They were shouting over the volume of the band.

"Signori," the conte interrupted. "What topic of discussion could possibly generate such passion?"

The Alchemist turned to face his host. He was wearing a gold half-mask, red leather hat, and a potions belt. Though the man's eyes were hidden, Lev could see from his grimace that the young man was flustered.

"We were debating the nature of God," the Alchemist explained. "My colleague was claiming that we are evolving into *Homo Deus*, while I was pointing out that we don't need another God who looks like us to understand our place in the universe."

Lev stepped into the conversation. "He who denies the existence of God has some reason for wishing that God does not exist."

"St. Augustine," the Doctor recognized the quote. He was dressed completely in black except for a white ruff around his collar. His *Il Dottore* mask covered only the forehead and nose signifying his character's strong thoughts and inquisitive intrusions. "I can see, sir, that you, unlike my brash young colleague, are a man of letters."

"Allow me to introduce you," the conte said. "Our *Medico Della Peste* is il signor Lev Veles, the acclaimed Ukrainian author. My wife tells me he is currently writing a novel set in Venice, so be wary because he will probe you for our darkest secrets. Our Dead Bride is la signora Angela Rose, a philanthropist from New York who is helping to restore our Venetian architectural treasures. Our *Il Dottore* is Dr. Jordan Brown, a Professor of Religious Studies from Northwestern University in Evanston, and our Alchemist is Dr. Elias Graf from the Max Planck Institute for Quantum Optics."

"You're quite young to have given up on God," Angela said eyeing Dr. Graf.

"Science is my religion, signora Rose. May I be so bold as to ask what you believe in?"

"I'm a girl without a philosophy," she replied.

From within the ballroom, the band struck up the "Forever Mine" waltz. Conte Rivelli offered his hand to Angela. "I believe, signora Angela, that they are playing our song."

Angela brushed back the yellow ribbons from her Dead Bride mask. She looked askance at Lev as if he had failed to save her. "Yes, let's dance and leave these scholars to their philosophizing."

Lev felt a tinge of jealousy. *So what if the conte is rich, aristocratic, and charming? He's also a pompous ass.* He saw his own macabre reflection in the glass of the open balcony door and regretted his choice of costume.

"And you, sir, do you believe in spirituality?" Professor Brown asked Lev.

"I'm a Byzantine-rite Catholic," Lev replied.

"Yes, but are you *spiritual?*"

"What's the difference?" Lev asked.

"Religion is a contract. Spirituality is a journey."

Lev looked over the balcony into the dark water of the Grand Canal. He was too young to remember the shock of the cold water as he was immersed into a baptismal font in the name of the Father, Son, and Holy Spirit, or anointed with the oil of gladness and swaddled in the white garment of righteousness. Someone had renounced Satan in his name. But those were not words he had spoken. Those were not choices he had made.

"Why do you say spirituality is a journey?" he asked.

"I'm sure you've wondered about the meaning of life," Professor Brown replied. "About why we are here?"

"My faith gives me the answers," Lev said. "I don't need to dwell on those questions."

Dr. Graf interjected. "But you *must*, sir. Socrates had said that 'the unexamined life is not worth living.' I'm surprised that you, a writer, haven't given it more thought."

A lone figure on an adjacent balcony was staring at them intently. He was dressed in a monk's robe with his face concealed in the shadow of the hood.

"That monk, or whoever he is in that costume, has been eavesdropping on our conversation," Lev said.

"That's Father Stephan," Professor Brown replied. "He's the contessa's spiritual advisor. He's promised to show her 'The Way.'"

"He's a real cleric?"

Father Stephan continued to stare at them, even though he could clearly hear that they were talking about him.

"He's a mystic," Dr. Graf said. "The contessa introduced us at one of her soiree's a few weeks ago. I'm not sure how much you really know about our hostess, but she dabbles in the occult: séances, tantric rituals, astral projection, and the like. I can't tell if it's from boredom or if she actually believes in this superstitious nonsense."

"That would explain her medicinal garden," Lev said.

"You should see her library," Professor Brown said. "It's something out of the Dark Ages. She let me peruse some of the volumes – original editions, some centuries old. It's her sacred place."

Lev had always assumed that Contessa Rivelli was just another decadent aristocrat whose main amusement was to trifle in the lives of others. He was intrigued that there was this other side to her.

"This library of hers. Where might I find it?"

"Hidden in plain sight," Professor Brown replied. "It's on the floor above us. You can reach it by going up the stairs on either end of the *portego*. There's a red door emblazoned with golden apotropaic symbols that opens into the library. The key has been in the door each time I've been up there. With all of the revelry down here, you might want to sneak up and take a peek."

"Will you accompany me?" Lev asked.

"No, we'll draw too much attention. Pretend you're looking for a bathroom."

"Perhaps another time," Lev said. "I'll ask the contessa to show it to me herself."

"It's been a pleasure talking to you," Professor Brown said. "You listen before you speak, unlike our brash Dr. Graf."

"I need a drink," Dr. Graf said and stormed back into the ballroom.

"Let me give you my card," Professor Brown said. "I'm currently doing a sabbatical in ancient heritage studies at Ca' Foscari University which is walking distance from here. I'd like to share some of my views on spirituality with someone like yourself, an enlightened man who might be willing to delve into the topic more deeply."

"I'd like that," Lev said, "but right now I need to rescue signora Rose from Casanova."

Lev noticed that the band had switched from the "Forever Mine" waltz to Italo disco several numbers ago. He reentered the ballroom where the bacchanalia was now in full swing. Scores of *Baute, Morette,* and *Gnaghe* – cat masks – swirled around him. He zigzagged through the dancers searching for his Dead Bride. Though they had arrived together by chance, her dalliance with their host was an affront to his virility. He had felt a connection with her when they first met at La Fenice two months before, yet despite her flirtations, he hadn't found the time to pursue her. His writing had gotten in the way. Now that a rival was seeking her attention, he needed to have her. He searched for her in each room of the *piano nobile* without success. He stopped at the foot of the marble stairs and decided to look for her on the upper floor.

The upper floor was a maze of odd-size rooms that had been reconfigured multiple times over the centuries. The one common architectural feature was a labyrinthine hallway illuminated with mirrored glass sconces. Generations of Rivellis stared down from the dark portraits that hung on its red velvet walls. Lev heard a panting from behind one of the doors. He opened it a crack to peek in. The beak of his Plague Doctor mask protruded through the crack in the chamber door. Angela was astride the conte on a four-post bed. They were naked except for their masks. As her hips rose and fell, the yellow ribbons of her mask flailed to and fro. The conte glanced at him through his ghost mask and continued his lovemaking unabated. Lev withdrew and closed the door.

I'm such a fool to believe that there was something between us. At the far end of the hallway, he saw a red, arched door engraved with gilded apotropaic symbols. A key was left in the lock, as if tempting the intruder to enter. *Why the hell not?*

He turned the key and opened the door. The faint light from the doorway revealed a cavernous room with a vaulted ceiling, ornate bookcases, and stained-glass windows. He flipped a switch, and clusters of milky-white bulbs suspended from a cross-beam chandelier illuminated the room like stars. The Sacred Seal of Solomon was inscribed on a midnight-blue wall. While Professor Brown had referred to the space as a library, it was actually an alchemic laboratory. Arcane instruments, such as cucurbits, alembics, and lutes were laid out on workbenches. Glass cabinets held sundry containers of powders, elixirs, and botanicals labeled with strange symbols. Contorted creatures, from amphibians to hominid-like fetuses, were preserved in bottles of formalin. A monastery table in the center of the room was strewn with books and occult paraphernalia. A fireplace at the end of the room had been converted into a smelting furnace.

As a writer, Lev was naturally drawn to the books. The tomes on the table spanned centuries. Several were written in Latin with names like *Clavicula Salomonis, Corpus Hermiticum,* and *Libro de San Cipriano.* Others were Italian translations of ancient texts, such as the *Coptic Magical Papyri* and the Arabic *Picatrix.* Lev paged through a book titled *Arbatel de Magia Veterum.* It appeared to be bound in human skin. Though he had studied Latin in secondary school, he was only able to decipher portions of the text. Cryptic symbols on the pages depicted the heavenly orbs.

"The magic of the ancients," a voice said behind him.

Lev turned around to see Father Stephan standing in the doorway.

The monk's face was hidden in the shadow of his hood. Lev wondered if he was yet another vision sent to torment him, some Rasputin returned from the grave. "You followed me?" Lev asked.

"You look lost, and I'm glad I found you."

"Do you even know who I am behind this mask?"

"The author, Lev Veles. I've read your novel, *The Storyteller*, about the Revolution of Dignity. I found your literary use of magical realism quite insightful." Father Stephan looked at the grimoires that were scattered on the long table. He had spent many hours in the contessa's library perusing her remarkable collection. "You seem drawn to the supernatural."

Lev looked at the brass crucifix that hung from around Father Stephan's neck. "Who are we to say what's real and what's not?"

"Faith, Mr. Veles, faith."

"I believe in God, but I also believe in demons."

"As do I," Father Stephan replied. "But have you seen them?"

Lev was surprised by the directness of the question. "I sometime see things that others do not."

"Visions can be part of one's spiritual journey. The supernatural creatures in your novel, *The Storyteller* – have you actually encountered them?"

Lev hesitated to bare his soul to a stranger. "Why are you so interested in what I have or haven't seen?"

Father Stephan lowered his hood. He was a round-faced man with a trimmed black beard, bushy eyebrows, and a disarming smile. His eyes, however, were piercing, as if they had seen things that no living man should see. "I apologize if I'm being overly inquisitive. It's for my doctoral research. But regardless of whether these beings actually exist, the events you foretold in your novel have come to pass. I too share a Ukrainian heritage – my parents emigrated to the United States after the Second World War. Do you regret leaving Ukraine?"

"Ukraine is a country for heroes. I'm an old man."

"Do not underestimate the power of words. Your pen is mightier than you think."

"You were eavesdropping on our conversation on the balcony below.

Why?"

"I've read about your political journey, your escape from the Soviet Union, your expatriate life in Paris, and your return to Ukraine to participate in the Revolution of Dignity. On the balcony below, I overhead you talking about embarking on a spiritual journey. I thought I could share some insights from my own research on the passage of the soul."

"Dr. Graf said you're a mystic."

"I am but a humble priest who leads others to God. There's a small, Byzantine-rite church by the name of San Basilio's on Campo Venere. Do you know it?"

"I've walked through the campo on my way to the seafood market, but can't say that I've noticed it."

"It's a simple, red stucco building with a Byzantine dome and cross which aren't visible from the street. I suspect that's why there are so few visitors. The interior, on the other hand, is marvelous. The mosaics in the iconostasis rival the finest in Ravenna. It's a beautiful place to pray."

"Are you the pastor there?" Lev asked.

"For the time being. Father Sylvester passed away from the pandemic, and I was reassigned to take his place until they can find another monk from my Basilian order who is more fluent in Italian than I am. I will then return to my studies."

"Professor Brown said that you are the contessa's spiritual advisor."

"The contessa expressed a desire to follow in the footsteps of St. Teresa. I'm showing her the way."

"Does the path involve studying the "magic of the ancients?" Lev asked, pointing to the *Arbatel.*

Father Stephan came up to the table and turned the fragile pages of the book to the title page. "The *Arbatel de Magia Veterum* is a fascinating grimoire. As you can see from the imprint, this particular edition was published in Switzerland in 1575. It focuses on the relationship between man and the celestial hierarchies, whomever you believe them to be. It contains ceremonial spells . . ."

"Curses? Black magic?" Lev asked.

"Unlike other grimoires, it actually exhorts the magus to help their community, favoring kindness, charity, and honesty."

"Are you telling me that the contessa is a *good* witch?"

"She is, as were her ancestors before her, a *Benandante*, a *good walker*. She strives to eliminate evil from the world."

"Does she also turn base metals into gold?"

Father Stephan smiled. "Alchemy is not what you imagine it to be. The purpose of alchemy, whether spiritual or physical, is to complete the work of perfection, bringing forth the 'latent goldness' which lies obscure in metal or man."

"I find it hard to believe that you, a Catholic priest, would condone this kind of magical thinking."

"For the contessa, alchemy is but a starting point in her spiritual journey. He waved his hand as if to discount the occult paraphernalia around them. "I'm helping her to transcend from the magical to the mystical, from the left-hand path to the right-hand path." With word "mystical," he crossed himself in the Eastern tradition, moving his right hand from his forehead to his heart and from his right shoulder to his left.

"Isn't magic just another form of mysticism?" Lev asked.

"Magic is the antithesis of mysticism. Magic wants to get, while mysticism wants to give."

"I don't understand."

"Magic is the deliberate exaltation of the will, until it transcends its limitations and obtains for the practitioner the power to manipulate the visible world. It's an individualistic practice, seeking reality for one's own purpose."

"I can see what magic wants to get," Lev said. "But what does mysticism want to give?"

"Oneself," Father Stephan replied. "It's the abolition of individuality."

"For what purpose?"

"For union with the Absolute."

Lev lifted his mask so he could look at Father Stephan face to face. "Can't we just wait until we die to meet our Maker?" he asked.

"Death is certain. Union with God is not."

Lev heard shouts in the hallway. "You demon!" Angela screamed.

He ran out of the library and saw the yellow ribbons of Angela's Dead Bride mask disappearing down the stairs at the other end of the hallway.

"I need to go after my friend," Lev said to Father Stephan. "Perhaps we can continue . . ."

"Come by San Basilio's church at any time," Father Stephan replied. "I'll be waiting for you."

Lev rushed down the hallway in pursuit of the Dead Bride. He glanced into the open bedroom where the Bauta, naked and shriveled from the neck down, bowed and tipped his tricorn hat. Lev caught up to Angela at the bottom of the stairs that led into the *portego*. The back of her wedding dress was unbuttoned. Her back was scratched. When he touched her on the shoulder, she recoiled and turned to slap him, until she realized who it was. She fell into his arms sobbing.

"That heartless prick!"

Lev gently fastened the buttons on the back of her dress without saying a word.

"He called me a *tola*!"

Lev lifted the mask off her face. Her mascara was running down her face. "Your mask can be a bit frightening."

"He said I was as *lifeless* as a wooden statue – a wedding dress on the outside and dead on the inside."

"What did you do?"

"I slapped him and told him I had had enough. He then said something even worse."

"What did he say?" Lev asked.

"He said that the only things that never say enough are the grave, the barren womb, the parched earth, and fire."

"It's a biblical proverb."

"I'm not dead on the inside, am I?"

"I've never known anyone more full of life than you."

She took his hand and slid it down to her hips. "I'm not a barren womb. I chose not to have children. It's not that I couldn't."

"You don't have to explain," Lev said.

"But I do. I want you to understand me. I *need* for you to understand me. He called me a Maenad. They're not lifeless, are they?"

"They're immortal," Lev replied.

Angela gave him an open mouth kiss. "That's what I want to hear," she said. "I want you to be my Dionysus, and I'll be your Maenad."

The role of Dionysus, the god of pleasure, sounded much more appealing to Lev than the role of a Plague Doctor.

Contessa Rivelli, surrounded by a gaggle of costumed revelers, emerged from the ballroom into the *portego* and began marching towards them. Angela donned her mask and turned away. Lev was still holding his mask in his hand. He stepped forward to greet his host, but the Black Widow and her entourage passed by him without so much as a glance.

He soon saw the reason for the slight. The Doge had just arrived via the *porta d'acqua* with a retinue of lavishly costumed nobles and noblewomen. A woman dressed as the Dogaressa entered the *portega* from the *porta d'acqua* a few steps behind the Doge. She was escorted by a macabre figure in a blood-splattered burial shroud with a mask that depicted the rigid face of a corpse.

Who are these people masquerading as the Doge and Dogaressa? Lev wondered. *And who has the audacity to come dressed as a victim of the pandemic? It's beyond indecorous. It's mocking the dead.*

Lev put on his mask to avoid their evil eye. As the figure in the burial shroud straggled past them, it stopped, turned to Lev and said in a last-breath voice: "You're too late, *Medico della Peste*. You won't be able to save them."

This can't be real, Lev thought. *I'm still having visions.*

Angela was standing behind him, hiding from the accusing eyes of the contessa.

"Did you see . . . did you hear that plague victim speak to me?"

"He said you're too late to save them," Angela replied.

Lev thought of the mandrake in the medicinal garden that looked like a corpse crawling out of its grave. He felt as if the roots were encircling his own body and dragging him under the ground. "We need to leave here while we still can."

"Will you save me?" she asked.

Lev didn't know from what or from whom. "I'll protect you."

"Then stay with me tonight," the Dead Bride asked. "I'm afraid to be alone."

* * *

Father Stephan hurried down the dark, winding streets and stone bridges to get back to San Basilio's church in time for Compline – the night prayers. The evening at the Rivelli's Carnival ball had given him hope. He had found a lost soul who could still be saved. He nearly collided with a gaggle of drunken revelers who were laughing, staggering, and threatening to push each other into the canals. Beggars were crouched under the lampposts vying for their attention. One was rocking back and forth on his hands with only stumps for legs. Another was pretending to put a dead rat into his mouth. Father Stephan crossed himself, pulled the hood over his head, and continued to walk straight ahead. He had nothing to offer them but his prayers.

Campo Venere was quiet for the first night of Carnival. Most of the celebrants who braved the pandemic had crowded into Piazza San Marco where they could see and be seen. Father Stephan unlocked the medieval door of San Basilio's church and entered into the serenity of darkness. He lit a thin, beeswax candle and placed it into the sand base of the votive candle stand in front of the iconostasis. The icons, assembled from thousands of pieces of multi-colored glass, stone, and shell by Byzantine masters, shimmered in the light of the solitary candle. Father Stephan knelt before the altar, bowed his head, and recited the Jesus prayer until the candle burned down to the sand and his mind transcended from the physical world into the realm of the spirit.

Lord Jesus Christ, Son of God, have mercy on me, a sinner. Lord Jesus Christ, Son of God, have mercy on me, a sinner. Lord Jesus Christ, Son of God, have mercy on me, a sinner . . .

CHAPTER 2

The Dead Bride

Storm clouds gathered over Palace Square in St. Petersburg. A wet snow began to fall. Sophia watched from her window as small groups of protestors gathered in front of the Winter Palace. She placed a vinyl record on the turntable and turned up the volume. The music from Shostakovich's *Symphony No. 7* echoed through the vaulted ceilings and marble floors of her spacious apartment. She returned to the window and watched as cordons of police, their faces covered with balaclavas, took their positions. In contrast to the rigid columns of helmets and shields, the protestors marched about freely, chanting "No War!" and carried makeshift signs that pictured *Putler* – Putin with a Hitler moustache and bloodied hand over his face. The crowd swelled from dozens to hundreds to over a thousand. Sophia saw a dozen police vans drive up Admiralteyskiy Prospect towards Palace Square. When a young woman unfurled and waved a blue and yellow flag, the riot police pounced. They tackled her to the ground and dragged her away by her hair. Within minutes the demonstration devolved into mayhem. The police beat young and old indiscriminately. Those who didn't scatter were hauled into the waiting vans.

Sophia heard Alex fumbling with the three locks that secured the steel door to their apartment. He entered out of breath, having rushed up the five flights of stairs lugging his video gear. The birdcage elevator, like most other amenities in the common space, no longer worked. Inside, however, the apartment was luxurious by Russian standards. It was a gift from Andropov to her late stepfather, Sergei Borodin, to reward him for his many years of diplomatic service.

She ran up to Alex and hugged him as if afraid to ever let him go. "I have something important to discuss with you," she said.

"In a moment. I first need to gather my things."

"You're leaving?"

"Just for a short while." Alex recognized the clash of strings against the brutal rhythms of trumpets and tympani. "You're playing Shostakovich's *Seventh Symphony*. You saw what's happening in the square below."

"The *Seventh Symphony* was my stepfather's favorite. It celebrates the defense of Leningrad and the fight against fascism. It gives me hope."

"Fascism is again rearing its ugly head," Alex said, "but not in Ukraine as Putin claims. The beast is rising right here in Russia. How can Ukraine be run by Nazis? Ukraine has a Jewish president whose grandfather fought in the Red Army against the Nazis! Putin is perverting the truth. We have to stop him before he leads us into World War Three. I need to show our countrymen what's really happening."

"Alex, you're scaring me." She tried to hide the quiver in her voice.

"Sophia, this is bigger than the two of us. I heard today that Putin is planning to recognize the independence of the Donetsk and Luhansk People's Republics. You know what that means: *war*. Surely you can't stay indifferent at a time like this. Your mother was Ukrainian, wasn't she?"

Sophia was about to answer, but held her tongue instead. She wanted to tell him that her mother and biologic father both were Ukrainian, but that he was a scoundrel who had broken her mother's heart. Her stepfather, who suspected that Sophia was not his own child, nevertheless raised her as his own and offered her the privileges of being among the St. Petersburg elite. Ever since her mother died, Sophia hid her Ukrainian heritage. Her stepfather had told her that Ukrainians were the lesser brothers and sisters of the Russians; they were peasants who lived in the outland of the empire. Russia was her motherland – Ukraine was the stepchild.

"You know we're under surveillance. Whatever you're planning to do will put us both at risk."

"I'm going to Kyiv to expose these lies. I'm hoping to stop this war before it starts. What are they going to do, shoot me?"

"Kyiv? The border is closed to Russian men."

"Except for humanitarian purposes. A Ukrainian filmmaker, Andriy Orishkevich, has managed to get me an invitation from UNICEF to investigate the plight of children who were displaced from the war in Donbas. I can take the train to Minsk, pick up my documents, then drive by car to the border crossing at Novi Yarylovichi. Andriy will be waiting for me on the Ukrainian side."

Sophia and Alex had met six months ago. He was an *avant-garde* filmmaker who knew how to navigate the dangerous straits between what the Kremlin would tolerate and what it would not. His blog had over three hundred thousand followers, including several full-time trolls from the Internet Research Agency. Sophia, at the age of thirty-nine, had reached the pinnacle of her musical career. She was the first woman to be named as the chief conductor of the St. Petersburg Philharmonic Orchestra. As a member of the cultural elite, she was under constant surveillance by the Kremlin. The FSB had warned her to keep a close eye on her filmmaker boyfriend. What the Kremlin gave, it could just as easily take away.

"We both need to get out of Russia before Putin turns it into a Stalinist gulag. You could be a conductor with the best orchestras in Europe: Vienna, Amsterdam, Berlin . . ."

"Russia is my home," Sophia replied.

"Mine too. We'll leave for a few months, maybe a year or two. We'll return when this nightmare is over."

"You know I can't leave."

"But I have to," Alex said. "I'll be back when we've finished filming."

"Alex, please, no heroics."

"Nothing you can say will change my mind. This is my opportunity to save Russia from herself."

"Wait, I need to give you something before you go." Sophia went to her jewelry box and returned with a pendant of the Blessed Virgin Mary on a gold chain. The antique silver medal featured the *Pokrova*, a full-length image of the Mother of God. The Blessed Virgin was extending Her veil as a sign of protection. Sophia hung the pendant around his neck. "I received this for my birthday when I was a child. My mother said the Blessed Virgin would protect me. May She now protect you."

"I'll wear it always," Alex said.

Sophia helped him pack a small rollaway suitcase that held enough clothes for a week of travel. He kissed her and set off for the train station. Sophia watched from the window as he got into a taxi in front of their building. She was proud of him for his courage. Her gaze turned to the snowflakes that drifted past her window to the square below. Each was unique and beautiful, yet ephemeral. Before they could accumulate, they were trampled by boots and reddened by blood, melting into rivulets that drained into the sewers below. In his haste Alex had forgotten to ask what Sophia had wanted to tell him: she was ten weeks pregnant and was debating whether to keep their child.

* * *

Lev awoke in Angela's bed. The morning light streamed through the arched windows that overlooked the Grand Canal. The plush mattress, down pillows, and white satin sheets made him feel as if he had slept on a cloud. The place next to him was empty, but he could tell from the depression in the pillow and her scent on the sheets, that he had slept with the Dead Bride. Surprisingly, he had no recollection of getting into her bed. He had dreamt of gods and goddesses, of centaurs and Maenads, of orgiastic dances, and the pleasures of the flesh. He sat up in bed and saw his Plague Doctor costume on the floor atop a crumpled wedding dress. The yellow ribbons of her Dead Bride mask were intertwined around the beak of his Plague Doctor mask in a macabre kiss. The beak of the mask was stuffed with herbs.

Angela stepped into the bedroom. Her wet hair was wrapped in a towel. A silk robe caressed the contours of her curves. She undid the towel and ran her hands through her long golden hair. Lev felt himself getting hard.

"That bastard called me a *tola*. What in hell is a *tola*?"

"It's Venetian slang for a flat-chested woman."

Angela opened her robe to reveal her soft, ample breasts. "Do I look like a *tola* to you?"

"Your breasts are like two fawns, feeding among the lilies . . ."

"You're also a poet?"

"It's a verse from the Song of Solomon, a sensual poem from the Bible," he replied. "How . . .?"

"How were you last night?" She leaned over and gave him a luscious kiss. "You were Dionysus himself. How do you know so much about *tolas*?"

"I'm researching local lore for my new novel. It's a contemporary take on Thomas Mann's *Death in Venice*."

"About a man enamored of a youth?" she asked.

"I'm imagining an author who longs for the innocence of his lost youth. Until he reconciles with his past, he can't embrace the last chapter of his life."

"Are you writing about yourself?"

Lev reflected for a moment. "Perhaps."

Angela sat down on the bed and put her hand on his thigh. "You'd rather be an innocent boy than a decadent author?"

"The devil robbed me of my youth."

Angela saw the hurt in his eyes. She laid her head on his shoulder. Her wet blond hair touched his bare thighs. He tried to focus on something other than her body.

"Why are you setting your novel in Venice?" she asked.

"Because Venice is a city in love with her past, and she can't let go – she's dying, yet she sees itself as immortal. Centuries go by yet Venice remains the same. She's forever reliving her youth."

"I'm still young, aren't I?" Angela said. She took Lev's hand and ran his fingers from her lips to her cleavage. "You were telling me about *tolas*."

"Yesterday I went to see the *Festa delle Marie* – the procession of the Twelve Marias. It's a Venetian tradition that dates back to the 10th century. I learned that *tola* is short for '*Maria de tola,*' or "Mary made of wood. It's a captivating story."

"Then captivate me," she said. "I love stories."

"The tradition began with an event that happened during the Feast of the Purification of the Blessed Virgin Mary. To encourage marriage, twelve beautiful girls were chosen from among the poorer in Venice. The nobility provided them with beautiful clothes and dowries including jewels from the Doge's collection. The brides-to-be and their fiancés gathered at the Church of San Pietro di Castello, the seat of the bishop's palace of Olivovo. After the weddings the brides and their dowries traveled in procession to Piazza San Marco, where they were invited for a feast in the Doge's palace. They then rode in the Doge's ceremonial barge up the Grand Canal to the Rialto and up to the Church of Santa Maria Formosa for further celebrations."

"It sounds like a fairy tale. Is there an evil twist?"

"There is. Dalmatian pirates kidnapped the brides and stole the gold and jewels. They were going to sell the women into slavery."

Angela sighed. "That's all men ever want of us, sex and submission."

"But the story does have a happy ending. A squad of brave Venetians rescued the maidens, killed the pirates, and recovered the gold and jewels. As a reward they asked that the Doge visit their church, Santa Maria Formosa, annually on the anniversary of the kidnapping. The celebration of the marriages of the twelve Marias resumed, and people from far and wide came to view the annual procession of the beautiful maidens. Getting close to the Marias was considered a good omen. The Feast of Mary was eventually incorporated into the traditions of Carnival."

"Why were they called 'Marias made of wood?'"

"Because, horrifically, their admirers sometimes raped them. The organizers of the festival had to replace the maidens with marionettes. The word *tola* became slang for a flat-chested woman. The populace didn't take kindly to the change, and the marionettes were often pelted with stones and garbage. The celebration of the Feast of Mary was suppressed and didn't resume again until seven centuries later."

"So, you went to see a procession of marionettes?"

Lev laughed. "Fortunately, when the tradition was revived in recent times, real women replaced the figurines. I followed the procession from San Pietro di Castello, down Via Garibaldi and Riva degli Schiavoni to the Doges' Palazzo and Piazza San Marco. The most beautiful of the Marias was selected to be the Angel for next year's Carnival. She took my breath away."

Angela lifted her head and looked into his eyes. "Was she more beautiful than me?"

He slipped the robe off her shoulders. "Let me see your wings."

She playfully pushed him away. "I just took a long, hot shower. We'll have plenty of time to play angels and demons over the next several days. You promised to protect me, and I'm not letting you go."

Lev stood up off of bed. He felt more vigorous than he had in years.

Angela admired his naked body. Watching his erection rise and fall and rise again with her flirtations made her feel irresistible. She relished the power that she had over men.

"Take a shower and get dressed. I'll wait for you in the salon downstairs."

Lev picked up his costume off the floor.

Angela took it from his hands and tossed it back on the floor. "No more hideous costumes. We'll wear some simple ghost masks instead. My ex left some of his clothes in the armoire: Valentino, Versace, Gucci – whatever suits your fancy."

Lev opened the armoire and selected a pair of slacks, a cashmere sweater, and a jacket that looked like they would fit. He stepped into the master bathroom that was as large as his apartment in Corte del Milion. It glistened with white Carrara marble and gold fixtures. The mirror was still steamed from Angela's shower. He rubbed away the condensation to look at himself in the mirror. Contessa Rivelli had once remarked that he reminded her of the Italian actor Marcello Mastroianni. His hair was peppered with grey and the fine lines in his face denoted experience rather than age. His eyes were seductive, but haunting. Behind the mask of his persona, they reflected his shadow self, a psyche tormented by guilt and madness. He looked away from the mirror and stepped into the shower. The rush of hot water washed away the disturbing memories from the night before: the human face of the mandrake, the grimoire of the *Magic of the Ancients*, and the masque of the Red Death. The only thing he couldn't remember was making love to Angela.

Angela was waiting for him in the salon on the *piano nobile*. Though smaller than the Rivelli's palazzo, the Roses' palazzo was every bit as opulent. Rather than portraits of dead ancestors, Picassos, Monets, and Pollocks adorned its storied walls. The salon was the beating heart of the building. Before she died, Angela's mother had regaled her daughter with stories of all of the famous people that she had entertained in that very room: poets, princes, artists, and luminaries from a bygone era. Some were lovers and some were friends. This would always be her mother's room, and Angela had not changed a single item of décor. Though they had houses all over the world, her mother was always drawn to their intimate palazzo in Venice.

Lev walked into the salon wearing her husband's clothes. Angela was sitting at the table dressed in a silk blouse and soft suede pants that were the antithesis of her garb from the night before. While yesterday's Dead Bride costume had screamed, "look at me," the outfit she had chosen to watch today's Flight of the Angel was understated haute couture. She had placed two porcelain ghost masks on the table, one for Lev and one for herself. The table was otherwise empty, except for a bowl of overripe peaches. Lev sat down and reached for a peach. It mushed in his fingers releasing a swarm of fruit flies.

"You remind me of Val in that sweater," Angela said. "I bought it for him last summer in Verona."

"I can change back into my Plague Doctor costume if you wish," he said.

"Don't be silly. We're separated."

"Do you miss him?"

"I miss the good times: the Palme d'Or in Cannes, the Golden Globes, the walk down the red carpet at the Oscars."

"So, you loved him."

"I loved the *star*. He was the sexiest leading man in Hollywood, and he swept me off my feet. But off the screen he was just a man. He was . . ." she searched for the word, "*conventional.* He said he'd be willing to give up his career to start a family. Can you imagine that? I *hate* conventional. I wanted a star, not a family. Before you know it, you have a baby at your breast sucking your youth away. Your hopes and dreams are gone."

"We live on through our children," Lev said.

"I don't want to live on through my children. I want to live *now*."

"You give your children the gift of life. They can experience the wonders of this world with all its joy and beauty."

"And its pain and suffering," she added. "Do you have children?"

Lev hesitated before answering. He lowered his eyes. "I have a daughter, Sophia, but we're estranged."

"So much for your moralizing," Angela said. "Let me guess. You got some poor girl pregnant, and you abandoned your child."

"It wasn't like that."

"What was it like?"

"Complicated. It was a long time ago. I loved her mother, and I still love my daughter."

"You writers and your romantic fantasies above love! What is love anyway?"

Lev thought for a moment. "It's trusting your heart to another."

"Why, so you can get your heart broken?"

The image of the Dead Bride astride a sardonic Conte Rivelli wormed itself into Lev's brain. Perhaps that's why he couldn't recall making love to her the night before. It was neither sensual nor spiritual. It was simply meaningless.

Lev looked up into her eyes. "What did we share last night?" he asked. "Love? Intimacy?"

Angela walked around the table, embraced him from behind, and purred in his ear, "Lust. You and I are alike in our selfishness."

He could feel the gentle heaving of her breasts against his neck. He could feel her nipples harden and her breathing quicken. He felt her luring him into her web of earthly delights. He was surrendering to her embrace, as if there was nothing more that he needed in life but the pleasures of the flesh. In his mind's eye, he saw a black widow spider about to devour her mate.

Lev broke away before she could consume him. "There has to be more to life than the pursuit of pleasure."

Angela pulled his head back and slid her tongue into his mouth. "There is this, just this, and nothing more."

"Is pleasure all you live for?"

"I live for every breath, every beat of my heart, every rush, and every thrill." Angela put on her ghost mask. She stepped in front of him and offered her arm. "Will you dance with me now?"

"Life is fleeting," he said without taking her hand. "There has to be some deeper meaning as to why we're here."

Rebuffed, she danced across the marble floor in the arms of an imaginary lover.

"The meaning of life is that there is no meaning of life."

As he watched her ghost dance, he recalled what Conte Rivelli had said to her the night before: that only the grave, the barren womb, the parched earth, and fire never have enough.

Angela danced over to a hand-painted table in the corner of the room that held a white Murano vase with a bouquet of black flowers. She pulled a flower from the vase and clenched the stem in her teeth. She again beckoned him to join her in her ghost dance.

"I've never seen flowers like that before," he said.

Angela stopped dancing. She took the flower from her mouth, came up to him, and brushed the petals against his face. It smelled of ash and burnt flesh. "They're black chrysanthemums."

"They're hauntingly beautiful. Where on earth did you find them?"

"They were a gift."

Who on earth would have given her black flowers? he wondered. *Did the conte taunt her before humiliating her?*

Angela saw the puzzled look on his face. "They're from my friend, Mara."

"Mara?"

"She's a young woman from one of the neighboring islands. She has a boat. She's been showing me some of the lesser-known islands. The black flowers grow on the island of Poveglia."

"Isn't that the haunted island?"

"Only if you believe in ghosts," Angela replied. "Or angels, devils, saints, and all of that other religious nonsense."

"My faith gives me hope," Lev said.

"Your faith is a crutch. We live, we die, we are no more. It's that simple."

Lev thought of the Epicurean mantra that he had seen inscribed on ancient Roman gravestones and repeated at the funeral services of some of his atheist friends: *I was not; I was; I am not; I do not care.* The finality had mortified him.

"How did you meet your new friend, Mara?" he asked.

"We met at the water parade on Rio di Cannaregio. She's unlike anyone I've ever known. She can tell you about everyone who's ever lived or died here, even if it was before she was born."

"Mara is a tour guide?"

"No, no, not at all. She's never asked me for money. She's just interested in people, in listening to their stories."

"What did you share with her?" Lev asked.

Angela smiled. "My darkest secrets."

"But you barely know her."

"Yes, but she knows me. It's as if she's always been a part of my life. But why are you asking me so much about her? At least she gave me flowers. You wouldn't even dance with me."

"You asked me to protect you. Black flowers symbolize death."

"So what if she's a bit gothic? You're not jealous, are you?"

"I'm a writer. People fascinate me."

"Then you have to meet Mara. I'll ask her to show you the outer islands. Promise me you'll tell her your story. There's no such thing as a free ride."

* * *

Lev and Angela arrived early at Piazza San Marco to be near the stage for the Flight of the Angel. The crowd at the piazza, though sparser than usual because of the pandemic, was still festive and growing. The costumes were more elaborate than those from the night before.

In addition to the traditional costumes, such as the characters from *Commedia dell Arte*, competitors from all over the world embarked on artistic flights of fancy with costumes such as the Stars of Love, Leda and the Swan, and Electric Dreams. With their simple ghost masks, Lev and Angela were spectators rather than competitors.

"Will the Flight of the Angel be in your novel?" Angela asked.

"Yes."

"Will I?"

"That depends," Lev replied. "Who would you like your character to be?"

"Make me an angel."

The music of Handel's Messiah filled the piazza. The sea of faces looked up to the top of San Marco's bell tower. A woman in a flowing, white dress and plumed wings stepped off the bell tower and, attached to a steel cable and harness, began her graceful glide to the stage below. Her countenance was majestic as she spread her wings, tossed angel dust to the crowd below, and descended in a glorious fugue of hallelujahs. Her flight was streamed to millions of viewers all over the world and digitally archived for posterity. When she touched the stage, the Doge and his court stepped forward to greet her. Television reporters bustled to be the first to get a live interview.

"This is the happiest moment of my life," Angela heard her say. The rest of her remarks were drowned out by the cacophony of the crowd.

"She's rapturous," Angela said.

"The most beautiful of the Marias," Lev said.

Angela rolled her eyes. "You and your Marias – you're obsessed with the cult of Mary."

"The veneration of the Madonna is central to the theology of Venice. She's the city's patron and protector. She's linked to the founding of Venice on Annunciation Day, March 25th, 421. The theme of Mary is found throughout the mosaics of the Basilica San Marco. In the 17th century Venice supplicated Mary to intercede with Christ for the cessation of the plague. It's not surprising that the veneration of Mary has been incorporated into the traditions of Carnival."

"More lore for your novel?"

"Carnival is rich in history and tradition. I want my readers to relive the experience."

"Then tell me the story of the Flight of the Angel."

Lev was happy to bring the conversation back down to earth. The Blessed Virgin Mary – the *Theotokos* or God-bearer – was a tenet of his Byzantine-rite faith and held a special place in his heart.

"In the 16th century a Turkish acrobat performed a daredevil feat in tribute to the Doge. He climbed to the belfry of San Marco's bell tower on a tightrope from a boat that was anchored on the pier. On his way down he stopped off at the Doge's palace balcony. Over the centuries acrobats continued to reenact the tightrope walk during each Carnival until one of them decided to wear wings while descending from the bell tower. The Flight of the Turk then became known as the Flight of the Angel."

"When did maidens replace acrobats?"

"Tragically, in the eighteenth century, an acrobat performing the Flight of the Angel fell to his death. After the fall, a wooden dove replaced the live acrobat, and the event was renamed the Flight of the Dove. The event ended with the fall of the Republic and Napoleon's banning of the historic Carnival. When Carnival revived, the wooden dove was replaced by a real woman, the most beautiful of the Marias, and the Flight of the Dove again became the Flight of the Angel."

Angela sighed.

"Why are you sad?" Lev asked. "It's a joyous event. You said we should celebrate life."

"I wish I was the Angel of Carnival. If even for a moment I could have been an angel – to see Venice from the sky, to feel the wind beneath my wings, to hear the chorus of hallelujahs as I descend into an adoring crowd – it would be heaven. For me, it would be enough."

"You'll be an angel in heaven."

Angela shook her head. "I'll never escape my flesh. My sins are of this earth, and I'll return to the earth from which I was made."

"Anyone can be redeemed," Lev said.

"You and your Christian myths," Angela said. "Your belief in God, final judgment, and eternal bliss is your excuse for enduring suffering and injustice in this world. I don't believe in the things that you do. For me, this life is all that there is. You have to take as much as you can, even if…." A painful memory clouded her face. She began to cry. "The conte's right, you know. I'm pretty on the outside, and dead on the inside."

Lev put his arm around her to console her. "You need to find faith," he said. "There's still time."

"It's too late for me."

"Last night, at the masquerade, I met a priest, Father Stephan. He's the contessa's spiritual advisor. He offered to show me the way. We can go to him together."

"The contessa's a witch. She practices black magic."

"I thought so too, when I first saw her occult library. But Father Stephan explained that she's a *Benandante*, a person who uses magic to battle evil."

"She's still a witch."

"He said that magic is just the beginning of her spiritual journey. She wants to follow the mystical path of Saint Teresa."

"You can follow some mystical path to God if you want to," Angela said. "For me, my path ends in the grave."

"You don't fear death?"

"I embrace living," Angela replied. "I imagine that we are like snowflakes, each of us unique in our beauty and complexity, that are created in the sky, enjoy our existence for a few brief moments, and then fall to earth and are no more. When you accept the impermanence of it all, then each passing moment becomes ever more precious."

"But Christ gave us hope of eternal life. You just need a spiritual guide to show you the way to heaven."

"Mara is the only guide that I'll ever need."

The crowd at Piazza San Marco abandoned any semblance of social distancing. Revelers in period costumes paraded up and down the piazza scattering the pigeons that were scuttling underfoot. The cafés were open, and waiters in tuxedos were hustling in and out of the bars carrying silver trays with wine and espressos to patrons seated at the hundreds of tables that lined the square. Each café had its own musical ensemble that competed for attention with tunes that were popular decades ago.

"All of this pageantry is starting to bore me," Angela said. "Let's just wander around and get lost in the maze of Venice."

"There's a place I'd like to visit," Lev said. "It's just on the other side of the Accademia Bridge."

"Another dead saint?" Angela asked.

Lev shook his head. "I want to see the home of one of the most infamous ghosts of Venice."

* * *

The house of Olga Rudge and Ezra Pound was on Calle Querini, a hidden street that jutted out from the Giudecca canal and ended before it barely began. It was a narrow, triplex house with a green door, barred windows, and a peeling, umber, stucco façade. A simple plaque above the door read:

In un mai spento amore per Venezia
EZRA POUND
Titano della poesia
questa casa abito per mezzo secolo
Comune di Venezia

"This is where Ezra Pound spent the last years of his life," Lev said. "He described Venice as a 'stone forest growing out of the water.' If I can recall his words, it was something like *'Flat water before me, and the trees growing in water, marble trunks out of stillness.'*"

"Why are you so fascinated by some dead poet?" Angela asked. "The man was a fascist and anti-Semite."

"Because fascism is rising from the dead in Europe. Pound was an enigma. I'm just trying to understand why he was the way he was."

"What's so hard to understand? The man was insane."

Lev was no stranger to insanity. "It's true that he spent the latter days of his life in an insane asylum before returning to Europe and settling in Venice. He recanted the views that he held in his youth. They say he barely spoke to anyone before he died. The Irish poet Desmond O'Grady called it 'Dantescan self-punishment' for the views that he held earlier in his life."

"So why even remember him?"

"Because I'm a writer. He was one of the greatest poets of the twentieth century. Pound was one of the founders of modernist poetry. He had an immense influence on many famous modernist writers whom I admire: Eliot, Yeats, Joyce, Lawrence, among others."

"Have you even read any of his work?"

"I've read the *Pisan Cantos*, the ones he wrote when he was incarcerated in a cage near Pisa by the U.S. Army on charges of treason."

"I hear they're incomprehensible unless you're a literary scholar," Angela said,

"The *Cantos* is an epic poem about his life journey. His poetry is more understandable than his life."

"What have you learned from his *Cantos*?" Angela asked.

"It's a journey in search of truth. On one level, it's a spiritual quest for transcendence, for individual enlightenment. On another it's a search for worldly wisdom, for a just world of order and harmony."

"Did he find what he was looking for?"

"No, I don't think that he did. In Canto CXVI, the last one he ever completed, Pound, as the mythical figure Odysseus, returns home. The home he returns to, however, isn't the place that he intended when the poem began, but is the earthly heaven of human love. In this last Canto he writes, *'I have brought the great ball of crystal; Who can lift it? Can you enter the great acorn of light? But the beauty is not the madness, Tho' my errors and wrecks lie about me. And I am not a demigod, I cannot make it cohere.'"*

"He admits that his life was a failure?"

"I think it's more complicated than that. I think that in the end of his effort, he comes to accept not only his own errors and madness, but the conclusion that it was all beyond him, and possibly beyond poetry, to do justice to the coherence of the universe."

"Is that what you want?" Angela asked. "To make it all cohere?"

"Yes," Lev replied. "I would very much want to make sense of it all before I die."

* * *

Contessa Rivelli, dressed in black, stood in the nave of San Basilio's church while Father Stephan circled the tetrapod swinging a censer and chanting the prayers of the *Parastas,* the memorial service for the dead. The aromatic smoke from the incense wafted through the air in puffs like agonal breaths. The contessa held a lighted candle and black prayer book. She responded to the priest's prayers with the refrain, *"Lord, have mercy."*
Father Stephan sang the *Requiem Troparium:*

> *Of old you called me out of nothingness into being, and honored me with your divine image; but because I transgressed your commandments, you returned me to the dust from which I was made. Restore me again to thy Image, and to my original beauty . . .*

The contessa responded to the prayers of the Troparium with the refrain: *I am like the lost sheep. Call me O Savior and save me.*

The *Parastas* ended with a hymn asking for eternal memory for the souls of the dead. The contessa blew out her candle. She placed a gold coin in the offertory box.

"God thanks you for your generosity in supporting this *Parastas* in memory of the departed," Father Stephan said.

"This pandemic has taken the innocent as well as the sinners," she replied. "I pray for the eternal memory of the innocent." The contessa turned her back on the altar and began to walk out toward the narthex.

"If you wish to follow the path of St. Teresa, you must let go of your anger and forgive those who have transgressed against you."

The contessa turned to face Father Stephan. She managed a sardonic smile. "I could have used my magic to turn them into mandrakes in my garden."

"Then you too would have been damned."

"It would have been more satisfying to mete out justice to the living rather than to the dead."

"Vengeance is God's."

"But the wrath is mine alone."

"Be angry, but do not sin. Damnation is for eternity."

"What is your vision of hell, Father? Fire? Brimstone? Eternal torment?"

Father Stephan considered her question for a moment and replied, "I think that hell is returning to dust without ever communing with God."

* * *

Darkness descended over the stone forest as Lev and Angela wandered through the maze of marble trunks and flat water on their way back to her palazzo. As the shadows grew longer, Lev imagined that they grew arms and legs and grotesque torsos that slinked over the stone. The shadows morphed into faces of people he had known, eyed him, and slid into the still water of the canals.

They walked into a small, unmarked campo built around a stone rainwater well. The three narrow *calli* leading out of the campo were indistinguishable from one another, except that the walls of one of the passageways was defaced with graffiti.

A young couple, dressed as Romeo and Juliet, gamboled out of the passageway. Juliet's bodice was unbuttoned and her lipstick was smeared.

Angela took Lev's hand in hers. "To be young again," she reminisced.

"So we can relive our mistakes?"

"When you're young, you have infinite opportunities ahead of you. You grow, you blossom, you reach for the sun. When you're old, you have only the choices that you've made. Each passing moment robs you of what might have been. In the end, you wither and die with your regrets."

Lev looked around the small campo. The doors were closed and the windows were shuttered. He thought of the generations of people who had come and gone to draw water from the well. All had hopes and dreams that were were now buried in San Michele cemetery or lost at sea. His mind was flooded with his own regrets.

"I can see the sadness in your eyes," Angela said. "Let me guess – loves lost?"

"My love wasn't enough to save them."

"Yet you were able to save yourself." Angela repeated the words that had stung him in her web: "You're as selfish as I am."

The receding rays of the sun slid up over the roofs of the buildings.

"We should get back to your place before it's completely dark," Lev said. "Which of these streets should we take?" he asked. "I'm lost."

"Let's go down the one with the graffiti. We might run into your ghost of Ezra Pound."

The narrow passageway was scribbled with messages of eternal love and despair. Spray-painted communist slogans defaced the street poetry. The pavement smelled of urine. After several twists and turns, it opened into a campo that Lev recognized.

"This is Campo Venere. I've walked through it before but through a different way. There's a church here somewhere, San Basilio's, that Father Stephan was telling me about. Let's see if we can find it."

They scanned the darkened facades of the buildings in the campo: a mask shop, a restaurant displaying *chiccetti* – Venetian sandwiches – in the window, and a bookstore, until they saw a nondescript building with two stone steps that led up to an arched wooden door. The red stucco was peeling from the brick. The door opened and a woman in black stepped out onto the stairs. She lifted her veil and stared directly at them.

Angela froze. "It's the contessa! She saw us!"

Angela turned and ran back down the passageway from where they had come. Lev caught up to her after a several meters.

"Stop! Why are you so afraid of her?"

Angela cowered in his arms. "She has the evil eye! She's put a curse on me."

"Why do you think so?" Lev asked.

"You *know* why. I know you saw me having sex with her husband during the masquerade."

Lev bit his lip. "I'm sorry I intruded on you. I'm sure the contessa didn't see you. She was occupied with her guests all evening."

"It's not just last night. The conte and I have been having an affair ever since I arrived in Venice."

Lev released her from his arms. "I see. You think she knows?"

"Of course she knows! She's a witch!"

"Is that why your husband left you?"

Though she was still wearing her ghost mask, Lev could see tears well up in her eyes.

"You don't have to tell me if you don't want to," he said.

"I got pregnant," Angela blurted out. "I didn't know whose baby it was, so I decided to abort it."

"Neither your husband nor the conte knew you were pregnant?"

"The conte knew. He gave me some potion that he found in the contessa's library and had me drink it. That same night I aborted. It was a bloody mess. The fetus had a face, little hands, little feet!" Angela was sobbing uncontrollably. She looked pale, as if the blood had left her.

"What did you do with the . . .?"

"I thought of throwing it into the canal, but I couldn't. I panicked. I put it in the velvet box that had held my engagement ring."

"What did you do with the ring box?"

"I tried to hide it, but Val found it. He opened it in front of me. I was mortified! He asked me if it was his baby, and I couldn't lie. I confessed my affair, I confessed my abortion, I begged for his forgiveness . . . but he wouldn't forgive me. He took the box and never returned."

"What about the conte?"

"I was vulnerable. He pretended to comfort me, but instead he became my tormentor. I tried to escape him. His wife must have put a curse on us, where we have to relive our unholy union and torment ourselves until the end of our days."

Lev turned to see if the contessa had followed them into the graffiti-defaced passageway.

"She's gone," Lev said. "She must not have seen us. Let's go back to San Basilio's church. Father Stephan must still be in there. Confess your sins to him."

"He's in league with her," Angela replied. "I don't want his absolution, and I don't want her forgiveness."

"Then why did you confess your secret to me?" Lev asked.

"Because I need someone to understand the choices that I've made.

You understand, don't you? You're just like I am."

Lev felt as if he was suffocating. *I'm not like you,* he tried to convince himself.

Lev felt the walls of the narrow passageway closing in. The graffiti looked like scratches on the inside of a crypt. *My spiritual journey can't end like Angela's, in the loneliness of the grave.*

He took Angela by the hand and led her back to her palazzo in silence. As they neared her palazzo, he saw a lone figure in a black cloak waiting by the entrance. A hood hid the face. The figure stood motionless as they approached. When Angela looked up and saw the figure, she let go of Lev's hand and ran into its embrace. A pair of delicate, white hands emerged from the cloak and stroked Angela's flowing, blond hair.

As Lev neared, Angela turned and said, "I want you to meet my friend, Mara. *She* understands me."

Mara pulled back her hood to reveal herself. Lev froze. With her midnight hair, dark eyes, and marble skin, Mara was the most beautiful woman he had ever seen.

"My dark angel," Angela said. "She's more beautiful than the Angel of Carnival."

Mara's eyes were as black as night. Her gaze beckoned Lev into the void. She kept Angela in her embrace.

"Will you join us?" Mara asked.

For what? Lev wondered. *A tryst?*

"A ride in my boat," Mara answered, as if she had read his thoughts. "You are lost, Lev. I can help you find your way."

How does she know my name? "Not tonight," he replied. "Perhaps another time."

Angela took off her ghost mask and turned to Lev to bid farewell. She no longer looked frightened. In Mara's embrace, she looked like she had found peace.

The apparitions that had been tormenting Lev emerged out of the shadows. It was as if Mara was beckoning them into the world of the living.

I need to leave this place before I lose my mind. He began to back away. He wanted to tell Angela that he could no longer protect her, but he couldn't voice the words. Mara smiled at him and sheltered Angela with her cloak.

Before he turned to flee, he heard Mara say to him, "Meet me at the dock at the Piazza San Marco at dawn."

CHAPTER 3

Poveglia

Lev was afraid to close his eyes. He tossed and turned in his bed. He had hung a crucifix above the bed to ward off evil spirits. His mind drifted between wakefulness and sleep, between lucid dreams and nightmares. He saw himself as a young boy standing in front of an open casket in a *Hutsul* church deep in the forests of the Carpathian Mountains. His grandfather, who had been the village priest, lay in the open casket, dressed in a white vestment embroidered in gold. An *epitrachelion* stole with seven embroidered crosses was draped around his neck. His cold hands clutched a pectoral cross. A priest from a neighboring village stood over the body waving a censer and singing the prayers of the *Parastas*. The burning incense filled the church with fragrance.

As the priest was reciting the Trisagion prayer, Lev's grandfather sat up in his coffin. Gasps and screams echoed through the small wooden church. Those in the back ran for the door. Others, frozen with fear, crossed themselves and begged God for forgiveness. The corpse's right arm contracted at the elbow. The fingers of the right hand formed a priestly blessing. The terrified parishioners bowed their heads, afraid to look if their pastor was climbing out of his coffin. The priest came up to the corpse's face and gazed into its clouded eyes. When he saw no signs of life, he called upon a few stout parishioners to help him bend back the body and nail shut the lid of the coffin. The corpse's head pressed up against the pine.

Lev sat up in a cold sweat. To this day he didn't know if he had witnessed a miracle or the involuntary contractions of rigor mortis. His grandfather had died in a chair while eating dinner, and Lev had not discovered the body until the next morning. The memory of his grandfather's resurrection haunted him. The forceful sealing of the coffin had shattered the illusion of the peaceful sleep of the dead. No amount of prayer or ritual could mask the finality of the decomposition of flesh and obliteration of consciousness.

Lev climbed out of bed and paced through his dark apartment. He pinched his thigh to make sure he was awake and not sleepwalking. He recited Psalm 23 out loud: *"Though I walk through the valley of the shadow of death, I will fear no evil . . ."* He tried to still his mind, but the image of Mara kept haunting him. There was something terrifying, yet consoling about her. When he was a little boy, his mother had told him the myth of Mara, the goddess of death and winter, the demon of nightmares. But the mysterious woman he had met the evening before was not some frightening demon – she was the most beautiful creature he had ever seen. For a moment he imagined her standing next to him at his grandfather's funeral. She put her arm around him and pressed him closer to her hip, as if telling him not to fear death. She told him not to seek consolation in the hope of salvation, but to find it in her embrace instead. He looked at the crucifix that he had hung above his bed. *Lord,* he prayed, *be my shepherd. Guide me through the valley of darkness. Lead me to the still waters and restore my soul.*

⁂

Sophia awoke from a nightmare: she had been clutching her mother's hand and refused to let go as the undertakers were taking the body away. Sophia threw off the stifling duvet cover, walked to the living room, and looked out the window onto Palace Square. It was a starless night. Not a soul was out. The protests had been extinguished, the litter picked clean, and the blood scrubbed off the pavement. She hadn't heard from Alex in days. It wasn't like him. She understood his need for discretion, yet in the past he had always managed to send her a message, from a public computer, a burner phone, or through a friend. If she kept their child, their lives would change dramatically. She hoped it would be for the better, but it was not a decision she wanted to make alone. Trying to contact him would place them both at risk. All she could do was wait. She felt as if her whole world was being sucked into a black hole that had swallowed the stars and what little hope was left in the world. She feared her child would be stillborn into the void.

Sophia battled her insomnia with work. Her days were hectic with rehearsals for an upcoming concert that had been hastily commissioned by the Ministry of Culture. The Ministry had selected the program and ordered that the orchestra be ready in days rather than weeks. The orchestra had performed several of the pieces before, such as the *Overture* from Sergei Prokofiev's *War and Peace* and Tchaikovsky's *1812 Overture*. Other pieces were less familiar and required more rehearsal, but shared the same themes of war, valor, and victory. At night when she tried to close her eyes, the rousing melodies still reverberated in her head, but rather than incite dreams of glory, they stirred nightmares of suffering, death, and destruction.

Sophia turned her gaze to the Hummel figurine that graced her coffee table. Her stepfather had given her the Hummel of a young girl playing the violin for her third birthday. She was grateful to him for compelling her to pursue her musical talent, but hers had been a life of singular focus, sacrifice, and unrelenting criticism. At night, in her loneliest loneliness, she longed for her mother, for her love and approval, for her touch, her voice, and her scent. She remembered how her mother would whisk her away from the confines of the embassy to an outside world of sunshine, parks and flowers where she could be a child, happy and carefree. One of her fondest memories was watching the Guignol puppet show in the Luxembourg Gardens with her mother . . . and her natural father.

Lev Veles was an enigma to her. He had been a part of her life from the day she was born. As hard as she tried, she could not erase him from her memories. Her mother had told her that he was a famous author and a dear friend. When Sophia reached the age of intuition, she saw that Lev inspired a joy of life in her mother that she didn't share with her husband. Lev was handsome and charming, yet he had a melancholy in his eyes that only her mother's smile could dispel. He was a wonderful storyteller and would take Sophia on imaginary journeys into enchanted places in search of golden eggs and magical fern flowers. Lev would speak to Sophia and her mother in Ukrainian, the language she had learned from her own mother. This secret language was a bond they shared. Sophia had an echoic memory, and Lev taught her beautiful songs that had been written by a friend of his who he said had gone to heaven. She knew in her heart that her mother had loved him, and for those first seven years of her life, she had grown to love him as well.

Their bond was broken when her mother, with her dying breath, confessed that Lev was Sophia's natural father. To this day Sophia wasn't sure if it was the shock of her mother's death or their betrayal that had turned her against him. Her world had been turned upside down, and she needed someone to blame. At her mother's funeral, an acquaintance of her father's named Georgiy warned her that Lev was not the person he pretended to be – he was a dangerous man with a reputation for drinking, drugs, and debauchery. Georgiy revealed that Lev had fled Ukraine because he was suspected of killing his girlfriend, or at the very least, had driven her to take her own life. He was prone to madness and hallucinations. Her mother's death was suspicious, and Lev was again under investigation.

Sophia returned to her bedroom, pulled a worn leather suitcase from beneath the bed, and opened it. The suitcase was stuffed with unopened letters and packages. They began arriving shortly after her stepfather passed away. Twice each year, on her birthday and at Christmas, Lev sent her a post. They were addressed by hand in a distinctive style that was a cross between printing and cursive. The stamps were commemorative and carefully chosen to reflect a theme that might strike a familiar chord: storybook heroes, musical instruments, or flowers. Most were from France, but occasionally a letter or package would be marked with stamps from Ukraine or Italy. She didn't have the courage to open them nor the heart to throw them away. He had once tried to approach her during Christmas time when her orchestra performed a holiday concert in Paris, but she had heartlessly turned him away. She remembered how, on her deathbed, her mother had closed her eyes and let go of her hand . . . Sophia closed the suitcase. Despite her father's efforts to reconcile, he was as good as dead to her.

* * *

Mara's voice beckoned him like a siren's song. After the night of uneasy dreams, Lev went to her. He left his apartment to meet her at the dock by Piazza San Marco. The moon was setting in the west. A cold, white mist hung over the water. The piazza was empty before dawn, except for a few pigeons that were scouring for crumbs between the paving stones. The four horses of San Marco Basilica stood watch over the piazza. The stage that had celebrated the Flight of the Angel the day before stood empty. Lev walked between the Column of the Lion and the Column of San Todaro towards the water. The locals considered it to be bad luck to walk between the pillars. The site had been the place of public executions, with the condemned facing the clock of the tower with their back to the lagoon.

Mara was waiting for him at the helm of an ebony launch. Unlike the night before, she was dressed in a flowing, white dress. Her black hair descended below her shoulders.

"I knew you would come," she said.

"You keep haunting me in my dreams. I need to know why."

"Because you are lost, and I will guide you."

"To where?"

"To where you belong."

Lev recalled his disturbing dreams from the night before. "In the realm of nightmares?"

"Would you prefer that I let you rest in peace?"

I'd prefer nightmares to nothingness.

Lev stepped into the launch. *I must be sleepwalking,* he convinced himself. *What if I can't awaken? What if this is the end of my journey?*

The elegant wooden boat looked like it belonged in a bygone era. The seats behind the wheel were upholstered in red leather. He sat at the starboard side so he could see her face as she steered. She started the engine and piloted the boat into the lagoon. The launch rose and fell with the waves. The whoosh of the water and the whistle of the wind drowned out the churn of the motor. "Where are we going?" he asked.

"Poveglia, my home island."

He watched the skyline of Venice recede in the mist as the sun rose in the east. The early morning light illuminated the silhouettes of the islands of La Grazia, San Clemente, and San Spirito. Fishermen were dropping their trammel nets around the islands in the lagoon. The island of Poveglia loomed to the south. A bell tower peeked above the trees. Mara's boat was the only one approaching the island.

"Why aren't there any fishermen around Poveglia?" Lev asked.

"Superstition," Mara replied.

"What are they afraid of?"

"For centuries Poveglia was used as a *Lazaretto* – a quarantine station for incoming ships. When the Black Death arrived, Venetians that were infected or presumed to be infected were brought to the island to either be treated or to die. One hundred and sixty thousand bodies have been burned or buried there in plague pits. The fishermen fear that the winds blow human ash off the island. Bones get caught in their nets.

"Is it still used to quarantine those with infectious diseases?" Lev asked.

"No. In more recent times it has served as an asylum for the mentally ill. The fishermen call it the 'Island of Madness.'"

"Is anyone still on the island?"

"Only the forsaken."

Lev had heard the island was abandoned. He was surprised to learn that it was still inhabited. The approaching shoreline was overgrown with gnarled trees. An octagon, that once held a Venetian fort, protected the inlet to the harbor. Mara steered the craft around the western shore towards a concrete dock. A lone figure was waiting for them on the dock.

Lev squinted to make out the figure. It was a tall man in a doctor's white coat. His white hair, trimmed white beard, and erect posture gave him the look of authority. The doctor raised a pair of quizzing glasses to his eyes to study the approaching passengers. He seemed familiar with Mara. His gaze fixed on Lev.

"You've brought me another patient?" he asked.

Patient? Lev's blood went cold.

"I've brought him here to show him my home," Mara replied.

"I see." The doctor bent over the dock to take a closer look at Lev. "You are not like the others."

Lev stood up in the launch. "My name is Lev Veles, and you are . . .?"

"Veles?" The doctor looked startled. He looked to Mara for confirmation.

"An ancient bloodline," she said.

The doctor took the rope from Mara and moored the boat. He kept his eyes lowered while helping Lev step onto the dock.

"Forgive my impudence, signor Veles," the doctor said. "I meant no disrespect. I'm honored to have you visit our island. Please make yourself feel . . . at home. For now, I must return to care for my poor souls." The doctor bowed his head and left towards the buildings.

A gust of wind rustled across the water. Lev thought he heard voices in the wind – distant cackles, shrieks, and screams coming from the interior.

"Who was that strange doctor?" Lev asked.

"The director of the asylum," Mara replied. "He's a pioneer in psychosurgery, and quite famous among his peers. He lets his patients wander freely around the island. The only escape is by boat."

* * *

Father Stephan pored through his voluminous notes. With the underlines, circles, and scribbles, his handwritten notes looked more like hieroglyphics than script. He preferred the feel of pen on paper to the tap on a keyboard. When he completed his initial drafts, he would transcribe the chapters of his dissertation onto his laptop for final editing. He was scheduled to defend his doctoral dissertation on "The

Dark Night of the Soul: from Myth to Metaphysics" at the end of the next semester, and now, with his assignment to San Basilio's parish in Venice, he was hopelessly behind. His research advisor in the Department of Patristic Theology at the Pontifical Oriental Institute in Rome had advised him to focus his dissertation on Christian mysticism, but Father Stephan's inquisitive mind had wandered from West to East and from "Anno Domini" to millennia before the birth of Christ. While studying at the Pontifical Athenaeum in Rome, he had become fascinated by Frazer's *The Golden Bough* and the study of comparative myth and religion. He found a unifying theme in Jung's concept of archetypes in the collective unconscious, but found Jung disappointedly agnostic on the question of life after death. For Jung the underworld was not real. It was a metaphorical representation of the collective unconscious, the depths that each person must travel through to become a whole, or individuated person. For Father Stephan, the realm of the dead was as real as the realm of the living.

Father Stephan received the order to transfer to Venice while he was delving into ancient texts in the École Biblique in Jerusalem. During the past summer and fall, he had traveled widely throughout the Near East to study the afterlife beliefs of the ancient religions. He had walked the Stations of the Cross, touched the Wailing Wall, and descended into the tombs in the Valley of Kings and the Royal Cemetery of Ur. He had sought out learned archimandrites, rabbis, and imams to learn secrets that were only passed on by word of mouth, such as the necromantic rituals to communicate with the dead. While the holy men were willing to share their secrets with a true believer, the Archimandrite of the Ecclesiastic Mission in Jerusalem warned him that the price of such forbidden knowledge was high. The Church could accuse him of heresy, and he could risk excommunication and eternal damnation.

Father Stephan organized the chapters of his dissertation by time, place and religious beliefs. For his bibliographic references he sought out the most faithful translations of ancient sacred and literary texts, even though many were long out of print. The research was arduous but illuminating. He had learned that the earliest written descriptions of the passage of the soul from life to death came from Mesopotamia about

3000 years ago. His sources included George Smith's 1872 translation of the Sumerian *Epic of Gilgamesh* and Pirjo Lapinkivi's 1901 translation of the Akkadian poem *Ishtar's Descent to the Underworld.* For the Mesopotamians, life did not end after physical death but continued in the form of a ghost dwelling in the netherworld. The ghost had to cross a demon-infested steppe, pass over the Khuber River and be admitted through the seven gates of the netherworld in order to be judged. In the Sumerian epic, Gilgamesh's friend, Enkidu, recalled a dream he had of the afterlife. He states of the passed souls that "dust is their food, clay is their bread . . . they see no light and they dwell in darkness." When Gilgamesh crossed the waters and death, he met a female tavern-keeper who denied the possibility of immortality and told him to cherish his life: "The life you seek you will never find: when the gods created man, they let death be his share, and life withheld in their own hands."

Father Stephan took a sip of his espresso as he read through his notes on the afterlife beliefs of the ancient Egyptians, Greeks, and Jews. The vintage brass espresso machine was one of the few luxuries that Father Sylvester had left behind in the tiny apartment that in more prosperous times had served as the sacristy of San Basilio's church. The modest accommodation befitted a monk. The steady shots of espresso helped Father Stephan maintain his focus as he labored over his dissertation during the witching hours.

The Egyptian *Book of the Dead*, written about 1500 BC, offered a more hopeful vision of life after death. Father Stephan had obtained a copy of Wallis Budge's 1895 English translation at the Libreria Antiquaria Borromini in Rome. The book of maps and spells that guided the deceased spirit to the afterworld incorporated the Pyramid texts, that were written on the walls of the pyramids in the time of the Old Kingdom, and the Coffin texts, that were inscribed on the coffin itself. After the mummified deceased was placed in his tomb, his spirit embarked on a perilous journey to the underworld by either land or water. He had to pass through Twelve Great Halls whose gates were guarded by serpents and gods. In each of these Halls, he faced trials that included the "Swallower of Sinners," the "Evil of Face," and the "Stinger." When the spirit reached the Hall of Final Judgment, he stood before forty-two divine judges and pleaded his innocence of any wrongdoing. His heart, which contained the record of all of his actions in life, was weighed against the feather of Ma'at, the goddess of truth and justice. If his heart were heavier than the feather, he would be fed to the goddess Ammit, "the Devourer." If the scales balanced, he would be taken before Osiris and allowed to pass through to a new life as a transfigured spirit.

His research into the religious beliefs of the ancient Greeks was based on Homer's *Iliad* and *Odyssey* and Hesiod's *Theogeny*. The ancient Greeks believed that at the moment of death, the soul was transported to the entrance to Hades. The soul carried a coin under the tongue to pay Charon, the ferryman, to take him across the river Styx. On the other side of the river, Cerebrus, the three-headed Hell Hound, guarded the gates to the underworld. Beyond Cerebrus the Judges of the underworld decided where to send the soul. Demigods and heroes went to Elysium, the Isles of the Blessed. The wicked were cast into the deep abyss of Tartarus for eternal torment and suffering. Ordinary souls, who did not commit significant crimes and who did not achieve greatness, were sent to the Asphodel Meadows, while those who wasted their lives on unrequited love were sent to the Mourning Fields. The souls were shades of their former selves, and their existence in the underworld paled compared to the life of the living.

Jewish beliefs in life after death evolved over millennia. In the earliest books of the Bible, the descriptions of Sheol bore similarities to the dark and desolate underworld of the Mesopotamian religions. It was an abode of silence where oblivion was the lot of those who entered. Sheol was located deep underneath the earth at the farthest possible point from heaven. The dead were sleepers in the dust, mere shadows without knowledge or feeling. The notion of resurrection seemed to have originated during Judaism's Hellenistic period. Isaiah announced that "the dead shall live, their bodies shall rise," and the "dwellers in the dust" would be enjoined to "awake and sing." The prophet Ezekiel in the Vision of the Dry Bones said that God "will open your graves, lift you out of them, and return you to Israel" while the Book of Daniel confirmed that "many of those that sleep in the dust of the earth will awake, some to eternal life, others to reproach." Some would be granted everlasting life while the wicked were consigned to an existence of shame and everlasting contempt.

Father Stephan sat at his desk in the early morning hours and pored through the prayers of the *Bardo Thodol*, the *Tibetan Book of the Dead*. He had ordered the 1927 English Evans-Wentz translation from the Maggs Brothers Ltd Rare Books and Manuscripts in London and, because of the pandemic, had waited months for it to arrive to his address in Venice. It was one of the few missing references for his dissertation. Tibetans believe that an individual's soul remains in *bardo*, a special zone for the newly dead, for 49 days after death. On each of the 49 days, the deceased passes through a new level, until they enter a new body (that of a human, a hell being, a god, or an animal) to start a new cycle of life, death and rebirth. The spirit begins in the Clear Light of Ultimate Reality and descends down to the level at which it will reincarnate. The prayers of the *Bardo Thodol* guide the spirit through these worlds hoping that it can hold in the highest Chakra and not plunge from the realms of illumination into the realms of demons and hungry ghosts. In the lower levels they encounter Yama, the Lord of Hell. With the head of a buffalo, three round eyes, and a crown of skull. Yama was as terrifying as any Christian depiction of Satan . . .

The bells of Venice rang at 7 a.m. Father Stephan opened his eyes. He had fallen asleep at his desk with his face in the *Tibetan Book of the Dead*. In less than an hour he would need to open the doors of San Basilio's church to celebrate the morning liturgy. He splashed his face with cold water, put on his cassock, and entered the church through the sacristy door. The inside of the church was dark and cold. With the flick of a switch, the lights of the *choros* chandelier illuminated the mosaics on the iconostasis, walls, and ceiling. The faces of the saints gleamed with halos of gold leaf. Father Stephan faced the altar, bowed his head, and crossed himself three times. He unlocked the front door of the church, as he did every morning, in the hope that someone, other than the dead saints, would join him for the Divine Liturgy of Saint John Chrysostom. But death still roamed through the streets and canals and even the most pious were afraid to venture outside their homes for fear of contagion. Father Stephan would again have to partake in the body and blood of Christ alone.

* * *

Though it was February, Poveglia's trees had not shed their leaves. It was as if they were trapped in a state of perpetual winter unwilling to give up their dead. There was no green in the trees, bushes, or grass – the island had renounced the life-giving energy of the sun. The only sounds were the wails of the wind whistling through the dead leaves. Mara led Lev up a path from the dock to a block of dilapidated buildings. A worn sign on one of the buildings read: REPARTO PSICHIATRIA.

"Why have you brought me to this godforsaken place?" Lev asked.

"To discover your roots. You are a shepherd of souls."

Lev heard a cry for help from inside one of the buildings. He rushed in to an abandoned ward to discover a young woman in full leather restraints tethered to a metal frame bed. She had an innocent, child-like face that was marred by black and blue circles around both eyes. Her red hair was matted. Her wrists and ankles were bruised from her violent struggle to escape. Her hospital gown was stained with blood and urine.

Lev turned to Mara for an explanation, but she was gone.

"I'll go find the doctor," he told the patient.

The woman shook her head violently and wrestled against her restraints. "No!" she cried. "*Mi farà del male. Deve lasciarmi andare!*"

Lev knew enough Italian to understand that the patient was terrified of her doctor and was begging to be released. He looked around the barren room. There were no sheets, no bedpan, and no towels. The radiator was cold, and the desperate woman was shivering.

This is inhuman, he thought. "I'll come back with help," he told her. "I'll find Mara. She'll understand what's happening here."

The woman lurched up against her restraints, but the force of her contractions sent her recoiling back into the wire frame bed.

Lev went outside to search for Mara. The asylum buildings looked abandoned. Most of the doors were shut and overgrown with dead vines. He peered through the dirty windows looking for signs of life.

Every now and then he thought he saw shadows flitting through the rooms. They seemed to be floating off the floor. *These can't be real,* he thought. *I'm still sleepwalking.* His calls for Mara went unheeded.

The bell tower of San Vitale was the tallest structure on the island. If he could reach the belfry, he would be able to scan the island to find Mara. The door to the bell tower was open. He heard the hum of a generator. He climbed the spiral staircase until he reached a landing. A single hanging bulb illuminated the interior of the windowless room. An antique examining table with a manual crank stood in the center. A box-like machine with dials and paddles was connected to the sole electrical socket. A metal tray next to the table held an array of surgical instruments, including forceps, a steel spike, and a hammer.

Lev heard footsteps coming down a ladder from the belfry above.

"Signor Veles," the doctor greeted him. "I see that you've discovered my operatory. I apologize for not accompanying you, but I presumed that Mara was giving you a tour of our humble asylum."

"I saw only one patient, a young woman . . ."

"Ah, yes – Valentina. I assure you that there are many more patients who roam the island freely, but she, I'm afraid, is a danger to herself and others and needs to be restrained." The doctor began to tidy up the operatory for his unanticipated guest. He took the forceps, plucked a wad of bloodied gauze off the rough-hewn floor, and dropped it into a metal waste bin.

"What's her diagnosis?" Lev asked.

"She has a debilitating sexual neurosis. It's a sad story, quite scandalous."

"But what could possibly warrant such harsh confinement? And what are those bruises around her eyes?"

The doctor did not take offense at the rude questions. He presumed that his guest was simply unaware of the latest advances in psychosurgery.

"Valentina," the doctor explained, "was referred to me by the courts. She was convicted of murdering her father."

"But how could someone so young be capable of such a heinous crime?" Lev asked. "She looks so . . . frail."

The doctor shook his head as if to contradict him. "It's a tragic story, full of twists and turns. She was a promising young woman, a medical student at the University of Bologna. She fell in love with one of her classmates."

"A tale of star-crossed lovers?"

"Darker still." The doctor looked at him with the eyes of someone who was about to reveal a horrendous secret. "Her lover, Cyrene, was a woman."

"I fail to understand," Lev said. "In this day and age . . ."

"Did you hear what I said, signor Veles? She fell in love with a *woman*."

"You said she killed her father."

"One ill-fated day her father discovered the lovers in the act. He had come to visit his daughter in her dormitory on her eighteenth birthday. To his shock and surprise, he found his daughter and her lover naked and locked in . . . I will spare you the sordid details. The father, quite understandably, flew into a rage at this debauchery. He strangled his daughter's lover with his bare hands. Imagine, signor Veles, what would you have done in his place?"

Lev took a step back from the doctor.

"Their classmates heard the cries, and when they opened the door, they saw Valentina standing by the broken window. Her father had fallen to his death below."

"How do you know it was murder?"

"At the trial Valentina claimed that she wanted to join Cyrene in death by jumping out the window, and that her father lunged to stop her. But you understand, signor Veles, that a person capable of such unnatural acts is also capable of murder. I testified that she was criminally insane and, rather than committing her to prison, the court put her in my care."

"So you shackle her like a wild animal?"

"The poor girl is a danger to herself. On her first day in the asylum, she tried to jump off the bell tower. She claimed that she had made a pact with death whereby she could spend eternity with her beloved. She clings to this delusion every time I treat her."

"How exactly do you treat her?"

"I am pioneering a new form of psychosurgery that advances the work of Dr. Moniz. My research has demonstrated that for her particular pathology it is not sufficient to simply sever the lobes of the brain. Sexual desire is controlled by the amygdala, which is a deeper structure with more complex neural connections."

"You cut into her *brain*?" Lev asked incredulously.

"It's not as complicated as it sounds," the doctor replied. "Allow me to demonstrate." He picked up the paddles of the electroshock machine. "Imagine that she is lying on the examining table. First, I place the paddles on her temples and administer an electric shock for several seconds. After a brief period of convulsions, she falls into a relaxed, postictal state."

"Does she feel pain?"

"Discomfort perhaps, but she remembers little to nothing about the procedure." He put down the paddles and picked up the spike and hammer.

"I then lift her eyelid and position the spike in the fleshy space between the eyeball and eye socket. With a few taps of the hammer, the spike pierces through the thin orbital bone and penetrates the brain. I then continue tapping until I locate the deeper structures."

"You tap into her brain blindly?"

"No, no, I have an exquisite understanding of neuroanatomy. I admit it can be a bit of trial and error before you sever the right connections, so I carefully test and record her reactions."

"How will you know when it's working?" Lev asked.

"Why, isn't it obvious?" the doctor replied. "When she renounces her love for Cyrene."

Violence, Lev recoiled in horror. *The seventh circle of hell,*

The doctor placed his surgical instruments back on the tray. When he turned around, his guest was gone. The doctor climbed up the ladder to the belfry to see if his guest had ascended to admire the view. The belfry was empty. The doctor raised his quizzing glasses and looked down through the tops of the trees. He saw his guest running towards the asylum.

"Beware, signor Veles!" he called out in alarm. "Valentina is cunning. Don't let her beguile you."

Lev didn't heed the warning.

Mara was still nowhere to be found. Valentina was writhing in her bed.

"Don't be afraid," Lev said. "I'm going to free you. My friend has a boat. We'll get you off this island."

He unfastened the leather restraint from her left arm.

Valentina pointed to her feet. "*I miei piedi!*"

She unfastened her right arm as he freed her ankles. She leapt out of bed and embraced her savior with all her might. Lev stiffened. *What if she is insane? What if she is guilty of patricide?* Her trembling, however, dispelled any fear that she was dangerous.

"We need to get to the dock now," he said. "We have a boat waiting."

Lev took her by the hand and led her down the path to the water. He imagined that demented faces were staring at them through the windowpanes of the abandoned buildings. As they approached the sea, they saw Mara standing on the dock.

Valentina froze. She refused to take another step.

"Why have you stopped?" Lev asked. "We're almost at the boat."

"*La morte!*" Valentina cried out. She let go of Lev's hand and fled back up the path.

For a second Lev thought of waiting for Mara but decided to pursue the panicked patient instead. If he lost sight of Valentina, it could take hours to find her.

Valentina veered off the path into the tangled brush. The brambles tore at her flesh and gown. Rough pebbles cut her bare feet. She ran north, away from the buildings. Lev was only a few meters behind, but the twisted roots and branches kept impeding his pursuit. He saw Valentina cross a dilapidated bridge to the Burning Grounds on the north part of the island. A narrow canal separated the asylum on the south from the pyres and plague pits to the north.

Lev followed her across the bridge to the Burning Grounds, where the bodies of the plague victims were burned and buried. The earth beneath his feet was an unholy mix of soil and human ash. It reeked of burned flesh. A cacophony of coughs and cries assaulted his ears. Here and there charred bones and black chrysanthemums sprouted from the earth.

"You can't save her," he heard a voice behind him.

He turned to see Mara and the doctor standing on the south side of the bridge.

"She has made a pact. She may relive her life over and over, but it always ends the same," Mara said.

"This is madness!" Lev shouted. "We have to save this innocent girl!"

"Poveglia won't give up her dead," Mara said.

A pestilent vog rose from the Burning Grounds. Lev saw faces in the sulfurous mist: the sick, the demented, and the forsaken. The wraiths circled around Valentina, clawing at her flesh and gown, trying to pull her into the Burning Grounds.

Valentina knelt down at Lev's feet and took hold of his ankles. She looked up at him with her blackened eyes and pleaded *"Salvami – Save me."*

The wraiths swirled around Lev, probing his soul to see if he too deserved to be damned. As they peered into his soul, he felt their agony and despair. *This can't be happening! I need to wake up from this nightmare!* He closed his eyes and crossed himself three times. When he opened his eyes, he was still in the inferno.

This is not my hell! This is yours! He broke away from Valentina's grip and fled the Burning Grounds. The doctor passed him on the bridge and said, *"Du hast mit Bedacht gewählt – You have chosen wisely."*

The doctor walked up to his cowering patient, pulled her up to her feet, and said, "We need to get you back to the operatory, my child." Her head was slumped to her chest, as if she was resigned to her fate.

Mara was waiting for Lev on the other side of the bridge. He took one last look at Valentina from across the canal and said, "I'm sorry for my cowardice. I'm sorry I couldn't save you."

Valentina lifted her head, smiled at him, and said, *"l'ho ucciso – I killed him."*

Her revelation pierced him like a spike through his brain. *Treachery: the ninth circle of hell.*

The wraiths in the mist began to breach the canal.

"We must leave now," Mara said.

Lev followed her to the boat without looking back. Mara untied the lines, started the motor, and steered the boat into the lagoon. When Lev found the courage to look back at Poveglia, he saw that the mist had engulfed the entire island. Only the bell tower was still visible from the sea. As the boat rocked through the waves, he thought he saw movement in the belfry. Suddenly a man in a white coat plunged from the opening, flailing at the air before he disappeared into the mist below. A woman with red hair appeared in the opening and looked out to the sea.

They headed back to Venice in silence. Lev was numb. Mara had taken him on a nightmare to the darkest reaches of his own mind. *Why is she putting me through this ordeal? Why is she tormenting me?*

As they were approaching the dock at Piazza San Marco, he asked her again: "Why did you take me to that infernal island?"

"The dead need their shepherd," she replied.

"God is my shepherd," Lev said.

"What does He offer you?"

"Redemption."

"You don't need Christ to guide you. I can help you discover who you truly are."

"What can you offer me other than redemption?" he asked.

"Eternal return."

*　　*　　*

Father Stephan heard a pounding on the church door. The Eucharistic celebration had ended hours ago, and he had closed the church so he could continue to work on his dissertation without interruption. He put down his notes and opened the door to see what poor soul was so in need of salvation. Lev burst into the church in a cold sweat.

"Help me, Father, I'm losing my mind."

Father Stephan did not seem surprised.

"I'm having a nightmare from which I can't awaken. I'm seeing demons. They tried to drag me into hell."

Father Stephan looked outside to make sure that nothing had followed him. He closed and locked the door. "I was hoping you would come," he said. "These demons, are you seeing them now?"

"They lurk in the shadows, except in Poveglia, where they roam in open daylight."

Father Stephan illuminated the *choros* chandelier to ward off any evil spirits that might be lurking in the darkness. The saints in the icons stood guard. The nave held no chairs, other than the *stasidia* that were lined against the walls.

"Come, let us sit," Father Stephan said, "and tell me what happened."

"I dreamt I was in Poveglia, the Island of Madness. I met a young woman, Valentina, a patient at the asylum. She was being treated – no, *tortured* by a sadistic doctor. I tried to help her, but she deceived me."

"How?"

"I thought she was an innocent victim, but she *was* a murderess. She killed her father. Now Mara says she must continue her torment in perpetuity."

Father Stephan clutched the crucifix that hung around his neck. "You saw *Mara*?"

Lev relayed his ordeal that morning in Poveglia.

"Fascinating," Father Stephan said after Lev finished his story. "She took you to the Burning Grounds."

"Fascinating? It was terrifying!"

"Forgive my morbid curiosity," Father Stephan apologized, "but I'm a relative novice in necromancy."

"Necromancy?"

"Communicating with the dead," Father Stephan replied.

"But they *weren't* dead." Lev insisted. "They were as real as you and I. I spoke to them. I held Valentina's hand."

"This Mara, can you describe her?"

"Young, dark, beautiful – but why are her looks important?" Lev asked.

"For my dissertation. I've heard her described in many different ways. Why do you think she took you to Poveglia?"

"She said the strangest thing, that the dead need their shepherd."

"Your name – Veles, do you know what it means?"

"My grandfather said that it's an ancient Slavic name with a pagan origin."

"In Slavic mythology it refers to the god of the underworld, the guardian of the gates that separate the spiritual world from the physical world. Mara is pulling you back to your roots. She wants you to believe that you are trapped in a perpetual winter with no hope of rebirth. What did she offer you?"

"Eternal return."

"Nietzsche's demon," Father Stephan said. "She wants you to abandon your spiritual journey in exchange for eternity."

"Who is Nietzsche's demon?" Lev asked.

"I'll be right back. I want to quote him exactly." Father Stephan went to the sacristy and returned with his laptop. He scrolled to his chapter on Dualism.

"I read Nietzsche while researching my dissertation on "The Dark Night of the Soul."

"I thought he was an atheist," Lev said.

"He rejected God, and he rejected the dualism of body and soul, but to be objective in my research, I had to understand both points of view. Ah, here it is – I'm quoting his work, *The Gay Science:*

> *What if a demon were to creep after you one night, in your loneliest loneliness, and say, 'This life which you live must be lived by you once again and innumerable times more; and every pain and joy and thought and sigh must come again to you, all in the same sequence. The eternal hourglass will again and again be turned and you with it, dust of the dust!' Would you throw yourself down and gnash your teeth and curse that demon? Or would you answer, "Never have I heard anything more divine?"*

"The demon offers you a choice to keep reliving your exact same life endlessly?"

"The eternal return," Father Stephan said.

Lev thought of Valentina's tragic life – her heartbreak, her sin, and her recurring torment. Her hell was to repeat the same life endlessly, making the same choices, the same mistakes, and suffering the same consequences.

"The choice of eternal return depends on how you have lived the one life you have," Lev reasoned. He reflected on his own life and the choices he had made. He thought of the hearts he had broken and the people he had betrayed . . . "If I return endlessly, my sins would always be my sins. I could never escape my past. There would be no hope of redemption."

"Ultimately, you must take responsibility for your life and all of the consequences, both good and bad, of your willful actions," Father Stephan said.

Lev imagined that the saints portrayed in the icons of San Basilio's church were awaiting his reply. Many of them had been great sinners themselves before they repented and took responsibility for their actions.

"I would curse the demon," Lev concluded. "I would rather be redeemed."

"Then let me help you," Father Stephan offered, "I can show you the way."

"What way is that?"

"The Mystic Way."

"Will it cure me of my visions? Mara comes to me in my nightmares and even in my waking hours. How can I escape her?"

"You can't," Father Stephan said. "She will haunt you no matter what you do."

"But why? What does she want?"

"She wants you to forsake Christ and reunite with her in the underworld."

"Reunite? I don't understand."

"Yours is an ancient bloodline that began long before the coming of our Savior. Our ancestors believed in the old ways. The myth of Mara is part of our collective unconscious. Your belief in her is what makes her real."

"What am I to do?" Lev asked.

"You must confront your demons if you hope to defeat them."

CHAPTER 4

The Black Widow

Contessa Rivelli awoke with a cough. It began as a tickle in her throat and then worsened with each tick of the clock. The bedroom was insufferably hot, and she threw off her satin covers. Her head was pounding. Her whole body ached, as if she had danced with the devil himself. She pulled herself out of bed and staggered across the hall to the library. The medieval chandelier illuminated the vaulted ceiling like a night with a thousand stars. She paged through William Cole's *Adam in Eden* in search of a remedy for her ailment. The doctrine of signatures maintained that God had made herbs for the use of men and had given them particular signatures, whereby a man could read the use of them. Plants that resembled human body parts had a special usefulness for those parts. The concept was promoted by the finest physicians of their times, including Galen and Paracelsus. The doctrine of signatures was a logical extension of the principle of homeopathic magic, in which things that resemble each other must somehow be the same.

She searched through her collection of dried herbs for skullcap, a lavender plant whose seeds resembled tiny human skulls, and lungwort whose leaves looked like lungs. The skullcap would soothe her headache while the lungwort would calm her cough. She ground the botanicals with a mortar and pestle, added honey to form an electuary, and diluted the mixture with a little red wine. As she drank the elixir, she was surprised it had no taste. She wondered if the herbs had lost their potency; yet even the honey was not sweet nor the wine mellow. She debated whether to call a physician in the morning. The television stations streamed unrelenting images of the pandemic: the sick being treated in hospital corridors, the dying being isolated from their loved ones, and refrigeration trucks being used as makeshift morgues. The thought of dying in such a place was mortifying.

An ornate bookcase concealed the entrance to the old family chapel. The contessa turned a wooden statuette of St. Dunston that stood atop the bookcase and engaged a system of levers, weights, and pulleys that had stood idle for decades. The bookcase creaked and groaned as it slid along the wall to reveal a six-panel, ward-lock door. Contessa Rivelli's great-great-grandmother had replaced the original door with one that only she could open. Each of the panels held a brass knob cast with the head of a fallen angel. The contessa had seen the door opened only once before, when as a little girl she had snuck and hid in the library shortly after her father's death. She watched from under the table as her distraught mother turned the statue of St. Dunston, uttered an incantation, and turned the heads of the fallen angels in a specific order to unlock the door and enter the chapel.

The young contessa had crept up to the open door. The image of her mother in the hidden chapel inspired both fear and wonder. She was standing before a black altar with a candle in her hand. An inverted crucifix hung over the tabernacle. The pentagram of Baphomet was painted in goat's blood on the chapel floor. She watched as her mother removed a black box from the tabernacle. As she was about to open it, her daughter exclaimed: "Is that the Eucharist?" Her mother gasped and shoved the box back into the tabernacle. She grabbed her daughter, pulled her out of the chapel and locked the door behind them. Her mother was crying. "Promise me you'll never open that door again," she demanded. "I should never have gone in there. Your great-great-grandmother desecrated the chapel. She broke our sacred *Benandanti* vow to never practice the dark arts. One day she sealed herself in the chapel and was never heard from again. Her body was never found."

Now, out of desperation, Contessa Rivelli was prepared to break her promise. She uttered the incantation of the *Alohomora*, the unlocking spell, and turned the heads of the fallen angels: Moloch, Chemosh, Dagon, Belial, Beelzebub, and Lucifer. The door opened for the first time in decades. The chapel was as she remembered it, with the inverted cross, black altar, and pentagram drawn in blood. The stale air stunk of the grave. She placed the candle on the altar, opened the tabernacle doors, and took out the black onyx box. She opened it and gasped – the story her mother had told her was true! She placed the box with its contents back into the tabernacle. As the ward locks clicked close and the bookcase creaked back along the wall, she decided she would have nothing to do with doctors. If her medicinal herbs failed her, she would rely on God or the devil instead.

* * *

Angela had vanished. Lev's calls and texts to her went unanswered. The pandemic case count was doubling every three days with the new Omicron variant, and he was worried that she had taken ill. When he stopped by her palazzo, he found the doors locked and the windows shuttered, as if she had left for the season. Not even a servant was left behind to answer the door. He wondered whether his pressing her about her affair and decision to abort her child had caused her to flee to some more carefree clime, where no one would pry into her personal affairs. He concluded that she needed her time and space, and that, for the time being, he would bother her no more.

But he was lonely without her. It wasn't just the warmth of her smile or the heat of her passion – it was her vulnerability. Beneath her façade of hedonism, she was as fragile as a little girl. She wanted to be an angel, but her image of herself was that of the Dead Bride, pure and white on the outside and dead on the inside. He decided that in his novel he would make her the Angel of Carnival, the most beautiful of the Marias. She would find her immortality in the world of his words.

Lev's apartment in the Corte del Milion overlooked the Byzantine arch that was all that remained of Marco Polo's ancestral home. The rent was exorbitant, yet its central location in the belly of the fish made it easy for him to wander and explore the hidden treasures of the city of water. Fewer and fewer tourists ventured into the courtyard. Some of the visitors continued to wear their Carnival masks believing that they would protect them against the new variant. Lev was convinced that he had already had it. He had felt unusually winded when he followed the procession of the Twelve Marias from San Pietro di Castello to the Doge's Palazzo. Yet he had regained his strength before the contessa's masquerade. He considered getting tested, but by the following day, he was feeling nothing at all. The only lingering effects were his visions and nightmares.

The thought of being found dead in his apartment crossed his mind. *What an ignoble way to die.* He imagined being discovered by the landlady after his rent was past due. The woman would most likely call the authorities late in the afternoon, so the body could be removed under the cover of darkness. A death notice might be posted in some local paper, yet it would be weeks before his friends in Paris or Kyiv would learn about his death. They would express a moment of grief, share some happy anecdotes, and drink a toast to his memory. His publisher would promote his posthumous works and then deeply discount them. Lev had not made arrangements for his death, so he would most likely be buried in some anonymous plot, or, if the cemetery at San Michelle was full, cremated and interred in an urn. He wished to leave his estate and royalties to his daughter, but she had not answered any of his letters over the past many years. He decided to try to write to her again.

The fountain pen that his daughter's mother had given him lay atop a blank piece of Venetian stationary on the writing desk. Crumpled pieces of paper filled the wastebasket. He struggled with the salutation. "My dearest daughter" or "My dearest Sophia" implied an intimacy that he did not deserve. He began simply:

Dear Sophia,

I hope that you are well and will find it in your heart to open my letter. In these dark times, I cannot help but fear the worst. I think about you every day. I can only guess what you have been told about me, but I confess that the worst of what you have heard is likely true. I am a deeply flawed man who has failed those whom he loved the most. I truly loved your mother, and I regret the pain that I have caused her. But I do not regret bringing you into this world. You alone make my world cohere.

I am in Venice working on a novel. I have dedicated my last novel, "The Storyteller," to you, and had sent it to you for your birthday. If you have read it, you might begin to understand and forgive me. The Revolution of Dignity changed me. I was in the company of heroes. I saw that truth can overcome power and that good can overcome evil. I fear, however, that the darkest times are still ahead. I pray for your safety.

I plan to leave all of my possessions and royalties to you. I will prepare a will and ask Father Stephan, the priest at San Basilio's church in Venice, to witness it. I hope that we can finally meet before this pandemic and war take us all.

Your father,

Lev

* * *

Father Stephan received the call after evening vespers. Contessa Rivelli's maid informed him that her mistress had taken ill and had requested to see him. When he asked what ailed her, she simply replied: *"pandemia."* He packed a crucifix, holy oil, and Eucharist in his Viaticum case and hurried to the contessa's bedside. He was prepared to hear her confession, anoint her with holy oil, and administer Holy Communion if she was able.

The maid led him to her mistress's bedroom on the second floor of the palazzo.

"Have you called for the doctor?" Father Stephan asked.

"The contessa refused. She asked to see you instead."

Father Stephan entered the bedchamber. The room was dark. He heard the sound of labored breathing from inside the canopy bed. The room had the ketotic smell of sickness. Before turning on the light, he opened the door to the balcony to let in some fresh air.

"Do you believe in the devil, Father?"

"You're awake. I opened the balcony door to let in some fresh air." He drew open the silk canopy and turned on the lamp by her bed. Her lips were blue.

"It might be too cold for you. I'll close the balcony door."

"You didn't answer my question, Father. Do you believe in the devil?"

Father Stephan had long struggled with the question of how an all-powerful, all-knowing, and perfectly good God could allow so much suffering in the world. Free will was the usual explanation. Yet why create a soul if you know it will choose evil and the eternal torments of hell? Father Stephan had no easy answers. "The Church teaches us that the devil is real," he said.

"But what do *you* believe?"

"I don't know what to believe," Father Stephan replied.

"But surely you believe in evil?"

"Do you mean a metaphysical evil outside of ourselves? I see suffering and injustice that we ourselves create. If there is a devil, then he hungers for reality that only we can give him."

The contessa coughed violently.

"Let me call a physician," Father Stephan suggested.

"No doctors!"

Father Stephan knew Contessa Rivelli well enough to not make the same suggestion twice. He opened his Viaticum case and put the *epitrachelion* stole around his neck.

"What are you doing?" the contessa asked.

"I thought you called me here to partake in the Sacred Mysteries of Confession and Holy Communion."

"What next? Last Rites?" she cried out. "I'm not dying!"

"Then why did you ask me to come?"

"To ask you if you believe in the devil."

"What do *you* believe?" Father Stephan asked.

The contessa sat up in bed and propped her back with pillows. Her black wig and dentures lay on the end table. She was an imposing figure in health, but now she was a frail old woman who had abandoned any semblance of vanity. The lamp cast her shadow against the wall. "I want to tell you a story."

The air in the room was cold but fresh. Father Stephan closed the balcony door, pulled up a chair, and sat down by the bed. "I'm listening."

The contessa took a deep breath and began her story. My father was Bernadino Rivelli . . ."

"You're a Rivelli by birth?" Father Stephan asked. "But your husband . . ."

"Is also a Rivelli – a distant cousin and a detestable man. Our marriage was arranged to preserve the purity of the bloodline."

"An unusual practice in this day and age."

The contessa took another deep breath but coughed it out before it reached the bottom of her lungs.

"Can I bring you some water?"

The contessa grabbed him by his hand and pulled him closer. He could hear the rumbling in her chest.

"My father died when I was eight," she continued her story. "I heard him arguing with my mother the night before. He was a modern man who preferred chemistry to alchemy. He founded the cosmetic company that bears the family name. My mother, on the other hand, preferred the old ways. Their quarrel was about me. He insisted that my mother abandon her magic. He said that the *Benandanti* way had brought the family nothing but misfortune. He said that evil had corrupted the family over the generations, and we were turning into witches ourselves. She replied that I was born with a caul over my head, and that God had chosen my path."

"Your father was just trying to protect you," Father Stephan said. "He wanted you to live a normal life."

The contessa cackled. "What is a normal life, Father? We suffer like the rest of the masses, we die, we are no more."

"We follow the teachings of Christ, the Way of Love, so that we can be saved."

"Poverty, humility, and sacrifice?" The contessa's eyes darkened. "There is an easier path to eternity."

Father Stephan tried to move back in his chair, but the contessa dug her nails into his wrist.

"The next morning," she continued, "my father was found drowned in the canal. Some say he slipped and fell. Others said he took his own life. The inquest was shrouded in secrecy."

"You must have been devastated."

"I blamed myself. I hid in the library in a nook behind the Hermetic cabinet. My mother took my father's death very hard. She loved him terribly. She entered the library without seeing me. I saw her slide back a bookcase and open the door to a family chapel that had been sealed for generations. I crept out of my hiding place and watched her take a box out of a tabernacle that rested atop a black altar with an inverted cross."

Father Stephan broke her grip. "Are you telling me your mother intended to evoke a demon?"

"Before she could open the box, she saw me. She sealed the chapel and made me promise that I would never enter it again. My great-great-grandmother, she claimed, had desecrated the chapel. She then told me the story of the Devil's Bridge."

"The bridge in Torcello?" Father Stephan asked. "I've heard the legend, but I can't imagine it was true."

"Nor I," the contessa replied, "until I saw the key with my own eyes."

Father Stephan looked through the open doorway at the library door across the hall. He had thought that the golden apotropaic symbols were meant to keep evil out. Now he understood that they were meant to keep the evil in.

"It's well past midnight, Contessa. You need your rest. I can return in the morning."

She grabbed his stole and pulled him closer to her face. "You must hear me *now*."

Father Stephan glanced at the library door again to make sure it was closed.

"My story begins during the Austrian occupation of Venice," the contessa said. "My great-great-grandfather was imprisoned for supporting the resistance, and the family had fallen on hard times. His wife, Leandra, was a powerful *Benandante* who provided for the family in her husband's absence by practicing white magic – ensuring harvests, healing the sick, and telling fortunes. But it wasn't enough, and she was forced to consider selling the palazzo that had been in our family for generations.

"One day a rich merchant from Torcello came to her with a proposition. His niece was suffering from a terrible depression. She would not eat, drink, or sleep. She did not respond to bloodletting or prayer. He explained that she had fallen in love with an Austrian officer. She was beautiful, with hair as dark as the Venetian night and brown eyes as deep as wells. Her parents were furious at her traitorous romance and banished her from Venice to stay with her uncle in Torcello. While she was in her uncle's care, her lover was murdered. When she learned of his death, she abandoned hope and wanted to join her lover in death. The merchant offered to pay Leandra twenty gold coins if she would use her magic to help his niece: ten now and ten more when his niece was cured.

"Leandra prepared potions to cure the girl's melancholy, and when those failed, she gave her potions to induce forgetfulness, again without success. The merchant was frustrated by her repeated failures and threatened to stop payment. Leandra then turned to the forbidden texts: *De Nigromancia*, *Le Dragon Rouge*, and the *Grand Grimoire*. But even these spells couldn't cure the girl's heartbreak. Leandra finally found an answer in the *Liber Juratus Honorii*. It contained an incantation to evoke the fallen angels. Lucifer had the power to reunite the girl with her dead lover, but he would require a pact and exact a terrible price.

"On October 31st she lit a black candle and entered the family chapel. She inverted the crucifix and, using goat's blood, painted the pentagram of Baphomet on the floor. She read the incantation to summon a demon. To her surprise and terror, the devil appeared. He knew of her plight and offered a bargain. He would reunite the girl with her lover if Leandra promised to deliver the soul of an unbaptized child on each

Christmas Eve for the next seven years.

"Seven souls for one?" Father Stephan asked. "Who could agree to such a bargain?"

The contessa looked past him towards the library door. She then pulled him closer and whispered in his ear, "She believed she could trick the devil. She agreed to the pact and signed it with her blood." She began to cough.

Father Stephan pulled back from her haggard face. Her eyes were sunken and black. "This legend is disturbing you," he said. "Let us pray instead."

"I must finish," she insisted. "It's *not* a legend. I know the truth. The devil told her to bring the girl and meet him at the Devil's Bridge on the last Sunday of November. The girl agreed, and on that day, Leandra brought her to the stone bridge in Torcello that crosses the Maggiore Canal. She gave the girl a lighted candle and gold coin and told her to cross the bridge. As the girl was crossing the bridge, a tall figure in a dark cloak appeared on the other side. The devil met the girl on top of the bridge, pulled the key to time and space out of his mouth, and dropped it into the canal. When he took the coin out of her hand, she saw her Austrian soldier appear on the other side of the bridge. She passed through the devil and disappeared to be reunited with her lover. The devil told Leandra that she owed him the souls of seven unbaptized children. He told her to bring him the first soul on Christmas Eve one month hence."

"Did she?"

"The ending of the story depends on who tells it. The legend says that a young man learned of the plot and killed Leandra to save the souls of the poor children. They say that the devil comes to this bridge every Christmas Eve waiting for his payment."

"What do you believe?" Father Stephan asked.

"Leandra never intended to fulfill her end of the bargain. When the devil disappeared, she dove into the canal and retrieved the key."

"What did she do with this key to the gateway to time and space?"

"We never knew until now. My mother told me that Leandra designed a ward-lock door to the chapel that only she could open. On Christmas

Eve she sealed herself in the chapel and disappeared. Her children never found her. They hid the entrance to the desecrated chapel behind a bookcase. It hadn't been opened until the day after my father's death, when I saw my mother slide back the book case, utter an incantation, and turn the heads of the fallen angels."

"Then how do you know that the legend of the Devil's Bridge is true?"

The contessa let go of Father Stephan's stole and fell back into bed. Her mouth was open but her eyes were closed. Her breaths were sonorous, her pulse rapid, and her forehead was burning. Father Stephan saw the contessa's maid in the doorway with her hand over her mouth.

"The contessa is delirious," he said. "Don't heed her ravings – there are no devils in this house. I'm hoping that her fever will break by morning. Let her rest, and I'll check on her again tomorrow." He crossed himself three times and went back to San Basilio's church to pray.

* * *

The greatest power of the *Benandanti* was astral projection: the ability to leave one's body and travel through the astral plane. On the Ember Days – the days of prayer and fasting near the beginning of each season – they embarked on nocturnal visionary journeys, during which their spirits traveled out of their bodies and into the countryside, where they would do battle with malevolent witches who threatened the local crops. The Rivelli line of *Benandanti* had learned how to project their spirits at will. In this day and age, there was no longer a reason to battle witches over fallow fields on the nights of the Ember Days. The malevolent witches had entered the daylight and roamed the power realms of politics and money. Contessa Rivelli had engaged in the ancient practice of astral projection only once before: to see if her husband was cheating on her with the American heiress. Her spirit hovered over the adulterers as they copulated in the heiress's bed on Christmas Day. When she returned to her body, she scoured through her alchemic laboratory in search of a poison that could be spread through semen, and which would bring them closer to mutual death with each act of betrayal. She decided she would project herself once more. Her spirit would travel to the Devil's Bridge to drop the key to time and space into the water.

Her spirit rose out of her flesh and stepped onto the bedroom floor. Her failing body lay on the bed, still pumping blood and breathing, though the breathing was shallow and the pulse erratic. If her magic failed, she knew she had to return to her body before her heart stopped if she was to open her eyes to the world once more. As a precaution she had taken an elixir made of mercury, precious metals, and gems to preserve her mortal body while her spirit traveled in the astral plane. She entered the library and unlocked the chapel door. The onyx box was in the tabernacle where she had left it. She opened the box and removed its sole contents: a silver key.

A boat was waiting for her outside the *porta d'acqua* below. Mara was at the helm of an ebony launch with red leather seats. The contessa and her guide set off for Torcello in the moonlight. As they traversed the lagoon, they passed islands whose names no longer mattered. The people who had lived on these islands had come and gone, their dust scattered by the wind and the tides. All that mattered was the bridge, the key, and the gateway to eternity. The launch entered the Magiorre canal, and Mara ferried her passenger to the foot of an arched stone bridge. The contessa climbed the three stone steps to the top of the bridge and stepped to the edge. There was no parapet to protect her. The night enveloped the bridge in darkness. It was as if the light from the stars and the moon had been extinguished by the void. She looked into the blackness, reached out her arm, and was about to drop the key, when she heard a voice say: "Only I can open the gateway to time and space."

She turned to see a tall figure with hollow cheeks and black holes for eyes ascend the bridge from the other side.

"Have you brought me my seven souls?"

"I am not Leandra," she pleaded. "It was not my bargain."

"Yet you hold my key."

The contessa tried to trick the devil in vain. "Leandra stole it from you. I came to return it."

The devil took the key out of her hand. "The debt must be paid," he said.

"I have nothing to give you."

"But you do," he replied. "Your soul." She stared into the void and passed through his eyes into the emptiness of oblivion.

* * *

It rained on the first Sunday of the Great Fast. It was a cold, dreary rain that chilled the bones. Lev decided to attend Sunday service at San Basilio's church. His visions were becoming more frequent and more frightening. Father Stephan's offer to "show him the Way" at least gave him hope – it was better than losing his mind. The pandemic had not abated as the authorities had hoped. Bravado had turned into fear, and fear would soon turn into panic. Lev planned to ask Father Stephan to witness his makeshift will, in the event that he too would become a statistic.

On the Sundays of the Great Fast, Father Stephan celebrated the longer Divine Liturgy of St. Basil the Great. Lev walked into the church as Father Stephan was chanting the Great Litany for the living. The few faithful who attended the Sunday Eucharist were mostly immigrant workers and refugees from Ukraine. Only a handful wore masks. The others, like Father Stephan, most likely believed that God would not allow the plague to enter His shrine. Father Stephan sang the service in a rich baritone. For Lev, the sacred chants and hymns of Church Slavonic were the most sublime forms of worship, as intricate and ancient as the mosaics of the saints that adorned the walls and iconostasis of the Byzantine church. The Gospel for the First Sunday of the Great Fast was John 1:43-51. Jesus's words to Nathanael gave Lev hope: "Very truly I tell you, you will see heaven open, and the angels of God ascending and descending on the Son of Man."

After Sunday service, Father Stephan took off his vestments and put on his cassock. He began extinguishing the candles and closing the doors of the iconostasis when he saw Lev in the back of the church.

"I'm so glad you've come," Father Stephan said.

Lev walked up to the iconostasis. "You offered to show me the way. I believe I'm ready."

"It's a difficult path, but I've followed it myself, and I can assure you that it ends in ecstasy."

"Before we begin, I have a more mundane request," Lev said. "I was hoping you would witness my bequest to my daughter."

Father Stephan hesitated. "Is it a legal document?"

"I haven't prepared an official will. I plan to meet with a lawyer once they reopen their offices after Carnival. For now, I wrote a letter to my daughter and told her that in the event of my death I would leave her everything I own."

"Where is this letter?" Father Stephan asked.

"I left it in my apartment in the Corte del Milion."

"Consider me your witness," Father Stephan said.

Father Stephan's phone vibrated in the pocket of his cassock. He looked at who the caller was and answered it. A look of consternation came over his face. "I'll be right there," he said.

"Trouble?" Lev asked.

"It's a call from the Rivelli palazzo. I'm afraid the contessa has taken a turn for the worse. I visited her last night, and she was suffering from fever and delusions. She refused Last Rites, and I fear for her soul. I need to bring my Viaticum case."

"Shall I accompany you?" Lev asked. "Perhaps I can be of some help."

Father Stephan considered his request. "Perhaps you can. But what I ask of you might seem unusual."

"In these dark times nothing is unusual."

Father Stephan and Lev hurried to the Rivelli palazzo. Except for a few intrepid tourists, the streets were empty due to the cold and rain. The contessa's maid answered the door. Lev was surprised that Conte Rivelli was not home but figured that the contessa may have thrown him out after his lurid romp with Angela during their masquerade. The maid led them up to the contessa's bedroom and opened the door.

The contessa lay in her bed motionless. Her eyes were open, and her face was contorted in terror. Father Stephan felt her forehead. It was cold. He put his fingers on her carotid artery to feel for a pulse. He felt none. Father Stephan looked around the room, as if to check if someone was hiding. He looked behind the curtains, in the armoire, and up at the ceiling. When he looked under the bed, he saw a purple vial that appeared to have been dropped from the bed. He poured a drop of the silvery liquid remnants into his palm.

"*Zuo Thar*," he said.

"What is that?" Lev asked.

"It's a Tibetan magical medicine given to the dying. It's meant to preserve the body during the forty-nine days that the spirit of the deceased passes through the Bardo states in its quest for rebirth."

"It's too late for all of that," Lev said. "She's dead."

"It takes many days for the body to truly die. What I don't understand is why I can't sense her spirit."

The contessa's maid crossed herself and closed the door behind her as if she feared that some exorcised demon might escape.

"There might still be time," Father Stephan said. He opened his Viaticum case, put on his stole, and took out his liturgical book and a small flask with oil. He placed the flask on the nightstand, turned to Lev, and said, "As I administer the ritual of Anointing you must tell me if you see her rise."

Lev was incredulous. "Do you mean rise from the dead?"

"Tell me if you see her soul."

Father Stephan began praying the *Our Father* followed by Psalm 142: "*Bring my soul out of prison, that I may praise thy name . . .*" He then recited the Litany of Peace, petitioning Almighty God to send down the Holy Spirit, first to sanctify the oil, and then to sanctify the sick, followed by the Prokimenon: "*May your kindness, O Lord, be upon us, who have placed our hope in you.*" He read the Epistle of St. James about anointing, read the Parable of the Good Samaritan, followed by the Insistent Ekteny, imploring God "*for mercy, life, peace, health, salvation, visitation and forgiveness of sins . . . send upon her the grace of deliverance from illness, raising her from her sickbed.*"

Father Stephan invoked the power of the Holy Spirit to descend upon the blessed oil and make it "*a perfect deliverance from her sins and an inheritance of the kingdom of heaven.*" He dipped his finger into the holy oil, recited the Prayer of Anointing, and anointed the contessa on her forehead, eyes, ears, nostrils, lips, hands, chest, and feet. He placed the

Gospel Book over her head and entreated the Lord: *"If she has committed any sins she will be forgiven."* Father Stephan closed his eyes, and then in a moment reopened them as if to witness a miracle. He saw nothing. He turned to Lev. "Do you see her?"

"I see only her dead body," Lev replied.

Father Stephan lowered his head. "I've failed her. I was her spiritual advisor. I should have stayed with her last night. I should have convinced her to take Last Rites. She chose to follow the left-hand path instead."

"I'm sure you did all you could," Lev said.

"No. I didn't believe her."

"About what?" Lev asked.

Father Stephan tried to close her eyelids, but they would not stay shut. He pulled back the duvet cover. Her right hand was clenched in a fist. He undid the fingers of her hand and looked at her palm. The center of her palm was burned with the imprint of a key.

CHAPTER 5

The Mystic

Sophia Sergeivna Borodin raised her baton for the concert's finale: the Overture from Sergei Prokofiev's *War and Peace*. With a downward wave of her hand, the one-hundred-piece orchestra filled the Bolshoi Zal with a patriotic suite of wind, string, brass, and percussion. The symbolism was not lost on any of the fifteen-hundred patrons in attendance. Prokofiev had been born in Sontsivka, a small town in Eastern Ukraine, an area about to be liberated by Putin's "Special Military Operation." The goal of the operation was the demilitarization and de-Nazification of Ukraine. After the finale, the audience rose and gave the orchestra and its brilliant conductor an eight-minute standing ovation. A young girl, dressed in a blue-and-white-striped *telnyashka* blouse – Russian naval uniform – ran up on the stage and handed Sophia a bouquet of red and white roses tied with a blue ribbon.

Amidst the thunderous applause, rumors of the invasion flared through the audience like a phosphorus fire: cruise missiles had been launched at Kyiv, Kharkiv, Odesa, and Donbas . . . troops had landed on the beaches of Mariupol and Odesa . . . Ukraine was surrounded in the north, east, and south . . . tanks were rolling in from Belarus and Russia in a pincer movement that would capture Kyiv within ninety-six hours. Putin had unleashed the dogs of war.

Sophia forced a smile for the television cameras as she bowed and clutched the bouquet of roses. The thorns on the stems dug into her hands. In her long black skirt and tuxedo blouse, Sophia was the epitome of grace and elegance. Her long black hair was woven into a four-strand braid that framed her dark eyes, strong cheekbones, and full red lips. Nikolai Barsky, the artistic director of the Philharmonic, joined Sophia on the stage and together they bowed to thunderous applause. He was a man of consummate talent and culture. He had mentored Sophia in her mercurial rise to be the first female chief conductor of the greatest orchestra in Russia.

"You have a guest waiting for you backstage," he said. "An unwelcome guest, I might add. Keep your poise. You are a national treasure. You have more power and influence than any of these parasites."

Irina Vasilivna, the Deputy Minister of Culture, was waiting for her by the edge of the curtain. She was a heavyset woman with orange-red hair and Gucci pumps that buckled under her weight.

"Sophia Sergeivna, a magnificent performance! I haven't seen such patriotic fervor since the liberation of Crimea. Thank you for complying with my request to conclude the concert with Prokofiev."

"A fitting finale for the mood of the country," Sophia said.

"The Ukrainian *khokhols* will greet our soldiers with flowers. We'll arrange to have our Philharmonic perform at the Kyiv Opera House on Victory Day."

"It would be an honor. But for now, I need to return to my apartment. I . . . I have some guests coming over."

"Your guests will have to wait. Colonel Besoviy from the Russian Federal Security Service has asked to see you."

"The FSB? But why?"

"Sticks and carrots, Sophia Sergeivna. When the Ukrainians see the futility of resistance, we must show them what they have to gain: security, stability, and most important, reintegration into *Ruski Mir* –

the Russian world – and our great Russian culture. You, my dear, are a standard bearer of that culture, the heroine who in the fog of war carries the flag with the double eagle."

Sophia knew that Colonel Besoviy was not a man one could refuse. "I need a minute, Irina Vasilivna, to gather my things."

"I'll wait for you in the car."

Sophia hurried to her dressing room and pulled her phone out of her purse. She tried to call Alex but received no answer, not even a ring. The attack may have temporarily disabled phone communication, she reasoned. A text might be able to get through: "Please text that you are safe." She debated for a second, and then added an emoji of blowing a kiss.

A black Aurus Senat limousine was waiting for her on Italyanskaya Street with the motor running. The windshield wipers were swishing away the sleet. The driver extinguished his cigarette, got out of the car, and opened the back door. Sophia sat down next to the Deputy Minister.

"Cognac?"

Sophia knew it was rude to turn down the offer. "Yes, of course."

The Deputy Minister pulled two crystal snifters and a bottle of Remy Martin XO out of the limousine bar. She poured two fingers worth of cognac into each of the snifters.

"I find it's better for the nerves to have a drink before meeting with the FSB," the Deputy Minister advised her. "They study you as they speak to you, analyzing every frown, every wrinkle, every eye movement. It's best to be shit-faced when you meet with them."

The driver pulled up to the Bolshoy Dom, the FSB Headquarters on Liteyny Prospect. A uniformed guard opened Sophia's door.

"You won't be coming?" Sophia asked the Deputy Minister.

"Not on your life," she replied. "Remember, my dear, you are a Maestra. Don't let them intimidate you."

Sophia was no stranger to the Bolshoy Dom. Her stepfather made frequent visits to the FSB headquarters while he was still in the diplomatic service. He would take Sophia along and have her wait with one of the guards while he discussed matters of state with the security service. She remembered that the visitors seemed to enter reluctantly and exit quickly. The guard led her through the metal detector, up the elevator to the fifth floor, and down a long corridor to a corner office. Colonel Besoviy looked up from his desk without getting up. The photo of Putin hung over his head. Sophia's first impression was that she was staring at a corpse. His pasty white complexion, combed-back hair, and pin-stripe suit looked he had just escaped from a funeral home. The colonel's thick round glasses magnified his strabismus. With each eye looking in different directions, one was not quite sure which eye was looking at you.

"Sophia Sergeivna, please sit down."

Sophia sat down in a cracked leather chair facing the desk. She noticed that the arms were missing several brass fasteners, as if they had been clawed out by nervous fingers.

"You've been drinking," the colonel said.

"A celebratory toast after our concert this evening," Sophia lied.

"Prokofiev's 'War and Peace.'"

"You were there?" Sophia asked.

The colonel didn't answer her question. "Do you know why you're here?" the colonel asked.

"I can't imagine."

"Your boyfriend, Alex Ivanovich . . ."

Sophia felt an insect crawling up her spine. She squirmed in her chair.

"When was the last time that you saw him?"

"A few days ago."

"Where was he going?"

"I'm . . . I'm not sure. I know he was taking a train. I believe it was related to his work."

"You've not spoken to him since."

"No."

"You tried to reach him today."

Sophia wasn't sure if it was a question or a statement. "I texted him. I asked him to text me back."

The colonel opened a thick dossier that was lying on his desk. "Your boyfriend is well known to us. We tolerate his boyish attempts to circumvent our surveillance because he can be useful to us when he behaves, but there are limits to our patience. We have reports that he went to film the joint military exercises in Belarus. I have an unconfirmed report that he may have crossed the border into Ukraine at Yarylovichi."

"Then you know more than I do."

"We are living in dangerous times, Sophia Sergeivna, when dissent could be viewed as treason. You are patriot are you not?"

"I am a loyal citizen of Russia."

"Out of respect for your late father, I will take you at your word. You will let me know if your boyfriend contacts you. You will share every detail, no matter how trivial. I've texted you my contact information."

Sophia felt a ping in her phone. The colonel pressed a button on his desk, and the guard who was waiting outside opened the door.

"We have a car waiting for you in front of the building. Private Orlov will escort you."

When they were in the elevator, the private pulled out the concert program and a pen. "Could I trouble you for an autograph?" he asked. "My wife is a big fan."

Sophia scribbled her name on the program and handed it to the private with a forced smile.

A "geliki" Mercedes-Benz SUV flashed its lights when Sophia exited the FSB headquarters. The private led her to the car, opened the door, and helped her into the back seat. "Thank you again for the autograph," he said and closed the door behind her. The driver was a heavy-set man in a black leather jacket whose head appeared to rest directly on his shoulders. He drove to her apartment on Admiralteyskiy Prospect without asking for directions. She let herself out and climbed the five flights of stairs to her apartment, relieved to have the day behind her. When she put her keys in the door, she found that only two of three locks were locked. She turned on the lights.

"Alex?"

No answer.

The apartment was empty. Her keen eye noticed that the Hummel figurine on the coffee table, a girl playing a violin, was facing in the wrong direction.

* * *

Father Stephan's hands shook as he placed a gold coin and black candle into his Viaticum case. The burn mark of a key on the contessa's palm had shaken him. He had believed that the devil was allegorical and that evil was a product of our own free will. Yet the Pope had recently reaffirmed that the devil was real. The ritual of Anointing had not worked as he had hoped. Her soul was lost in a realm he could not reach. Once, during one of their late night soirees, the contessa had shown him where she kept her collection of forbidden books. They included the *Ars Notaria,* a thirteenth century grimoire on demonology that focused on communicating and summoning angels for assistance. Demons were fallen angels, so there was still a chance he might plead with them to save her soul. He had learned the rituals of the practice of necromancy from the Archimandrite in Jerusalem but had sworn never to use them to conjure demons. The Archimandrite warned that Pope John XXII's papal bull, *Super illius specula* (Upon the Watchtower) stipulated excommunication for anyone who summoned demons for the purpose of receiving any kind of help from them. It was the clergy's mission to save lost souls, but not if it meant forfeiting their own. But what if someone else descended into their world? Someone who had not summoned the demon themselves? Father Stephan's only hope of saving her soul was to ask the unthinkable: to ask Lev to come face to face with the devil.

Father Stephan called the Rivelli Palazzo and instructed the staff not to move the body until he returned later that morning. He said that he needed to complete his prayers over the contessa's body to try and save her immortal soul. He asked Lev to accompany him. Father Stephan was convinced that Lev had entered the astral plane in Poveglia. He was already communicating with demons. The contessa's soul had just begun its forty days of wandering. If Lev could enter the astral plane again, find her, and convince her to return to Christ, there was still hope of saving her soul.

They entered the palazzo through the pedestrian gate and garden.

"Where is Conte Rivelli?" Lev asked. "Shouldn't he be handling the arrangements for the funeral?"

"When was the last time you saw him?" Father Stephan asked.

"At their masquerade several nights ago."

"The conte is . . . away."

"He's a despicable man, if you ask me," Lev said.

"Theirs was a marriage of convenience," Father Stephan replied. "It was a loveless, childless affair, arranged to preserve the family's name and fortune. The contessa, herself, is actually a generous soul. She's the main benefactor of San Basilio's church. Without her we would be forced to close the church and make it yet another Venetian architectural monument. The church was built in the 12th century. The mosaics are an ecclesiastical treasure."

Lev was surprised to hear Father Stephan speak of Contessa Rivelli in the present tense. They were in fact entering her home to pray over her corpse.

The lady's maid let them in and led them up to the contessa's bedroom. The body had not been moved, as Father Stephan had instructed. He turned to the maid and said, "Leave us." He pulled down the sheet that covered the contessa's corpse. Her face was as he had left her: eyes open and mouth agape in terror. Rigor mortis had not yet set in. Perhaps the *Zuo Thar* was working as it was intended.

Lev envisioned the look on the face of a poor soul who had been buried alive.

Father Stephan opened his Viaticum case, put on his stole, and handed Lev the gold coin and the black candle.

"Place your right hand on her forehead."

Lev pulled his hand back. "Touch her? I thought we came here so you could pray for her soul."

"I am going to pray for her soul. The Anointing last night didn't work as I had hoped. I fear her soul is lost in its wandering. I want to try and bring her back."

"To life?" Lev asked incredulously.

"No, to God."

"Why do you need me?

"Because you can see with the eye of the soul. You've seen Mara. You've been to the Burning Grounds. These visions you're having are not hallucinations. They are very real. You, like the contessa, can enter the astral plane."

"The astral plane?"

"The plane of consciousness that lies beyond our sensual perceptions. It's mentioned in many religions and belief systems: the *Yesod* of the Kabalah, the "Perfect Land" of old Egyptian religion, the world of the Jinn, and the 'Third Heaven' of the Bible."

Lev hesitated. He had thought his visions were a curse brought on by madness. But perhaps his ability to see with the eye of the soul was a gift. His mother had been able to see and experience a world beyond mere human perception. It was not a world of either good or evil, real or unreal. It simply *was*.

"As I read these prayers, I need you to concentrate. I need you enter the astral plane and tell me what you see. If you stray, I promise I will bring you back to the light."

As Father Stephan began the orations of the *Ars Notaria*, Lev placed his right hand on the contessa's cold forehead. He held the coin and candle in his left hand. He cleared his mind of any and all distractions: the cold draft seeping through the window, the lavender perfume that the maid had sprinkled on the bed to mask the smell of death, the anxious beating of Father Stephan's heart. He closed his eyes and was engulfed by darkness. There was no up, no down, no left, and no right. There was no before or after. There was only Now.

"Darkness. I am nowhere – and everywhere," Lev said.

Father Stephan continued the oration and lit the candle in Lev's hand. "Tell me what you see."

With the light of the candle, the darkness slowly began to assume shape and form. Above him was a starless sky. Below him was black water.

"I see moving water."

"Look for a bridge," Father Stephan said.

Lev saw that he was standing by a canal. A stone bridge arched over the black water.

"I see it," Lev said.

Father Stephan paused.

"What shall I do?" Lev asked.

"Walk to the top of the bridge. Do not cross it. Tell me if you can see the contessa on the other side."

Lev climbed the three steps to the top of the bridge.

"Do you see her?" Father Stephan asked.

"No . . . wait. There is someone on the other side."

"Contessa Rivelli?"

"No. It's a tall figure in a dark cloak. He's climbing the bridge." Father Stephan crossed himself.

"His face – he has hollow cheeks and black holes for eyes."

"Ask him if he's seen the contessa. Offer him the gold coin."

Lev's hand was shaking. The candle flame went out. "He's . . ."

"He's what?

"He's asking me if I brought him the soul of an unbaptized child."

A loud knock on the door jolted Lev out of his trance. He opened his eyes. "Where in hell did you take me?" he cried out.

The contessa's maid opened the door to admit two men with a gurney and a body bag. Father Stephan waved them away and said, "I'm not finished."

"*Mi scusi*, Father," the maid replied, "but you've been praying over the body for hours. The men from the funeral home have been patiently waiting, but they say they can wait no longer. They will return the body once it's been embalmed. The family has requested that the visitation be held here in the palazzo in three days' time."

Father Stephan and Lev stepped back from the contessa's bed and watched as the men zipped the body into a black bag, lifted it onto the gurney, and carried it down to the *porta d'acqua* where a boat hearse was waiting. The waves from the wake of the vaporetto rocked the hearse as it motored away.

"I ask you again, Father. Where in hell did you send me?"

"The Devil's Bridge in Torcello. The contessa believed in the legend. I thought you might find her there."

"The Devil's Bridge. That apparition that I saw . . .?"

Father Stephan didn't answer.

"I asked you to free me of my hallucinations. Instead, you send me into a place darker than Poveglia."

"I had you follow her down the left-hand path in hope of saving her. I am in her debt. San Basilio's church would have closed without her. But the left-hand path leads to oblivion. We cannot undo her choice. But I can still show *you* the way."

"To where?"

"To union with the Absolute. I can lead you down the Mystic Way, the Path of Perfection. I've taken it myself. I'll come by your apartment later today and explain everything. But first I have to get back to my notes to transcribe what we experienced today."

* * *

Lev had suffered from visions since childhood. His first occurred at the age of five, when he found his mother drowned in a pool at the base of a waterfall. After her funeral, he ran away up the mountain. When the villagers found him two days later, he claimed he had met the *Didko* – the devil – in the woods. His grandfather, the village priest, had prayed to exorcise his demon. His second break with reality occurred when he was at the university at the age of twenty, after he found his sweetheart hanging from a weeping willow. He claimed she had turned into a *mavka* – a forest nymph – and tried to tickle him to death. His friends from the Komsomol helped him flee the country before he was accused of her murder. His third break occurred at the age of forty, when he was a writer in Paris. After his paramour, the mother of his daughter, had died of heartbreak, he claimed that she haunted him for forty nights. He was hospitalized for a month in the Sainte-Anne Hospital Center with a diagnosis of grief-related psychosis.

Lev knew full well that at times of stress he was in danger of losing touch with reality. The pandemic, with its death and isolation, was taking its toll. Russia's invasion of Ukraine had upended his view of the world – oppressors were victims, Jews were Nazis, lies were truth. George Orwell's apocalyptic vision of the totalitarian state – "War is Peace, Freedom is Slavery, and Ignorance is Strength" – was resurrecting in Russia. Lev had thought that good had overcome evil on the Maidan, but now the evil had returned even stronger than before. Death was all around him. He was trying to hold on to his sanity, but Father Stephan was convincing him that his visions of Mara, the Burning Grounds of Poveglia, and the demon on the Devil's Bridge were real: he had the gift of seeing into the astral plane. Lev was hoping to escape his demons, and Father Lev was forcing him to confront them.

From his window Lev saw Father Stephan enter the Corte del Milion through the carved Greek arch that was all that remained of Marco Polo's ancestral home. Lev's landlady met Father Stephan by the well in the middle of the courtyard and led him into the building. *Let the woman earn her exorbitant rent*, Lev figured, *and escort him right to my door. But before I let him guide me on my spiritual journey, I need to settle my earthly affairs. I need him to witness my will. He's the one person who believes that I'm still of sound mind and body and will attest that my will is valid.* Lev had addressed his letter to Sophia but had not yet sealed it. If needed, he would ask Father Stephan to deliver it as well.

The landlady let Father Stephan into Lev's apartment without first knocking. Father Stephan thanked her and closed the door.

"She's an irascible woman," Lev said. "She lets herself into my apartment whenever she pleases."

"On the contrary, I found her quite entertaining. She told me that the Corte is haunted."

"I presume she told you the story of the ghost of Marco Polo's wife. She repeats it to everyone who enters our building."

"She said that Marco Polo had married a daughter of the Great Khan and brought her to Venice. His sisters became jealous of her, and when he was captured in battle by the Genoese, the envious sisters told her that her husband was dead. Reeling in grief she set fire to her clothes and jumped from the window of Marco Polo's house into the underlying canal. Sometimes, your landlady said, when she looks out your window at night, she can see a white figure floating in the air or hear a strange song of oriental origin. Have you perhaps seen . . .?"

"The ghost of Marco Polo's wife? I may be suffering from visions, but no, I'm not seeing ghosts from seven hundred years ago."

"Yes, of course. It was foolish of me to ask."

"Father, please sit down. I helped you with your rituals to try and save the contessa's soul. I need a favor from you in return. Do you remember that you promised to witness my will?"

"I'll do whatever you ask."

Lev pointed to the letter on the desk. I wrote this letter to my daughter, Sophia, who lives in St. Petersburg, Russia. I don't know if she'll open it and read it, but I wanted someone I trust to witness my intention."

Father Stephan picked up the letter and read it.

"I would be happy to serve as your witness."

"Thank you, but even so, I fear that my letter won't reach her. The war between Russia and Ukraine has begun. My daughter is the conductor of the St. Petersburg Philharmonic Orchestra. She's a public figure, so she's probably under surveillance. The FSB will most likely read the letter before it gets to her. I have a history with the security services. I fear that . . ."

"I promise you I that I'll deliver it to her." Father Stephan carefully folded the letter and put it in his cassock pocket.

"You would do this for me?"

"We clergy minister to the heart and soul."

"You have no idea how much peace that gives me."

"I'm happy to do it for your daughter. Now allow me to help you. Do remember at the Rivelli's masquerade ball when Professor Brown asked you if you are spiritual?"

"He told me that spirituality is a journey."

"Yes. But it's not a journey outward. It's a journey *inward*."

"To find yourself?" Lev asked.

"No," Father Stephan replied. "To *lose* your Self."

"I don't understand."

"I didn't either, at first. My personal journey covered half the globe before I found the answers I was looking for. I knew when I was an altar boy in Philadelphia that I wanted to serve God. I could have entered the St. Josaphat Ukrainian Catholic Seminary in Washington D.C., but I chose a more academic path instead. I entered the Basilian Christ the King Monastery in Rome and completed my Ecclesiastical Bachelor degree at the Pontifical Athenaeum of Sant'Anselmo. I then obtained my Ecclesiastical Master's Degree in Patristic Theology at the Pontifical Oriental Institute. But after being ordained, I suffered a crisis of faith. At the advice of my abbot, I took a retreat at the monastery of the Exaltation of the Holy Cross in Buchach, Ukraine. A monk by the name of Brother Theodosius took me under his wing and introduced me to meditation through the Jesus prayer. Over and over, I would breathe in "Lord Jesus Christ, Son of God," and breathe out, "have mercy on me, a sinner." Each time I said the prayer I sank deeper and deeper into an awareness of Jesus's presence. With time I went through the mystic stages of awakening, purification, and illumination. I suffered through my dark night of the soul before finally abandoning myself and achieving union with the Absolute. I saw that God is everywhere, and even I, who was wracked with doubt, found God within me. It was sheer ecstasy!"

"Then why didn't you stay at the monastery?"

"I wanted to share my discovery with others. I returned to Rome and enrolled in the doctoral program at the Pontifical Oriental Institute. I wanted to research the "Dark Night of the Soul" to learn how other religions approached the soul's spiritual journey to eternity. I found remarkable similarities across ages and religions in the stages of the search for union with the Absolute. I met with holy men – Christians, Jews, Muslims – who showed me how to communicate with those in the spirit world."

"You can *see* the same things that I see?" Lev asked.

"Not exactly. You can't separate what you see from who is seeing it. Reality is one with the observer. But I can understand why you see the things that you do."

"Like Mara?"

"Yes, she appears different to whoever interacts with her. I've only read about and listened to what others have told me. You describe her as a beautiful woman."

"Beautiful beyond belief."

"Others have had very different perceptions. But what's important is how she appears to you."

Lev looked out the window into the Corte Milion. "Is that why you asked me if I see the ghost of Marco Polo's wife?"

"Forgive my naivete," Father Stephan replied. "I understand now that the ghost of Marco Polo's wife has no meaning for you. Your other visions are all connected to you in some way. My worry is that you'll be lost in the world of the Burning Grounds. You need to find a way out. I truly believe that orison, the Mystic Way, can help you unite with God before it's too late."

"What would you have me do?"

"Pray."

"I pray when I feel that all else is lost."

"Prayer is much more than a way out. It's a way *in*. All major religions practice forms of meditation. Buddhist meditation is perhaps the most well-known, but there are many paths to the Great Liberation. We Christians use meditative prayer. But there are also the Kabbalah in Judaism, Yoga in Hinduism, and Sufism in Islam among many others. Meditation is a spiritual practice regardless of your religious beliefs."

"Where will orison lead me?" Lev asked.

"You will pass through five stages on the Mystic Way. Jung had said 'Who looks outside, dreams. Who looks inside, awakens.' You have already experienced the Awakening of the self by embarking on your spiritual journey. Next you will go through Purification, in which you become aware of your imperfections and the impurity of your thoughts and feelings. Once you can cleanse yourself of these thoughts, you can reach a state of Illumination, a raised and more intuitive consciousness, before questioning your faith and entering your Dark Night of the Soul. If you can survive your dark night, you will achieve Union with the Absolute."

"I will … pray on it," Lev replied. "But before I try to save my soul, I need to try and reconcile with my one and only child."

* * *

Contessa Rivelli's wake was held on Shrove Tuesday, the last day of Carnival. She was laid out in the ballroom of her palazzo in an open mahogany casket with white velvet interior. She was dressed in what appeared to be an antique wedding gown. Scores of elaborate funereal wreathes formed a winter garden around the casket. The intricate carvings in the mahogany reminded Lev of the apotropaic symbols he had seen emblazoned on her library door. He wondered if she had the casket made in anticipation of her death to ward off any evil that might try to disturb her eternal rest. The interior of the ballroom was illuminated with a thousand candles. The mourners included her family and a few close friends. Most of the guests from the masquerade had opted not to come, given the likely cause of death, and had sent flowers and condolences instead. Unlike the elaborate masks from the Carnival ball, the mourners in attendance wore simple facemasks to protect themselves from the contagion. A few mourners went so far as to wear latex gloves. Lev had debated whether he should come to pay his last respects, but Father Stephan assured him that he would be welcome. To the chagrin of the Latin clergy, the contessa had willed that she wanted Father Stephan, an Eastern-rite Catholic priest, to perform the *Panachyda,* the prayer for the repose of the soul of the deceased. She had bequeathed a fair sum of money to support San Basilio's church. Lev now understood why Father Stephan was so intent on saving her soul.

After the singing of *Vichnaya Pamyat* – Eternal Memory – the mourners approached the casket in a single file to pay their last respects. Some knelt and said a prayer. Others touched the casket and moved on. Those closest to her heart touched her hand or kissed her on her cold forehead. Lev approached and took one last look at the *Benandante*. She appeared to be in agony, even though the funeral director had gone to great lengths to give her an expression of peace. He had stitched her eyelids shut with hidden sutures, filled her mouth with cotton, and severed some facial muscles to enable her to close her jaw. He had placed a crucifix in her lace-gloved hands and folded them over her chest. Lev couldn't pretend that he knew her well, although he had touched her dead forehead and risked his sanity searching for her soul in the astral plane. As he passed the casket, he saw that her right hand was no longer gripping the crucifix. He gently lifted her hand to fold it back on the cross and stopped. The burn mark of a key was emblazoned on her palm. He let go of her hand, crossed himself, and turned away.

Conte Rivelli was sitting in the front row of seats that were reserved for the immediate family. He was not wearing a mask. He gave Lev a wry smile and squeezed the hand of the woman sitting next to him. Her face was covered with a veil, but from her build and the color of her hair, Lev was certain that it was Angela. She did not so much as look up at him. From her downcast demeanor, Lev concluded that her sadness was profound, as if she was resigned to spend eternity with her tormentor.

Lev spotted Professor Jordan Brown by one of the windows in the back of the ballroom. Lev came up to him and asked, "You're not coming up to pay your last respects?"

"We're unwelcome strangers here," the professor replied.

"Then why did you come?"

"Curiosity. I was wondering if our mystic, Father Stephan, was going to raise her from the dead."

"You're being irreverent."

"How much do you know about him?" the professor asked.

"He followed me to the contessa's library on the night of the masquerade ball. I've come to know him since. He was born in Philadelphia and completed the seminary in Rome. He began his mystical journey in a monastery in Ukraine. He wanted to share his journey with others and is writing a doctoral dissertation on the 'Dark Night of the Soul.' He truly is a holy man."

"A holy man, you say? The man's a Rasputin."

"He believes that there are many paths to union with the Absolute, no matter how esoteric they might be. He's even involved me in some of his . . . rituals."

"Did you know that he was accused of getting a girl pregnant while he was in the monastery?"

"What?" Lev couldn't fathom the accusation.

"A young girl, a novitiate nun, accused him of seducing her. She got an abortion, gave up on her vows, and left the convent."

"I find that hard to believe."

"The Church covered it up. Before the local authorities launched an investigation, they sent him to some monastery in Ukraine until it blew over or until they paid her off."

"You think that this whole spiel about following the "Mystic Way" is a charade?"

"I don't know if he found Jesus or the devil in that monastery. I do know that he's not as holy as you think he is. At the masquerade you promised to meet with me so we could continue our discussion on the true nature of spirituality. I hold you to that promise."

That evening Lev stood on the Accademia Bridge and watched the Silent Regatta as it slowly glided down the Grand Canal. The procession of boats was the last public event of Carnival. The electricity along the Grand Canal had been switched off and the lavish palaces, like the Rivelli's Palazzo, were illuminated with thousands of candles. The boats were draped in black with crews in black. The last boat was an ebony launch with red leather upholstery. Lev recognized the boat and the woman at the helm. She pulled down her hood, looked up at him on the bridge, and motioned with her long white fingers for him to join her. The madness of Carnival was over. His had just begun.

— 96 —

CHAPTER 6

Il Dottore

Lev found his mother submerged in the green pool. Her face was visible beneath the froth where the mountain stream cascaded over the waterfall into the pool below. Her eyes were open, and her dark hair swirled in the vortex like seaweed. At first, he thought she was playing. He lay next to her, held his breath, and put his head under the water. He opened his eyes. The sky and the water were one. When he lifted his head out of the water, he saw that she still had not moved. He lifted her head, and her wet hair draped back over his arm. He shook her to wake her, but she did not respond. Her mouth and lungs were filled with water. He felt his heart pounding. He pulled her to the bank and rested her on a bed of ferns. Her embroidered shirt clung to her bosom, but her chest was still. He called to her, but she would not answer. He hugged her as hard as could. When he could hug her no more, he closed her eyes, put his head on her bosom, and cried.

The mountain pool, with its lush fern banks, moss covered boulders, and cascading waterfall was their sacred place. His mother would take him there when the quarreling in the home was too much to bear. They would sit on the bank with their feet in the swirling water, and she would tell him how the river flowed from a spring in a lake on top of the mountain. The water in the lake was as pure and blue as the sky above. She told him a tale that she had heard from her own mother. A golden egg lay at the bottom of the lake high atop the mountain. It had been there since the beginning, long before the land had a name – before it was called Ukraine, the Soviet Union, or Kyivan Rus. It was there when the sun, the moon, and the wind were alive, and the life-giving energy of the cosmos was in all things. She told him about the magical fern flower that blooms only once a year, for an hour before midnight during the summer solstice. Whoever found it would be granted eternal youth and eternal life, but it could only be found in the most magical parts of the forest by those who are truly in love. She told him stories about the denizens of the ancient forest, whom to respect and whom of fear. "The *lisovyk*," she had said, "protects the forest and the *vodianyk* protects the streams. Beware of the water and forest nymphs. The *rusalkas* will lure you into the water and drown you, while the *mavkas* will entice you into the forest and tickle you to death. Beware *Mara,* who appears to you in nightmares, torments you, and traps you in a world of perpetual winter. But most of all, beware of the devil that lurks in these woods. He goes by many names. Our ancestors called him *Didko* and your grandfather calls him *chort,* but he is one and the same ancient evil. Whatever he promises you, his real intent is to rob you of your soul."

Her father, Ihor, who was the village priest, chided her for filling his grandson's head with folklore and superstition. When Christianity came to these mountains, God the Father, Son, and Holy Ghost supplanted the ancient gods and nature spirits. The winter equinox became Christmas and the Festival of Kupalo became the Feast of the Birth of Saint John the Baptist. Perun, the God of thunder, became Saint Elijah, and saints and angels now watch over the faithful the way that local deities had watched over the ancient clans. *Didko* was the devil himself.

When Lev could no longer cry, he ran back to the village to search for his father. The house was empty, and the carved chest with their valuables was gone. Lev found his grandfather in church and led him back to the green pool. Father Ihor crossed himself three times and prayed over his daughter's body. He lifted her in his arms, carried her down through the forest and meadows and brought her to his house. Though he was old, he was strong for his age and refused to let any of the villagers help him carry her. Rumors surrounding her death quickly spread through the village. They said her husband was an abusive drunkard and philanderer and was often seen sneaking around the village at night. He fled the village before her body was discovered. Some said that she had taken her own life out of despair. Others said that he had pushed her down the waterfall. Lev preferred to believe that his mother had slipped while climbing the rocks of the waterfall in search of the golden egg.

The entire village attended the funeral. After the *Panachyda* the pine coffin was placed on a horse-drawn cart that carried her to the cemetery in the meadow above the church. Before the coffin was lowered into the ground, her father, firmly holding his grandson by the hand, took a handful of dirt and formed the sign of the cross over the head of the casket. Lev placed a bunch of her favorite wildflowers on the lid over her heart. He could feel his grandfather's pain in the strength of his grip. The finality struck Lev as the coffin was being lowered into the ground and the mourners sang *Vichnaya Pamyat* – Eternal Memory. He broke away from his grandfather's grip and bolted up the mountain. He ran and ran until he could no longer hear the yells of the men who were chasing him. *If I find the golden egg*, he thought, *it will bring my mother back to life*. He followed the stream up the mountain, past the green pool; past the oak, beech, and spruce; to where the stone pines and juniper eked out of the rock towards the life-giving rays of sun.

On the top of the mountain, he found the source of the stream: it flowed from a lake as blue as the sky above. The reflection of the sun shimmered in its icy water. As he came nearer, he saw a light shining from within. A golden egg lay at the bottom of the lake, bathing all that surrounded it with the yellow glow of the sun.

"Son, bring me the golden egg."

Lev looked up to see his father standing atop a crag overlooking the lake. "Father, mother is . . ."

"Gone," his father said. "Your mother was too fragile for this world.

We live in a world of perpetual violence, of eat or be eaten, of kill or be killed. The things she wanted you to believe in – love, hope, and happiness – are illusions. They are as fleeting as your reflection in the water. The only thing that matters is power. Dive into the lake and bring me the egg. Within it are all the riches of the earth. Bring me the egg, and I will share them with you."

Lev began to climb the crag to hug his father, but his father stopped him. "First bring me the egg."

Lev dove into the icy water and swam down towards the golden egg. As he was about to touch it, a hand grabbed his wrist. He turned to see his mother in the water, just as he had seen her in the green pool. Her eyes were open and her hair swirled in the water, but now he could hear her voice in his head.

"Don't let him deceive you. The egg belongs to all things. If he acquires its power, he will keep it only for himself, and all that is good in this world will wither and die."

He wanted to stay with her beneath the water, even if it meant drowning. The water enveloped him like a womb. She smiled and pointed up to the sun and the sky. "I will always be with you," she said.

Lev swam up and took a breath of air.

"Do you have the egg?" his father called out.

"Mother said to let it be."

His father screamed. It was not a scream of pain. It was a scream of anger, the blood-curdling scream of a beast. Lev saw that his father's head was bigger than he remembered. His eyes were hollow, and his legs were spindly and hairy, like the legs of a spider. His father, or whatever the creature was, began to climb down the crag. Lev swam to the opposite shore and careened down the mountain. Now and again, he thought he saw his mother appear from behind a boulder or a tree pointing the way. The sunlight streamed through her without casting a shadow. He heard the primal screams behind him, at first near, and then ever farther as he zigzagged down the mountain. He ran into a meadow and hid in the lush mountain grass until the screams died away. He closed his eyes and imagined his mother cradling him in her bosom.

A shepherd found him days later. Lev was suffering from hypothermia and dehydration. When he was brought back to his grandfather's house, Lev told him what he had seen. His grandfather blessed him with holy water, burned incense, and uttered prayers to cast away demons. His grandfather went into the church archives and found Lev's birth records. He crossed out the father's name and left only his mother's maiden name: Veles. The grandfather mourned his daughter for forty days. The villagers brought them food: polenta, sheep's cheese, and borscht. Rumors again began to spread through the village. The older women whispered that the boy had met the *Didko* high up the mountain. The younger women concluded that the poor orphan had simply lost his mind.

Lev ignored the gossip. He knew in his heart that his mother would always be with him.

* * *

The night train to Minsk rolled through the bloodlands. The moon shone over the barren, snow-covered fields where the Nazi and Stalinist regimes had committed mass murders of civilians. The passenger train passed slow-moving trains laden with military equipment. Alex looked at his reflection in the window. He wondered if any one man could make a difference in the horror that was about to be unleashed on Ukraine. During the Revolution of Dignity, the Ukrainians had said that: "alone we are a drop; together we are an ocean." Perhaps he could be the drop that changes the tide. The only other person in his train compartment was a pale woman with dark eyes and midnight black hair. She stared at him with a bemused look, as if deciding whether to engage him in a conversation. Alex kept looking out the window into the darkness.

A young Uzbek met him at the railway station in Minsk. He was holding a cardboard sign that read "UNICEF." Alex followed him to a Lada Niva in the parking lot and handed him a roll of U.S. hundred-dollar bills. The man counted the bills and asked, "What about the border guards?"

Alex reached into his camera case and took out another roll of bills. "Do you have the papers?"

The Uzbek showed him the invitation. It was on official UNICEF stationary with the obligatory signatures and stamps. He had procured it through the usual chain of connections and bribes. "I'll take you through the Belarusian border guards," he said. "The Ukrainians are your problem."

The driver took the back roads from Minsk to the border to avoid as many checkpoints as possible. Each unnecessary stop involved a risky conversation and a bribe. The road led through abandoned villages and desolate marshes that were uninhabitable due to the Chornobyl accident. Nature had taken over where man had fled. Every now and then Alex would ask the driver to stop, to get a glimpse of rare European bison and Prsewalski horses that foraged for radioactive grasses and sedges that were hidden beneath the snow. South of Gomel they veered onto E95 towards the border crossing at Novi Yarylovichi. They passed columns of armor – tanks, personnel carriers, Grad and Typhoon missile launchers – waiting for the order to attack. Conscripts sat in the turrets nervously smoking and cursing about the ineptitude of their commanders.

As they approached the border crossing, the Uzbek pulled the car off the road. "We walk the last kilometer," he said.

Alex didn't ask why. He assumed his driver didn't want to run the risk of having his car confiscated. When they reached the border, Alex was surprised that the guards didn't ask why they had traveled on foot. He saw the driver hand the guard the roll of hundred dollars bills. The entire crossing, with its perfunctory questioning, stamping of passports, and passage of money, was a well-orchestrated charade.

Crossing into the Ukrainian side was more difficult. The Ukrainian border guards kept him in a locked room for hours as they examined his passport, searched through his luggage, and checked with Kyiv regarding the authenticity of his documents. Alex pleaded with them to at least return his video camera, if they would not allow him to enter. Towards evening a border guard informed him that he had received the necessary clearance. A colleague of his, Andriy Orishkevich, had arrived to take him to Kyiv. Andriy had brought a document from the SBU – Security Service of Ukraine – allowing the issuance of a temporary visa.

Andriy was waiting by a ZAZ 968 outside the guard station. He shook Alex's hand and kissed him thrice on the cheeks.

"I'm sorry for the delay," Andriy said. "I had to make some stops along the way, delivering body armor and night vision glasses to our territorial defense groups in the Chornobyl zone. What does the other side of the border look like?"

"Ominous. Columns of armor as far as the eye can see."

Andriy looked across the checkpoint into the radioactive wasteland. "Let the 'orcs' come. We will welcome them to hell."

* * *

Lev crossed the Accademia Bridge into Dorsoduro for his rendezvous with Professor Jordan Brown. Ca' Foscari University was located in a gothic palazzo that overlooked the Grand Canal. The professor's office was furnished with an 18th century walnut desk and chair that befitted the stature of visiting academics. The desk was piled high with stacks of books and papers. The antique bookcase behind the desk held a collection of curiosities: a wooden talisman, a straw-filled doll, a Dybbuk box, and a charred human skull. Lev cringed. Visions of the dead in Poveglia crawled out of his brain.

Professor Brown peeked up from behind his desk. He was a fidgety man with

a cocked eyebrow that appeared to judge if you were worthy of his time. His hair was dyed a purplish black. He stood up and offered his hand. "Mr. Veles, I'm so delighted you came. I promise you a most interesting morning."

Lev kept staring at the skull without responding.

Professor Brown smiled. "I see you're admiring my reliquary. I've collected these items from various curiosity shops during my sabbatical in Venice. The professor lifted up the skull. "Allow me to introduce you to Father Gregorio Ricci. He was accused of heresy by the papal inquisition in the seventeenth century for questioning the worshiping of saints. When he refused to recant, he was excommunicated and burned at the stake. His skull was saved to warn others about the consequences of heresy. The other objects in my collection are also 'unholy,' each in its own way. They are relics of spiritual journeys that didn't end well."

Professor Brown pushed the stacks to the side so they could speak face to face. He placed the skull back on the bookcase.

"You appear to be working on something important," Lev said.

"The culmination of my life's work! I'm writing the definitive treatise on sacred places."

"Churches?"

"More than just churches," the professor explained. "Sacred places are where we enter the realm of divinity. They can be churches, mosques, temples, and tombs. But they can also be places in nature – mountains, rivers – that hold a special meaning for us. Cities such as Mecca and Jerusalem are sacred because religiously significant events occurred there. The Jews believe that God gave them Israel, and to them the entire land is sacred. In some religions, such as Tantric yoga, the sacred places are within our own bodies."

"Your work must bring you closer to God."

Professor Brown laughed. "I'm a religious scholar, but I'm not a religious man."

Lev was surprised. "At the Rivelli's ball you made a point about the need for spirituality."

"Spirituality, yes; religion, no."

"I don't understand."

"Religion seeks to cement the world order. It promises you eternal life if you follow the terms of the contract: believe in the one true God, follow the commandments, and support the church, even if it means waging holy wars, inquisitions, and burning nonconformists at the stake. Spiritual seekers aren't so easily satisfied. They seek to escape the constraints of organized religion. They are looking for more."

"What do they seek?"

"The historian Yuval Harari said that the spiritual journey is a lonely path that takes you in mysterious ways towards unknown destinations. It's different for everyone. Tell me, Mr. Veles, what places have had special meaning for you in your life journey? What places have had the power to transform you?"

Lev thought of his childhood in the Carpathian Mountains, his coming of age at the university in Chernivtsi, his ex-pat life in Paris, and his return to Ukraine during the Revolution of Dignity. "There's a sacred wood in the mountains where I was born where a waterfall empties into a green pool. My mother would take me there and tell me stories about the spirits that inhabited the forest. That place holds special meaning for me."

"Go on."

"In the foothills above Chernivtsi, there's a hidden meadow, a magical place with a weeping willow where my girlfriend and I first made love. We promised ourselves to each other and hoped to find the magical fern flower on the night of the summer solstice so we could be forever young."

"Your first awakening," the professor said.

"There's a church in Paris, St. Volodymyr's, where I first met Vera, the mother of my daughter. I believe that God had brought us together so we could bring Sophia into the world."

"Which place is most sacred?"

"Each has had special meaning for me at different times in my life. Today, the most sacred place for me is the Maidan in Kyiv. That's where I learned about human dignity and the strength of the human spirit."

"A postmodern revelation! Now your journey has brought you to Venice. Is there any place here that you would consider sacred?"

"The pandemic has cast a pall over the city. There are places I would consider unholy: Poveglia, the Devil's Bridge in Torcello, the contessa's library . . . the only place in Venice where I truly felt close to God was in San Basilio's church. With Father Stephan's help, I found solace there."

Professor Brown put his hands on the desk and brought his face closer to Lev's, as if to reveal a major insight. "Your spiritual journey – your growing up from a child to an adolescent to an adult – parallels the evolution of religion from primitive man to the present. Our stone-age ancestors believed in animism in which the spirit was in all things, like the spirits that you believed inhabited your sacred wood in the mountain. We then evolved to magical thinking where we believed that we actually had control over the spiritual forces around us, like your quest for the magical fern flower. Magical thinking evolved into mythical thinking where gods and heroes determined one's fate. Most men today still believe in the myths of the great religions. The more enlightened have moved beyond these beliefs."

"What's more enlightened than belief in God?"

"Belief in *ourselves*."

"What's so special about us?" Lev asked.

"You found your answer on the Maidan – you discovered the dignity of man and the strength of the human spirit."

"I witnessed the best of humanity and the worst of humanity."

"And which prevailed?"

"We overcame evil in that sacred place."

"It became sacred because you made it sacred."

"All of us who were there – Christians, Muslims, Jews – felt a spiritual presence there, something greater than ourselves."

"There is nothing greater than ourselves."

"Why? Copernicus showed us that we're not at the center of the universe. Darwin showed us that we're just another animal. What makes us greater than all of God's creations?"

"Our *consciousness*," the professor countered.

"We're aware of our own insignificance."

"Have faith in us, Mr. Veles, we are noble creatures. You're a writer. You must have read Hamlet: *'What a piece of work is a man! how noble in reason! how infinite in faculty! in form, and moving how express and admirable! in action, how like an angel! in apprehension, how like a God!'*"

". . . and yet, to me, what is this quintessence of dust? Lev completed the quote in his head. He thought about Russia's brutal invasion of Ukraine. *Are we truly noble, or are we just like all the other creatures on earth, living by the algorithm of kill or be killed? I fear that war is inherent in our nature. The* Didko *had told me that the only thing that matters in this world is power.*

"You truly believe that we humans, who murder millions in the name of God, are greater than God?" Lev asked incredulously.

"Not yet, Mr. Veles, but in time. Look at how far the universe has evolved over billions of years, from a primordial plasma to a wondrous natural world of highly complex systems, including stars, minerals, atmospheres, and life. We tend to think in simple terms of order and disorder but the missing law of nature is the law of emergence, the evolution of increasing complexity. Evolving systems become increasingly ordered with time. Our consciousness is the culmination of this evolving complexity."

"I don't understand."

"Our evolution doesn't end here, Mr. Veles. We are destined to become *Homo Deus*."

"If we don't destroy ourselves and all life on earth first."

"Look at how far we've come in the short time that we've been on earth," Professor Brown pressed his argument. "We've mapped our DNA and read the Book of Life. We've discovered the fundamental building blocks of the universe. We've created artificial intelligence. Science is the new religion."

"I believe in science, but I also have faith in something greater than ourselves."

"What is greater than ourselves? If I can't convince you with science, then how about art? Look around us, Mr. Veles, at this miracle called Venice, an impossible city built in the sea. Let's see who we can discover here, God or man? It is *we* who created her art and architecture. It is *we* who have made her sacred, not God or some Evangelist. Allow me to convince you. My sabbatical has allowed me to uncover some of the most interesting examples. Are you up for a stroll?"

Lev welcomed the change of air. The professor's office was stuffy with its books, curios, and hot air. He hoped that a tour of Venice's sacred places might uncover some hidden gems for his novel. The professor's atheistic humanism robbed Venice of her soul. John Ruskin had called Venice "a splendor of miscellaneous spirits." Lev decided he preferred the company of poets to the company of academics.

Professor Brown began his tour with a visit to the Auditorium Santa Margherita which was part of Ca' Foscari University. The vault was decorated with a fresco by the painter Antonio Zanchi that depicted the martyrdom of Saint Margaret of Antioch.

"This place has a long and troubled history. From the 9th century to the early 1800's, it was the Church of Santa Margherita, one of the oldest religious buildings in Venice. It was closed and deconsecrated in

1810, and since then has had a number of uses: as a tobacco storehouse, a depot for marble from other deconsecrated churches, and a private studio for the sculptor, Luigi Borro, before being again transformed into an Evangelical church. Later it became the home of the Chamber of Labor, then a cinema, and finally an auditorium of the university."

"What's your point, professor?"

"My point, Mr. Veles, is that over time a place can transition from being sacred to profane than back to sacred again. God does not dwell in this place. It is we who put Him here whenever we so choose."

Their next stop on their walk was the Church of San Giacomo by the Rialto market, believed to be the oldest church in Venice. The façade featured a large 24-hour clock with just one hand and rotated quadrant, which put noon on the left and midnight on the right. The inscriptions on the apse invited the Rialto merchants to be honest.

"San Giacomo's location in the Rialto market evinces the difference between sacred and profane. The word profane," the professor expounded, "originates from the classical Latin *profanus*, '*pro*' meaning outside and '*fanum*' being temple or sanctuary. Profane is the homogeneity of the mundane, here exemplified by the Rialto market, whereas sacred is that which causes breaks in that homogeneity, exemplified by the church. You see, Mr. Veles, the mystery of the sacred imposes order on the profane. It keeps simple people in check. The clock," he chuckled, "never tells the right time. And now, let's explore what many consider the most sacred place in Venice."

"San Marco Basilica?" Lev asked.

"The 'Golden Basilica,' the professor affirmed as they crossed the Rialto Bridge into San Marco. "The seat of power, piety and plunder."

San Marco Basilica, with its domes, multi-colored columns of rare marbles, and magnificent gold mosaics, dominated the piazza. Lev had been to the Piazza San Marco for the Flight of the Angel, but had not yet visited the Basilica. During Carnival it had been swarming with tourists. Now, between the Carnival and the Biennale, few people remained in the old city. Even fewer ventured into the public spaces due to the pandemic.

"The mosaics on the façade depict the story of the patron saint's arrival to Venice," the professor explained. "The first mosaic, on the right, tells the story of how St. Mark's body was stolen from Alexandria by two Venetian merchants: Bono from Malamocco and Rustico from Torcello. They hid the body in a large basket covered with fruits, vegetables, and pork to conceal it from the Muslim customs agents. The second shows the arrival of the relics in Venice. In the third we see the Doge and his government in adoration of the relics, and the fourth, which is called the *Reception,* depicts the Doge and his retinue in a procession carrying the body into the Basilica. The Latin inscription reads: *'The people place him here with worthy praises and reverence him with hymns in order that he guide the Venetians and rule over the land and sea.'* The body of the saint not only consecrates the Basilica, it gives the Venetians the religious justification for their imperial expansion and plunder. They pillaged and plundered art, relics, and treasures that had been the symbols of Byzantine sacred rule. The Triumphal Quadriga, the four bronze horses that you see above the main entrance, were taken from the Hippodrome in Constantinople during the fourth Crusade."

How similar to Russia today, Lev reflected. *Moscow is claiming to be the 'Third Rome' destined to restore Christianity to a godless world. They justify plunder, rape, and murder in the name of God.*

When they entered the Basilica, Lev lifted his gaze to the vaults and cupolas that glittered with gold mosaics. The mosaics were like the ones he had seen in San Basilio's church, though here they were depicted on a celestial scale. He felt like he had entered heaven on earth. The iconography encompassed Christian history from Creation to the Apocalypse. In contrast to the marvels above, the marble tiles beneath his feet were imperfect and wobbly. Water was seeping up from beneath the stone floor.

"San Marco's is sinking," the professor said. "It sits on flooded wood pilings that are slowly rotting away as the sea seeps in with the tides. I'm afraid that prayers won't save her."

The professor pointed out the marble iconostasis before the altar. With its eight columns and fifteen statues of the Cross of Christ, the weeping Virgin, St. John, and the Twelve Apostles, it separated the nave from the sanctuary.

"A true Byzantine iconostasis displays icons rather than statues," the professor expounded. "This one was designed by the Dalle Masegne brothers in the 14th century and is an amalgam of Byzantine and Italian Gothic styles. Nevertheless, the purpose is the same. The iconostasis is the doorway between the world of humanity and the world of the divine. As they pass through the doors of the iconostasis, the priests move between these two realms."

Behind the high altar, a Byzantine Golden Altarpiece – *Pala d'oro* – was studded with more than a thousand gems, including pearls, emeralds, sapphires, and rubies. The enamels in the top section portrayed the Archangel Michael at the center with six images of the life of Christ on either side: the Entry into Jerusalem, the Descent into Hell, the Crucifixion, the Ascension, Pentecost, and the Dormition of Mary. The enamels in the bottom section portrayed Christ surrounded by the Evangelists, the Twelve Apostles, the Last Judgment, the Second Coming, and the life of St. Mark.

"Your Christian myths, "Professor Brown said, "are illustrated in one, magnificent *'Pala d'oro.'* Tell me, Mr. Veles, do you now feel closer to God or to the artists who created these masterpieces?"

The mosaics on the cupolas, vaults, and walls of San Marco Basilica were a pictorial illustration of the gospel. They showed Lev a path to heaven that had been followed by the saints and countless faithful before him. *Who am I to doubt their veracity?* he asked himself. *What do I seek in my spiritual journey? I seek to know God's love, to love and be loved by others. I seek freedom from the forces of sin. I seek a life that provides love, joy and peace. I seek Jesus, who has the power to transform the world. Even if it relies on the mystery of faith, it is a worthy path to follow.*

"In truth, I feel closer to God."

The professor's eyelid began to twitch. "I concede that the grandeur of this basilica evokes awe in all who enter," he said. "But what inspires me is not that we have entered some magic doorway into the divine. What inspires me is that these are the creations of *man*. We created these myths, this art, and this glorious edifice. We seek the same things, you and I: knowledge, power, and eternal life. But these are all within the grasp of man. Don't you see, Mr. Veles, it is *we* who are divine and not some God in heaven."

"Pride goes before destruction, a haughty spirit before a fall," Lev quoted Proverbs.

The professor winced. "You say that you feel God's presence in this sacred place. But what did your mythical God create here? Doge Giustiniano Participazio brought the myth of the evangelist to life; Doge Domenico Canterini designed the basilica; Doge Enrico Dandolo plundered Constantinople to steal the treasures contained herein. San Marco Basilica is the work of man and not God."

"God created us in His own image. The Doges built this church to worship Him."

"What if it is *we* who created God in *our* image and built this place to glorify our own creation?" the professor countered.

"The holy relics make it sacred."

"Mr. Veles, they *stole* the relics. Not only the body of St. Mark. In the reliquary they also have the fragments of the True Cross, Christ's Holy Blood, and thorns from the Crown of Thorns. Without us empowering these symbols, they have no inherent meaning. Don't you see? It is we who make this place sacred."

Lev turned his gaze from the *Pala d'oro* to the man who aspired to be God. "Lucifer thought that he too was greater than God."

The professor was exasperated by Lev's blind faith rather than the light of reason. "Another myth meant to subjugate us to religion."

For a moment Lev considered sharing his visions of the *Didko* with the spindly legs atop the mountain or the demon with the empty eyes on the Devil's Bridge, but decided against it. The rational professor would think him insane.

"The power of the sacred is not in the hands of God or the devil," the professor continued. "The power is in *our* hands. Allow me to introduce you to the men behind the myths."

The Palazzo Ducale, immediately adjacent to the basilica, was the heart of the political life and public administration of the Venetian Republic. A grand staircase that led from an inner courtyard to the government chambers on the first floor served as the official entrance to the Palazzo.

"Venice, Mr. Veles, was an ideal republic for half a millennium, between the constitutional reforms of 1297 and the Republic's end after the city's occupation by Napoleon in 1797. It was an aristocracy governed by a Great Council of nobles who elected the Doge, as the representative of the city. It was marked by good government and protection of political and religious liberty. A city ruled by the wisest . . ."

"And richest," Lev added.

"The most highly educated," the professor countered. "The power of Venice comes not from the relic of the Evangelist; it comes from the men who were clever enough to appropriate the power of the myth. In the Palazzo Ducale you will see the true nature of man: the power, the beauty, the nobility."

As Lev and the professor climbed the staircase, the professor pointed out the two giant statues that stood guard at the top of the stairs.

"Mars and Neptune. They represent Venice's power by land and by sea. The Venetians didn't limit themselves to Christian mythology."

They passed through several rooms before entering the Chamber of the Great Council. The chamber was more grandiose and magnificent than Lev could have imagined. The walls and ceiling were entirely covered with golden moldings and works of the most famous artists of the period. One the paintings, *The Paradise,* by Tintoretto covered the entire width of the chamber while the other walls were decorated with episodes from Venetian history. The ceiling was decorated with the Virtues and individual examples of Venetian heroism. A frieze that ran below the ceiling displayed the portraits of the first seventy-six doges.

"The noblemen who sat in the Council were the guardians of the laws of the Republic," the professor continued with his lecture. "They elected the Doge who served for life. Only one Doge ever betrayed the Republic." The professor pointed up to the frieze. "His portrait is represented by the black cloth. He was not only condemned to death, but also to the total eradication of his memory and name."

The portraits of the Doges continued into the next room, the *Sala della Scrutinio.* The room, however, was closed to visitors. A sign read: "Closed for work on upcoming exhibition by German artist Anselm

Kiefer for the 59th Biennale."

"The *Sala della Scrutinio* is the chamber where the Doge was elected," the professor said. "It's decorated with scenes from the Venetians' military battles. They include the *Battle of Lepanto* by Anerea Vicentino, the *Victory over the Turks at the Dardanelles* by Pietro Liberi, the *Conquest of Tyre* by Antonio Aliense, and the *Venetian Naval Victory over the Egyptians at Jaffa* by Sante Peranda. Let's sneak in and take a peek."

The immense room with its magnificent ceiling and triumphal arches was draped from ceiling to floor with canvases by Anselm Kiefer that depicted a very different history of Venice. The massive paintings by Tintoretto and Jacopo Palma the Younger that portrayed the glory of Venice were draped and covered with equally massive works that depicted chaos and destruction. The fourteen Kiefer paintings included scenes of a frozen lagoon, an empty casket of St. Mark above a barren landscape, and the arcades of Piazza San Marco in flames. The Palazzo burned beneath the wings of a lion. The ashen pallets were a fugue of oil paint and sundry materials such as straw, ash, resin, and molten gold and lead poured over the surface. Three-dimensional objects affixed to the canvases evoked the city's true history: charred books, a wooden ladder to heaven, an open lead coffin, uniforms splashed with blood-like blots, and shopping carts tagged with the names of the city's rulers.

The professor was aghast at this desecration of Venetian history.

Lev read the exhibition description on a standing poster and smiled. "Not quite as noble as you expected professor?"

"It's profane!"

"The title of the exhibit is *'these writings, when burned, will finally give some light.'* It's a quote from the Venetian philosopher, Andrea Emo. I find it quite revealing."

"What's so revealing about these scenes of death and decay?"

"You claim that we are destined to become gods. These paintings depict a very different future. Our legacy is war and chaos. We're trapped in an endless cycle of life and death, creation and destruction, an inevitable march towards entropy. We try to transcend it, but perhaps we should just accept the impermanence of it all."

"No, no!" the professor protested. "We *can* transcend our human condition. We have it in our power to eliminate war, hunger, and disease. Eventually even death. Divinity is within us, just waiting to be realized."

"What is it that makes one a god, professor?" Lev asked. "Infinite power, infinite goodness, or infinite love?"

* * *

The bullet-riddled sign for Bucha marked the highway to hell. The Russian invasion, which began on February 24, had stalled 15 miles northwest of Kyiv due to stiff Ukrainian resistance. The Russian invaders, including the 234th and 237th Guards Airborne Assault Regiments and the Russian 64th Separate Motor Rifle Brigade, had dug in awaiting supplies to launch the next assault. The few civilians who had escaped Bucha told of unspeakable atrocities committed by their captors, including torture, rape, and murder.

Alex and Andriy navigated their ZAZ through cratered streets, scorched armor, and metal "hedgehogs" designed to block advancing tanks. A flattened car lay on a shoulder where it had been crushed by a tank. The street signs had been taken down or painted over to confuse the enemy. Andriy knew the route to Bucha by heart. His cousin, Irina, and her family had relocated to Bucha from Donetsk in 2014. He would often visit their home by the lake on weekends to grill pork *shashliks* – kabobs – and enjoy the fresh vegetables from their garden. On the outskirts of Kyiv, they stopped at the last Ukrainian-controlled checkpoint. Several men in camouflage jackets, helmets, and body armor were positioned behind the burned-out hulks of armored personnel carriers.

A grizzled old man in a green Territorial Defense fleece brandished his AK-47 and ordered them to get out of the car.

"Papers!" he demanded.

Andriy showed the man his Ukrainian passport. When Alex pulled out his Russian passport the soldier stuck the barrel of the gun in his chest dand ordered him to lie down on the pavement with his hands behind his head.

"My companion's a journalist," Andriy explained. "He has a letter of safe passage from the SBU." Andriy pulled the document out of Alex's jacket and showed it to the soldier.

"If you're heading towards Lviv, you need to turn around and take M09. The road to Bucha and Irpin is closed. If the orcs don't shoot you, you'll get blown up by landmines or artillery fire."

"I need to go to Bucha," Alex insisted. "I need to document what's happening there."

The soldier eyed Alex as if he were a saboteur. "If you want to get killed by your own orcs, go ahead. You," he said pointing to Andriy, "must stay. You're young enough to serve. Why haven't you joined the Territorial Defense forces?"

"I'm a documentary filmmaker," Andriy replied. "I contribute to our defense on the information front."

"A filmmaker, you say?" He pointed to the other members of his detachment. "Maksym is an Olympic boxer. Antin plays in a rock and roll band. I'm a watchmaker. We're all volunteers defending our homes. We could use a filmmaker."

"I'm on special assignment from the Ministry of Information."

"Then take a video of us and post it on social media," the old man said. "Our families and friends will be glad to see that we're still alive."

Andriy humored him and took a brief video of the motley band of defenders as they shouted "Glory to Ukraine!" to the camera.

"Regardless of your special assignment, you need to turn around and go back to Kyiv. We need all the defenders we can get."

Alex got up off the ground. "How can I get to Bucha?" he asked.

"It's 34 kilometers up the devil's ass. You can walk or take one of those bikes." A pile of bikes lay in a heap against the rubble of a collapsed apartment building. "You'll need to travel under cover of darkness if you have any hope of making it alive. Just follow the path of destruction. The artillery blasts will light up the road."

"Alex, we both need to return to Kyiv," Andriy said. "It's too dangerous to travel now. We'll return when the Ukrainian army has recaptured the territory."

"You go back. Your country needs you," Alex said. "I'll be in touch by cell phone."

Andriy shrugged. "My cousin lives in Bucha in a house by the lake. It's close to the medical clinic. She works there as a nurse." Andriy showed Alex a photo of the house on his phone. "She'll shelter you, but whatever you do, don't put her or her family in jeopardy."

Alex rode off for Bucha on a bike under a moonless sky. The road was strewn with debris: twisted metal, broken glass and the occasional children's toy. Every few hundred meters he passed the scorched hulk of a tank or the mangled remains of a private car. The territory between Kyiv and Bucha was a literal no-man's land. The only signs of life were the dogs and birds that scavenged for food. He saw a murder of crows pecking at something inside a turret-less tank. Every several minutes, artillery rounds whistled over his head and burst over the horizon, bathing the black and grey landscape in hues of orange and red. When he was five kilometers from Bucha, he ditched the bike and proceeded through the woods on foot to avoid sentries. He looked at a map of Bucha on his phone.

The most direct route to Irina's house led through a densely wooded area where the Russians hid their Grad rocket launchers out of sight of drones. The tanks were parked in vegetable gardens in back of homes. He entered the yard of the *Promenysty* children's camp on the outskirts of town. Swearing and drunken laughter blattered from inside the building. The freshly dug soil under his feet was lumpy. He looked down and to his horror saw a woman's hand with a severed ring finger sticking out of the ground. He knelt and dug deeper with his hands. The top layer of soil covered a pile of mangled bodies. Some were naked. Most had their hands tied behind their back. What they shared is that they all appeared to be civilians. He took a video of the mass grave and tried to text it to Andriy, but the cell signal was too weak to transmit the file.

Alex zigzagged through the backyards keeping away from any lights and sounds. He nearly bumped into a drunken soldier who had staggered outside to piss. Yablunka Street, the main road through Bucha, was strewn with corpses: a man next to his bicycle, a family inside a car that had been sprayed with automatic weapons, a blackened corpse of a woman who had been set on fire. The soldiers were too lazy or drunk to clear the day's dead. As he videoed the carnage, the sky began to lighten. He had to make it to Irina's house before daybreak. The GPS on his phone guided him to a one-story, brick house on the shore of the lake. He circled around and knocked on the back door. No answer. He knocked again – still no answer. He peered through the window and glimpsed someone moving inside.

"I'm not a soldier. I'm a friend of Andriy's."

The door opened and a woman yanked him inside. "Has anyone seen you?" she asked.

"No, I was careful to avoid the sentries."

The woman looked to be in her thirties, with dark hair and large, saucer-like eyes. "They won't let us leave," she said. "My neighbors tried to flee, and they were shot in the street."

"Are you alone?" Alex asked.

"Oksanochka, come here. It's all right." A ten-year old girl crawled out from under a table, ran to her mother, and clung to her skirt.

"It's just me and my daughter. My husband is fighting in Mariupol. I haven't heard from him in days. How do you know my cousin, Andriy?"

"I'm a fellow filmmaker, from St. Petersburg."

Alex showed her the videos he had taken on his phone.

Irina froze. "If they find that phone, they'll kill you. They'll kill all of us."

"I'm trying to show my Russian people what's really happening in Ukraine. I couldn't imagine the . . ."

"Inhumanity," Irina added.

"We need to get you and your daughter out of here."

An armored personnel carrier rumbled up the street. It stopped in front of the house and turned its machine gun towards the door.

"You need to hide," Irina said. "Take my daughter into the root cellar and stay still. I'll try to send them away. No matter what happens, promise me you'll protect my daughter."

"I promise," Alex said.

"Mama, I want to stay with you!" Oksana cried out.

"Oksanochka, please. Bad men are coming. You have to hide."

"I need to get Zoya!" Oksana cried out. She ran to her room and returned with her *motanka* doll. She hugged her mother and clutched her doll. "You won't leave me, promise."

"God willing," her mother replied.

The access to the root cellar was through a trap door in the pantry. A ladder descended into a cold, dank cellar. Alex and Oksana climbed down the ladder. Jars of pickled vegetables from the summer garden – tomatoes, cabbage, and cucumbers – were stacked on a table against the wall. A naked bulb hung from the ceiling. Alex unscrewed it and huddled with Oksana in a corner. Light from the upstairs seeped in through cracks between the wooden floor planks.

A fist pounded on the front door. Irina closed the trap door and covered it with a sack of potatoes.

"We know you're in there," a soldier called out. "If you don't open the door, it will be much worse for you."

Alex heard the door open. From the sounds of the voices and stomping of the boots, he counted four men.

"Who's this in the photograph?" the commander of the group asked.

"My husband and my daughter. My husband took her to Rivne to stay with his mother."

"What does your husband do?"

He's a bricklayer."

"Make us some food."

Alex heard Irina shuffling about in the pantry above them. He heard the clatter of pots. Oksana huddled next to him without saying a word.

Over the next several hours the voices and the boots came and went. The clatter of pots continued with lunch and dinner. "Where do you keep the alcohol," he heard a voice say. Irina entered the pantry and took a bottle of vodka off the shelf. Someone followed her in. "Get your hands off me!" she yelled.

"Where are you hiding your money and your jewelry?" the man demanded. "I couldn't find them in your bedroom."

"My husband took our money with him to Rivne. I have only a few hundred hryvnias. Take them, just leave me alone!" She broke away from him and left to serve the vodka.

The man stayed in the pantry to search for valuables. Lev feared that he and Oksana would be discovered at any moment. The man's phone rang. He placed it on top of the sack of potatoes, put it on speaker, and continued to rummage through the shelves so he could find and steal any valuables before his comrades did.

"*Serdenko* – sweetheart, why haven't you called me?"

"Katerinochka, my love, I've been busy with my duties," the man replied as he kept knocking over bottles and jars.

"Where are you?" a female voice answered.

"Some hell hole called Bucha. These *khokhols* hate us. Putin said they would greet us with flowers. They greet us with javelin missiles instead."

"But you're safe."

"The commander's a prick. He made me kill them." "Who?"

"*Khokhols* – men, women, some children. 'Just shoot them in the head,' he said. We made them strip naked. I told them to yell 'Glory to Russia!' before I shot them. They begged and pleaded for their lives, but I shot them anyway. It was easier than you think."

"The Patriarch said that killing Ukrainians is not a sin."

"I wanted to ask your permission for something," the man said.

"What?"

"There's a woman here. She reminds me of you. I haven't been with a woman in weeks. I was wondering . . .?"

"If you could rape her? I guess it's OK. Just use a condom and pretend you're making love to me. But don't let her live to talk about it. Bring me back some souvenirs."

"Like what?"

"I don't know what they have. A microwave, some appliances . . . whatever you think we could use. Vova brought his wife a washing machine."

Alex covered Oksana's ears. He debated what he should do. He could not overpower four armed soldiers. Irina had begged him to protect her daughter no matter what. He decided to wait.

Alex heard Irina scream, and the soldier left the pantry to join in the debauchery. The alcohol stoked the ardor of the animals upstairs. Alex heard shouts and slaps. He heard thumping. The soldiers were laughing, swearing, and singing. After a half hour he heard the thumping again and again . . .

Near daybreak he heard jars break and chairs turned over. He heard appliances and fixtures being ripped out the walls. The soldiers stomped out of the building. He heard the armored personnel carrier rumble away. He waited for Irina to let them out when it was safe. No sounds came from above for hours. Near nightfall he climbed the ladder and pushed open the trap door overturning the sack of potatoes. He waited for a response but there was only silence. The house was ransacked. He stepped over empty bottles. Appliances had been ripped off the walls. The soldiers had defecated on the floor. He found Irina on the bed. She was naked and motionless with bruises on her breasts and neck. Used condoms soiled the bed. Alex felt for a pulse and found none. He covered her with the sheet.

He returned to the pantry and motioned for Oksana to climb up the ladder. "We need to leave," he said.

Oksana grabbed her doll, Zoya, and climbed up the ladder. "What about my mother?

"She's gone ahead," Alex lied. "She said we should meet her in the woods behind the children's camp." He took the pendant of the Blessed Virgin off his neck and placed it over Oksana's head. "Wear this medal. The Blessed Virgin will protect you."

The house was dark. Shelling had knocked out the electricity to the city. As they snuck out of the house, Alex saw occasional headlights from personnel carriers and scattered garbage fires. He plotted their escape route. Holding Oksana by the hand, he backtracked the way he came. He led her towards the summer camp from where they could make their escape through the forest unseen.

As they passed the children's camp, Oksana cried out: "Mama, where are you?"

The headlamps of a parked personnel carrier illuminated them.

"Halt!" a soldier barked out.

"Run!" Alex told Oksana. As they ran towards the woods, Alex felt a sharp pain in his right calve. He tried to run but his leg collapsed beneath him. "Keep running and don't look back!" he yelled to Oksana. The girl disappeared into the woods.

Alex began to text "Oksana . . ." when he felt the blow of the butt of a rifle to the back of his head. He awoke in the basement of the summer camp building, naked with his hands tied behind his head. He was shivering uncontrollably. His calf was bleeding from the bullet wound. Several more bodies were lying next to him, face down, with their hands bound.

"I'm a Russian citizen," he said to his captors.

A soldier grabbed him by his hair and pulled him up to his knees. "We have your passport and your phone. You're a traitor."

"I'm a journalist. I'm just reporting the truth. This is not your war. This is Putin's war. Call Moscow. They'll tell you who I am."

Alex tried to keep his composure. One of the other captives, a young woman dressed only in a fur coat, was crying. Her husband lying next to her was telling her to be brave. He had been shot through both knees. After several minutes, the interrogator returned.

"We heard back from Moscow," the interrogator said. "Sasha, you know what to do."

"One shot," Sasha said.

Alex recognized the voice. He turned his head to look at the rapist. He was a youth with acne and dead fish eyes.

"Say 'Glory to Russia.'"

"Go to hell." Alex replied. He thought of Sophia playing Shostakovich's Seventh Symphony and asking him not to leave for Ukraine. *It can't end like this*, he thought.

Sasha walked up to Alex and put a bullet through the back of his head.

* * *

The last day of February began with a cold rain. Winter lingered longer than it should. Lev was not looking forward to continuing his discussion with Professor Brown. What Lev found most human about people were their flaws. The professor's aspiration to make men gods robbed them of their humanity. Still, the professor was challenging his core beliefs. It was a gate that Lev had to pass through on his spiritual journey. He agreed to meet the professor at the church of Santa Maria Gloriosa dei Frari, in the Sestiere di San Polo to continue their discussion.

Professor Brown was waiting for him inside the church. He was standing in front of a marble pyramid. Statues of mourning mythological figures decorated the entrance.

"The tomb of Antonio Canova," the professor announced. "The greatest sculptor of the 19th century. Do you recognize the symbolism?"

"Masonic?" Lev guessed.

"Excellent!" the professor replied. "I knew when I first met you that you are worthy of embarking on a spiritual journey. I discovered this monument within a few days of starting my sabbatical. This tomb, more than any other place in Venice, illustrates my thesis about sacred places. Here, inside a Catholic church, we find the occult symbols of a prohibited mystery religion. We find the sacred within sacred, though for each the other is considered heresy."

"A curious shape for a tomb," Lev observed.

"The pyramid is the symbol of the Great Architect of the Universe, the supreme deity of the Freemasons."

"God?" Lev asked.

"For Christians, He is the God of the Bible. For Muslims, He is Allah. For Hindus, He is Vishnu. Some scholars of the occult believe that the Supreme Architect of the Universe is none other than Lucifer. Masonic rituals have their origins in the mystery religions, dating back to paganism in ancient Egypt and Babylon. Canova's students designed the tomb in homage to their master and 'brother.' His heart is entombed here in a porphyry urn. The rest of his remains are buried in Possagno, his birthplace."

"What do the figures represent?" Lev asked.

"The angel with open wings is the custodian of the soul passed to the sky. The sleeping winged lion holding a closed book is a symbol of the wisdom that the artist has carried away. The winged figure is death while the one with the lit torch symbolizes immortality. The two women with the flower wreaths are Hope and Charity."

"You have an intimate knowledge of these symbols. Are you perhaps . . .?"

"A Freemason? I was until I discovered that *we* are the Great Architects of the Universe. The secrets and mysteries of the Freemasons go back to the wisdom of the ancients, but I understood that to continue our progress towards *Homo Deus*, we needed to break the shackles of ancient doctrines. I was understandably expelled from my lodge. You asked me before what will make men gods. I believe that the answer is *infinite knowledge*. Knowledge is power, and power will make us gods."

"What about infinite goodness?"

"There are no such things as Absolute Good or Absolute Evil. What's good for me may be evil for you."

Lev thought of the tall figure with hollow cheeks and black holes for eyes that had asked him for the soul of an unbaptized child on the Devil's Bridge. "You don't believe in the devil, professor?"

"We created God, so we had to create the devil."

"And what of infinite love?"

"With infinite knowledge there will be no need for love. Love is an illusion. It's a biological necessity to ensure our reproduction and evolution. Darwin robbed us of our souls. Knowledge will allow us to escape our biology through genomic engineering, artificial intelligence, and algorithms. We will become masters of our own evolution."

"Father Stephan says that 'he who does not love, does not know God, because God is love.'"

"What does a priest know about love?"

"Have you ever loved, professor?"

"My work is my life. I devote myself to mankind, rather than any one individual."

"Then yours is a lonely life indeed."

"My passion, Mr. Veles, is for *knowledge*. My great frustration in life is that for most of my academic career I have been mired in mediocrity. My current research is revolutionary. I will be the one who dispels the myth of God. My thesis will be nailed to the doors of every church, mosque, and temple. In the 17th century," he chuckled, "I would have been burned at the stake for my beliefs."

"I'm curious, professor."

"About what."

"In this monument to their master, why did Canova's students choose to inter his heart and not his head?"

"*Bon mot!* Mr. Veles. Spoken as a true romantic. But it was you who pointed out that we live in a universe of violence and decay. Who but man has the power to overcome chaos?"

Who but man? Lev reflected how in 1945 the greatest minds in the world had gathered in Los Alamos to build the greatest weapon in the world. *Was this the power to overcome violence and chaos?* He remembered Oppenheimer's famous words, when he witnessed the first atom bomb explosion: "Now I am become death, the destroyer of worlds." He thought of how in 1994 Ukraine had given up its nuclear weapons in exchange for guarantees of peace and security, and how Russia, a signatory of the Budapest Memorandum, was now killing, raping, and torturing Ukrainians in the name of *Ruski Mir* – Russian peace. He thought of how Russia had weaponized information and perverted the meaning of language, where peace means war, Jew means Nazi, and liberation means annihilation . . . of how Russia had desecrated the word of God, where a Russian patriarch blessed missiles and preached that the killing of Ukrainians would wash away sins. . . how Russia was threatening the world with nuclear war . . . all because one little man believed that he was greater than God. *No, infinite knowledge will not make us gods.*

"What is our true nature, professor? Are we angels or demons?"

"We are imperfect creatures seeking perfection. Come I have more sites to show you. We must visit the Basilica of Santa Maria on San Donato. The bones of a dragon are what make the place sacred. From there we'll go to Poveglia to experience the profane. I've taken the liberty of chartering a boat."

The rain had deadened to a drizzle. A white mist hung over the Grand Canal.

Lev froze. A black launch with red leather seats was waiting for them at the dock of San Toma. A pale woman in a cloak was at the helm.

"I'm sorry, professor. But I can't accompany you. This cold rain will be the death of me."

"Another time," the professor said as he stepped into the launch. "I need to visit these places to complete my research. Are you sure you won't join me? Don't let some dragon bones or ghost stories scare you away."

The fear of God is the beginning of knowledge, Lev's grandfather used to say. Mara looked back at Lev and smiled.

Lev watched as the launch disappeared into the mist. *My spiritual journey will continue. But I fear that yours, professor, ends here.*

CHAPTER 7

The Alchemist

The concert to celebrate the liberation of Kyiv was canceled. The Russian special military operation had not gone according to plan. Sophia flipped through the St. Petersburg television channels. Channel One was reporting that President Putin had just signed a new law that called for prison sentences of up to 15 years for people who distribute "false news" about the Russian military operation in Ukraine. CTC was running a story about a heroic Russian paramedic who delivered a child for a woman in Mariupol who had lost her leg due to Ukrainian shelling. The dramatic video, filmed in a destroyed apartment, was enhanced with the dubbed sounds of artillery fire. The Rossiya 1 channel was displaying a graphic on how a Sarmat nuclear missile could reach London in 202 seconds. Sophia turned off the television. She checked her phone for messages for the third time in the last hour.

Sophia heard a knock on the door. Her guest had arrived fifteen minutes earlier than expected. Anna Vladimirna Karkova was a brilliant young violinist in the St. Petersburg Philharmonic. She was a darling of the critics who eagerly anticipated her rise to first violin. Sophia unbolted the locks and invited her in.

"Anna Vladimirna, I'm so glad you accepted my invitation."

"The honor is mine," Anna replied. Sophia took her lynx coat. Anna wore a simple red dress with a string of pearls. Her blond hair was tied tightly in a bun. She was as cool and beautiful as a porcelain doll. The table in the parlor was set with a hand-painted tea set and a chrome-plated Soviet samovar. Honey, slices of lemon, and a decanter of cognac completed the presentation.

"Tea or cognac?" Sophia asked.

"Tea," Anna replied.

Sophia admired Anna's exquisite looks and demeanor more than her skill. Her violin technique was perfect but exaggerated. During their performances she drew the attention of the audience to herself rather than to the music.

Sophia boiled the water in the samovar, scooped six teaspoons of black tea into the teapot and placed it on top of the samovar. When the leaves floated to the surface, she poured the brew into the teacups through a strainer. She added water from the samovar until the color of the tea changed from dark brown to red to amber. Sophia drizzled her tea with honey. Anna added lemon.

"You're wondering why I've invited you for this . . . tête-à-tête," Sophia said.

Anna smiled.

"Your skill and progress have not gone unnoticed. I've been thinking of promoting you from second to first violin."

Anna feigned surprise. "Sophia Sergeivna, I . . ."

"With my guidance and time, I could see you becoming concert-master."

Anna leaned forward and her pearls draped her décolletage. She placed her hand on top of Sophia's. "I've always been attracted to beauty and power," she said.

Sophia pulled her hand away to take a sip of her tea. "There is a favor I need to ask of you."

"Anything," Anna purred.

"My private life has been private, and I want to keep it that away. I have a boyfriend, Alex . . ."

Anna pulled her head back, straightened up, and took a sip of her tea. "A very lucky man," she said.

"He's a bit of a nonconformist, if you know what I mean. The authorities are not supportive of our relationship."

"What does that have to do with me?" Anna asked.

"I have a simple request. I want you to help me contact him."

Anna picked up the decanter of cognac and poured a little into her tea. "Why don't you just call him yourself?"

"I've tried, but I can't get through. These are sensitive times. As the conductor of the Philharmonic, my every phone call, email, and text are being monitored. I fear he's not responding because he knows I'm under surveillance."

"Will it get me in trouble?"

"No," Sophia insisted. "Of course not. You have no relationship with him. You're not . . ." Sophia was going to say important enough, but changed midsentence. "You've given them no reason to be under surveillance."

"Where is your boyfriend now?"

"Ukraine," Sophia replied.

Anna took a long sip of her tea. "You say all I need to do is to put you in contact with him?"

"He has a colleague in Kyiv who he's been working with, a filmmaker by the name of Andriy Orishkevich. If you can contact Andriy, then he can help me find Alex."

Anna relished her newfound power. She took her phone out of her purse. "A simple phone call?"

"Yes."

She put her phone back in her purse. "Then I want something in return. I want to be promoted to first violin today, not tomorrow. Once you fulfill your part of the bargain, then I'll fulfill mine."

* * *

Lev had not seen Professor Brown since he had departed in Mara's boat. He hoped that his vision of Mara at the dock of San Toma was just another daymare. Lev visited the professor's office twice over the next two days. The first time the door had been locked. The second time it was open, but the piles of books, papers, and curios had been boxed and sealed. The shipping labels indicated they were being sent to Northwestern University in Evanston, Illinois. Lev tried to ask anyone with a Ca' Foscari ID badge about the professor's whereabouts, but to no avail. The university was on pandemic lockdown. The few people he encountered in the hallways would not even make eye contact. He attributed their reluctance to engage to the fact that he had forgotten to wear his mask.

The professor's desk had been cleaned out but the waste paper basket had not yet been emptied. Lev searched through the crumpled pieces of paper for some clue as to where the professor might have gone: a hotel address, an itinerary, or correspondence. The only thing he found was a scribbled note on the prayer card that was handed out at the contessa's memorial service. It read: *Graf, Bar Canale, Tuesday, 10 a.m.* Lev interpreted the note as a rendezvous. At the very least, Dr. Graf might know what had happened to his colleague.

The morning of March 1 was cold. The Bar Canale was located at the rear of the Hotel Bauer with an open terrace facing the Grand Canal. Lev expected to find them inside at the breakfast buffet. To his surprise he found Dr. Graf sitting at an unset table on the terrace beneath the statue of *L'Italia Turrita*. Without his mask he looked even younger than Lev expected. He had the intensity of a mathematician on the verge of solving an insolvable problem.

Lev noticed that the doctor's socks were of different colors.

"Dr. Graf," Lev announced himself.

"Is Professor Brown with you?" Dr. Graf asked.

"I was hoping he was with you." Lev replied. "I haven't seen him since he left on his excursion to Poveglia. I found a note in his office that suggested he was going to meet you here today."

"It's not like him to miss our colloquy on God."

"You meet to discuss the existence God?" Lev asked.

"Not the existence God," Dr. Graf corrected him. "The *nature* of God. The professor and I first met in the contessa's palazzo several weeks before you arrived in Venice. The contessa organized a small coterie – she and I, Professor Brown, and Father Stephan – to meet in her palazzo on Thursday evenings to share our thoughts on metaphysics. We were all on our own spiritual journeys and thought we could learn from one another. We were following different paths searching for the ultimate reality. Father Stephan was on the Way of Christian mysticism, Professor Brown on the path of humanism, and I was on the path of science."

"And the contessa . . .?" Lev asked, though he already knew the answer.

"She was an enigmatic woman. Father Stephan referred to her as a *Benandante*, or white witch. She began her journey on the right-hand path, but as the pandemic progressed, her worldview became darker, and she began to explore the left-hand path."

"What's the difference?" Lev asked.

"The right-hand path follows ethical codes and conventions; it seeks union with and dependence on God. The left-hand path seeks an even higher law based on knowledge and power. It abandons morality. Some believe it's the path to true freedom."

"She's a Catholic. I'm surprised Father Stephan didn't intervene."

"Father Stephan may be a Catholic priest, but he's a sinner like the rest of us. He feels his church has failed him, and he seeks union with his God, wherever that path might lie."

"I too have embarked on a spiritual journey," Lev said "but it's been terrifying rather than enlightening. I fear I'm losing my grip on reality," he confessed. "I see people who have died. I see demons."

"What kinds of demons?"

"Father Stephan insists that my visions are real. He believes I can see into the astral plane. When the contessa died, he asked me to accompany him to her bedside for Last Rites. He asked me to follow her spirit to the Devil's Bridge in Torcello."

"I'm familiar with the legend. Were you?"

"No. Why is that important?"

"I find it curious that you came face to face with a demon from a legend that you've never heard of before."

But Lev had seen those empty eyes before – in the *Didko* that he had encountered by the lake atop the mountain. "Are you saying that my visions are real?"

"You want to know if the devil really exists or if it is you who created him."

"Yes."

Dr. Graf leaned forward as if to share a secret. "Your visions are real only in the sense that you make them real. You see, Mr. Veles, I believe that we create our own reality."

"I don't understand."

"It doesn't seem that Professor Brown will be joining us. I actually prefer your company to his. The man farts higher than his ass."

"Why do you say that?"

"I listen to his arguments, but he doesn't listen to mine. He tries to convince me that we're destined to become gods. But I contend that we're just an anomaly in this vast universe, an emergent biochemical entity that has achieved self-awareness. We've evolved over hundreds of millions of years incorporating millions of entities into our essence, from bacteria to fish to dinosaurs to mammals. We're able to stare back at ourselves in the mirror and ask: Why? I find this remarkable, but I don't believe it makes us gods."

"What is it that *you* believe," Lev asked.

"If you want to learn more about the true nature of reality, then meet me here at the same time tomorrow. But promise me one thing, Mr. Veles."

"What's that?"

"You must come with an open mind."

* * *

The Church of Our Savior on Spilled Blood was deconsecrated. The magnificent edifice on the bank of the Griboyedov Canal in St. Petersburg was constructed in the style of Russian nationalism on the spot where Emperor Alexander the Second had been assassinated. With its multicolored, gilded domes and magnificent mosaics, it rivaled

St. Basil's Cathedral in Red Square. It now served as museum and semioccasional venue for concerts and funerals.

Sophia heard choral music emanating from the cathedral on her walk home from rehearsal at Philharmonic Hall. The cathedral was open that evening for a patriotic concert by the St. Petersburg Concert Choir to celebrate the imminent de-Nazification of Ukraine. The male choristers wore tuxedos while the women wore black dresses and red scarves. The few hundred seats closest to the choir were filled with uniformed officers and their consorts. Behind them stood a throng of pensioners who were nostalgic for the glory days of the Soviet Union. When a military usher recognized Sophia at the entrance, he rushed to escort her to a seat in the front, but she declined. She preferred to listen from the back with the civilians.

The choir was nearing the finale of its two-hour program. The choristers sang "The Sacred War" followed by "Farewell of Slavianka." They capped their performance with "On the Wages of Servicemen," a Cold War song that lionizes the crew of a Soviet nuclear submarine on its way to bomb Washington."

Sophia couldn't believe what she was hearing.

"Forgive us, America, fair America, but 500 years ago they discovered you for nothing," the choir sang in four-part harmony.

"Rousing, isn't it?" Sophia turned to see Colonel Bezoviy breathing down her neck.

"To glorify nuclear war in a cathedral? It's sacrilegious!"

"Do not delude yourself, Sophia Sergeivna. God does not dwell here. In Moscow they have their Cathedral of the Russian Armed Forces. I'm thinking we should dedicate our own Cathedral of our Savior on Spilled Blood to the FSB."

The lines, *"Set the target on Washington city, Petrov . . . burn in half the land of our adversary,"* drew wild cheers and applause. The cries for war reverberated through the nave and rose up to the domes like a mushroom cloud.

Sophia broke away from Bezoviy when the officers rose to give the choir a standing ovation. She pushed through the crowd, until she found herself standing before the icon of the Blessed Virgin Mary and

Infant Jesus. Sophia was not devoutly religious, but she took the sudden encounter with the icon as an omen. Her mother had told her that the Blessed Mother would always protect her and had given her the medal of the *Pokrova* that she had now given to Alex. Sophia hoped that the Blessed Mother's veil would protect him as well.

"Holy Mary, Mother of God," Sophia invoked her patron under her breath, "I pray for your guidance. I've made a grave mistake. I never thought I would bring a child into this cruel world, but now I realize that this life inside me is my sacred obligation. I want to keep our child, but I was afraid that Alex would not. I was afraid he would reject us, so I kept silent. But if he learns that he's a father to be, he might abandon his suicidal quest to prevent the war and return to us. I made a second grave mistake. I entrusted his safety to a woman whom I know is not trustworthy rather than risk looking for him myself. Music has been my whole life. If I'm discovered protecting him, it could jeopardize my career. But now that we have a child, everything has changed. Please tell me what I must do."

Sophia hoped for an answer but heard only the unending claps and cheers for bloodlust. The icon before her portrayed the Blessed Mother sitting on a throne holding Infant Jesus. Her loving gaze was fixed on her son. Sophia placed her hands over her womb. "I know what I must do."

* * *

"You would betray your mentor?"

Anna Karkova shifted in the leather chair. She tried to determine which of Colonel Besoviy's eyes was looking at her. She turned her gaze to the portrait of Putin.

"I'm doing my patriotic duty," she replied. "Let me know if I'm wasting your time."

"Sophia Sergeivna is a celebrity. Some would say she's a national treasure. You are, I believe, a second violin."

Anna flinched at the stinging remark. The chair she was sitting in seemed designed for maximum discomfort. One had to strain to sit upright. Her back muscles were as finely tuned as violin strings. She straightened her spine and adjusted the pin in her hair.

"Perhaps I've made a mistake in coming to you," she said. "I have friends in the FSB. I should have consulted them to make sure I'd meet someone at the appropriate . . . rank."

Colonel Besoviy rose from his desk and walked over to her chair. He stepped behind her and placed his hands on the back of her neck. He ran his fingers down her spine probing for points of tension. She tried to breath normally. When he reached a pressure point on the edge of her left scapula she flinched.

"It must be difficult to hold a violin for hours on end," he said.

"Do you play, colonel?"

He tilted her head back so she was forced to look up at him.

"What is it that you would like to share?" he asked.

"She asked me to contact her boyfriend, Alex. She was afraid to contact him herself. She's concerned you're watching her."

Colonel Besoviy let go of her head. He began to pace up and down the length of the long table aisle. "Go on," he said.

"She said that her boyfriend went to Ukraine to meet a fellow filmmaker, a man by the name of Andriy Orishkevich. She believes I can contact her boyfriend through this Andriy."

"And have you?"

"No, I decided to come here first."

"What do you seek to gain by coming here?"

"Gain? Nothing. As I said, I'm simply doing my patriotic duty."

"Anna." He did not give her the respect of addressing her by her patronymic. "We know all about you. We know whom you've slept with and whom you've compromised. We know you tried to seduce Barsky but failed. We even know what kind of tea you drank this morning. I'll ask you again. What do you seek to gain from coming to us?"

"I want to advance in my career."

"Sophia Sergeivna has already offered you first violin."

Anna Karkova turned white. How could he have known? She wasn't sure who was betraying whom.

"You aspire to be concertmaster?"

"I simply wish to be recognized for my talent."

"You are a woman of many talents, Anna. You could be of use to us. How were you to contact Andriy Orishevich?"

"Sophia Sergievna gave me his cell phone number."

Colonel Besoviy picked up his phone and issued some commands to an underling. Moments later, a woman brought in a cell phone plugged into a laptop computer. Anna Karkova noticed the woman's pointy bra under a tight white sweater and her candy red lipstick.

"Make the call," the colonel instructed. "It will appear as if you're calling from Paris."

Anna tapped the numbers that Sophia had given her. The phone rang four times before going into voicemail. The colonel motioned for her to speak.

"Mr. Orishkevich, my name is Anna Karkova. I'm a friend of Sophia Sergeivna Borodin. We're currently on tour in Paris, and she asked me to call you to see if you had any information about her friend, Alex. She's been unable to reach him, and for reasons you understand, she did not want to call from her own . . ."

The call went out of voicemail. "How did you get my number," a voice said.

"Alex gave it to Sophia, and she gave it to me."

"You say you're a friend?"

"A friend and co-worker. We're both with the St. Petersburg Philharmonic."

"Are you alone?"

"Yes of course."

"Tell Sophia that I haven't seen him for over a week. We were on our way to Bucha but the Ukrainian Territorial Defense stopped us. They made me turn back, but he insisted on going ahead. He understood the danger."

"Where are you now?" Anna asked.

Colonel Besoviy bristled at the naïve question. He waved his hand to tell her to shut up.

After a long pause, the voice on the other end said, "East," and hung up.

"I'm sorry if I said the wrong thing," Anna said. "I'm new to this intrigue."

"You did well," Colonel Besoviy said. "Your patriotism is noted. I will put a good word in for you with Barsky. I'll attribute your flirtations to your youth. You may leave."

Anna Karkova stood up and left without another word.

Colonel Besoviy put on his leather coat and called for a driver. "Admiralteyskiy Prospect," he instructed.

The traffic was bumper to bumper. Cars were honking and inching along in the sleet. An ambulance that was three cars ahead of them flashed its lights and wailed its siren but had no place to pass. After fifteen minutes it turned off its siren. The colonel called his office in Bolshoi Dom and asked them to track Sophia Borodin's phone. Her phone was off the grid. He instructed them to contact her building superintendent to meet him at her apartment with the keys.

The wire cage elevator in the building was not working. Colonel Besoviy climbed the stairs. The superintendent was waiting for him by her door. The colonel knocked, but no answer. He instructed the superintendent to open the door. The apartment was dark. The colonel called his office and asked them to check the bookings and security cameras at the airport and train stations. He walked through the apartment looking for clues. The bed was made, and the dishes were put away. The stove was cold. His phone rang.

"Colonel, we've located her. She's booked a plane ticket to Warsaw through Dubai on Emirates Airlines. The flight was scheduled to leave at 16:00."

He checked his watch: 16:10.

"Is it still on the tarmac?"

After a minute, he heard: "It's taken off. Shall we order the pilot to turn it around?"

"Who else is on the flight?"

"Some Russian nationals, but mostly Emiratis. A few journalists."

Colonel Besoviy sucked on the inside of his cheek. "No, let it continue. Contact our embassy in Warsaw. Apprehend her when she lands and bring her back to me."

* * *

Dr. Graf was at the same table at Bar Canale where Lev had left him the day before. It was as if he had never left.

"What do you know about quantum mechanics?" the doctor asked.

"Only that nobody understands quantum mechanics."

Dr. Graf laughed. "Tell me, Mr. Veles, when you look out over the Grand Canal, what is it that you think you see?"

The view from the terrace of Bar Canale was one of the most beautiful in all of Venice. Lev looked over the stone fretwork at the gondolas that glided down the blue-green water of the Grand Canal. Across the canal, the white dome of the Basilica di Santa Maria della Salute glistened in the winter sun.

"I see a glorious view of Venice. The kind you see on postcards."

"Illusions," Dr. Graf replied. "If you and I were not here observing these things, would they still exist?"

"Naturally."

"Perhaps . . . perhaps not. Quantum mechanics predicts that they come into existence only because you are looking at them."

"That doesn't make any sense."

"Einstein was as skeptical as you are about the implications of quantum mechanics. He famously asked the question 'Do you really believe the moon is not there when you're not looking at it?'"

"I'm confused."

"Good. That means you're listening. What I'm going to tell you defies all logic. What was it that Heisenberg said? 'Not only is the universe stranger than we think, it is stranger than we can think.' You're familiar with the dual nature of particles?"

"Vaguely."

Dr. Graf paused. His discourse on the nature of reality might have to be more elementary than he had hoped. Yet he saw that Lev's desire to learn was genuine, so he continued. "In the early part of the last century, physicists like de Broglie and Schrödinger showed us that fundamental particles like electrons and photons behave as both particles and waves. A better description is that they behave as wave functions – evolving mathematical functions that indicate a particle's probability of having various properties."

"The probability of having properties?"

"It's difficult to comprehend, Mr. Veles, but these fundamental particles don't assume their properties, like location, color, or spin, until you *look* at them. Your act of observation collapses their wave function and makes them real to you."

"I still don't understand."

"Let me give you a simple example. When you picture a hydrogen atom, with one proton and one electron, what do you see?"

"I see the electron orbiting the proton, like our earth orbits the sun."

"Classic, but wrong," Dr. Graf said. "In reality the electron is *anywhere* and *everywhere*. It's in what we call 'superposition.' Think of it as a cloud of probability that collapses to a specific point, your electron, when you observe it. Until then, it's in an amorphous cloud of probability."

"How does that impact our understanding of reality?"

"In your perception of reality, you believe that the physical universe is actually physical. You believe that the smallest particles, like your electron, exist independent of whether we observe them or not. Consider this statue before us. Let's delve into its essence. Look at it, touch it, and tell me what you perceive."

Lev stood up and examined the 3.6-meter statue that was facing the Grand Canal.

"I see a stone statue of a woman in a toga holding a torch and a shield."

"*The Towered Italy*," Dr. Graf said, "the work of Carlo Lorenzetti. What does she feel like?"

Lev ran his hand over the statue. "Cool, smooth, and hard."

"Imagine now that you have the world's most powerful microscope. If you more closely examine the stone from which she is made, what would you see?"

"I assume some sort of crystals."

"And with a higher magnification?"

"I would see the molecules that comprise the crystals."

"And higher still?"

"The atoms that comprise those molecules."

"And higher still?"

"Electrons, protons, neutrons."

"And higher still?"

"The subatomic building blocks of matter. The fundamental . . ."

"Fundamental what?"

"Particles? Waves? I'm not sure what they are."

"At the quantum level, what you perceive to be solid matter diffuses into fuzzy clouds of energy. These clouds spread out as ripples in the quantum field, and the ripples themselves are mathematical configurations in hyperspace. Your act of observing collapses their wave functions. They become real because you ask the question 'What are you?' and Nature obliges you with an answer. You must abandon this idea of a world made of *things*. They only become actualized when we look at them. Reality, Mr. Veles, is an illusion."

Lev returned to the table and sat down. Dr. Graf's description of reality was beyond weird. It was beyond comprehension. What Lev perceived to be solid matter was fundamentally a sparkling world of dancing energy in which particles twinkle in and out of existence. He too was energy, interacting with the energy around him and actualizing it into existence.

"But why is *my* perception so important to its realization?" Lev asked. "You're looking at the same statue. Doesn't your act of observing make it real? If my consciousness is creating – actualizing – what I'm seeing, then how do I know that you're even real?"

"Because you're asking the question."

Lev looked perplexed.

"It gets stranger still," Dr. Graf said, satisfied that his revelation had elicited the desired effect of bewilderment. "When fundamental particles, like electrons, are created in pairs they become entangled. They remain linked together no matter how far apart they are in space. Allow me to give you an example. Let's say we have two coins that are entangled such that whenever one comes up heads the other must up tails and vice versa. Now imagine we are on opposite sides of the world – I'm in Venice and you're in the Australian outback – and we flip our coins simultaneously. Furthermore, we are barred from communicating to know what the other person has flipped. Because the two coins are mysteriously entangled, when I flip heads, you will flip tails, and when you flip heads, I will flip tails."

"But how is that possible?" Lev asked. "It's over 10,000 km from here to Australia. How does one coin know if the other has come up heads or tails? That information would have to travel faster than. . ."

". . . the speed of light," Dr. Graf added. "It seems impossible, doesn't it, and yet when we study entangled pairs of fundamental particles, we get the same result over and over again. Einstein called it 'spooky action at a distance.'"

Lev pondered Dr. Graf's description of illusory reality. Reality as we experience it seems to be the result of human consciousness interfacing with the quantum levels of existence that are pure waves of energy. He thought of Prospero's description in Shakespeare's *The Tempest*: *"We are such stuff as dreams are made of."*

"What is your view on the nature of God," Lev asked.

"I will give the same answer that Einstein gave when he was asked the same question. 'I believe in the God of Spinoza.'"

"I'm not familiar with Spinoza."

"Baruch Spinoza was a 17th century Jewish-Dutch philosopher who wrote that 'All things are in God, and everything which takes place takes place by the laws alone of the infinite nature of God, and follows from the necessity of His essence.' He didn't believe in an anthropocentric God: an external being acting on the world of human affairs, dispensing rewards for devotion and punishments for transgression. He was branded a heretic, and his *Theologico-Political Treatise* was condemned as a book forged in hell by the devil himself. His *Ethics* was placed on the Catholic Church's index of forbidden books. Many accuse him of being an atheist, but he was not an atheist."

"If he didn't believe in God as portrayed in the Bible, then what did he believe in?"

"Spinoza argued that whatever exists is in God. He is not some distant force, but is all around us. Nothing in nature is separate from Him: not you, not me, not animals nor plants, nor inanimate objects. Everything is 'being in God.'"

"Being in God?" Lev asked.

"I have to thank Father Stephan for that phrase," Dr. Graf said. "The Father pointed out that this conception of the divine actually follows well-established Christian tradition. Saint Augustine wrote in the 4th century AD that 'all things are in God.' The 8th-century monk, John of Damascus, said that 'Toward God all things tend, and in God they have their existence.' Saint Anselm, in his *Proslogian* prayer, says to God: 'In You I move, and in You I have my being.'"

"Does Professor Brown share this pantheistic view of God?"

"Professor Brown takes the concept of our being in God to the extreme. He believes that because the divine is within us, that we ourselves are gods. Spinoza rejected the idea of God as a king ruling over men. He would have been appalled by Professor Brown's belief that because the divine is within us, we have the right to rule over all things, animate and inanimate. The universe is vast Mr. Veles, and we are a puny part of it. Who are we to claim that we are more divine than the rest of the universe?"

"But we're conscious, we're aware of our own existence."

"And how do you know, Mr. Veles, that the rest of the universe is not? I've spent my entire career searching for these answers. The more deeply we delve into scientific reality, the less substance we discover."

"Is there nothing that we're certain of?"

"Only that the universe exhibits certain regularities. We like to call them laws, but laws are merely human constructs." Dr. Graf sighed. "I was close to unlocking the secrets of the universe, Mr. Veles. I had a doctoral student, Johann Gregor, just a few years younger than me, who was working on solving the mystery of the magic number."

"Magic number?" Lev asked.

"Why 137, of course, or more accurately 1/137: the fine structure constant. It characterizes the strength of the electromagnetic force affecting charged particles such as electrons and protons. If it were any other value, say 1/138, stars would not be able to create carbon, and life as we know it would never have come to exist. Why 1/137? Some say it's random, just a cosmic role of the dice, but Einstein believed that God does not play dice. My student, Johann Gregor, was a strange young man – with his shock of red hair and piercings you would not have figured him for a scientist. Mathematics, Mr. Veles, is the language of the universe, and Johann was more fluent in that language than I."

"What happened to him?"

Dr. Graf paled from the memory. He took a moment to collect himself. "Three years ago, on New Year's Eve, he called me in the middle of the night and claimed that he had solved the riddle of the magic number. He said that the reason no one had figured it out before was because it was so *obvious*. Obvious! Can you imagine? I attributed it to drink, since it was New Year's Eve. I rebuked him for waking me up told him to come to my office after the New Year to discuss his discovery. But he never came."

"Why? What happened?"

"I thought he had left the university for the holiday. But he didn't show up to class when the new semester began. Two weeks passed with no word from him. Finally, I became concerned and went to his flat. I knocked on the doors and windows but no one answered. I called the police and they told me the building was unsafe and had been condemned several months ago. I relayed my concern, and they forced open the door."

"What did you find?"

"Rats."

"Had Johann left?"

"No. We found him on the floor. He had been dead for two weeks. The coroner said that he died of pneumonia. There was no heat, no food . . . The only thing we found were his papers – pages and pages of mathematical calculations. Over the last three years I've attempted to make sense of them, but I could not. They began with the conventional formulas of quantum mechanics, but then he seems to have invented, or discovered, a new branch of mathematics. From the little I could follow it was beyond brilliant . . . it was celestial; it was the language of God."

Lev could see the pain in his face.

"I failed him, Mr. Veles. In my arrogance I didn't realize that my pupil was destitute and starving, living in an abandoned building in the dead of winter. He wanted to share his joy of discovery with me, and I cared only for my own comfort. He needed more than my mentorship – he needed my friendship. I should have invited him to my home, fed him, nurtured him. Instead, I cared only for what he could do for me."

"How could you have known that he was in such desperate straits?"

"The truth, Mr. Veles, is that I didn't care. He was a means to an end. I used him to try and help me unlock the secrets of the universe. The irony is that I let him take his secret to the grave. It was my vanity in thinking that I alone could make it all cohere. Now he haunts me."

"How?"

"Every night I dream that he comes to me and tells me that he's solved the riddle of the magic number. But every night I tell him to go away and come back the next day. It's my punishment for having failed him. You must think me a monster."

"No, Dr. Graf. I don't think of you as a monster. I have my own demons to contend with."

* * *

A message from Anna Karkova pinged on Sophia's phone when she landed at Chopin Airport in Warsaw. It read: *I suggest we add the Polovtsian Dances to our repertoire for the upcoming season.* Sophia knew the piece well. The music of the Polovtsian Dances was the highlight of Alexander Borodin's opera *Prince Igor*. The opera was based on *The Lay of Igor's Host*, a medieval epic poem from Kyivan Rus that described Prince Igor Svyatoslavich's failed campaign against the Polovtsians. The main themes of Borodin's opera were betrayal and alliance. Sophia immediately grasped the meaning of the cryptic message: Karkova had betrayed her, either intentionally or through coercion, and by warning her, she was hoping to salvage their alliance.

Sophia passed through immigration using her French passport. Whoever had been sent to apprehend her would be waiting outside customs. She dropped her phone into a trash can. The luggage area was chaotic but secure. Flights were arriving from all over the world, and the passengers were eager to find their luggage and reunite with their loved ones. She scrutinized the arriving passengers looking for potential cover. She found her target: a young man with a Cubs baseball cap who had just flown in on the flight from Chicago. He was loading a score of blue duffel bags onto three luggage carts. When loaded, each stacked cart was over two meters high. Sophia approached him and said in English:

"You seem to have your hands full."

"I just need to get these bags through customs," the young man said. "I have friends waiting to receive them on the other side."

"What's in the bags?" Sophia asked.

"Military gear for the Ukrainian territorial defense forces: miniature drones, night vision glasses, medical kits, helmets."

"I only have a carryon," she said. "If you'd like, I'll help you wheel these carts through customs. I'm not taking any responsibility for any contraband."

"I've got the customs paperwork from the Polish embassy. It won't be a problem. But I could use a hand wheeling these through. My name is Roman and you are . . . "

"Sophia."

The customs officer did a perfunctory inspection of two of the bags. The blue bags loaded with military gear had been coming through the Warsaw airport in an endless convoy for the past two weeks. This was Roman's third trip as a courier.

As they were wheeling the luggage carts through the exit doors, Sophia said, "I have a confession. There's someone outside the exit who's stalking me – my old boyfriend. Can you help me sneak out?"

From the look on her face, her concern seemed genuine. "Sure, why not?" Roman answered. "Just duck between the bags."

When Roman and the overladen carts appeared in the exit, two young men rushed up to help him. Roman pushed the first cart and the two men pushed the carts behind him. Sophia crouched between them. The waiting area was mayhem. The eager crowd ignored the roped cordon and rushed the exit to greet their family and friends. Young men met their girlfriends with flowers. Mothers met their husbands with children in their arms.

Sophia spotted the FSB agents before they spotted her. A short woman with rimless glasses was checking the faces of the passengers as they emerged from the exit. A lean man with a cord in his ear stood behind her. Hidden by the stacked baggage carts, Sophia slipped through the chaotic crowd unseen.

A vintage Plymouth Voyager was idling by the curb. It had been rigged to run on both gasoline and LPG. The police were not chasing it away. Roman and the two young men loaded the bags into the van.

"Where are you going?" Sophia asked.

"To the Ukrainian border," Roman replied. "It's about a five hour drive. From there, the bags go to Lviv, and from Lviv they go to the front."

"Can I travel with you to Lviv?" Sophia asked.

"We're only going as far as the border."

"Can you take me to the border?"

"You look wealthy enough. Take a train," Roman said. "How do we know you're not some Russian spy?"

Sophia showed him her French passport. "My name is Sophia Borodin. I'm the conductor of the St. Petersburg Philharmonic Orchestra. My partner traveled to Kyiv two weeks ago to film a documentary on the war. I haven't heard from him since. I'm under surveillance. The people I'm trying to evade at the airport are FSB agents. I'm sure they're watching the airport, buses, and trains. You can google me."

Roman took out his phone and searched for Sophia Borodin. The search registered thousands of hits. "It says here that you're Russian."

"I have dual citizenship. My mother was French, and I was born in France. Please, they'll abduct me if they find me."

Roman went over to his two companions and explained the situation to them in Ukrainian. He showed them her online profile, and they deliberated for a few minutes. Roman returned looking noncommittal.

"What did they say?" Sophia asked.

"They're asking if you know any Ukrainian composers."

"Lysenko, Lyatoshynksy, Leontovych, Skoryk . . . I not only know who they are, I play and conduct their music."

Roman went over and relayed the information. He returned with a request.

"My friends say they'll give you a lift to the border if you promise to play Lysenko's "Overture" from *Taras Bulba* at your next concert."

"I promise."

"Then hop in the van."

Roman and Sophia sat in the back seat as the van headed southeast on the five-hour drive to the border. The back of the van was stuffed with blue duffel bags so the driver had to rely on the side mirrors to change lanes. The highway through the Polish countryside was built to European standards, unlike the Russian roads that turned from potholed asphalt to gravel once out of the city. The highway both to and from Warsaw was congested with cars, trucks, and buses. The drive to the border seemed interminable.

"Unusually heavy traffic for the countryside," Sophia said.

"The cars and buses are bringing refugees from the border," Roman replied. "The trucks are taking provisions for those who are waiting to be relocated. Fifteen-hundred refugees are passing through the border crossing at Medyka each hour, mostly women and children. These are the people who are fleeing Putin's liberation."

Sophia felt ashamed to be Russian. These innocents were being displaced from their homes and separated from their families. The Russian press had kept silent on the number of refugees and civilian casualties. The two young men in the front seat conversed in Ukrainian, and Roman would occasionally join in. Sophia understood much of what they were saying. She had sat quiet for most of the journey but tried to understand why these foreigners, an American and two Poles, were so vested in helping the *khokhols*, as the Russian press derisively referred to their Ukrainian "little brothers."

"How is it that you know Ukrainian?" she asked Roman. "You flew in from Chicago."

"I'm a Ukrainian-American," Roman replied. "I was born in the states. I learned the language from my parents, and my parents learned it from theirs."

"And your Polish friends?"

"You ask a lot of questions," Roman replied.

"I don't mean to pry. It's just that in Russia we know little about this war – she stopped herself – 'special military operation.' I would be arrested in Russia for calling it a war."

"It's a hellacious war. Tens of thousands of people have died, including women and children. Millions have been displaced from their homes. Your military's idea of liberation is reducing cities to rubble with missiles and artillery, including thermobaric and cluster bombs. Your 'Rashists' have committed countless war crimes among the civilian population, including rape, torture, and murder."

"I find that very hard to believe."

"You'll soon witness the horror with your own eyes."

"How did you, an American, become involved? Are you CIA?"

"No, I'm a lawyer. My wife and I were in Kyiv before the war began. She was doing a Fulbright Fellowship with the Ministry of Health. The State Department evacuated us to Warsaw. We're now doing what we can to help the war effort."

"And your friends?"

"They're Polish nationals whose parents immigrated from Ukraine. We connected through Plast, a Ukrainian Scouting Organization."

They arrived at Medyka after nightfall. The picturesque village of 2,800 had swelled into a refugee camp of tens of thousands. The public buildings, such as the town reception center, schools and sports hall, had been converted into temporary shelters for those who were not eligible for visa-free travel through the European Union: students and migrant workers from Africa, Asia, and the Middle East. Outside, others huddled around campfires. Mothers sat on their luggage swaddling their children with blankets to shield them from the cold. The lucky ones stood in queues waiting to board buses to the larger cities. Officials in green and orange fluorescent vests directed the refugees to the queues that distributed food, clothes, medicine, and other humanitarian aid. Empty plastic water bottles were piled next to cans overflowing with garbage.

Sophia got out of the van when they stopped at a warehouse to unload the bags.

"Where can I find a toilet?" Sophia asked.

Roman pointed across the street to a lot crammed with trucks and buses. Rows of port-a-potties were arrayed in an adjacent field. Sophia had expected to inhale a breath of fresh mountain air. Instead, she became nauseated from the diesel fumes of idling trucks and buses, wafts of cigarette smoke, and stench from rows of port-a-potties. She entered one to relieve herself. Inside a message in Ukrainian was scribbled on the wall: *Do not get into a car with strangers. Trafficking human beings does not sleep."*

Roman was waiting for her by the van.

"This is where we part," he said. "We've brought you as close to the border as we can. We're heading back to Warsaw tonight. You can take the train from here to Lviv. The station and border are guarded by Polish troops. I doubt your pursuers would follow you there."

"They have eyes everywhere. It's too risky to travel by train," Sophia said.

"Then you can cross on foot. It's about three kilometers to the border crossing. There are empty cars and buses on the Ukrainian side of the border that will be returning to Lviv to pick up more refugees. You can try and catch a lift with them."

"Thank you for your help," Sophia said.

"Every little bit helps," Roman said. "Good luck. I hope you find whomever you're looking for."

* * *

Dr. Graf asked Lev to meet him at the Hotel Bauer on the morning of March 5. He was returning to Munich and was hoping for one last word. When Lev arrived Dr. Graf was already waiting on the hotel dock for his launch to the airport.

"I'm so happy you came to say goodbye," he said to Lev. "You've helped unburden me by hearing my confession. I was hoping we could part as friends. Please call me Elias. May I call you Lev?"

Lev welcomed the gesture of friendship. The pandemic repelled people from one another. It felt human to reconnect. "Yes of course,

Elias." He was surprised that Elias did not have any luggage other than a worn leather briefcase.

"I see that you're staring at my briefcase," Elias said. "I've sent my luggage ahead. The briefcase contains Johann's notes. They're my only hope of understanding the world."

"We've had some most interesting discussions," Lev said. "I'll miss our time together."

"Perhaps we can continue our correspondence by mail. I wanted to tell you that I ordered your novel, *The Storyteller*. It should be waiting for me in Munich. From the excerpts that I've read it seems that you too are an outsider."

"Outsider?" Lev asked.

"Conflicted about your place in your country. My grandparents were outsiders in Germany. We are Jews. They were respected members of their community until the Nazis came. My grandparents sent my parents to Switzerland to stay with an uncle while they tried to make sense of the world. They died in Auschwitz."

"I'm truly sorry for what the Nazis did to your grandparents, but I fail to understand how that relates to my situation."

Elias looked puzzled. "The war, Lev, the war. The fascists have invaded your country. From your book I can see that you love your country, yet you choose to remain in Venice. You must have your reasons for not returning. I suspect that because you're an intellectual, you, like my parents, are on a list for liquidation. I presume you're waiting for this war to end."

Why am I here and not in Ukraine? He thought of his mother's face submerged in the green pool and his first love hanging from the weeping willow.

"I left Ukraine because I failed to save those whom I loved. I left my homeland to escape my past."

"Yet you returned during the Revolution of Dignity to write your novel."

"To seek redemption. You confessed your regrets to me. I too have regrets. The truth, Elias, is that I'm a coward. On the eve of my engagement to the first woman I ever loved, I found her hanging from a tree. I should have had the courage to find out why. Did she take her own life? Was she murdered? Did she confront some unspeakable evil? Instead, I fled for fear that I was somehow to blame. When the mother of my daughter was dying at the hands of Soviet doctors, I should have had the courage to confront her husband and insist that she seek the best medical care in Paris. Instead, I said nothing and watched her die. She asked with her dying breath that I care for our daughter, Sophia. I failed Sophia as well. You see, Elias, I've failed them all. I have little hope of redemption."

"Look within Lev. Don't forsake them. Continue your spiritual journey. There is always hope of redemption."

Lev saw the black launch approaching from the lagoon. Mara was at the helm. "What if I die before I'm redeemed?" he asked.

"The real questions, Lev, are what is death, and what is time?"

Mara steered the launch towards the Bauer dock.

"My time on earth ends with my death," Lev replied.

"Does it?" Elias asked. "Einstein's theory of Special Relativity sees the universe as a four-dimensional space-time block that exists as one entity. Your birth is out there in space-time. Your death is out there in space-time. Every moment of your life is out there in space-time. The past, the present, and the future all exist and are equally real. If you believe in eternalism, as most physicists do, then when you die you are not really gone, because every moment of your life up to that point continues to exist in space-time."

Lev looked at Mara. *Nietzsche's demon,* he thought.

He turned to Elias. "If everything that might happen has already happened, if everything is predetermined, then how can I hope to change things? If I don't have free will, how can I hope for redemption?"

"I said *most* physicists. I believe in an evolving block universe where the present is the boundary of space-time as it expands into the future. Quantum uncertainty tells me that in the dimension of time, the future is not determined until it's happened. I still believe in the arrow of time, the spirit that moves through all things. I believe in free will, in *becoming* through our own choices and not simply *being*. The present is where the uncertainty of the future changes into the certainty of the past. While you may exist eternally in your past, you can still shape your future."

Mara moored the launch to the dock and called Dr. Graf by name.

"My launch has arrived, Lev." He reached out his hand. "We must keep in touch. If I decipher Johann's notes, you will be the first to know."

Lev did not say a word. He stood on the dock staring at Mara. Elias Graf was not her only passenger. Sitting on the leather seats inside the cabin was a young man with piercings and a shock of red hair.

CHAPTER 8

Purgation

Lev awoke as the bells tolled for Divine Service. He pinched himself to see if he was still dreaming. His visions of Mara as a psychopomp ferrying souls to the underworld could not be real. Dr. Graf had asserted that we create our own reality, yet how could that be true? How could he even be sure that Dr. Graf was real? Perhaps their conversations had taken place in his dreams, yet Dr. Graf had revealed insights about the nature of reality that Lev could not have imagined – superposition, entanglement . . . these are the stuff that dreams are made of. He decided to seek Father Stephan's counsel, even though Professor Brown alleged that the man had broken his vows and been ostracized to avoid scandal. Lev entered San Basilio's church just as Father Stephan was chanting the Holy Gospel. To his surprise, the church was filled with the faithful. Father Stephan chanted the gospel in Ukrainian, in a Galician dialect that had survived in the diaspora during the decades of Russification in Soviet Ukraine. Lev knew the dialect well. It was his native language in the Carpathians. The faithful in attendance were mostly mothers and children who were among the millions that had recently fled Ukraine during the Russian invasion. They found refuge wherever they had friends or relatives who had taken jobs in the European Union before the war began. Father Stephan sang the liturgy of St. Basil the Great in Slavonic chant and the faithful responded. Lev knew the music and responses to the liturgy by heart from the days when he served as an altar boy for his grandfather.

The Gospel for the Second Sunday of the Great Fast was Mark 2:1-12, about how Jesus had healed and forgiven a paralyzed man. When Jesus cured the paralyzed man and told him that his sins were forgiven, the teachers of the law accused him of blaspheming: "Who can forgive sins but God alone?" Jesus answered: "Which is easier: to say to this paralyzed man, 'Your sins are forgiven,' or to say, 'Get up, take your mat and walk'? But I want you to know that the Son of Man has authority on earth to forgive sins."

But Lev was accused of sins he could not remember committing – and if he was indeed guilty of these sins, he wondered if he still had the faith to seek forgiveness. He had been baptized and raised as a Christian, but these were his parents' choices, not his. Until the night of the Carnival ball, he had taken his faith for granted; but now it was time to decide for himself. His discussions with Angela, Professor Brown, and Dr. Graf had shaken his faith. He was, as Father Stephan had observed, a lost soul. He had been accused of betraying and even killing the ones he loved, yet he had no recollection of having committed physical violence. His repressed memories had paralyzed his psyche. *Will the truth free me of my sins or tear apart my soul?*

After the Divine Liturgy was over, Father Stephan saw the torment in Lev's face.

"Jesus gave his disciples the authority to forgive sins. Let me help you unburden yourself."

"I'm afraid to face my sins."

"Jesus will help you," Father Stephan replied.

"Are you, Father, free of sin?"

"What do you mean?"

"I heard that you were sent away to avoid scandal."

Father Stephan closed the church door so the two of them could be alone with God.

"It's one thing to be accused," Father Stephan said. "It's another to be guilty."

"I don't mean to pry into your personal affairs," Lev said. "It's just that I *want* to trust you. When you first met me in the contessa's library you said that I was lost. You offered to show me the way. Dr. Graf told me that you, he, Professor Brown, and Contessa Rivelli would meet at her palazzo to discuss metaphysics. All of them except you rejected Christ. They opened my mind to other interpretations of who or what God might be and made me question the very nature of reality. How is that you, after being ostracized by your own order, can still believe and preach the gospel to others?"

"I don't claim to have all of the answers or to pretend that I understand the true nature of reality," Father Stephan replied. "What I know is that there are many paths to the Great Liberation, and that the way of Christ works best for me."

"As professed in the gospels?"

"Yes. I find my salvation in Christ. I saw that you came in during the reading of today's gospel."

"About how Christ forgave the paralyzed man."

"To seek forgiveness, you must confront your past," Father Stephan said. "You are paralyzed with regret and guilt. You need to confront *her*. You need to confess your sins."

"To Mara?" Lev asked incredulously.

"To yourself. You need to give up your Self to God."

"But why to Mara?"

"Before you can give up your Self to God, you must go through your dark night of the soul. Mara will pretend to absolve you of your sins. She will feed on them. She will try to seduce you. She will do whatever she can to convince you to not seek union with God."

"Then what must I do?"

Father Stephan looked him in the eyes. "You will find this difficult to accept, but to achieve the Great Liberation, you must first die."

* * *

At midnight Lev sat at his writing desk with an open laptop trying to work on his novel. The green, hand-painted desk dated to the 1920s and was decorated with painted scenes of Venice. Lev ran his fingers along the curved contours trying to comprehend that this fine piece of furniture that was born in the imagination of a long dead craftsman was made of illusory particles that emerge and vanish out of fields of probability, like the fleeting crests of waves in a rolling ocean of space-time. He looked out his window at the Corte del Milion and half expected to see the ghost of Marco Polo's wife floating above the Corte singing a song of longing for her homeland. He smiled nervously and continued to write his novel. His opening chapter began with an expatriate author in Venice who was following the Procession of the Twelve Marias. He felt a presence behind him. He turned to see Mara standing in the doorway. She was even more beautiful than he remembered her. Her eyes were black as night and her face as serene as the moon. He had seen her visage before, on primitive paintings and idols that dated back to the dawn of man, on frescoes and statues of Persephone, and on Renaissance paintings and statues preserved in museums, churches, and graveyards. She wore a hooded cloak that she let drop to the floor. Beneath her cloak she wore a gossamer gown as sheer as moonlight that clung to her like spiderwebs. She sat down on his four-poster bed beneath the white velvet canopy.

"Who are you?" Lev asked.

"You *know* who I am."

"My mother told me stories about you."

"I've been with you since your first breath, just a heartbeat away."

She's a creature of my imagination, Lev reasoned, *emerged from my subconscious. Father Stephan told me I must confront her. I need to face my demons . . . and resist her temptations.*

But Lev felt fatally attracted to her, like a mate to a black widow spider. It was more than her beauty. She offered serenity, an escape from his world of doubt and torment: the peace of the grave. He could lie down beside her and never awaken.

"What do you want from me?" he asked.

"I want to *know* you so you can know yourself."

"I'm a writer . . ."

"From when you took your first breath."

Lev turned his chair to face her. Her eyes were drawing him into the abyss.

"Tell me your story," she asked.

"Where do I begin . . ."

I remember my life in fragments, like a shattered mirror. I don't know if what I'm about to tell you actually happened, or if my reflections are like you, figments of my imagination. I was born in the village of Dzerelo, high in the Carpathian Mountains. My first memories are from Christmas time. The frost etched ice ferns on the windows. My mother put her finger to the glass and traced the outline of a rabbit hiding in the ferns. I remember going with my father into the forest to cut down a Christmas tree just as the first snow began to fall. The snow transformed the forest into a white winter wonderland. It's my fondest memory of him. My mother and I decorated our tree with fancy glass ornaments that my great-grandmother had brought back from Vienna. My mother added her own hand-made ornaments: spider webs made of straw and a garland of silver beads, cotton, and straw. She lifted me on her shoulders so I could place an angel on top of the tree. She sang Christmas carols about a newborn king.

"The magic of winter," Mara said. She began to hum the melody of a carol that his mother used to sing.

"Yes, that's it," Lev said. "The *koliada* celebrates the birth of Christ."

"The *koliada* is far older than Christ," Mara said. "It marks the winter solstice. Your ancestors believed that during the dark and cold winter, the border between the spiritual and mortal worlds is the thinnest. On the darkest night of the year, the *koliada* welcomes back the newborn sun. Your mother knew this."

Lev knew that his mother was a child of nature, as much as she was a child of God. Perhaps they were one and the same. He dove into the depths of his memories. He told Mara the story of her tragic death, how he found her beneath the water of the green pool, and how he tried to bring her back to life by searching for the golden egg in the lake on the top of the mountain. Mara was not surprised by his tale or by his encounter with the *Didko*. They seemed as natural to her as they did to him. *"Mara understands me,"* Angela had said. Lev continued the story of his youth deep into the night. He wasn't sure if he had been reminiscing for minutes or hours or days. When he opened his eyes, he thought Mara would be gone, like awakening from a dream. Instead, she had picked up his laptop, and her fingers were flying over the keys.

"What are you writing?" Lev asked.

"The story of your life."

"But my novel?"

"Why lose yourself in fiction when you can find yourself in your own story? Tell me about your first love."

My teenage years were turbulent. I had hoped to become a priest like my grandfather, but the communists closed the seminaries. Instead, I enrolled in the philology program at Chernivtsi National University with the goal of becoming a writer. It was difficult. I was a Hutsul orphan from the mountains who spoke broken Russian and had little hope of advancement. I decided to join the university chapter of the Komsomol – the Leninist Young Communist League – to try and improve my prospects. I pretended to be interested in Marxism-Leninism and suddenly doors opened for me. I was able to take courses in English and French in addition to philology. I was invited to write for the student paper."

"Tell me about your *mavka*," Mara said as she leaned back in the bed.

Her request sent a chill down his spine. "How could you possibly know about her, unless I'm just talking to myself?"

"*Mavkas* are inhabited by the spirits of girls who've died a tragic death. I see her in your dreams."

"You must confront your past," Father Stephan had said. *"You need to confess your sins."* Lev began to unearth a secret that he had buried decades ago.

> *Lida was in her second year at the university studying music. She had organized a student club to preserve and celebrate the themes and melodies of Ukrainian folk music. Her own songs about love and freedom were popular among the students and were spreading faster than the Communist Party could censor them. Her club had organized a rally to commemorate the dissident Ukrainian poet, Vasyl Symonenko, who had died at the age of twenty nine after being arrested and beaten. Symonenko's poetry was banned, and Lida put his words to music. My group leader at the Komsomol suggested that I attend the rally and report on her counter-revolutionary activities. When I first saw her, I was smitten. Instead of a nationalistic firebrand, I found a courageous young woman who believed in the ideals of love, the strength of the human spirit, and our right to determine our own destiny. I still see her in my dreams. She had raven hair, dark brows, and verdant green eyes . . .*

"Your dark passion," Mara purred.

> *She was the first girl I had ever been with. I found the courage to approach her and told her that I was deeply moved by her performance. I expected that she would brush me off, but to my surprise she smiled and said that I spoke the purest Ukrainian that she had ever heard, uncorrupted by Russian. We became friends. I expected to be rebuked for befriending a nationalist, but my comrades in the Komsomol encouraged me to pursue my relationship with her. They simply asked that I share whatever I knew of her compositions, so they could help me keep her out of trouble.*
>
> *She read my short stories and convinced me that I had*

talent. She encouraged me to write in Ukrainian rather than Russian and to focus on themes that reflected what was in my heart even if they broke societal norms. I began to write about my childhood in the Carpathians, about the characters in my village, and about the magical forest where the moon and the sun and every plant and animal were alive with the spirit of all things. When I was free to write about the things that mattered to me, the words flowed from my subconscious like water from a hidden spring.She became my muse.

Over the winter we became close friends. We shared our hopes and fears. She dreamed that one day she would sing her songs on the Maidan in Kyiv and awaken the nation to the beauty of their own poetry and music. I dreamed of being a novelist. But underneath her brave face, she was vulnerable. She was afraid that the authorities would silence her, the way they silenced her hero, Vasyl Symonenko. I promised I would protect her and help make her dream come true. My friends in the Komsomol advised me that the best way to protect her would be to convince her to temper her lyrics and return to Soviet mainstream music. They would pry me for her latest compositions. "Those lyrics are much too radical," they would say, "and will get her in trouble with the Party." Other times they would say, "Ukrainian is so provincial! Govorit po cholovitske – speak human! Tell her she must compose some songs in Russian if she ever hopes to be a popular singer." I would repeat these comments to her as if they were my own, and they would anger her. She told me to resist Russification and communist brainwashing and to celebrate my own culture instead. Her songs, rather than being tempered by my suggestions, were becoming more nationalistic and anti-establishment.

Mara reclined on the bed and bent her knee. Her gown slipped down her thigh. "Tell me about the first time you made love."

In the spring Lida invited me for a picnic to her favorite place in the foothills above Chernivtsi: a hidden meadow with a meandering stream surrounded by an old-growth beech forest. A lone weeping willow arched its branches over the stream. We sat under its shade and shared our humble feast of bread, honey, and dried fruits. I brought a bottle of moonshine that I had made from wild berries. She awakened feelings in me that I hadn't felt since childhood: wonder, hope, and trust. We talked and laughed and kissed. I . . .

Lev turned silent.

"Why did you stop?" Mara asked.

"It's too painful to continue," he said.

"The bittersweet agony of heartbreak," Mara whispered. "Come, sit by me, and we can reminisce together."

Lev yielded to her invitation, rose from his desk, and sat beside her on the bed. He saw that she had transcribed every word that he had said. He read them again out loud. Mara tilted her head against his as he read. She sighed when he sighed and smiled when he smiled. She savored every recollected emotion, as she fed on his memories. She was a succubus usurping Lida's place in his heart. Her long hair draped over his neck and shoulder. He felt as if her hair was coming alive, its black tendrils enveloping him in rhythmic waves of dark energy. She brought her pale lips close to his as if to inhale his breath. He pulled away.

She rose and put on her cloak and said, "Embrace your suffering. I'll return when you're ready to continue your story."

* * *

"What do you mean you didn't apprehend her!" Colonel Besoviy shouted into the phone.

"She didn't emerge from customs," the woman's voice on the other end replied. "The locater on her phone indicates that she never left the airport. I've forwarded you the security footage."

The colonel opened the encrypted email file on his desktop computer. Sophia Borodin's name was on the passenger manifest of the flight from

Dubai, so she had to have gone through immigration and customs. He studied every person who emerged from the exit, freezing the frame and replaying any suspicious video footage. He scrutinized them for disguises: women in babushkas, men who looked like women, persons in burkas . . . he stopped when he spotted the luggage carriers piled head-high with blue duffel bags. Two young men met a third who was exiting customs to assist with the carriers, but how did the man with the baseball cap manage to push all three on his own? The swarm of people who jammed the exit to greet the arrivals obscured the video footage.

Colonel Besoviy was familiar with the blue bags. The Ukrainian diaspora was sending military gear through commercial airlines, and the Polish authorities were assisting them. The GRU was monitoring the shipments from start to finish and had identified the informal network of suppliers, carriers, and distributors who were supporting the Ukrainian National Guard battalions. The Plast scouts were the main movers, but they were overseen whether they knew it or not by the U.S. and Polish intelligence services. The supplies would be too little too late the GRU had reasoned, since the Ministry of Defense had predicted the fall of Kyiv within three weeks of the invasion. If the offensive stalled, then the GRU would have to develop a strategy to disrupt the shipments.

It was possible, even likely, that Sophia Borodin had ditched her phone and eluded the waiting FSB agents by hiding between the luggage carriers. But why would the Plast scouts have helped her, a Russian citizen? More importantly, who had alerted her to the threat? The colonel asked an assistant for Anna Karkova's electronic communications. Within minutes the files appeared on his computer. He found the text within seconds: *I suggest we add the Polovtsian Dances to our repertoire for the upcoming season.* He called in his underling.

"Why didn't you alert me to this text?" he demanded.

The young FSB lieutenant tried not to squirm. "It seemed innocent enough. I didn't want to trouble you."

"Trouble me? We're an intelligence service. Trouble is our business. Perhaps your skills are better suited to the front lines. Apprehend Karkova and bring her back to me."

"We have a problem, colonel."

Colonel Besoviy gave him a dead stare. The lieutenant imagined himself looking through the sights of a T-14 Armata tank at an approaching Javelin missile. "She left for Estonia this morning," he replied.

Colonel Besoviy picked up the phone and called the FSB headquarters in Warsaw. "Sophia Borodin has eluded you with the help of Plast scouts. She will undoubtedly try to cross the border at Medyka. Alert your agents to watch the train station and monitor the border crossing."

"Medyka is heavily guarded by the Polish military. It will be a difficult abduction."

"Then kill her and make up some story about Ukrainian Nazis."

* * *

Despite her French passport, it had taken Sophia all night to cross the Polish-Ukrainian border on foot. She hadn't slept for twenty-four hours. Local volunteers had assumed she was a Ukrainian refugee and had given her food and water at the crossing, but the wait and review of her documents had been grueling. In the hours that she waited, she saw thousands of refugees – mainly women, children, and the elderly – fleeing into Poland with what precious little they could carry. They had left their husbands, brothers, and fathers behind to defend their homes against her countrymen.

A Kia Sportage stopped to offer her a lift as she was walking away from the Ukrainian side of the border crossing. The driver, Ignasi, was a debonair man with white hair who looked like he could be sipping an espresso in a seaside bar in Monte Carlo rather than shuttling refugees to the Polish border. They tried to communicate in multiple languages and settled cn English. A truck ahead of them with Belgian license plates was belching thick black exhaust whenever it had to downshift to climb a hill. It had "Emergency Help for Ukraine" spray painted on its side. Sophia vomited on the dashboard.

Ignasi apologized for the diesel fumes that were seeping into the car through the heater.

"I'll pass the truck in front of us on the next straightaway. You can then open your window for some fresh air. I have some bottled water in the back. Please help yourself."

Sophia took a bottle of water off the back seat. She took a gulp, wetted her scarf, and cleaned up the mess as best as she could. This was her first pregnancy, and her first bout of morning sickness. She worried that the cold, lack of sleep, and diesel fumes would affect the health of her unborn child. On the opposite side of the highway, an endless caravan of cars, vans, and buses filled with women and children inched towards the border. In desperation, a pregnant woman and her daughter had abandoned the car they were in and were walking the last few kilometers. The woman held her daughter by one hand and lugged a suitcase in the other. The daughter clutched a stuffed toy rabbit. Sophia realized that her discomfort was nothing compared to the trauma that these refugees were experiencing. She started up a conversation to take her mind off of her own worries.

"I noticed that your car has Spanish license plates. Have you returned to Ukraine to aid some friends or relatives?"

"No," Ignasi replied. "I live in Lviv. I'm volunteering with the 'Save the Children' foundation to help reunite refugee children who were separated from their families."

"They're separated when fleeing the war zone?" Sophia asked.

"The lucky ones are able to reunite with their families. For others, their parents have been killed, and we try to find orphanages that will accept them. The children who remain in the occupied territories are being abducted and taken to Russia for repatriation."

"But that's a war crime!"

Ignasi nodded sadly.

"How is it that you know English?" Sophia asked to change the subject.

"I learned it in school, and then had the opportunity to use it when I worked in South Carolina."

"Ukrainians are allowed to work in the United States?" she asked.

Ignasi smiled. "I'm honored that you mistake me for a Ukrainian national. I am Catalan. I was born and raised in Barcelona."

"Why did you come to Ukraine?"

"Love," Ignasi replied. "I was studying to be a priest when a Ukrainian dance group from Munich performed in Barcelona. I was sitting in the front row when I saw her. Marta, in her embroidered blouse and flowered wreath with flowing ribbons, was for me the epitome of feminine beauty. I caught her looking at me, though to this day she denies it. I came up to her after the performance to introduce myself, but while I spoke multiple languages, I didn't know German or Ukrainian."

"What did you do?" Sophia asked.

"I learned Ukrainian. For three years I took lessons from a priest in Barcelona in the hope of seeing her once again. When I felt I was fluent enough, I took a train to Munich to find her. I had not yet been ordained and decided that before I devoted my life to God, I should first offer my heart to Marta."

Sophia closed her eyes and imagined that she was Marta, a woman so enthralling that she could capture a man's heart with a single glance . . . a woman for whom a man would sacrifice his own calling for her love.

"I was able to locate her through the pastor of the Ukrainian parish in Munich. She came from a famous Ukrainian family. Her uncle had been a member of the Ukrainian government in exile and had been assassinated by the Soviets during the Cold War. Everyone in the Ukrainian diaspora knew them. I was hoping against hope that she would at least give me a chance."

"You just showed up at her door?"

"I knocked on her door, and her father answered. I told him in Ukrainian that I was studying to be a priest and had come to see his daughter. How could he refuse?"

"How did she react when she saw you, a total stranger?"

"At first, she pretended that she didn't recognize me, but I saw the gleam in her eye. I told her that I had learned Ukrainian so I could at least tell her that I loved her. I told her if she rejected me, I would return to Barcelona and take my vows."

"What did she decide?"

"My prayers were answered. We fell madly in love. We married and made our home in Barcelona. We honored and maintained both our Ukrainian and Catalan heritages. We worked and traveled throughout the world and have two wonderful sons who speak both languages. Now we're retired and bought an apartment in Lviv. We spend our winters in Barcelona and our summers in Lviv."

What a remarkable love story, Sophia thought. *A Catalan man and a German woman of Ukrainian descent chose to cherish their heritage and live in Barcelona and Lviv . . . are these the Banderites who threaten the Russian way of life?*

"That is my story," Ignasi said. "Now tell me yours."

Sophia was afraid to tell him who she really was. She was ashamed of her willful ignorance and temerity in challenging Russia's invasion of its peaceful neighbor. Her partner, Alex, was the brave one. He had left for Ukraine to try and stop this madness. All Sophia wanted was for this conflict to end and to love and be loved as much as Ignasi and Marta.

"I'm pregnant," she said. "I'm searching for the father of my child."

* * *

Father Stephan found Lev at his desk.

"What are you writing?" he asked.

"The story of my life."

"She came to you?"

"She has come for all of us," Lev replied. "Angela, Contessa Rivelli, Professor Brown, Dr. Graf . . ."

Father Stephan crossed himself three times. He looked at what Lev had written. "You're writing about your youth in Chernivtsi." The autobiography began with "I." The last sentence he had written began with "I" and stopped.

"It's too painful. I've been trying to write the next sentence for days, but I can't do it without her."

"Let your anguish be your grace," Father Stephan said.

"My anguish? Mara said the same thing, that I should embrace my suffering."

"Purgation is the second step of the mystic journey."

"Why must I relive my suffering? Why should I trust you? You've not revealed your own secrets."

Father Stephan sat down on the bed. "I told you that I was at the Basilian monastery of Christ the King in Rome and went through my own crisis of faith. What I didn't tell you was why."

Lev closed his laptop to listen.

"Shortly after I was ordained, a novitiate nun came to me and asked me to hear her confession. She was a deeply troubled young woman. She was penniless and had neither family nor friends. She told me she had a vision of the Blessed Virgin Mary who told her to become a bride of Christ. I made the foolish mistake of trying to heal both her spirit and her psyche. She confessed that she had become pregnant by a boy who didn't love her. She asked me if she should keep the child and leave the convent or have an abortion and stay. It was a Hobson's choice. I'm a Catholic priest, so how else could I answer her but tell her to keep the child? She begged for penance, and I told her to pray to the Blessed Virgin. But while God forgave her, she was unable to forgive herself. She returned to the monastery every day and insisted that I, and only I, hear her confession. She prayed the rosary till her fingers were raw, and she stopped eating and drinking. The abbot became concerned that I was spending too much time with her. I was worried for her health, both mental and physical, and feared for the health of her unborn child, so I continued to see her. I realized, however, that I was hurting her more than helping her and suggested that she find another confessor. That's when my trials began."

"Why? What happened?"

"She accused me of being the father of her child."

"Are you?" Lev asked.

Father Stephan took a moment to answer. "My abbot asked the same question. No, I am not the father of her child."

"Couldn't you disprove her allegation with a DNA test of the baby?"

"She was hospitalized with anorexia and depression. She elected to have an abortion. My abbot decided to send me to a monastery in Buchach so I could find my way back to God. I was spiritually lost and anguished. Why did God use the plight of this poor girl and her unborn child to try me? Who was testing me, God or the devil? My faith was shaken to my core."

"But you did go to Buchach."

"At first reluctantly. I left Rome and traveled east in the company of Basilian nuns who were taking the train to Lviv. One of them was like myself, a Ukrainian-American who had finished college in the states and then received the calling. She had a doctoral degree in Eastern Christian Spirituality from the Pontifical Oriental Institute and had been invited to be a guest lecturer at the Ukrainian Catholic University in Lviv. I told her I was going to Buchach to find myself, and I'll never forget what she said: 'To find God you must lose your Self.'

"From Lviv I took the train to Chortkiv where I switched to a locomotive pulling a single carriage that rocked and swayed as it climbed the hilly terrain toward Buchach. After an hour of climbing, we entered another world: the Canyon of the Strypa, carved by one of the wildest rivers of Ukraine. We crossed a bridge, entered a tunnel, and were in Buchach, a 13th century town from the time of the kingdom of Halych Volynsk. The monastery of the Exaltation of the Holy Cross was on the Fedir Hill.

"No one met me at the train station, and I walked to the monastery on foot. I was given a tiny room with a window overlooking the river below. The river reflected the sky, and the movement of the sun, the clouds, and the moon marked the passage of time. I spent my days and nights in prayer: Matins and Lauds in the early morning, Prime in the first hour of daylight, Terce in the third hour, Sext at noon, Nones in the ninth hour, Vespers at sunset, and Compline at the end of the day. I kept asking God, why? Why had He put me through this terrible trial, but He never answered. I began to spend time in the monastic library between prayers to seek answers. I had read St. Augustine of Hippo in the seminary, but here, in the Monastery of the Exaltation of the Holy Cross, I discovered the ancient works of the Desert Fathers, Paul of Thebes and Anthony the Great. I read the *Apophthegmata Partrum*, the Sayings of the Desert Fathers, and it opened my eyes to a purer form of Christianity, unrestrained by dogma.

"One evening, after Vespers, an old monk came up to me and introduced himself as Brother Theodosius. He said he had been praying for me since I arrived at the monastery. He said that God had asked him to show me the way. 'Orison,' he said, 'is not simply a petition to God. Orison is a spiritual communion with God.' I told him that I prayed so that God would help me understand myself. He repeated what the sister on the train had said: 'To find God, you must lose your Self.' I accepted his offer to show me the way. 'We begin,' he said, 'with the Jesus prayer: *Lord Jesus Christ, Son of God, have mercy on me, a sinner. Lord Jesus Christ, Son of God, have mercy on me, a sinner. Lord Jesus Christ, Son of God, have mercy on me, a sinner.*' How often do I repeat the prayer, I asked? 'Until you see God,' he replied.

"Did you … see God?" Lev asked.

"In time, with Brother Theodosius's guidance, I began to achieve Illumination. I prayed and prayed and prayed until I was in a state of infused orison in which I was seeing, feeling, and thinking all at once. My mind was filled with gladness, and I forgot my pain and wretchedness. The eyes of my soul were open, and I beheld the plenitude of God in all things. But before I achieved the Unitive State, I was again stricken with doubt. I went through the 'Dark Night of the Soul' and faced my own demons. It was only after I emerged from the darkness that I was able to achieve Union with the Absolute."

"Was it all you had hoped for?"

"It was ecstasy. My soul was lifted into union with God so close and so complete that I was merged in the being of God and lost the sense of any separate existence."

"If you achieved union with God in the monastery, then why did you leave?"

"St. Basil said that the purpose of the monastic life is to be like God in love, and not only to practice love on one's own prayer and work, but towards others by word and deed. I felt that I had a responsibility to share what I had learned and to help others achieve union with God. I decided to study the mystic path in many ancient and modern religions and learned that while the paths may be different, the goal of union with the Absolute is the same."

Lev felt guilty for judging him. Father Stephan's motivation to help him was sincere, even if it meant sending him into terrifying realms. He decided he would listen to him and try to find grace in his own anguish.

"I'm still puzzled," Lev said. "If you've been able to achieve union with God through Christ, why did you engage in the metaphysical discussions with the contessa, Professor Brown, and Dr. Graf. To convert them?"

"No, to learn from them and to share my own beliefs. I've learned that each of us takes his own path to the Absolute."

"But Professor Brown believes that men are divine. How could you reconcile your beliefs with his?"

"In the fourth century, the Church Father Athanasius had said that 'God became man so that man could become God.' Saint Basil, the founder of my order, had said, 'The human being is an animal who has received the vocation to become God.' The purpose of the incarnation was to establish full communion between God and humanity, so that in Christ humanity can find adoption and immortality. The Fathers called this 'deification.' The sacrifice of Jesus accomplished the eternal plan of the Father to unite humanity with divinity."

"So, you agree with Professor Brown?"

"Where I disagree is believing that we are greater than God. Lucifer, too, thought he was the self-reflection of God."

"And what of Dr. Graf's belief in the 'God of Spinoza?'"

"I believe that God is all embracing love that unites the universe into one indivisible whole, the being of all beings. Everything is in communion with God."

"But how do you *know* this?" Lev asked.

"I know it in my heart."

Lev understood the concept of Oneness, but he did not yet feel it. His sins were too great to be forgiven. The world around him was disintegrating into madness, and he was ready to succumb, if chaos would bring him peace. Mara had carried away those around him and now she had come for him. He wondered where she would take him. Dr. Graf implied that we create our own reality, so perhaps we create our own hell. Dostoevsky had said that hell is the suffering of being unable to love. Yet he had loved but had lost them all. Perhaps Mara was forcing him to retell his story to rob him of whatever love he had left. Mara had told him to embrace his suffering. Father Stephan had told him to embrace his anguish. He decided to continue his story.

* * *

Mara appeared again after midnight. Her radiance was increasing like the waxing of the moon. Her face was beyond youthful – it was immortal. Her gossamer gown exposed her neck and shoulders before plunging to her breasts and hips. Her lips were blue.

He lay next to her, closed his eyes, and continued telling his story. She leaned her head against his so she could capture every word, every breath, every beat of his heart, as he continued the story of his first love.

> *Spring had arrived in our secret meadow. It was teeming with wildflowers and lush with grasses. The air was filled with a symphony of trilling, chirping, and humming. The weeping willow, with its yellow catkins, formed a glistening canopy that hid us from sight. I teased Sophia that the Mavky might be watching us, and she began to laugh and tickle me. We sipped our moonshine and shed our inhibitions. Lida wore a Bukovyna blouse with floral designs, an embroidered skirt, and a red coral necklace. When she pulled off her blouse, her raven hair cascaded over her shoulders and breasts. Passion pulsed through our veins with each beat of our hearts. We lay down beneath the dappled shade of the weeping willow. We kissed and caressed before I entered her. It was the first time we had consummated our love, and we were united in our ecstasy. Afterwards I carved our initials into the willow tree, and we promised each other eternal love.*
>
> *Our romance burgeoned into the summer. I wrote my short stories while she composed her songs and performed at the local music festivals. Her popularity was growing, yet despite all the adoration from her fans, she had eyes only for me. Her lyrics were becoming ever more radical, and my comrades in the Komsomol warned me that my tolerance of her civil disobedience was jeopardizing my membership in the Party.*

I assured them that she was just going through a rebellious phase that would soon pass.

On the eve of Ivana Kupala, we were going to be engaged. In our Ukrainian culture, on that magical night a girl weaves a wreath made of wildflowers, places a lit candle in the wreath, and lets it float down the river. Whichever boy picks up the wreath will be her mate. Together we would search for the magical fern flower that blooms only on the night of Ivana Kupala. It has the power to grant eternal youth and eternal life to those who are truly in love. I received a note under my door to meet her that evening in our secret place. She would wait for me by our willow tree and release the wreath into the stream so that only I would catch it. But when I came to our sacred place . . .

Lev stopped.

"Embrace the suffering," Mara said.

She was hanging from our tree! Her hair was green. I ran up to her and grabbed her legs to lift her, and she opened her eyes. She undid the noose around her neck, and I gently lowered her to the ground. She put her arms around me and kissed me. She was naked and I could feel her breasts press against my chest. She was trying to tell me something, as if to warn me, but I couldn't hear her words. When I tried to embrace her, her back was gone! The bones of her spine were exposed!

"You panicked," Mara said.

"I let go of her and ran."

"You were afraid."

"My mother had warned me about girls who die, turn into a *mavka*, and seduce and tickle their lovers to death. What else could I have done?"

"Do you think she killed herself?"

"No, she would never do that. It was the eve of Ivana Kupala. We were going to be engaged."

"What do you think happened?"

Lev looked into the abyss of her eyes. "I think she encountered some unspeakable evil in that meadow. Midsummer night's eve is the shortest night of year, when spirits, both good and evil, are the most active. I've seen the *Didko* with my own eyes. I know this sounds crazy, but I fear that he got to her before I did."

"Did anyone believe you?"

"I wandered through the forest in shock until my friends from the Komsomol found me. When I told them what had happened, they asked me if I had gone berserk and killed her. They said the police would come looking for me. They convinced me that I needed to flee the country and that they would help me escape."

"Did you kill her?"

"How could I have killed her? I *loved* her."

"Yet you betrayed her to the Komsomol."

"I was naïve. I thought I was protecting her." Lev began to weep. Mara cradled him in her arms.

"I'm such a coward. I'm trapped in this purgatory of guilt. What if she did hang herself because she thought I had betrayed her? Why did I panic and flee? Why didn't stay, find out the truth, and defend her memory? I hate myself more than I can endure."

"The divine sorrow in the heart of things," Mara whispered. "You will not be alone in your suffering. I will be with you."

The Dark Night of the Soul

CHAPTER 9

Illumination

Sophia took the overnight bus from Lviv to Kyiv. Ignasi had driven her to the bus station and helped her exchange some of her Euros to *hryvnias* – Ukrainian currency. The bus had stopped in Rivne and Zhitomir to pick up and drop off passengers. Those who continued to Kyiv were mostly men volunteering to defend the capital. They had the innocent faces of boys who had not yet heard the sound of artillery. Sophia slept most of the way. She awoke with her head resting on a man's shoulder. He had been kind enough to let her sleep.

She awoke as they were nearing Kyiv.

"I'm sorry," she said to her fellow passenger in Ukrainian as she awoke. "I didn't mean to fall asleep on your shoulder."

"I'm afraid I don't speak Ukrainian," the man replied in English. He was a ruggedly handsome man in his late forties.

"You're American?" Sophia asked in English.

"My name's Eric. I'm an emergency medicine physician from Boston.

I'm giving some lectures on the recognition and management of chemical warfare agents to the medics in your armed forces."

Sophia was reluctant to admit that they weren't her armed forces.

"Why would an American come here?" she asked.

"Because this isn't just your fight. This is a turning point for democracy and freedom."

"Putin says it's just a special military operation."

"Invading your peaceful neighbor isn't just some special military operation. It's a violation of the United Nations charter that's brought us the most peaceful era in world history. Think about it. Since the end of the Second World War, there hasn't been a single case of an internationally recognized state being annihilated through foreign conquest. Putin's trying to unravel this world order. Ukraine believed in the rule of law. Ukraine gave up her nuclear weapons in exchange for guarantees of her territorial integrity."

"Putin says that the current world order is only good for the West," Sophia countered. "What about Russia and the rest of the world?"

"The global order is based on the ideals that all humans deserve the same basic liberties; that no human group is inherently superior to all others; and that all humans share core experiences, values, and interests. You fought for these values in your Revolution of Dignity. Forgive me for asking, but are you truly Ukrainian?"

"I'm French," Sophia replied.

"You'll soon see what I mean with your own eyes. Why are you in Ukraine?"

"I'm searching for the father of my child. He's a Russian filmmaker. He left for Ukraine to document the war and disappeared. I know someone who saw him last, but I've lost my phone and his contact information."

"Maybe I can help," Eric replied. "What's his name?"

"Andriy Oriskhevich. He's a Ukrainian documentary filmmaker."

Eric googled the name on his phone and came up with a hit. "I found something that might help. According to this link, he's a founding member of the 'Prosvita' group of independent Ukrainian filmmakers. They recently had a film festival at Mysteckyi Arsenal. Someone there might know how to reach him. You can get there by metro from the train station." He reached into his backpack. "Here, I have a map of Kyiv with the metro system. You can keep it."

"Thank you for your kindness," Sophia said and closed her eyes for the rest of the journey.

Sophia rode the metro from the Kyiv train station to the Arsenalna metro stop. When she exited the subway car, police officers instructed her and the other the commuters to hunker in the subterranean station until the air raid sirens passed. The piercing sound echoed through the subterranean hall and tunnels. Sophia unfolded Eric's map of Kyiv to plan her route to the Mystecky Arsenal National Art and Museum Complex once the sirens stopped. The route down Ivana Mazepa Street and Lavrska Street had few shelters and several potential military targets. She doubted that the Russians would risk bombing the route, even with their most advanced guided missiles for fear of hitting the Pecherska Lavra, the seat of Christianity in Kyivan Rus. Putin had received the blessing of the Russian Orthodox Church for his war on Ukraine and in the eyes of the Russian faithful, the Lavra monastery and catacombs were sacred.

The street lamps were turned off. She sprinted to the Mystecky Arsenal under cover of darkness. The building that housed Ukraine's largest museum and art exhibition complex was once a workshop for the manufacture, repair, and storage of ammunition and cannons. In 2005 President Viktor Yuschenko had converted the site into a museum complex by government decree. When Sophia arrived, the gates were locked. A guard informed her that since the Russian invasion the museum had enacted a security plan to safeguard the cultural treasures. Sophia showed him her French passport and insisted on speaking to the museum director. The guard dialed his phone.

"Forgive me for disturbing you Yuriy Oleksandrovich, but I have a French woman here who insist on speaking with you. Her name is Sophia Sergeivna Borodin." After a moment the guard handed her the phone.

"Yuriy Oleksandrovich," Sophia said. "I am the conductor . . ."

"I know who you are," the director replied. "We're closed because of the war. You're a Russian celebrity. Why are you here?"

"I'm trying to find a Russian filmmaker by the name of Alex Ivanovich. He was filming a documentary on the war and disappeared. He's a friend of Andriy Orishkevich."

"Are you alone?" the director asked.

"Yes."

"Wait by the gate. Someone will come for you."

It began to snow. She watched as the snowflakes fell from the sky. She recalled the night of the protests at the Winter Palace, when Alex told her he was leaving for Ukraine. She shivered as she shifted her weight from one foot to the other. As the snow accumulated, her hair and coat were covered in an aura of ice crystals. The feeling of cold in her toes came and went. A young woman in a hooded parka was watching her from across the street. Sophia had no idea how long she had been there. The woman abruptly crossed the street.

"Sophia Sergeivna," the woman said without asking.

"Did the director send you?"

"Follow me," the woman replied.

They walked back in silence to the Arsenalna metro station. The woman handed Sophia a green token and inserted her own into the slot to open the gate. Sophia followed. They caught the next train, exited at the Teatralna station and transferred to the train towards Syrets. The woman did not speak until they exited the train at Zoloti Vorota.

"Forgive my rudeness," the woman finally said, "but I needed to be sure that we weren't being followed. My name is Ruta. Andriy asked me to meet you and escort you to his flat."

"I understand," Sophia said. "Precautions are necessary during this special military . . ."

"War," Ruta corrected her.

"War," Sophia finished her sentence.

Andriy's apartment was located on the third floor of an old building on Yaroslavivniy Val Street that overlooked the *Zoloti Vorota*. The Golden Gates were the main gate of the 11th century fortification of Kyiv during the time of Kyivan Rus. The stairs and common area were lit by a single bulb and smelled of urine. Ruta knocked four times, and Andriy opened the door. He was a handsome man of forty with disheveled hair and a week-old beard. He was wearing a clean white shirt.

"Thank you for escorting her, Ruta," he said. "I'll take care of her from here."

Ruta gave him a light kiss on the cheek and left.

"Your girlfriend?" Sophia asked.

"My apprentice," Andriy replied. "I apologize for the intrigue, but you can imagine that your visit, though not unexpected, is bound to raise questions."

"With whom?"

"Anyone and everyone: the SBU, the FSB, the Armed Forces of Ukraine. Let me take your coat and your suitcase. You must be cold and hungry. Please sit down."

Sophia sat on the leather sofa and took off her boots. She rubbed her toes with her hands until they began to hurt. Andriy returned with a cup of steaming hot tea and a slice of poppy seed cake.

"You said you were expecting me," Sophia said.

"Alex spoke of you. I assume you came to Kyiv to find him. I was taken aback when I received a call from someone who claimed to be your friend."

"Anna Karkova."

"Why didn't you call yourself?" Andriy asked.

"I'm under surveillance by the FSB. They tried to apprehend me in Warsaw."

Andriy looked out the window at the Golden Gates. "The horde is back," he said. "You're lucky to have gotten away. You know they'll keep trying to find you."

The hot tea helped Sophia come to herself. The cold had numbed her body and her mind. "Will you help me?" she asked.

Andriy sat down next to her on the sofa. "I'll do whatever I can. Alex is a friend . . . and a hero. Our heroes don't always make it back."

Sophia steeled herself. "Do you know what happened to him?"

"Two weeks ago, we set off for Bucha. I have a cousin who relocated there with her family eight years ago when the Russians first invaded Donetsk. Bucha is on the front line, and we heard rumors of atrocities being committed against the civilians. We thought we could sneak in to film and document the horrors. I was turned back by the territorial defense. Alex decided to go on alone. He thought his Russian passport would protect him."

"Have you heard anything from him?"

"A single-word text from the following day: *Oksana.*"

"Oksana?"

"My ten-year old niece."

"Have you heard from her?"

"No."

Sophia stood up from the sofa. "I need to go to Bucha."

Andriy took her by the hands and pulled her back down to the sofa. "You don't understand. Bucha is the entrance to hell. It's not just a military front line. The few civilians who have escaped have told us of unspeakable horrors being committed upon the residents. We have to wait for the Ukrainian army to recapture it to know what happened and to pray that there are still survivors."

The hard truth shattered her composure. She buried her head in her hands and began to cry. "You don't understand," she said fighting her tears. "Alex is not just my boyfriend. He's the father of our unborn child."

Andriy put his arm around her and hugged her. "You must stay here with me until we find him. You can have my bedroom. I'll sleep here on the couch. You need to take care of yourself and the baby. It's what Alex would have wanted."

"If your niece escaped, perhaps we can find her. She might know what happened to Alex and her mother."

"I've been searching for her without success. There are millions of refugees fleeing west. She could be among them or she could be . . ."

"She's among them," Sophia insisted. "I know someone who can help us find her. A man by the name of Ignasi helped me when I crossed the border. He volunteers in an organization that reunites refugees with their families. I'll call him first . . ."

Before Sophia had finished her sentence, she was fast asleep. Andriy gently lifted her, carried her to his bed, and covered her with the blanket. He felt her forehead to see if she had a fever. He uttered a silent prayer to the icon of the Virgin Mary above the bed and closed the door.

* * *

Lev returned to San Basilio's church on the third Sunday of the Great Fast. Father Stephan stood before the Royal Doors and chanted the Gospel about the Way of the Cross from Mark 8:34-9:1 in which Jesus said to his disciples: "For whoever wants to save his life will lose it; and whoever will lose his life for my sake and the sake of the gospel will save it."

"For whoever wants to save his life will lose it," Lev repeated the words to himself, *"but whoever loses his life for my sake and the sake of the gospel will save it." Father Stephan said that to achieve the Great Liberation I must first die. But am I ready to give myself entirely to God?*

Lev waited until the Divine Service was over, and he was alone in the church. Father Stephan told him that he could stay for as long as he needed to contemplate and pray. Lev walked up to the iconostasis, the gateway between the world of humans and the world of the divine. The iconostasis dated back to the construction of the church in the 12th century. Lev gazed at the icons trying to grasp their meaning. The icons, rather than painted on wood, were mosaics inlaid with thousands of pieces of stone, glass, tile, and shell. They were masterpieces of Byzantine art that seemed beyond the artistry of mere men. The Royal Doors depicted the Annunciation and the Four Evangelists. The icon to the left of the Royal Doors was the *Theotokos*, the Mother of God holding the Infant Christ. The icon to the right was Christ Pantocrator, the Almighty. To His right was the icon of St. Basil, the patron of the church, and to the left of the *Theotokos*, the icon of St. John the Baptist.

The way to salvation appears before me, Lev thought. *The Angel Gabriel announced the good news that the Virgin Mary would bear a son, Emmanuel, meaning "God with us." The* Theotokos *with the Infant Christ is the beginning of the time of salvation and Christ Pantocrator will sit in judgment at the end of time. Father Stephan had said there are many paths to the Great Liberation, and the way of Christ worked best for him. I pray it will work for me.*

Lev stood before the icon of Christ Pantocrator. He closed his eyes and tried to envision Christ revealing his divine nature to his apostles:

the Transfiguration. Lev's visions to this point in his life had been about spirits, ghosts, and demons. He hoped that Father Stephan could help him illuminate his inner vision and see the world as it truly is, under God. He knelt before the icon of Christ and began to recite the Jesus prayer as Father Stephan had taught him:

Lord Jesus Christ, Son of God, have mercy on me, a sinner. Lord Jesus Christ, Son of God, have mercy on me, a sinner. Lord Jesus Christ, Son of God, have mercy on me, a sinner . . .

As he recited the words over and over, he felt his anxiety begin to ease. His guilt over his sins began to lighten. He began to escape the cell of self-knowledge to appreciate the vastness of creativity in which his individual life was immersed. His life was like a piece of the mosaic before him, infinitesimal yet integral. Beholding the icon, he saw goodness, truth, and beauty.

Lord Jesus Christ, Son of God, have mercy on me, a sinner. Lord Jesus Christ, Son of God, have mercy on me, a sinner. Lord Jesus Christ, Son of God, have mercy on me, a sinner . . .

He immersed himself in the icon and beheld light, life, and love. He hoped beyond hope to behold a vision of the transfigured Christ, His face shining like the sun and His clothes white as light.

Lord Jesus Christ, Son of God, have mercy on me, a sinner. Lord Jesus Christ, Son of God, have mercy on me, a sinner. Lord Jesus Christ, Son of God, have mercy on me, a sinner . . .

As he journeyed deeper within, he entered the Divine Darkness, the Desert of the Godhead. He felt his Self – his doubts and fears, his hopes and dreams – fading away, as if he were returning to the womb where it all began. He stared into the Abyss of Unknown Nothingness, and stopped . . .

* * *

"The priest is leading you to oblivion," Mara said. She lay on the bed in her gossamer gown. Lev could see her breasts swell and fall as she inhaled and exhaled the words that told the story of his life. Lev knew she was a phantasm, a creation of his own imagination, yet her sexuality was beyond corporeal; it was carnal. She wanted to devour him. "Come lie with me," she said.

Lev surrendered and lay down beside her. The brief illumination he had felt while meditating before the iconostasis had been fleeting. The Divine Darkness he had entered, albeit briefly, seemed like a place of no return. Father Stephan had told him that to achieve the Great Liberation he must first die. But Lev did not want to die. The Divine Darkness had terrified him. He continued his story:

I escaped to Paris. The Franco-Soviet Friendship Society helped me secure a job as a correspondent for the French newspaper, L'Humanité. The Society introduced me to Georgiy Volkov, a cultural attaché at the Soviet embassy, who was looking for someone to share his spacious apartment in the 2nd arrondissement. Georgiy knew everyone in French high society. He was a bon vivant with a passion for women and wine. But underneath those seductive eyes and rakish moustache, he was a voyeur who got his thrills by spying on the affairs of others. In my eagerness to start a new life, I fell into his den of corruption. I began to drink and carouse with the best and the worst of Paris's beau monde. The parties at our apartment were infamous. Our guests included artists, politicians, and members of the diplomatic corps who were looking for something more risqué than the diplomatic balls. I often had to climb over passed-out, naked bodies to make it out the door for my morning espresso.

I wrote for L'Humanité during the day and for myself at night. My assignment at L'Humanité was to write articles about class struggle, proletarian internationalism, and the Soviet utopia – the very same lies that Lida had given her life to expose. But what else could I do? I was indebted to the Franco-Soviet Friendship Society for giving me a new lease on life. I rationalized my complicity by convincing myself that what the Didko said was true: that love, hope, and happiness are illusions, as fleeting as my reflection in the water. At night

I retreated into my imagination . . . into a fantasy world of erotic love. I began to write under a pseudonym, Daniel Verchant, to avoid the ire of my employer. To my surprise my stories about the pleasures and torments of love became wildly popular. Within a year I had made enough money to pay my fair share of the rent. One night, after we closed down Harry's New York Bar, Georgiy confronted me about my clandestine writing. He said he'd been aware of my deceit for months and was waiting for me to fess up. We were best friends, after all. I confessed that I was a communist in name only and believed in the intrinsic worth of each individual rather than the masses. I didn't see the need for World Revolution; the liberal democracy in France seemed to be doing just fine. As we were walking back to our apartment, Georgiy admitted that he too had his doubts about communism. He encouraged me to not only continue writing the stories that I wanted to write, but to publish them under my own name. From that night onward, I trusted him with my life.

I completed my first novel during my fourth year in Paris. Laure was a story about the wife of an American ambassador who falls madly in love with a French author named Arsène. One critic described it as "Sagan meets André Pieyre." Once the true identity of Daniel Verchant was revealed, I became both famous and infamous. I was accepted as a member of the "literary tout-Paris" and moved in circles that were previously closed to me. Everyone wanted a piece of my fame. Men wanted to boast that they knew me. Women wanted to brag that they had slept with me. Fellow authors wanted to claim that they had influenced my writing. I was swept into a maelstrom of sex, alcohol, and drugs. Even Georgiy lived vicariously through me; he pressed me for the salacious details of every one of my exploits. People used me, and I used them. The young man who had once wanted to search for the fern flower with his true love was turning into a jaundiced cynic unable to love anyone but himself. I was becoming Arsene in my own novel – pathetic, not tragic, for I had no heights from which to fall. I hated the person I'd become and would have drunk myself to death, or overdosed, or succumbed to a venereal disease had I not met Vera. She was beyond beautiful

. . .

"The dance between love and death, Thanatos and Eros," Mara whispered. Her fingers were flying over the keyboard as he told her his story. When he said the name, Vera, she stopped typing and ran her forefinger from his forehead, down his nose, to his lips. He was on the bed next to her with his back against the headboard. She turned towards him and gave him an open mouth kiss. Her breath was cold. She took his hand and placed it on her thigh. He felt himself rise as she plunged her cold tongue into his mouth. *She's living through me. She's feeding on my memory of Vera, the mother of my daughter.*

"Stop!" Lev said. "I'm not ready to surrender. I want to finish my story."

Mara smiled and picked up the laptop.

"Vera," she said. "You were telling me about Vera."

Vera was the wife of the Head of the Economic Sector in the Soviet embassy in Paris. I met her in the Taras Shevchenko square adjacent to the Cathedral of St. Volodymyr in San Germain. I was covering a commemoration in honor of Princess Anna Yaroslavna for L'Humanité. Princess Anna was the youngest daughter of Yaroslav the Wise, the Prince of Kyivan Rus in the XI century. She married Henry 1 and became Queen of France and the ancestor of all the subsequent kings of France. During the commemorative Divine Service, I stepped out into the square for a breath of fresh air. I saw Vera standing under the bust of the poet Taras Shevchenko ruffling through some papers. She was dressed in a blue Dior dress, and her hair was as golden as sunshine. A cloudburst caught us by surprise, and a gust of wind blew the papers out of her hand. They scattered throughout the square, and I stooped to pick them up before they blew out onto the street. I saw that they were notes handwritten in French and Ukrainian. When our eyes met, the sun burst through the clouds – she was Laure from my novel! Even with her wet hair and clinging dress, she displayed a grace and elegance that belied her sensuality. I handed her the notes, and said I was delighted to meet a fellow Ukrainian.

She looked at herself in her makeup mirror and blushed. I offered her my handkerchief so she could wipe the mascara from her cheeks. As she fixed her makeup, she explained that the organizers of the event had asked that a representative from the Soviet embassy say a few words about Queen Anna in both languages. She admitted that she was not used to public speaking, but her husband insisted. She was surprisingly open and talkative for the wife of a Soviet diplomat. She said her father was a French engineer whose company had sent him to Soviet Ukraine to work on the construction of nuclear reactors. Her mother was a Ukrainian schoolteacher. They fell in love and returned to live in France. Vera was born and raised in Bordeaux and had met her future husband at an economic forum in Paris where she was working as an interpreter. They married two years later. She spoke Ukrainian with her mother, French with her father, and Russian with her husband. I felt she was as attracted to me as I was to her. I could tell by the way she smiled, the way she tilted her head when she spoke, and the way she brushed her fingers through her wet hair . . . she was flirtatious, yet ingenuous. When I told her I was an author, she confessed that she had not read any of my books or stories. I offered to send her my novel, Laure, and she gave me her husband's business card with the address of the Soviet embassy.

When I told the story of our encounter to Georgiy, he winked and offered to deliver my novel to her personally. He explained that the embassy staff screened all incoming mail, and that a mysterious package to the wife of a Soviet diplomat would raise unnecessary questions. I inscribed my novel: "To Vera, may you be as great a gift to France as Anna of Kyiv" and signed my name. A few weeks later Georgiy handed me a handwritten note inviting me to join her for lunch at Le Grande Cascade restaurant in the Bois de Boulogne. I tried to dress the part of a writer – a corduroy jacket, blue linen shirt and jeans – and utterly failed in my attempt at understated style. The maître d' eyed me disapprovingly before leading me to her table by the window that overlooked the park. Vera was dressed in a red St. John dress with a long string of pearls. The décor of the restaurant, with its Florentine marbles, crystal chandeliers, and posh furniture, made it seem like we had traveled back in time to the Belle Époque. She apologized for choosing a restaurant outside the center and explained that she and her husband were well known in Paris, and people might get the wrong impression about her rendezvous with a dashing writer. Dashing was her word, not mine.

I asked her how she liked my novel. She said she was intrigued by Laure, but found Arsène to be selfish and vain. He mistook lust for love and eroticism for passion. "How could someone so in love with themselves find true love?" she asked. She blushed when I told her that she reminded me of Laure in my novel. I remember little of the rest of the meal, other than we sampled all sorts of delicacies, from artichokes to urchins. There was something mesmerizing about her. If Lida, with her dark hair and green eyes, was born of the earth, then Vera was born of the sky. She had azure eyes that could see the beauty in others. I needed to know if our connection was real, or if it was just my imagination, my vanity of falling in love with a character in my own novel. I knew it was a forbidden desire. Still, for my own sake, I had to know if I was still capable of love or if I was like Arsène, too selfish and vain. I began to woo her. We discussed art and literature. She especially liked the American expat authors, like Hemmingway and Fitzgerald, who wrote in Paris during the twenties. We shared our appreciation of the impressionist collection at the Musée d'Orsay. I told her that she dispelled my melancholy like a ray of sunshine. After sharing a soufflé aux fruits rouges, I suggested that we meet again. We had so much in common, and there was so much more about each other that we wanted to learn.

"What about her husband?" Mara asked.

Sergei Borodin was a complicated man. He was much older than Vera and cared for her the way a man might cherish a Fabergé egg. In time, at Vera's urging, I became a frequent guest in their home. Sergei and I discussed politics over vodka and the need for openness and reform. He was an accomplished politician and rose in the diplomatic ranks. When Gorbachev became president of the Soviet Union, he appointed Sergei as the ambassador to France. Sergei considered me his friend.

"At the same time, you were sleeping with his wife," Mara said.

Our relationship didn't begin that way. We were both lonely. We enjoyed each other's company. It was only later that we succumbed to our passion and our relationship became an affair. I don't remember who of us initiated it. She was tired of being cherished but not loved. I was looking to end my downward spiral. We fell into each other's arms and then into each other's beds. But it was never only about sex. I loved her and wanted to have all of her – her heart, her body, and her soul. I often suggested that we run away together and start our lives all over again. Two years into our affair she told me she was pregnant. She didn't say it was my child, so I assumed that she still had a conjugal relationship with her husband. I stopped talking about running away. But I couldn't give her up. I was hers, body and soul.

"Until you broke her heart," Mara said.

* * *

Sophia awoke to the sound of armored personnel carriers rumbling down Yaroslavivniy Val on their way to Makariv. The sun was streaming through the window. She was alone in the bedroom. Her outer clothes were neatly folded on a chair. Her boots were on the floor and her suitcase was beside the bed. She took a fresh change of clothes and tiptoed to the bathroom in the hallway. When she finished showering and dressing, she heard the whistle of a tea kettle. Andriy was waiting for her in the kitchen. He had prepared a simple breakfast of hardboiled eggs, bread, and tea.

"I didn't want to wake you after your long journey," he said.

"How did I . . .?"

"You fell asleep on the couch as you were talking. I carried you to my bed – I slept on the couch. I tried to make you comfortable. I hope you don't mind."

Andriy looked youthful in the morning light. Sophia saw that the lines around his eyes were from stress and not age. He had shaved off his days-old beard and put on a white linen shirt and blue jeans. He reminded her of Alex.

"I told you last night that I think I can help you find your niece. Do you have any photographs of her?"

"I have a photo of Oksana and Irina from my visit to Bucha this past Christmas. Let me find it."

Andriy scrolled through his phone until he found the photo he was looking for: Irina and her daughter, Oksana, were standing in front of the Christmas tree in their home. The tree had been decorated with homemade ornaments and spiderwebs made of straw. Mother and daughter were wearing their *vyshyvanky* – traditional embroidered blouses.

"How about this one?" Andriy asked.

"Perfect. They're very pretty. I'll need to use your phone to text the photo to Ignasi."

Sophia found Ignasi's phone number on a piece of paper in her purse. She took Andriy's phone and texted him the photo with the following message:

> *Ignasi, this is Sophia. Thank you for your kindness in helping me reach Kyiv. My friend, Andriy, and I have a favor to ask. His cousin, Irina Dekaylo, and her daughter, Oksana, who are in the photo, were in Bucha during the invasion. He has lost contact with them. They may be refugees. Can you please help us search for them through your contacts?*

After several minutes, Andriy's phone pinged with a message.

> *I am happy to hear that you are safe. I will send the names and photo to our "Save the Children" network. I will let you know what I find out.*

"All we can do now is wait," Andriy said. Over the next several hours they told each other their life stories. Sophia talked about her rise in her music career, from second violin to first violin to conductor. She spoke highly of her mentor, Nikolai Barsky. She told Andriy about Alex, how they had met and fallen in love. She related the tragic story of her mother's death and confided in Andriy that Sergei Borodin was not her biologic father.

"Have you ever met your real father?" Andriy asked. He would not pry for her father's name unless she chose to reveal it.

"Yes, we were very close when I was growing up." She grimaced as if she felt a pang in her heart. "He was a writer, my mother's best friend. He was often at our house. My mother and he would take me on excursions to parks and museums and to my violin recitals when my father was too busy with work. They would speak to me in Ukrainian so I would learn the language. He was a wonderful storyteller. He would captivate me with stories about the magical denizens of the mountains, forests, and streams. My favorite was the one about a brave young boy who searches for a golden egg deep in the lake on top the highest mountain to save his mother from an evil demon with a large head and spindly legs. When I turned five, he gave me a book of *kazky* – Ukrainian fairy tales – for my birthday.

"You could read at the age of five?"

"I was just beginning. I mostly looked at the pictures. I was proficient in language, but my real talent was in music. My father would teach me Ukrainian songs that were written by a friend of his. I would memorize the notes and lyrics in no time at all and replay them on my violin."

"You are a prodigy in music, an internationally acclaimed conductor." Andriy said. "I wish I had half of your success in filmmaking. I've won awards with the Ukrainian Film Academy and the Eastern European International Film Award, but I've yet to attract a popular audience. I'm currently working on a documentary about how the Russians are destroying our cultural heritage. They're targeting museums, libraries, historic buildings, and even churches. I recently learned that I'm on the Russian's hit list."

"Hit list?" Sophia asked.

"The list of people targeted for elimination after the Russians occupy our territory. They prepared it long before the invasion. It's straight out of Stalin's playbook. The list includes not just political, cultural, and religious leaders, but also teachers, artists, writers, and filmmakers. Anyone who might resist occupation and Russification."

They continued talking well past dark when Andriy's phone rang. Sophia watched his face as he listened. His expression changed from concerned to hopeful. At the end of the conversation, he tried to smile.

"Ignasi thinks they may have found Oksana," he said.

"How about Irina?"

"A girl who closely matches the photo was found alone. She had been wandering through the fields west of Bucha when a Ukrainian reconnaissance team found her. They transported her to a children's hospital in Vinnytsia. She hasn't spoken a word since they found her."

"We need to go to her now," Sophia insisted.

"There's a nightly curfew until 6 a.m. We can leave at first light. The roads to the west are still secure. We can take my car."

Sophia tossed and turned in bed, hoping that the girl was Oksana, and that she could provide some hopeful news about Alex. Andriy lay on the couch with his eyes open.

Sophia and Andriy set out for Vinnytsia at dawn. The 270 km drive from Kyiv to Vinnytsia passed through multiple checkpoints. The road west was jammed with cars and buses filled with refugees who were fleeing the fighting. The traffic east was mainly columns of military vehicles that were advancing towards the front lines. Whenever a soldier would call out, "Glory to Ukraine," Andriy would proudly respond, "Glory to heroes."

They arrived at Vinnytsia Regional Children's Hospital on Khmelnytsky Highway in the late afternoon. Andriy relayed the information that Ignasi had provided to the clerk at the entrance. She made a phone call and after several minutes, a pediatrician with a white coat and tall white medical hat met them in the lobby. He asked to see the photo of Oksana and Irina.

"This could well be her," the pediatrician said. "Are you relatives?"

"I'm her uncle, and this is my . . . friend."

They ascended the elevator to the general ward. "You need to be prepared when you see her," the doctor said. "Physically, she's suffering from frostbite and dehydration. Still, she's one of the lucky ones. We have children here who've lost their limbs. We have girls with torn vaginas."

Andriy clenched his fists. "Did the orcs. . ."

"No, she wasn't physically assaulted. But mentally, she's in a state of shock. She has traumatic mutism. She hasn't spoken a word since they brought her here. Perhaps you can get her to speak."

The girl was lying in a fetal position on a bed in the corner. She was clutching a doll to her chest. Andriy came up to her and gently turned her face towards his to see if she was indeed his niece. At first her stare was blank. As Andriy caressed her face, her stare changed from bewilderment to recognition.

"Uncle Andriy?"

"Oksana, I'm here. You're safe with me."

Sophia stood behind Andriy not wanting to confuse the girl. The medal and chain around her neck looked familiar.

Oksana began to whimper. She then began to cry. She reached her arms out to Andriy. He lifted her from the bed and hugged her with all his might.

"This is my niece," Andriy said to the doctor. "When can I take her with me?"

"You'll need to complete some paperwork. We need to verify your identity. You'll need to assure us that you'll be taking her someplace safe where she can continue to receive counseling."

"Her grandmother lives in Moryntsi. She'll be safe with her there for now."

"What about her father?" the doctor asked.

"He's defending Mariupol."

"Where's mama?" Oksana cried out.

"I don't know. I was hoping you would tell us."

"Alex said she'd be waiting for us by the children's camp," Oksana said.

"You met Alex?" Sophia asked.

"He gave me this medal. He said it would protect me."

Sophia's heart sank. She recognized the medal of *Pokrova* that she had given him before he left for Ukraine. "I'm Alex's . . . friend," Sophia said. "Can you tell me what happened to him?"

"She's still in a state of shock." Andriy interrupted. "Perhaps it's too soon to ask."

"No, I need to tell you," Oksana said. "When the soldiers came to the house mama hid us in the cellar. We were hiding for a long time. It was cold, and I had to pee on the floor. Alex held me in his arms so I wouldn't freeze. He told me to be as quiet as I could and not to cry. I told my doll, Zoya, not to be afraid. I heard a lot of noise and yelling upstairs. I closed my eyes and tried to dream about Baba Maria's house in Moryntsi with Kozak and the cherry orchard. When I woke up, the soldiers were gone. We waited for mama to let us out, but she didn't. Alex climbed out of the cellar to look for her. He came back for me and said that she was waiting for us by the children's camp on the edge of town. It was dark when we left the house. We snuck between buildings so the soldiers wouldn't see us. I saw my friend, Maya, lying in the street next to her bike." She began to sob.

"You don't need to tell us everything now," Andriy said.

"No, I must! When we reached the children's camp, mama wasn't there. I called out for her. That's when the soldiers saw us. Alex told me to run, and they started to shoot. When I turned around, he was lying in the snow. The soldiers lifted him off the ground and dragged him away. He shouted for me to keep running, and I ran into the forest. I ran as fast as I could. I heard bullets hit the trees around me. I heard soldiers chasing me, so I hid beneath a fallen tree. It was dark, and they didn't see me through the branches. I waited till they passed, and then I ran in the other direction. I ran and ran until I couldn't run anymore. I hid from everyone I saw. I ate the snow because I was so thirsty. It's my fault that they saw us!"

"No, you're not to blame. Your mother and Alex are heroes to have saved you."

Oksana looked at Sophia and saw the tears welling in her eyes. She took off the medal of the *Pokrova* and gave it to Sophia. "Please give this back to Alex when you find him," she said. "Thank him for being my hero."

Sophia accepted the medal from Oksana and hung it around her own neck for safekeeping She covered her face and began to cry.

"I'm sorry," Andriy said. "There may still be hope. We won't know what really happened to him until we retake Bucha."

* * *

Lev opened his eyes. His head was on Mara's lap. He jerked himself up.

"How long have I been asleep?"

"Did you dream?" Mara asked.

"I can't tell the difference between dreaming and waking anymore. I'm losing my mind."

"You are *opening* your mind, unencumbered by the world around you. You are free to be who you truly are. Your dreams are as real as your waking moments. But now, you must continue your story."

> *When Sophia was born, I was both happy and sad. I was happy for Vera and Sergei that they had a daughter. I was sad for myself, that I did not have my own family. Vera saw my distress and did her best to include me in theirs. I loved Vera and Sophia as if they were my own. I was there for every birthday, every holiday, every recital. Sophia was a very*

special girl. She was bright, inquisitive, and incredibly talented in music and language. She loved fairy tales. When she was old enough to read, I brought her books for her birthday. She loved stories that took her to faraway places. She was fluent in French and Russian. Vera even taught her Ukrainian, which was the native language on her mother's side.

"Your affair with Vera?" Mara asked.

It continued, but it was love and not lust. Sophia was more precious to Vera than I was, which I fully understand. But the more I loved Sophia, the more Vera loved me. We were a family, if I can use that word given that our love was forbidden. I again suggested that we should run away together, this time the three of us, but she wouldn't hear of it. She was afraid it would disrupt her daughter's life. The more I knew about Vera – her fears, her anxieties – the more I loved her. About the time of Sophia's seventh birthday, Vera's health began to fail. She was becoming more introverted and was reluctant to share her suffering with me. Her skin became pale, and she had little appetite. She said she was losing feeling in her hands and feet and was having difficulty walking and holding a fork or a pencil. I urged her to see the best doctors in Paris, but the embassy insisted on using only their own doctors. The Soviet doctors said her bone marrow was failing, and that there was little they could do.

One day when her husband was away, Vera called me to her bedside. Sophia was with her holding her hand. Vera said she wanted to share a secret with the both of us. Her voice was faint, like a whisper. I remember that I knelt by Sophia's side so Vera would not have to raise her head off her pillow. Her words struck me like an arrow through my heart. She confessed to the both of us that Sophia was my daughter. She made me promise that I would love and care for our daughter when she was gone. My heart broke for the both of them. Yet

Sophia's reaction was the opposite. She said it was a lie. She said her mother would never betray her and her father. She blamed me for breaking her mother's heart. She blamed me for her illness. She started to cry and said she never wanted to see me again.

"What did you do?" Mara asked.

What could I do? I wanted to hug and console the both of them. But Sophia's anger put a wall between us, a wall that I have never been able to breach. The next morning Georgiy told me that Vera had died during the night. I was devastated. I wanted to rush over to see Sophia, but he said I was no longer welcome at the embassy. For the second time in my life, I had failed to protect the woman I loved. I was allowed to attend the funeral for the sake of appearances, but it was clear that no one wanted me there. I waited till the others had left to place flowers on her grave. I promised myself that while I failed her, I would not fail our daughter. That night it began.

"What?" Mara asked.

The haunting. The night after she was buried, Vera came to me in my dreams. She didn't say a word. I saw a profound sadness in her eyes, and I wanted to comfort her, but she was the one comforting me. I had suffered from visions before and ascribed her visit to my grief. Still, I held on to her until daybreak. When I awoke, she was gone. The next night she came again. I told her that I wanted to die so I could join her. I thought that if death reunites us with the ones we love, then I welcomed death. She shook her head no. I reasoned that it was because I had promised to care for our daughter. I craved Vera's nightly visits. I didn't want to let her go. You see, I was sane in my insanity. It was only when she stopped coming that I began to lose my mind. I fell into despair. I stopped eating, drinking, and sleeping. I tried to write but I could not. Georgiy saw my physical and mental health slipping away, and he had me committed. He said it was for my own good. I spent several weeks in a mental institution suffering from a grief-triggered psychosis. When I was released from the hospital, Sophia and her stepfather were gone. They had left Paris and moved to St. Petersburg. I tried to contact Sophia over the years that passed, but she never responded. She was convinced that I was somehow responsible for her mother's death, and I began to believe her. I was told that my deceit had killed Lida, so perhaps my deceit had killed Vera as well.

Mara stopped typing. She cradled Lev in her arms. She was pulling him into the Burning Grounds. But he didn't care. He was sharing his darkest secrets without judgment. He was not sure what she wanted from him, other than everything. Was she a succubus, a demon lover who seduced men in their dreams? He was sure she was a phantasm, a creation of his own imagination. Yet she felt more than real. She craved sensuality, as if it were something she could not have without feeding on his. If he lay with her, would it be a sleep from which he would never awaken?

* * *

Colonel Besoviy lit a Sobranie Black Russian cigarette with his Bulgari gold lighter. He eased back in his chair and admired the view from his penthouse on the Griboyedov Canal: the illuminated Church of Our Savior on Spilled Blood, the site where Tsar Alexander I had been assassinated, reflected in the black water. He was about to pour himself 50 grams of vodka when his phone rang.

"Colonel Besoviy, we have 'Zmiy' from the Ukrainian SBU on an encrypted line."

"I'm listening," Besoviy replied as the call was transferred.

"We've located her, colonel. She's staying with the filmmaker Andriy Orishkevich. They traveled from Kyiv to Vinnytsia to pick up his niece from the Children's Hospital."

"He has family in Vinnytsia?"

"The girl is a refugee. He has family in Bucha."

The colonel took a deep drag of his cigarette. "I see," he finally said.

"It's only a matter of time before she discovers what happened to Ivanovich. What will you have me do?"

A sharp knock on the door interrupted their conversation.

"Wait on the line," he told Zmiya. He left his phone on the chair and walked down the long hall to the front door. He looked through the peephole and saw three plain-clothed FSB agents. One of them was his deputy. He unlocked the door to rebuke them.

"This must be urgent to. . ."

Before he could finish the sentence, two of the agents twisted his arms behind his back.

"What's the meaning of this!" the colonel shouted.

"You're under arrest," his deputy replied.

"On what charge?"

"Treason."

"This is outrageous. I'm a decorated FSB colonel. I demand to speak to General Vodkin."

"That won't be possible," his deputy replied. "The General is under house arrest. He's blaming you for the intelligence failures in Ukraine."

Colonel Besoviy knew that the special military operation was not going according to plan. His office had predicted the fall of Kyiv within days of the invasion. The Kremlin needed someone to blame. His whole department was being purged to whitewash the failure. Then why was his deputy here?

"Aren't you going to cuff me?" Besoviy asked.

His deputy opened the French doors to the balcony. A blast of cold air blew into the 12th floor apartment.

Besoviy twisted and kicked to break free, but the two agents who were restraining him lifted him off the ground by his arms and belt. Before he could plead with them, they hurled him off the balcony into the night air. The last thing he saw before striking the embankment was the illuminated Church of Our Savior on Spilled Blood.

Zmiya waited on the line for the colonel to return with his orders.

He heard the distant knock on the door and unintelligible shouting. His safety as a mole in the Ukrainian SBU was in jeopardy. He hung up the phone. The matter with Sophia Borodin would have to wait. If the colonel or his superiors wanted her dead, they would have to do it themselves.

The Dark Night of the Soul

CHAPTER 10

The Dark Night
of the Soul

Spring did not arrive on March 20th. Dark clouds blocked the sun, and the stone forest was void of warmth and color. Lev's walk to San Basilio's church for the fourth Sunday of the Great Fast took him over the Rialto bridge, where he had met the Dead Bride on their way to the Rivelli's masquerade ball. Now she was gone, the Black Widow was gone, Il Dottore was gone, the Alchemist was gone. . . only he and Father Stephan remained. Lev had immersed himself in his autobiography, and Mara was his muse. Father Stephan had found a new calling: being a shepherd to the Ukrainian refugees who were flocking to Venice to escape the war.

San Basilio's church was filled with faithful. Lev saw hope in their eyes. They had found something of their own culture in this foreign land. Father Stephan was assisted in the service by Yuriy, the new church deacon, who had just emigrated from Ukraine with his daughter because he was told he was too old to fight. The Gospel for the fourth Sunday of the Great Fast was Mark 9:17-31 about how Christ had healed a boy possessed by an evil spirit. The boy had been convulsing and foaming at the mouth and throwing himself into water and fire. Before driving out the unclean spirit, Jesus said to the boy's father: "If you can believe, all things are possible to him who believes," to which the father replied: "I believe. Help my unbelief!"

Help my unbelief, Lev pleaded to God. *Mara is possessing my body and soul, and I have no relief from her haunting. Jesus's disciples were not able to cast out the unclean spirit. I fear that Father Stephan will not be able to cast her out as well. "This kind can come out only through prayer and fasting," Jesus had said. But I have prayed and I have not eaten and still Mara keeps returning. There is no hope for me. There is no salvation.*

Father Stephan saw Lev walk out the church when the Gospel had ended. *It's beginning,* he said to himself: *the Dark Night of the Soul.*

* * *

Mara was waiting for Lev in his apartment.

"I told you the priest will lead you into oblivion."

"He wants to bring me closer to God."

"Don't you see?" Mara asked. "God has abandoned you. But I have not. Come lay with me."

At first Mara's visits were sporadic – the mysterious friend of Angela, the woman in the launch, the night visitor. Now she seemed omnipresent. Lev could not sleep a night without her. She wove her seduction like a web, strand by strand, word by word. He was caught between love and death, Eros and Thanatos. He wanted to lay with her and lose himself in her. He did not want union with the Divine. He wanted union with death. Yet she would not give him peace until he reached the climax of his story. She wanted more than his body. She wanted everything that made him who he is – every hope, every fear, every desire.

Mara lay on his bed with her elbow bent, resting her head in her palm. It was an enticing pose that reminded Lev of Canova's masterpiece, *Venus Vitrix.* Her gown had slipped to her hips, unveiling her perfect torso. She was the epitome of female beauty. Lev wondered if he was conjuring her from his imagination to create the perfect woman. He first touched and caressed her foot. He ran his hand up the back of her leg, up her calf and thigh, probing for a taboo. She took his hand when he reached the inside of her thigh and brought it up to her lips. She put his fingers in her mouth and gently sucked them. She lifted her head to his and brought his hand to her breast. He could feel her breathing accelerate. She opened her mouth and invited his tongue. His lust for her was becoming unbearable. He began kissing her on the neck and breasts. He grabbed her gown and pulled it above her hips . . .

"Wait," she said. "You must finish your story. Then you'll be mine."

Lev took a moment to collect himself. He was burning with desire, and she was as cold as death.

"Will you write it down?" he asked.

She took his computer and placed it on her bare lap. Lev closed his eyes to the temptation.

After Vera was laid to rest, Sergei left Paris and moved with Sophia to St. Petersburg. I never saw him after that. I wrote to Sophia, but she never returned my letters. It was as if I was dead to her. I tried to call Sergei, but he never returned my calls. He must have known that I was Sophia's true father. Perhaps Vera had confessed to him on her deathbed, the way she had confessed to Sophia and me. I wanted to travel to St. Petersburg in the hope of reconciling with them, but Georgiy advised me against it. He said I already had a KGB file because of Lida's death, and if I returned to the Soviet Union, I risked arrest. I went back to my writing and wrote three more novels, but I was never able to recreate the passion of Laure.

Sergei Borodin died in the spring of 2003. His death offered hope for a reconciliation with my daughter. I even thought of attending the funeral, but my Soviet passport was no longer valid. I considered applying for a Ukrainian passport but was afraid that the circumstances of my self-exile would come to light. The editor of L'Humanité convinced me that a French passport would allow me a wider freedom of travel and helped facilitate my application. I made up a story about being a political refugee.

"You didn't tell them that you were running away from yourself?" Mara asked.

Lev continued his confession without answering.

The following winter I learned that the St. Petersburg Philharmonic Orchestra would be performing a concert at the Palais Garnier in Paris over the upcoming Christmas holidays. I bought a ticket for the opening performance in the hope of seeing my daughter. I had followed her mercurial rise in the world of music from afar, through newspapers, magazines, and the internet. She had completed her studies at the St. Petersburg Conservatory and by seventeen was the youngest member of the St. Petersburg Philharmonic.

I remember it was the first snow of the season. It was a time of peace and goodwill. I hoped it would herald a new beginning for us. I sat in the balcony of the Palais Garnier and spotted Sophia with my opera glasses. She played second violin in an ensemble of one hundred musicians, but in the symphony of strings, woodwinds, brass and percussion, I heard only her. After the performance I waited for her outside the musicians' exit. I wrapped a present of my novels and a photo of us with her mother at the puppet theater in the Luxembourg Gardens. But when she came out into the cold and saw me, she froze. She said I was a stranger to her, that I was a man without a home, a family, or a country. She asked that I stop sending her letters. She said she never wanted to read any of my novels, because she might find a piece of me there.

I was heartbroken. Despite her rejection, I will always love her. I see the both of us in her: Vera's radiance and my darkness. Borodin had given her education, luxury, and a stepfather's love. We had given her ourselves. We would be forever united within her. The irony was that Sophia too had forsaken her home, her family, and her country. She was Ukrainian and French by birth, and Russian by choice. But who am I to judge? She was right; I am a stranger in my own land. I had abandoned my birthplace, my culture, my language to live in a foreign land. As Dr. Graf had pointed out, I would always be an outsider.

The following year I was offered an assignment by my former newspaper, L'Humanite: to travel to Ukraine to cover the events of the Orange Revolution. I took Sophia's criticism to heart – that I was a man without a country – and hoped to redeem myself in her eyes. I convinced myself that now that Ukraine was independent, my Soviet KGB archives were buried forever. I accepted the assignment and returned to Ukraine under the protection of my French passport for the first time in twenty-five years. The people's presidential candidate, Victor Yuschenko, had been poisoned with "Agent Orange" and the election was stolen. The popular uprising, known as the Orange Revolution, reversed the outcome of the election, and Yuschenko became president. It was a time of great hope and promise. It was also a time of great disappointment. Ukraine was riddled with corruption. Yuschenko himself admitted that the system corrupts people faster than he could reform it. Ukraine needed to purge itself of its Soviet past if it was to become a nation. I decided to use the opportunity to return to the village where I was born to rediscover my roots.

I arrived in Dzerelo in late January, 2005, after Yuschenko's inauguration. For the last several kilometers, I had to ride up to the village on a horse-drawn sleigh. I saw my grandfather's Hutsul church which was in a state of disrepair. I saw the pastor's house where I was raised. I walked to the cemetery above the church to visit my mother's grave. The gravestones were covered in snow. As I was clearing her grave, a young priest came up to me. He said that he had noticed the stranger in the village and wondered if he could help me. I told him that my name was Daniel Verchant, and that I was a writer from Paris. I was researching Ukrainian ethnography for a new novel and had heard a legend about a boy who had met the devil in these woods.

The priest knew the story well. The boy was the grandson of Father Ihor, a former village priest. The boy had found his mother drowned in a pool up the mountain. He claimed that the Didko had killed her. Many people in the village believed that she had committed suicide, and they did not want to give her a Christian burial. Father Ihor insisted that her death was accidental, and that the shock of finding her had precipitated her son's delusions. The daughter's husband, who was a drunkard, had disappeared. Father Ihor raised his grandson until his dying day. After Father Ihor died, the grandson tended to the church, attended school in a village down the mountain, and relied on charity to survive. When he was eighteen, he left for the university and never returned. It was a tragic story, because the boy was the last in his bloodline.

"The story of an author, in love with his youth, who can't let go," Mara said.

"You mock me," Lev said.

"On the contrary, I cherish your roots."

"My childhood died with my mother. There was no going back to the life I had, though the hardship made me who I am. I was a stranger in my own birthplace. I still feel a kinship with the villagers – we share a collective unconscious, a belief in the spirit in all things, natural and supernatural. They were kind to me after I was orphaned. Before I returned to Paris, I donated money to the village priest to repair the church bell that had been broken in a great thunderstorm on the night that my grandfather died. I had spent my boyhood in that church. I had rung that bell for Divine Liturgy on Sundays and Holy Days. I wanted to be remembered as the boy who rang the bell to call people to church rather than the orphan who met the devil in the woods."

"Do you know how your mother died?" Mara asked.

"I know that she would never take her own life. She would not have abandoned me."

"Perhaps for her, death was preferable to life."

"I can't believe that."

"Why? Do you fear death?"

"I fear the not knowing. What happens to us when we die? Where is Angela? Where is Contessa Rivelli, or Professor Brown, or Dr. Graf?"

"They are each in their own place and time."

"Where are these places? Angela believed that she will be no more. Contessa Rivelli believed in an afterlife of devils and demons. Professor Brown believed that he is a god. Dr. Graf believed that everything is God. Father Stephan believes in heaven . . ."

"What do you believe?"

"I don't know what to believe. But Father Stephan says that I can experience union with God by following the Mystic Way, even before I die."

"What do you imagine union with God to be like?"

"Father Stephan says that it is ecstasy. I imagine merging into a Divine Light, my energy becoming one with the universe."

Mara gave him a grim smile. "Union with the Absolute requires losing your Self. You will need to give up everything that makes you who you are: your hopes, your dreams, your memories. You will become one with the Divine Darkness. Is that what you want?"

Lev hesitated with his answer. "I want to be who I am, Lev Veles. I don't want to lose myself and meld into everything – or nothing. I want to live forever, at least in memory. I want people to know who I am or was."

"As do I," Mara said.

* * *

The Russians were advancing on Kyiv from the north, east, and northwest. Andriy and Sophia drove his niece from the Vinnytsia hospital to his aunt's house in the village of Moryntsi in Cherkassy oblast. The 250 km drive through the snow-covered fields and gently rolling hills of central Ukraine seemed a world away from the scorched earth of the Donetsk, Luhansk, and Kharkiv oblasts. The Russians were advancing on Zaporizhzhia from the south, but the front was still 500 km away.

Andriy's aunt's house was a traditional peasant home, with white mud-plastered walls and a straw roof. The home had been in the family for generations, dating back to the time of the national poet, Taras Shevchenko, who had been born in the village in 1814. It had been updated with electricity, but still had an outhouse, vegetable garden, and cherry orchard in the back. The front of the house was decorated with hand-painted sunflowers that rose from the ground to just below the snow-covered roof line.

Oksana recognized the house as they drove up to it on the one-lane road that also served as a cow path. Oksana had spent several carefree summers with her grandmother while her parents worked in the city. Young adults had abandoned the villages even before the war. The women went to work as maids or caregivers in the European Union. The few young men who stayed in the villages either farmed or drank. Now, most had gone to war and left the villages to the pensioners.

Andriy parked his ZAZ along the wattle fence that separated the house from the cow path. A dog was barking inside the house. Oksana got out of the car and ran through the ankle-deep snow towards her grandmother's house. When Baba Maria opened the door, her terrier, Kozak, darted into Oksana's arms. Kozak licked her face as Oksana nuzzled him. Andriy hadn't seen Oksana so happy since Christmas. Kozak sprung to the ground to sniff the intruders. He recognized Andriy but pranced around Sophia feigning nips and bites until he was satisfied that she posed no threat.

Andriy's aunt waited at the threshold as her dog reconnoitered the stranger. A red babushka framed her gaunt face and world-weary eyes. The babushka had been a gift from a distant cousin in America who had sent it to her during the Cold War. She opened her arms to greet her granddaughter and hugged her with all her might.

"Baba Maria, is mama here?" Oksana asked.

"No, Oksanochka, but I'm sure she'll join us soon. Come, I've got some hot borscht and your favorite *varenyky* – potato dumplings – on the table."

Oksana ran into the house with Kozak, while Maria waited at the threshold to greet her nephew and his companion. She saw in her nephew's downcast eyes that there was little hope of reuniting with her daughter. Andriy kissed her three times on the cheeks according to custom. She took hold of his hands and kissed them.

"Thank you for saving my Oksana," she said.

"It was not my doing. This is my friend, Sophia. She located Oksana in a hospital in Vinnytsia. Her friend, Alex, rescued Oksana in Bucha. We still have no word about his fate or Irina's. Have you had any word from her father?"

"He's defending Mariupol. Come inside. Eat, drink, and rest. There's much to talk about."

The modest home consisted of two rooms separated by a central hallway. The living quarters contained a wood-burning oven that was also used for heating, along with two beds, and a wooden table and chairs. The room on the other side of the hallway was used for storage. The table was set with an embroidered table cloth and laden with multiple courses: pickled herring, pickled vegetables, pork fat, rye bread, *holubtsi* – cabbage rolls, and *varenyky*. In the center was a bottle of mineral water and a bottle of *samohonka* – moonshine.

Once at the table, Maria poured three shot glasses with *samohonka* and raised a toast: "*Budmo!* Let us be." She and Andriy downed their shots. Sophia followed and coughed. The *samohonka* was distilled from horseradish. Oksana took a sip of mineral water.

Maria loaded their plates with pickled tomatoes, pork fat, and raw garlic. After several bites she looked at Andriy to refill the glasses so he could raise the second toast.

"Glory to Ukraine!" he said.

"Glory to heroes," Maria and Oksana replied and finished their glasses as well.

Sophia took a sip from her glass. *May my hero return to me,* she wished.

The borscht, which was served as the second course, was the best that Sophia had ever tasted. It was deep red and steaming hot, with copious slices of beets and other vegetables, along with boiled pork, and a dollop of sour cream sprinkled with dill. It was served with hot garlic rolls.

Before serving the *holubtsi* and *varenyky*, Andriy refilled the glasses and asked Sophia to raise the next toast. "It's customary to raise the third toast to women," he said.

Sophia thought of raising a toast to their host, but then looked at Oksana and said:

"Let's raise a toast to Oksana. May she live in a world without war."

"God willing," Maria added as she finished her glass. "You have an unusual Ukrainian accent," she said. "It's not quite *surzhyk* – a mixture of Ukrainian and Russian."

Andriy gave Sophia a look imploring her to not unsettle his aunt.

"My mother was half-Ukrainian and half-French," Sophia said. "I grew up in Paris."

"And your father?" Maria asked.

Sophia waited a moment before answering. "He was . . .Ukrainian."

Maria sighed with relief. "At least you're not a *Moskalka,* a Muscovite sympathizer."

"Nor a Nazi," Sophia added.

"The winter is not as cold as last year's," Andriy interjected trying to change the subject.

"The coldest winter I remember was 1943, when the Nazis occupied Moryntsi," Maria said.

"You suffered under Nazi occupation?" Sophia asked.

"I fought the Nazis," she replied. "I was in the Red Army. She pointed to a display case with Soviet medals that hung between an icon of the Blessed Virgin and a portrait of Taras Shevchenko. A quote scribbled on the wall beneath the portrait was from Shevchenko's poem *Caucacus*. It read: '*Fight – you will prevail. God is helping you.*'"

Sophia stood up from the table to examine the medals.

"You were a Hero of the Soviet Union and received the Order of Lenin!" Sophia exclaimed. "What did you do to merit such honors?"

"I was a sniper," Maria replied. "I killed . . . the count is not important. I did what I had to do to liberate my homeland."

"Your family must be so proud of you," Sophia said.

"Yes and no. My brother fought in the Ukrainian Insurgent Army. He thought I was a traitor."

"He was a Banderite?"

"He was a Ukrainian nationalist. He was killed by the Nazis."

"But I thought the Banderites *were* Nazis," Sophia said.

"It was a complicated time. We all fought the Nazis. My brother also fought against the Soviets and the Poles – anyone who would deny independence for Ukraine."

The moonshine was going to Sophia's head. "I heard that Ukraine is still overrun by Nazis."

"What Nazis, child!" Maria exclaimed. "This is a myth the Russians have created to justify their invasion. We have a Jewish president whose grandfather fought with me in the Red Army. The only fascists you'll find in Ukraine are the 'Rashists' with the 'Z' on their tanks."

Sophia sat quiet for the rest of the meal. Andriy and Maria discussed the war and the future of their family. Oksana left the table to play with her doll, Zoya. Kozak sat under the table hoping for a dropped morsel. At the end of the meal, Maria served a compote made from dried fruits.

Andriy rose from the table before evening fell. "Aunt Maria, Sophia and I need to return to Kyiv. It's about a three-hour drive. We need to return while the southern route is still open."

"Wait," she said. She opened a chest and pulled out her antique Dragunov SVD sniper rifle and a box of armor-piercing bullets. "Here, take this. You'll need it in Kyiv."

Andriy declined. "Aunt Maria, you'll need this with you to protect Oksana."

The terrible truth was not lost on Sophia.

As they drove north to Kyiv, Andriy said: "Thank you for sharing that your father is Ukrainian and nothing more. If my aunt knew that you had rejected him to pursue your life in Russia, it would have been awkward."

Sophia nodded. "I didn't want her to hate me." She closed her eyes on the drive back to Kyiv and wondered if she would ever have to lie to her own child about who she really was.

* * *

Father Stephan walked to the Post Office on San Polo to check for his mail. His post office box had a single returned letter that he had addressed to Sophia Borodin in St. Petersburg two weeks before. He had not sent Lev's original letter for fear that it would be lost. He sent his own letter instead, explaining that her father had asked him to witness his will, and that he needed to speak with her personally. He included his phone number and email. The letter was stamped with "Return to Sender" in Russian. There was no explanation as to the reason. A lone clerk sat with his back to the counter reading Kafka.

"Can I resend this as certified mail requiring a signature?" he asked the clerk.

The clerk looked up from his book surprised that he had a customer. "Yes, but it may take several weeks to receive a notice of receipt. There's a war on, you know."

"I'm afraid I don't have that much time."

Father Stephan took the letter back to his apartment in the sacristy. As he tore open the envelope, he noticed a line of glue that extended beyond the seam of the flap. It looked as if the letter had been steamed opened and resealed. He wondered why the FSB would be reading Sophia Borodin's mail? She was a Distinguished Artist of Russia. What threat could she pose to them?

His previous attempts to contact her by phone, email, and text message had all gone unanswered. Her Facebook page had not had any updates for weeks. When he googled her, he got tens of thousands of hits, but few dated after February 28. He recalled that Father Demetrius, one of his classmates from the Pontifical Oriental Institute, was conducting his doctoral research on the suppression of Catholicism in Russia. He had been working from the Church of St. Catherine of Alexandria in St. Petersburg. Father Stephan looked through his old contacts and decided to try his colleague's Italian mobile number. To his surprise, someone answered.

"Glory be to Jesus Christ," Father Stephan said.

"Glory forever. Father Stephan, is that you? Are you here in St. Petersburg?"

"No, I'm still at San Basilio's in Venice."

"Chasing ghosts for your dissertation?"

Father Stephan laughed. "Something like that. But seriously, I need your help. I'm trying to reach Sophia Borodin, the conductor of the St. Petersburg Philharmonic. I'm sure you've heard of her. I've tried calling, emailing, texting, and sending her a letter without any reply. Is there a way you could contact her to let her know that I need to speak with her?"

"I can walk over to the Philharmonic and make some inquiries."

"You'll need to be discreet. I believe she may be under surveillance by the FSB."

"FSB? Now you've really piqued by interest. I have some contacts in the FSB. Even they get remorseful from time to time and ask me to hear their confessions. They're afraid to go to their own Orthodox priests for fear they'll report them."

"Thank you, Father Demetrius. You can reach me on this phone number. But please look into it quickly. It's a matter of great urgency."

* * *

Andriy nudged Sophia awake. She rubbed her eyes to see him standing over the bed fully dressed. He was holding his winter coat.

"What time is it?" she asked.

"A little before noon. I didn't want to wake you earlier. You were sleeping so soundly."

"I was dreaming about my childhood in Paris. It's a way to escape the horror of this war."

"What was your childhood like?"

"Lonely. Rather than send me to school, my stepfather hired tutors. He said it was for my own security. I was taught to play the violin at the age of three. He told my mother that I was a prodigy in music, and that

I should practice my violin rather than play with friends. I had wanted a doll for my birthday, and he bought me a Hummel figurine of a girl playing a violin instead."

Andriy saw that he had stirred a painful memory.

"I became like that porcelain figurine," Sophia continued, "someone to be showcased rather than embraced. I retreated into the fantasy world of fairy tales and storybooks where I could pretend to be a princess, fall in love, and live happily ever after."

"What about your mother?" Andriy asked. "Did she showcase you as well?"

"No, my mother loved me for who I am. She was as lonely as I was, but at least we had each other. As I told you before, she had one very close friend, who I later learned was my natural father. I remember when they would take me with them on day trips to Versailles, Giverny, Mont Saint-Michelle. We would laugh and play and share stories. We were like a family. They would hold hands and sneak kisses when they thought I wasn't looking."

"It sounds like you have some fond memories of your natural father."

"I did . . . until he killed her."

"Killed her? Andriy asked in disbelief.

"At my mother's funeral, my stepfather's friend, Georgiy, told me that my father was an evil man who had fled the Soviet Union because he was suspected of killing his girlfriend."

"From what you've told me, he loved your mother very much. I can't believe that he would have killed her."

"Then my mother died of a broken heart. She must have learned the truth about him."

Andriy put on his coat. "I'll be back in a few hours. I need to conduct an interview for my documentary on preserving our cultural heritage. The Russians invaded not just to seize our land and natural resources. They invaded to erase our cultural identity. They're destroying everything that makes us Ukrainian. Our music, literature, movies, and museums are not just recreation. They're battlefields. My camera is my weapon."

"Alex used much the same words."

Andriy sat down on the bed next to her. "Not *all* Russians. There are a few, like Alex and you, who oppose this war."

"Then let me help. Let me go with you."

Andriy looked uncomfortable with her request. "I don't know."

"Please," she asked. "War I can't understand – culture I do."

She jumped out of bed to get dressed. She was wearing one of his shirts as a pajama.

"Let me make a phone call to see if they'll agree."

Andriy made his call as Sophia got dressed. She turned her back to him and took off the shirt. Her long black hair fell down her back. Andriy admired her body as she dressed. Beauty like hers was scarce in these terrible times. She turned her head to see him staring at her. He left the bedroom to let her dress in private.

"Hello, it's Andriy. I'm calling about our interview this afternoon. I'm sheltering a friend of a friend. She's asking if she can come along."

"Who is she?"

"Sophia Sergeivna Borodin."

There was long silence on the other end of the phone.

"Her partner, Alex Ivanovich, and I were working together on the documentary. He went to Bucha to investigate the rumors and has gone missing. Sophia's searching for him. I can vouch for her."

"Very well. You can bring her along. But under no circumstances can she know where we'll be moving the museum pieces. She's probably under surveillance, if not by the FSB, then by our own SBU. There are many in our own security services who would betray us."

"You needn't share the details of your relocation during the interview."

"Come to the Mystetskyj Arsenal in an hour. After the interview, you can give us a hand packing our exhibit."

Sophia emerged dressed and ready to go. For the first time since Andriy had met her, she appeared confident and rested.

"Where are we going?" she asked.

"Mystetskyj Arsenal to interview the director of the Museum of the Maidan. He asked us to be there within the hour."

"I didn't realize that there's a museum dedicated to the Maidan revolution. Is it located in the Arsenal?" she asked.

"No. It's a living museum that organizes cultural and educational programs and hosts temporary exhibitions."

"It doesn't have a permanent location?"

"There are architectural plans to build a museum and memorial complex on Institutska Street where many of the protestors were killed, but, like many other things in Ukraine, its mired in politics and bureaucracy. With the war, everything's on hold."

"Then what does a 'living museum' do?" she asked.

"How can I best describe it? It's a space, not necessarily a location, where people come together to reflect and remember. The museum began as a way to collect and disseminate the stories and struggles of the people on the Maidan, especially the 'Heavenly Hundred' protestors who were killed by government forces. Over time it evolved from a Museum of the Revolution of Dignity to a Museum of Freedom that preserves the history of our struggle for national and personal freedom, dignity, and human rights. The director is one of the true cultural heroes of Ukraine."

"I'd be honored to meet him," Sophia said.

Andriy and Sophia took the metro to Arsenal, retracing the route she had taken a few days before. Sleeping bags, toys, and books were strewn over the station floors. People were trying to live their ordinary lives between air raid sirens. City workers swept the station and collected garbage. A group of children were connecting to an American teacher in Chicago on their iPads. Three teenagers played the banduras and sang patriotic songs from the Ukrainian Insurgent Army hoping to lift people's spirits.

They found the director of the Museum of the Maidan in the back storage area of the Arsenal Museum complex. He and a group of volunteers were packing paintings, photographs, books, and artifacts into wooden crates for transport to an undisclosed location. The director was a handsome man in his forties with chiseled features and steel blue eyes. His visage conveyed resolve. He greeted them with a firm handshake and a smile.

"Sophia Sergeivna," the director said. "Andriy told me about Alex. He's a brave man to have gone to Bucha alone. I'm hoping that your countrymen won't harm one of their own."

"Alex is against this terrible war . . . as am I. Andriy said that culture is a battleground in this war. Perhaps I can help."

The director looked at Andriy to see if her offer of help was genuine. Andriy shrugged his shoulders.

"Before we start the interview, I'd like to show you some of our collection. We were one of several museums that participated at an international exhibition here at Mystetskyj Arsenal called 'Revolutionize.' Thirty contemporary artists and art groups from fifteen countries participated. The exhibit analyzed the Revolution of Dignity through the language of art. It included installations, paintings, photographs, videos, books, and multimedia."

"Art lets one escape the tragedy," Sophia said.

"On the contrary," the director replied. "Art makes us witnesses. It gives us strength to resist. It gives us hope."

The items in the collection had been taken down after the exhibition and placed in temporary storage. Volunteers were cataloging the items, carefully covering them in bubble wrap and re-packing them into wooden crates by type and size. One group of items included homemade flags, helmets, protest banners, makeshift weapons, and purloined police shields. A tent graffitied with revolutionary slogans was waiting to be folded.

A miniature of an artificial Christmas tree caught Sophia's eye.

"A representation of the 'Yolka,'" the director explained. "The original is a 35-meter-high, metal structure that was the official Christmas tree of the city of Kyiv. Rather than pine boughs, it was decorated with flags of Ukraine and the European Union and plastered with political posters and street art. It stood on the Maidan and became a symbol of the Revolution of Dignity. One day we hope to place it in the lobby of our future museum and memorial complex."

"I'm sorry that the war has derailed your plans to commemorate the Maidan revolution. Hopefully, one day you'll be able to resume your work."

The director looked at her with surprise. "One day? Today is that day. The war is a continuation of the Maidan."

Sophia was embarrassed to think that the war had suppressed the spirit of the Maidan.

"We're moving this collection to a secure location so the Russians won't destroy it. We are number one on Putin's list for liquidation. But we focus not only on the past, but on the present and future. We are living through a special time. It's our job to preserve this moment. We go into the areas that have been liberated and collect objects that tell symbolic and emotional stories, symbols of terror and resistance."

Andriy walked up to them and said, "I've set up my camera. We're ready for the interview."

"It's best if I give you some space," Sophia said. "I'll wait in another room."

Andriy and the director did not disagree. "We're still cataloging the books from our collection in one of the other rooms," the director said. "You may want to browse through them. One of our volunteers will show you the way."

A young woman escorted Sophia to a room where books had been laid out on tables alphabetically by name of author. A metal shield inscribed with "Library of the Maidan" rested against one of the tables. It pictured a protestor in a winter hat and scarf sitting atop a pile of tires beneath a Ukrainian flag reading a book.

"I'll be fine here," Sophia said. "Please tell Andriy that I'm here once he's done with his interview."

The books laid out on the tables included nonfiction accounts of the Maidan revolution, photobooks, poetry, and novels. They were written in multiple languages. Towards the beginning of the alphabet, she found a novel called *The Storyteller*, by Lev Veles. It was written in Ukrainian. Next to it was a French translation. After a moment of hesitation, she picked up the novel.

As she turned the pages, she was drawn in deeper and deeper. The voice of the narrator was one she had heard in her youth, captivating her with stories of magical forests, nymphs, and evil creatures with spindly legs. For Lev, the supernatural world and the real world were one and the same. When she was a little girl, he had held a special place in her heart. But there was a darkness in him that her mother had not known when they first fell in love. On her death bed, her mother had told her the truth: that Lev was her natural father, that she loved him, and hoped that Sophia would continue to love him as well. Her mother's forbidden love for him had sapped her of her strength, initially year by year and then day by day. Sophia was convinced that her mother could no longer live with the lies and had lost her will to live. How could her parents have betrayed her the way they did? Yet she realized that without their love, she would not have been born.

"Are you enjoying the book?"

Sophia looked up to see Andriy looking over her shoulder. She was so absorbed in her reading that she had not heard him enter. The minutes that she thought had passed were actually hours.

"*The Storyteller,*" Andriy said, "is one of my favorite books about the Maidan. It won the European Book award. It's been banned in Russia and the occupied territories. I had met the author on the Maidan, and we became friends. He's a remarkable man."

"He may be a good writer, but he's not a good man."

Andriy looked surprised. "Do you know him?"

Sophia closed the book. "I do. Lev Veles is my father."

* * *

Lev opened his eyes. He was no longer sitting at his desk pretending to resist his seductress. He was lying in bed with her astride him. Her gossamer gown was on the floor. Her black hair cascaded over her shoulders, each strand tingling with desire. She was as beautiful and comforting as the night. He reached up to caress her. He yearned to enter her.

"Wait," Mara said. "You must finish your story."

She picked up his laptop from atop the bed, placed it on his chest, and typed as he spoke.

> *The Maidan in Kyiv is my sacred place. Lida had shared her hope of one day performing on the Maidan so millions could hear her songs and share her dream of love and freedom.*

When the Revolution of Dignity began in the fall of 2013, I had to go. I had promised Lida I would make her dream come true.

I was a witness to history. The only way I could understand the events of that winter was to write about them. I wanted to know what brought ordinary people to the Maidan. Was it love of country? A yearning for freedom? A belief in the dignity of each and every one of us? Through my pen I was able to give voice to the maidantsi – the protestors who gathered on the Maidan. As I began to write my novel, The Storyteller, I realized that I could no longer be a detached narrator of other people's stories. The Storyteller gave voice to myself.

During the Christmas holidays, the Maidan was a sanctuary of hope and peace. The Yolka, the official Christmas tree of the city of Kyiv, stood at the center of the Maidan and was decorated with flags, posters, and street art rather than Christmas decorations. An open stage was constructed near the Yolka that featured all types of performances: poetry readings, political speeches, rock concerts, and plays. Tents sprang up within the barricades, each posting the city where the people were from. People came to the Maidan from all walks of life. They were not only Ukrainians. They were Belarusians, Russians, Armenians, Americans – it was not ethnicity or religion that brought them there. It was the hope that we can live together as brothers and sisters and respect the dignity of each and every individual.

But the barricades and television cameras couldn't keep out the forces of oppression. At first the attacks were covert. People disappeared. Titushky – paid thugs – were bused in to terrorize the protestors. When they failed, The Berkut – police of the Ministry of the Interior – encircled the Maidan like a python. But the people resisted. In the beginning the police shields and clubs were met with music and flowers. But when the Berkut resorted to violence, shields were met with shields, and clubs with clubs. The Berkut used water cannons in the subfreezing temperatures to turn the Maidan into a frozen wasteland. The protestors responded to the ice with fire.

In February of 2014 the protests turned violent. The Berkut had tried to storm the Maidan but were repulsed by the barricades of burning tires and the self-defense forces. That's when the mass killing began. Government snipers picked off one protestor after another. Over one hundred died, shot in the head and neck. They were laid in rows in front of the makeshift hospitals. I thought that the Maidan had failed, but I was wrong. Rather than surrender, the maidantsi rose up by the hundreds of thousands. They threatened to overturn the government if the president who ordered the killings did not flee – and the tide turned. The coward fled. We won our freedom. In that moment everything was illuminated: our past, our present, and our future. I finally felt that I was part of something greater than myself.

Mara stopped typing. "Did you fulfill your promise to Lida?"

"The storyteller in my novel is a *kobzar,* an itinerant bard who sang stories about Ukraine's past and present, including songs written by a brave, young songwriter from Chernvitsi named Lida. I wanted to immortalize her through my novel. It was my best work as a writer."

"If you found your purpose on the Maidan, then why are you here in Venice?"

Lev reflected for a moment. "I was afraid my past would catch up with me. The *maidantsi* were demanding that the new government open the KGB archives to the public. In Chernivtsi the *Komsomoltsi* had convinced me that I was somehow responsible for Lida's death. I was afraid of exhuming the dead. I was in the company of heroes, and the opening of the archives would expose me as a coward who had fled his country. At least on the Maidan, for those few months of solidarity, I was accepted. I felt that my sins were forgiven."

"Your worst sin is that you sacrificed yourself for nothing."

Her remark stabbed him in the heart. A sense of despair descended over Lev like a shroud. Had it really all been for nothing? Good had triumphed on the Maidan, but Mara was right: the evil had returned stronger than before. Missiles rained down from the sky. Tanks rumbled over the earth. Warships plowed the seas. He pictured the horrors of war . . . the torture, rape, and murder of innocents . . . the twisted metal and mangled limbs . . . the stench of abandoned bodies . . ."

"What troubles you?" Mara asked.

"The war. I feel helpless to stop it."

"No one can stop it. The prophecy is being fulfilled. The Prince of Rosh has begun his march to Armageddon."

"I feel the agony. . ."

Mara inhaled his words and began to sway her hips against his. "And the ecstasy . . ." she added. "War excites me."

Lev recoiled from her lust for war. "How can you desire war? It destroys goodness and truth."

"War is both a maker and a destroyer of truth," Mara replied.

"But the evil?"

"There is no good without evil, no order without chaos, no hope without despair."

He tried to escape from her, but she pinned him with the weight of his sins. Her lust was possessive. She began to thrust rhythmically. She was deathly beautiful atop him with her hair blacker than night, her funereal skin, and her eyes deeper than the void. He wanted an end to his torment. He was ready to surrender to her, to the corruption of the flesh, and to the beauty of chaos. He wanted the peace of the grave.

"Who are you?" he asked.

"You *know* who I am."

"But are you real?"

"I'm as real as you are."

I'm creating my own reality, Lev convinced himself. *But why her? Why Mara?*

"What do you want from me?" he asked. "I am but a man."

"I want you to be who you are, and who you have always been, born of this earth and returned to this earth: Veles, a harvester of souls. Yield yourself to me."

* * *

Father Stephan chanted from 2 Corinthians 2: 17-21.

> *Brothers and sisters:*
> *Whoever is in Christ is a new creation:*
> *the old things have passed away;*
> *behold, new things have come.*
> *And all of this is from God,*
> *who has reconciled Himself to us through Christ."*

As he was reading the gospel, Father Stephan scanned the faces in church to see if Lev was among them. San Basilio's church was filled with refugees, but Lev was nowhere to be seen. He was worried for his friend. He decided to check on him after the service.

Outside the church, Venice was as cold as the grave. Spring had failed to arrive. Father Stephan crossed the Rialto Bridge on his way to the Corte del Milion. Lev had given him a key in the event of the worst – that the pandemic had taken him, and he had died alone and undiscovered. Father Stephan climbed the stairs and turned the key to the door.

He froze in the doorway. Lev was lying naked on his bed. A haggard crone straddled him. Her burial shroud lay on the floor. Withered skin draped her skeletal frame. Her shriveled breasts pressed against his chest. Her long fingernails dug into Lev's temples. Strands of white hair clung to her skull. Her mouth was over his, inhaling his breath and sucking out his soul. When she turned her face towards him, Father Stephan saw despair – the end of hope, the end of love.

She bared her teeth and shrieked, "Be gone priest! He's mine."

Father Stephan crossed himself three times. He clutched his pectoral crucifix and began to say the prayer of "Anima Christi" out loud:

> *Soul of Christ, sanctify me; Body of Christ, save me; Blood*
> *of Christ, inebriate me; Water from the side of Christ, wash*
> *me; Passion of Christ, strengthen me; O good Jesus, hear me;*

within Thy wounds, hide me; let me never be separated from Thee; from the evil one, deliver me; at the hour of my death, call me and bid me come to Thee, that with Thy saints, I may praise Thee forever and ever. Amen.

Mara climbed off of Lev and stood between him and Father Stephan. "He does not want your salvation. He does not want your union with God. He wants to be who he is and who he has always been."

Father Stephan raised his crucifix to her face and continued to pray:

The Lord is my salvation; whom should I fear? I will not fear evil because You are with me, my God, my strength, my powerful Lord, Lord of peace, Father of all ages. Yes, Lord our God, be merciful to us, Your image, and save your servant, Lev, from every threat or harm from the evil one, and protect him by raising him above all evil. We ask You this through the intercession of our Most Blessed, glorious Lady, Mary ever Virgin, Mother of God, of the most splendid archangels and all Your saints. Amen!

"You will not have him. He will not give up his Self for Christ. You will see. I will return for him." She bent over Lev, kissed him on the lips, and vanished.

Lev did not move from the bed. He lay there like a corpse. It was is if every hope, every memory, and every dream had been sucked out of him.

Father Stephan put his hand over his friend's heart. "It's not too late," he said. "There's still time. You can still overcome your dark night of the soul. Say the words with me: 'Lord Jesus Christ, Son of God, have mercy on me, a sinner.'"

Lev opened his eyes to see Father Stephan praying over him. He clasped his friend's hand and began to whisper the words over and over again. "Lord Jesus Christ, Son of God, have mercy on me, a sinner. Lord Jesus Christ, Son of God, have mercy on me, a sinner. Lord Jesus Christ . . ."

CHAPTER 11

Union

Sophia awoke on the sofa with her father's book in her hands. The director of the museum had given it to her as a gift at Andriy's suggestion. She had read deep into the night before drifting off into dreams. The narrator of the novel was a mythical *kobzar*, an itinerant bard who wandered between place and time telling and collecting stories. The author portrayed him as a blind old man in a peasant shirt with an *oseledets* – a long lock of hair on his otherwise bald head – a drooping white moustache, and a *bandura* – a traditional Ukrainian string instrument. He sang about the old myths, the glories of the past, and the hope for the future. The people on the Maidan would give him food and coins, but what he asked was to listen to their stories so he could sing them to future generations.

In the novel, the kobzar told the myth of Mara, the daughter of Perun, the god of thunder, and Mokosh, the Great Mother. Mara was once a nature goddess. When she was young, her twin brother, Jarylo, was kidnapped by Veles, the god of the earth and underworld, who raised Jarylo as his own. When Jarylo returned from the underworld, he brought fertility and spring. The twins did not know they were related, and they fell in love and married. The marriage brought temporary peace between Perun and Veles. But Jarylo cheated on her, and Mara killed him for his betrayal. She became bitter and turned into the goddess of winter and death. Their tragedy begot the cycle of the seasons.

The kobzar told the story of a hero's search for a golden egg, the same fairy tale that her father had told her when she was a little girl. He told how Batu Khan and the Mongols had destroyed Kyiv when the city refused to surrender. He sang wailful *dumy*, the epic poems of the Cossacks, and about Catherine the Great's destruction of the Zaporozhzhian Sich. He described the horrors of Stalin's Holodomor and how millions had died of starvation when the fields were plentiful with wheat. He told how Stalin had invited the brotherhood of kobzar*s* to attend a Congress in Kharkiv, and then executed them all. The kobzar sang songs of hope, composed by a young songwriter from Chernivtsi, who had defied the Communist Party and given her life to compose in her own native language. In return the *maidantsi* told him their stories. The Crimean Tatars spoke about the *Surgun*, their forced exile from Crimea, and how they had returned once Ukraine became free. Students recalled the first nights on the Maidan, when they were beaten by the Berkut, and how the small group of a few hundred had grown into hundreds of thousands.

"I didn't want to wake you," Andriy said. "Are you enjoying your father's book?"

"There are stories, passages, that I heard in my youth. When I was a little girl, my father told me fairy tales that he learned from his own mother. They were wonderful stories about a magic egg, *mavky* and *rusalky*, and scary creatures who were half-human and half-spider. He claimed he saw them with his own eyes, and I believed him."

"He seems to have cared for you, perhaps even loved you."

"I was naïve. I could see that my mother loved him, so I wanted to love him as well. I couldn't see the darkness in him."

"I know you're estranged, but how well do you really know your father? You haven't seen him in decades. Perhaps he's changed."

"He took my mother away from me. How can I ever forgive him?"

Andriy sat down next to her on the sofa. "You only know what you think you know. The truth could be very different."

"Why are you defending him?"

"Because I knew him. We spent many days and nights together on the Maidan. He's a complicated man, but he's not capable of murder. He may be haunted by the demons of his past, but in that place and in that time, he rose above them. We all did. Think of the passages you just read in *The Storyteller*. They're filled with hope and compassion."

"He's a writer, not a husband or a father."

Andriy stood up from the sofa. "I need to run an errand. I'll be back before nightfall. I suggest you finish the novel. I'm convinced there's more for you to discover."

* * *

Father Stephan sat back at his desk. He had been writing for hours, recollecting every detail about his encounter with Mara. It was one thing to experience one's own visions – it was part of the mystical experience. To see and hear the visions of another was extraordinary. At first, he had believed that Mara was a Jungian shadow, a creation of Lev's imagination. But if Mara was real outside of Lev's imagination, then so was the devil who met the contessa on the Torcello bridge. Perhaps Mara had appeared to Father Stephan because she was now coming for him. He debated whether to include his eyewitness account of Mara's haunting of Lev in his dissertation but decided against it. He was afraid that his doctoral committee would judge him insane and fail him.

His phone rang. The caller ID showed that the call was coming from Father Demetrius.

"Father Stephan, I've located her."

"Glory be to Jesus Christ. Where is she? How can I contact her."

"My information comes from a junior FSB officer whom I've helped with some personal issues. Not everyone in the security services is in favor of this 'special military operation.' I can't disclose his name, but I assure you that the source is reliable."

"Is she in St. Petersburg? Can you visit her to deliver a message."

"Unfortunately, no. She's in Kyiv?"

"Why Kyiv?"

"Her partner, Alex Ivanovich, is a Russian filmmaker who snuck into Ukraine in late February, shortly after the war began. He's friends with a Ukrainian colleague, Andriy Orishkevich. Apparently the two of them were planning to go to the Bucha to investigate the rumors of atrocities. Andriy Orishkevich never left for Bucha. Alex Ivanovich never returned."

"And Sophia?" Father Stephan asked.

"She left for Ukraine to find Alex. She's met up with Andriy. I was able to get his cell phone number."

"So, she's safe?"

"Not entirely," Father Demetrius replied. "According to my contact, an FSB colonel was having her tracked. Plans were being drawn up to have her eliminated."

"Why did you say 'not entirely'? It sounds like she's in mortal danger."

"Perhaps. Perhaps not."

"Why?"

"The FSB colonel who was about to issue the order fell to his death off a 12th floor balcony."

* * *

The Archive of the Security Service of Ukraine was located in a yellow, nine-story building one block away from Andriy's apartment. Andriy was a frequent visitor to the Archive while researching his documentary on Russia's destruction of Ukraine's cultural heritage. In September, 1991 the Presidium of the Supreme Soviet issued a decree ordering the transfer of KGB files to the State Archives. After the decommunization reform in 2015, the archives were declassified and opened to the public. The building on Zolotovoritska Street contained over 224,000 volumes of KGB files. These included political cases: search warrants and arrest warrants, interrogation records of defendants and witnesses, fingerprints, photos of the arrested and their families and friends, search logs, descriptions of confiscated property, indictments, confessions, documents related to stay in forced labor camps, appeals, and conclusions on the futility or likelihood of rehabilitation. The archives also contained lists of those who were executed without the travesties of show trials.

Andriy showed his identification papers to the guard at the entrance and proceeded up the stairs to the director's office. He and the director had stood together on the barricades of the Maidan in the winter of 2013. The director had called him shortly after the archives were open to encourage him to delve into the secret history of state terror and oppression. The secretary smiled at him and opened the double doors to the director's office to let him in. The director was at his desk reviewing a digitized archive.

"Andriy, I see that you've befriended my secretary, Katerina. She no longer needs to announce your presence."

"My apologizes for intruding," Andriy said, "but I have a pressing need to review a file in the archives."

"You're lucky to have come before we shut down."

"You're shutting down the archives?"

"Temporarily," the director said. "Moscow would like nothing more than to destroy these files and erase the evidence of their crimes. We're expecting one of their missiles to come crashing down on us any day. We've digitized about half the files. The others we need to box and move to a more secure location. Whose records are you looking for?"

"Lev Veles, the author. He was born in western Ukraine in the sixties. He's spent much of his life abroad."

"Do you think he was under surveillance during the Maidan?" the director asked.

"I have a feeling his history with the KGB goes back much earlier."

The director typed the name Lev Veles into his computer. "We have a record, but it hasn't been digitized. You'll have to sift through it by hand. If it hasn't been packed yet, you should find it on the sixth floor, file number 60-17845."

"Thank you," Andriy said. He rushed out the door and climbed the stairs to the sixth floor.

Hundreds of thousands of uniform cardboard boxes were neatly stacked on rows of metal bookcases, that if lined together would stretch for 7 kilometers. The fluorescent lights gave the room an eerie glow. Hundreds of thousands of lives were reduced to sheets of paper that had yellowed with time. Heroism, betrayal, pain, and suffering were dutifully recorded, catalogued and stored in musty boxes that were never meant to see the light of day. Andriy had hoped that he might find some record that could exonerate his friend in the eyes of his daughter. On the other hand, it might reveal his crimes.

Andriy was as familiar with the system as any archivist. He expected he would at most find a single box with a few surveillance notes. Instead, he found five densely-packed boxes. He pulled them off the shelves and placed them on the floor. The musty boxes were organized by time and place: two from Lev's early years, two from his decades in Paris, and one from his months on the Maidan. The files from Lev's early years were surprisingly detailed. Some were typed and others were handwritten. The typed records were officially stamped in blue ink. Every detail of every conversation with the members of the Komsomol was transcribed. There were signed testimonials from his fellow students. Some of the files seemed superfluous: his grades from the university, the books he checked out from the library, parish records from his boyhood church in Dzerelo. The files contained his early attempts at creative writing, including short stories and poetry. There were black and white photographs of him with a pretty girl with dark hair and a guitar in her hand. There was . . . Andriy stopped – a photo of the same girl hanging naked from a tree. From the bruises and cigarette burns, it was clear she had been tortured before she was hanged. A tied packet of papers contained the police records and the results of the investigation. Andriy laid the most important documents on the floor from one end of the room to the other and began to photograph them with his phone.

The documents from the two boxes of his life in Paris were even more revealing. Andriy spent hours sifting through the documents. They included transcriptions of phone conversations; troves of surveillance reports from a man named Georgiy Volkov; photos in both color and black and white, some of Lev entangled in a mass of naked bodies after nights of drunken revelry; names of socialites who attended Lev's parties. The box included Lev's writings: every newspaper and magazine article, every short story, every novel. Sections were flagged and annotated in red as evidence of counter-revolutionary rhetoric. A separate folder held photos of Lev with Sophia's mother, including several with Sophia as a toddler. The file on Sophia's mother was unusually thick. He began to peruse the file and could not believe what he was reading. Yet there it was, authorized with an official stamp of the KGB.

* * *

The stairwell was dark when Andriy returned to his apartment. He wondered if someone had intentionally unscrewed the light bulbs, or if they had failed on their own which was not unusual. He turned on the light on his phone and climbed the stairs, stepping softly so they would not creak. To his relief, his door was still locked. He turned the key. Sophia was still where he had left her, sitting on the sofa immersed in her father's novel. He locked the door behind him.

"Where have you been?" she asked.

"The State Security Archives. I found your father's file."

Sophia put down the book. "Was he under surveillance or was he one of *them*?"

"You need to see for yourself. I took photos of the most important documents."

Sophia took Andriy's phone and began scrolling through the photos of the documents. She flipped through the first few, seemingly nonchalant. She slowed as she read the next several pages, expanding the screen to reread each important detail. As she read on, her face changed from aloof to incredulous.

"This can't be true."

"I'm afraid it is. I've read through enough KGB files of Soviet dissidents to know what the bastards are capable of."

Sophia read about the young man who had been ensnared by an incomprehensible evil. Her perception of him was turned upside down. The system preyed on the naïve and the vulnerable. Those who refused to be corrupted were manipulated and destroyed. The files exhumed long-buried truths. She began to understand why her mother and father had fallen in love. Their love was an escape from the world they were trapped in. When she reached the file on her mother's death, she stopped.

"I can't read any more. It's too painful."

"Healing comes from revealing the truth," Andriy replied.

As Sophia read on, she realized that she had never truly known her father. She regretted shunning him all these years. The more he had tried to love her, the farther she had pulled away. Now she knew more about him than he knew about himself. She read through the last few documents as if she were walking on shards of glass. Each step was painful. Each sentence stuck and bled. The last was too much to bear.

"This can't be true!" she cried.

Andriy's phone rang. The call came from abroad. He stepped away to give Sophia some space. When he returned, he handed her the phone.

"It's for you – a Father Stephan from Venice. He claims to know your father."

Sophia took the phone and listened. Andriy could not hear what Father Stephan was saying. He saw tears well up in Sophia's eyes. When the call ended, he said, "You seem distraught."

Sophia looked up at him and said, "I need to go to Venice. I need to leave now."

* * *

Lev arrived early for the morning service. The door to San Basilio's church was open, but the nave was still dark. The only light came from the flickering candles that had been arranged in the votive candle stand in the shape of the cross. The candlelight was reflected in the myriad pieces of colored stone, glass, tile, and shell that comprised the mosaics on the iconostasis. The Royal Doors of the iconostasis were closed, separating the world of men from the world of the divine. A *tetrapod* – covered table with an embroidered Ukrainian cloth – stood in front of the iconostasis. A Murano urn rested atop the tetrapod. The urn was deep green in color and reminded Lev of the sacred wood in the Carpathians where the water, ferns, and rocks came alive with his mother's stories.

The church was as silent as a tomb. *A good time to pray*, Lev thought. He approached the iconostasis. The mosaics glimmered in the flickering candlelight. *Father Stephan had said that icons are a window to heaven. He had said there are many paths to the Great Liberation, and the way of Christ worked best for him. I was baptized and raised a Christian. I pray this path will work for me.* Lev stood before the icon of Christ the Teacher. It was a masterpiece of Byzantine art. *The artist who made this mosaic must have had a vision of heaven. If I can look through his eyes, perhaps I can see what he had seen.* Lev looked into the icon and began to recite the Jesus prayer: *"Lord Jesus Christ, Son of God, have mercy on me, a sinner."*

Father Stephan had taught him the Jesus prayer as a way to reach communion with God through meditation. Lev was sincere in his supplication, but the true power of orison came from repeating the prayer – tens, hundreds, thousands of times. Unwanted thoughts drifted in and out of his consciousness like clouds, and he had learned that through prayer he could let them pass without judgement. If he tried to engage, they would darken and storm. The tempest during his dark night of the soul had drowned him in a torrent of doubt. If Father Stephan had not come to save him, he would have been Mara's, joined in an unholy union, separated from any hope of salvation. *Lord Jesus Christ, Son of God, have mercy on me, a sinner.*

As he prayed, he imagined that the light in the pieces of the icon of Christ the Teacher emanated from within. The gold-leaf background shone like the sun. Jesus held an open book with the letters A and Ω, the "Beginning" and the "End," displayed on opposite pages. His right hand was raised to give a blessing. His fingers made a symbol of the letters: IC and XC, the monogram of "Jesus Christ" in Greek. He was dressed in a red robe, covered with a blue cloak. The red symbolized divinity and blue humanity. The halo around His head contained the Cross of Salvation. Each of three arms that symbolized the Trinity was inscribed with a letter: O Ω N, "He who is." *Lord Jesus Christ, Son of God, have mercy on me, a sinner.*

Lev prayed for faith but the clouds of doubt kept rolling in. *If I surrender myself to God, what awaits me? If I could peer through the icon, what kind of heaven might I see?* He pictured the fresco on the ceiling of the Rivelli's palazzo, in which the Father and Son sat on heavenly thrones with the Holy Spirit hovering above them. The eyes of the angels, saints, and faithful were raised to the Holy Trinity in worship. *Would I raise my eyes to heaven or look back to earth like the artist who painted the fresco?* He looked at the green urn. *Will my mother be waiting for me among the angels and the saints in the clouds or will she be waiting for me by the lush ferns and moss by the green pool? I long to see her as she was, young and beautiful and full of life, one with nature. If I could spend another moment with her by the green pool . . .*

His reverie was rippled by an image of her face beneath the water. *Why did you leave me when I needed you? Why did my father abandon us? Why did the Didko try to trick me into stealing the golden egg?* He realized that the world of his youth was not as idyllic as he had remembered it. He longed for his lost innocence. He returned his gaze to the icon of Christ the Teacher. *Lord Jesus Christ, Son of God, have mercy on me, a sinner.*

He thought of Lida, his first love. Her love was like the rays of the sun that wake the dormant roots and stir the verdant shoots to reach for the sky. She had helped him become a man, but what had he given her in return? He was like the moon that reflected her sunlight but was cold and barren without her. He remembered the ecstasy when they consummated their love and carved their initials into the willow tree. *If only I had caught your wreath on the eve of Ivana Kupala. If only we had found the fern flower on that magical night and earned eternal youth together. If we meet in an afterlife, will you still love me? My youth is gone, and you'll stay forever young. I kept my promise and shared your songs on the Maidan. Thousands sang your songs during the Revolution of Dignity. It gave them hope. It helped them persevere. I tried to preserve your legacy through your music. I taught your songs to my daughter. I wrote a novel about a kobzar on the Maidan who sang your songs. If I could not be your hero in real life, then I could at least pretend to be a hero in my stories.* His mind turned dark. In a flash of lightning, he saw Lida hanging from the weeping willow with her eyes open. Her hair was green and her back was gone. She came down from the tree to embrace him . . . *Lord Jesus Christ, Son of God, have mercy on me, a sinner.*

He tried to quell the storm by thinking of Vera. He recalled how they first met in a cloudburst in the Taras Shevchenko square in Paris, and how she had smiled at him and brushed her fingers through her wet, golden hair. He remembered their first intimate lunch at Le Grande Cascade and how she had blushed when he told her she reminded him of Laure in his novel. He recalled their Sunday strolls through the gardens of Paris where they could escape from the embassy to be alone with their daughter. They would walk hand in hand among the climbing roses and flowering fruit trees, stealing a kiss when Sophia wasn't looking. She would hide behind bushes and frolic in the fountains without a care in the world. *Vera, you loved me, when I had given up on love. You saved me from myself. Despite our sin, our love brought our beautiful Sophia into this world.* Repressed memories hailed into his consciousness: Vera lying on her deathbed, pale and too weak to hold his hand, struggling to smile . . . Sophia crying at her side and renouncing him as her father . . . Vera's ghost haunting him for weeks after she died. *My love suffocated you. I destroyed your marriage and the life you had. I promised to take care of our daughter, and I failed. I wish you had been there to help me raise her. But what if I never see you again? What if there is no heaven, no reuniting with the ones we love? No chance at forgiveness? No chance at redemption? Lord Jesus Christ, Son of God, have mercy on me, a sinner.*

What if Angela was right? What if there is no afterlife, only the one life we have now? Our lives, she said, are as ephemeral as snowflakes, each unique and beautiful in their complexity, that appear in the sky, fall to earth, and are no more. Perhaps there is this, just this, and nothing more. Even so, the brief time I've been alive has been the most wondrous and rarest of gifts. My chance of having being born – of my parents having fallen in love and of my being conceived, and their parents before them, going back countless generations to the dawn of man – is infinitesimal.

My life is a miracle, a cosmic roll of the dice. I've witnessed the wonders of the universe. I've seen the sun reflected in a sky-blue mountain lake. I've seen a first snow turn a deep green forest into a white winter wonderland.

I've heard the laughter of a child watching a puppet show in the Luxembourg Gardens. I've heard the songs of freedom on the Maidan during a winter of ice and fire. I've felt the joy of a first kiss and the heartbreak of a last embrace. I've experienced love and loss, hope and fear, and anguish and joy. I've given this gift of life to my daughter, what more can I want? Only to be remembered by the ones I love . . . to have someone, somewhere, someday read my words to know that I was once here, in this place, in this time. Lord Jesus Christ, Son of God, have mercy on me, a sinner.

Lev could still not see into heaven through the icon. He looked upon the face of Jesus. What struck him was not the cruciform halo or the mystery of the divine. What he saw in the face of Jesus was the ultimate of humanity: love and compassion, utterly bereft of Self. Before His Transfiguration, Christ appeared as man, just like the rest of us. While His humanity paled to the divine, it was nonetheless miraculous. *What if Professor Brown was right, and we are destined to become Homo Deus? Father Stephan had said that "God became man so that man could become God." We are made of elements that were born in the stars. For billions of years, we've been evolving in configurations of ever greater complexity. We contain in our DNA each and every major holon that evolution has brought forth and emerged since the Big Bang. From quarks to subatomic particles to atoms to molecules to prokaryotic cells to eukaryotic cells, to the fundamental biochemistry of life, to instinctual drives of food and sex of the reptilian brain stem, to mammalian emotions of the limbic system, to symbols of the cortex, to thoughts and consciousness – we incorporate in ourselves every major level of the Great Tree of Life. Evolution is spirit in action, the breath of the Holy Ghost.*

But who's to say that we will evolve into Homo Deus and not devolve into devils? After Russia's invasion of Ukraine, I have ceased to understand the world. Rather than guide us to salvation, the Russian Orthodox church has desecrated the word of God. It condones the torture, rape, and murder of my countrymen. It erects churches to the gods of war. It blesses arms with holy water. Its priests tell their soldiers that it is not a sin to kill their brothers. The Russian leaders, like the Doges, have appropriated the myth in their quest for power.

Lord Jesus Christ, Son of God, have mercy on me, a sinner. Lev had asked Professor Brown what makes one divine: infinite power, infinite goodness, or infinite love? "Infinite knowledge," the professor had replied. Lev envisioned Kiefer's paintings of war, death, and decay. He thought of Oppenheimer's words when he witnessed the horror of his own creation: "Now I am death, the destroyer of worlds." He thought of Putin's threat of using nuclear weapons, and how with the push of a button, he could bring about the end of the world. *No, infinite knowledge cannot make it cohere. It will not make us gods. The only thing that can make us divine is infinite love.*

Lev opened his heart. His love for Lida, Vera, and Sophia filled his soul, yet he could still not see into heaven. *What more can I give, other than my entire Self? What if Elias was right and reality is only an illusion? What if we are just quantum fields of energy interacting and entangling with the fields around us? What if we are such stuff as dreams are made of? What if our consciousness, the very "I" of our being, is but quantum information stored in the microtubules of our brain? What happens when we die? Is this information that makes us who we are dispersed in the cosmos and lost forever, or is it retained as an eternal soul? And what if Einstein was right, and every moment of our life – past, present, and future – all exist and are equally real? Then when we die, we are never really gone, because every moment of our life continues to exist in space-time. We are a timeless thread in the fabric of the universe.* Lev thought of the last line of Ezra Pound's the *Last Canto:*

"But the beauty is not the madness, Tho' my errors and wrecks lie about me. And I am not a demigod, I cannot make it cohere."

* * *

Sophia arrived at San Basilio's church in time for the service. She had spent the last thirty-six hours in transit: by train to Warsaw, by plane to Venice through Zurich, and by boat from Marco Polo airport to the old city. A cold fog hung over the city like a shroud and chilled her to the bone. Father Stephan was waiting in the narthex of San Basilio's church.

"Sophia," he affirmed and welcomed her in. "Thank God you were able to come. As I explained on the phone, time is of the essence."

"Is he here?" she asked.

"In spirit," he replied.

"How did . . .?"

". . . he die?" Father Stephan crossed himself. "Your father died forty days ago on the first day of Carnival. The pandemic raged through Venice in February. From what I understand, he walked in the March of the Twelve Marias and was having difficulty breathing. He returned to his apartment in the Corte del Milion that evening. The next morning the landlady found him dead. At the inquest, the coroner listed Covid as the cause of death. He left some things for you: a letter indicating you were his sole heir, a few personal possessions, and his laptop. It looks like he had begun to write his autobiography."

"He died alone?" Guilt welled up within her like the water in Venice that seeps up from the cracks between the stones below.

"He had friends and acquaintances, but many of them died at the peak of the pandemic. Others were afraid to venture out."

"Who were his friends?" Sophia asked.

"He was close with an American heiress by the name of Angela Rose, but she died the same night that he did. He knew the Conte and Contessa Rivelli. The conte died before Carnival, and the contessa died a few days after a masquerade ball that she hosted. I'm afraid that many of her guests were infected that evening. I know that he knew a Professor Brown and a Dr. Graf, but I'm not sure if he knew them before or after he died."

"After he died? I don't understand."

"Are you a Christian?" Father Stephan asked.

"I was raised in the Orthodox faith, but I'm not practicing."

"In our eastern-rite faith, we believe that the soul wanders the earth for forty days before moving on to the next. During that time, the soul faces its demons and tries to reconcile with its sins."

"I want to . . . no, I *need to* believe you," she said. "There are things I want to share with him. There are things I should have told him years ago."

Father Stephan looked towards the altar. "There is still time."

Sophia walked up to the tetrapod and looked at the green urn.

"His ashes," Father Stephan said. He looked towards the iconostasis and saw Lev's soul standing before the icon of Christ the Teacher. He was in a trance reciting the Jesus prayer. Father Stephan walked up to him and said, "Your daughter has come to see you."

Lev turned around to see Sophia standing before the tetrapod.

"She can't see or hear you," Father Stephan said. "But I told her you are here."

Lev watched as his daughter placed her hands on the green urn. She was crying. He came up to the tetrapod across from her and put his hands on hers to console her. She did not see or feel them.

"Your spiritual journey has come to an end," Father Stephan said.

The revelation of his own death did not shock him. The epiphany was that he was still here, in this place, in this time. His physical self was gone, but his soul had lived on and begun its passage to heaven or hell, eternity or oblivion. For the past forty days, his soul had wandered through space and time trying to make sense of his life. He had searched for the Absolute in the bottom of a lake on a Carpathian Mountain, on the dead-end street of Calle Querini, in the Burning Grounds of Poveglia, on the Devil's Bridge in Torcello, in the Golden Basilica of San Marco, and the sparkling realm of quantum reality on the Bar Canale. *I am not a demigod I cannot make it cohere. All that matters is that you are here.*

"Father Stephan," Sophia said. "Can you give me few minutes with . . . my father."

Lev had never heard her say those words before.

"Of course," Father Stephan said. "I'll go put on my vestments for the *Parastas*. Let me know when you're ready to begin the service."

Sophia wiped her tears to muster the courage to speak. "Father, I pray you can hear me. I know you must think me heartless for rejecting you all these years, but I was just a little girl when I knew you. I lost my mother, I lost my childhood, and I blamed you. I now know the truth, that I hadn't known before. I read your KGB files. I know it's too late, but I'm hoping you can forgive me. Even if it's too late for you, it's still not too late for me. Healing comes from revealing the truth."

I am ready to face my sins.

"I wanted to tell you that my mother loved you. I know you know, but I wanted you to hear it from me. When she told me you were my father, I felt betrayed. I felt ashamed. When she died, my trust and innocence died with her. I became selfish and cynical. But now I know that your love for each other was the purest love in the whole world. Heartbreak didn't kill my mother. Your friend, Georgiy, did. He worked for the KGB. They were threatened by my stepfather's support of Gorbachev's policies of openness and reform. They tried to recruit my mother to spy on her own husband. When she refused, Georgiy needed to silence her. He began to poison her. He put thallium in her tea, a little bit at a time, so she wouldn't suspect. Over several weeks she kept getting progressively weaker. She lost feeling in her hands and feet. She lost her hair. She wore a wig and makeup to hide her illness from you."

Georgiy? My most trusted friend? I bared my soul to you. I can't fathom the depth of your betrayal. You took away my Vera, my Sophia, my sanity. But why?

"Georgiy needed another way to compromise my stepfather, so he told him about the affair. He said that if the scandal was revealed, my stepfather would be disgraced, and his career would be ruined. The only way out of the scandal would be if he let my mother die from natural causes. The KGB brought in their own doctors who diagnosed aplastic anemia. They said there was nothing they could do. In revenge for her betrayal, my stepfather refused to seek outside care. He never took her to a hospital. He just let her die. At my mother's funeral, Georgiy took advantage of my grief to further manipulate me. He told me that you had fled Ukraine because you were suspected of killing your girlfriend. He said you were an evil man capable of murder. He made me believe that you were the one who had killed my mother."

Lev recalled the *Didko's* words above the lake in the mountain: '*We live in a world of perpetual violence, of eat or be eaten, of kill or be killed. The things she wanted you to believe in – love, hope, and happiness – are illusions.' But my love for your mother is not an illusion. The time I shared with the both of you was the happiest time of my life. I love you, my daughter, with all my heart. I never gave up hope to reconcile with you.* Lev felt the demon of regret crawl out of his soul.

"Your girlfriend at the university – the songwriter, Lida. You didn't kill her. The KGB did. Moscow had given the order to silence her. I read their secret reports. It was awful. They abducted her, tortured her, and hanged her. They reveled in their cruelty. They tried to force her to sign a statement that said that she was afraid of you and that you were stalking her. They wanted to frame you for her murder. When she refused, they faked her suicide and convinced you that you were somehow responsible. They made you believe that you were losing your mind. They used your guilt to manipulate you all these years. They murdered her, but they couldn't silence her music. You taught me her songs, and I will share them with the world."

Her revelation exorcised the demon of guilt that had tormented him his whole life. He was purged of hate and anger towards those who had wronged him. He saw the frailty in himself: he was an orphan desperate for love and belonging, an outcast who trusted those who betrayed him. As he lost his mother, Lida, and Vera, he withdrew deeper and deeper into the safety of his own imaginary world. He lived through the characters in his books. For his entire adult life, he had carried the sins of others. Sophia had set him free.

"I read your book, *The Storyteller*, Sophia said. "It was beautiful and inspiring. Especially now, in these terrible times, it gives me hope. I find you in fragments in your stories, and I wish with all my heart that I could have known you more. You returned to Ukraine to give voice to the *maidantsi*. I won't let the Russians silence you. I'm proud to be your daughter."

Her words cast the last demon out of his soul.

"I wish I could have said these words to you when you were still alive. I wish I could have told you that I love you."

You have made my life cohere.

"I have news that would have made you happy." She put her hands on her belly. "I'm pregnant. The father, Alex, you would have liked him. He's like the heroes in your book about the Maidan. He's an idealist, ready to . . ." Sophia could almost not say the words, "sacrifice his life for a noble cause. He's a filmmaker. He went to Bucha to expose the atrocities. I'm praying that we'll be reunited soon."

I gave you the gift of life, and now you will give it to my grandchild.

Lev saw a soulful young man standing in the back of the church. The young man walked up to Sophia and put his arms around her waist. From her sigh, she seemed to sense that he was there.

"Father Stephan," Sophia said, "I'm ready to begin the memorial service."

Lev stepped back from the tetrapod. He turned to face the icon of Christ. *Now I can face my final judgement. Whether I see Divine Light or the Abyss of Unknown Nothingness, it will be what it will be. I am grateful for the miracle of my life and to have been a witness to this wondrous universe. I have tried to live a decent life, as best as I knew how. I have loved and was loved. I have given the gift of life to my daughter, and she will give it to her child. I need nothing more.*

Father Stephan opened the Holy Gates of the iconostasis and carried down a *Peresopnytsia* Gospel that had been passed down from one pastor to another over the centuries. He was wearing an epitrachelion and phelonion, the traditional vestments of the *Parastas*. He lay the Gospel on the tetrapod and handed Sophia a prayer book so she could respond if she so chose. The prayer book was in Ukrainian, rather than old Slavonic, and she was able to follow the service. Father Stephan was pleased that she would actively participate in praying for the repose of her father's soul and the forgiveness of his sins. He handed her a lit beeswax candle. He raised the censer and circled the tetrapod three times, waving the censer back and forth, so the smoke would raise their prayers to heaven.

He began the *Parastas* with the words:

Blessed is our God, now and ever and forever.

Sophia responded: *Amen.*

Father Stephan continued with Psalm 90 of the Kontakion:

As a shield his truth shall cover you.
You shall not fear the terror of the night,
Nor the arrow that flies by day,
Nor the plague that lurks in the darkness
Nor the demons that lay waste at noon.

Lev heard their prayers, but they were like voices that were coming from a faraway realm. With each wave of the censer, the chants drifted farther away. Lev looked into the icon. Christ the Teacher was also Christ the Protector. Lev was finally shielded by truth. He no longer feared the terrors of the night: the *Didko* with the spindly legs who had asked him to steal the golden egg; the Masque of the Red Death at the Rivelli's masquerade who had told him he could not save his friends; the tortured dead in Poveglia who had tried to pull him into the Burning Grounds; the devil with the hollow cheeks on the bridge in Torcello who had asked if he had brought him the soul of an unbaptized child; and he no longer feared, nor desired Mara, the seductress who would have made him a harvester of souls.

The hymns of the *Parastas* grew ever fainter as they rose to heaven. Lev heard only fragments of the prayers.

> *Let us pray for the repose of the soul of the departed servant of God, Lev, and that his every transgression committed deliberately or through human frailty be forgiven him, let us pray to the Lord. Lord have mercy, Lord have mercy, Lord have mercy.*

Lev stood before the icon of Christ the Teacher.

> *Christ, show me the way. I know now that I could not have saved my mother's life – I was but a child. I did not drive Lida to despair – our love was courageous and true. I did not break Vera's heart – our love brought Sophia into this world. I should have been stronger and believed in myself. My sins were sins of frailty and not malice. I wanted to protect the women I loved, but it was they who protected me. My mother saved me from the Didko when he tried to trick me into bringing him the golden egg. Lida did not renounce me to her KGB killers. Her spirit took the form of a mavka to tell me that she had died a tragic death and warn me that I was in mortal danger. Vera did not disavow our love, even on her deathbed. Her spirit*

came to me for forty nights after her death to show me she loved me. If I could be reunited with their love, it would be my heaven.

Father Stephan sang the prayer of supplication.

O God of spirits and all flesh, Who have trampled death and overthrown the devil, and granted life to your world; now O Lord, grant rest to the soul of your departed servant, Lev, in a place of light, a place of green pasture, a place of refreshment where all pain, sorrow, and sighing have fled away.
Lev peered into the icon of Christ the Teacher searching for heaven. Father Stephan told me that if I have faith, You will show me the way. Will You lead me to Divine Light or Divine Darkness?

The elementary particles in the bits of glass, ceramic, shell, and gold that comprised the mosaic were formed from the energy of the universe in the very beginning. Their light emanated from within. Over billions of years, they took countless forms: they were stars, meteors, mountains and oceans; they were the building blocks of life, from primordial plants and organisms to humans. They comprised a sparkling world of dancing energy in which particles twinkled in and out of existence, forever changing, forever creating. In the mosaic they created beauty and meaning. We exist in a reality of Form and not Emptiness. We are energy interacting with energy, spirit in action, forever present, transfiguring, evolving in a universe of creativity and consciousness. Father Stephan sang the Doxology.

For you are the resurrection, the life, and the repose of your departed servant Lev, O Christ our God, and we glorify You, together with Your eternal Father, and Your all-holy good, and life-giving Spirit, now and ever and forever. Amen.

As Lev looked into the icon, the body of Christ was transfigured. His face shone like the sun. His robe and cloak, rather than red and blue, were white as light. He now understood that the purpose of the incarnation was to establish full communion between God and humanity, so that in Christ humanity can find immortality. Christ had come to show us that we too are in God. Whatever exists is God, and everything is "being in God." God is all embracing love that unites the universe into one indivisible whole, the being of all beings. Lev was immersed in light and love. He shed his doubts and fears, his hopes and dreams, all the trappings of the Self that now seemed but an infinitesimal part of the universal whole. He was in communion with God. He understood that eternity is not time going on forever. Eternity is a moment without time. In each and every moment, there is this, just this, and nothing more.

As Father Stephan sang the *Podoben*, the Hymn of Farewell, Sophia touched the urn and kissed the cross that he held in his hand. Father Stephan concluded the *Parastas* with the prayer:

> *In blessed repose, grant, O Lord, eternal rest to the soul of Your departed servant, Lev, and may his memory be eternal.*

Sophia replied:

> *Eternal memory. Eternal memory. Eternal memory.*

CHAPTER 12

The Death of Mara

The fishing boat was waiting for them at the San Basilio dock before dawn. It was a wooden *sanpierrota*, painted black and red, with a single outdoor motor. Rather than nets and traps, the bottom held a mysterious cargo covered with a canvas tarp. The lone occupant motioned them aboard. From his light brown hair, roundish face and deep blue eyes, Sophia guessed that he was Slavic rather than Italian. A cigarette was burning down to his fingers.

"Sophia, meet Yuriy," Father Stephan said. "He's the deacon in my parish. Have you prepared the effigy as we discussed?"

Yuriy crossed himself and pointed at the canvas tarp. "As our people have for thousands of years."

Father Stephan placed a crucifix over the tarp. The boat set off into the darkness of the lagoon.

"Where are we going?" Sophia asked.

"Deep into the lagoon," Father Stephan replied. "Off the coast of Poveglia."

The temperature was just above freezing. The bow of the boat rose and fell as it cut through the waves. Sophia closed her eyes. The rocking was lulling her to sleep. She hadn't slept since the *Parastas* service the day before.

"Stay awake!" Father Stephan cautioned.

The wind was chilling her to the bone. She took hold of the tarp to cover her knees. Father Stephan grabbed her by the hand.

"Do not disturb her. Let her lie."

"Do you really believe in these superstitions?" she asked.

"There are many things in this world that I don't understand," he said, "but I still respect them. Your father believed in them."

"Then explain them to me. If I'm to participate in this ritual, then I need to understand it."

"What do you know of the gods of ancient Rus?"

"Before Christianity? Very little."

"These myths are engrained in our Slavic collective unconscious. In the Carpathians, where your father was born, many people held on to their pre-Christian beliefs, even though they were practicing Christians. From what your father told me, your grandmother believed in the old ways even though her father was a priest. She passed them on to your father through the stories she told. Do you know the significance of the name Veles?"

"I saw a reference to an ancient god by that name in my father's novel, *The Storyteller.*"

"In Slavic mythology the world was pictured as a Tree of Life whose branches and trunk represent the living world of heaven and mortals, while the roots represent the underworld, the realm of the dead. Perun was the ruler of the living world and sat atop a sacred oak tree from where he kept watch over the world. Veles was the watery god of the underworld, who was able to change forms, and often crept into the living world to steal from Perun. According to the myth, Veles transformed himself into a snake and slithered up the tree to kidnap Perun's son, Jarylo. He brought Jarylo back into the underworld and raised him as his own, where he grew up to be a major fertility deity. Perun was enraged by the kidnapping of his son, and the two gods battled each other in a great storm."

"Are you saying that I'm descended from some ancient Slavic god?"

"I'm saying that your bloodline is rooted deep in the Carpathian forests."

Sophia looked out over the dark water. The black silhouette of Poveglia loomed in the distance. "It's a dark legacy indeed," she said.

"It depends on your world view," Father Stephan said. "Veles was the god of the underworld, but he was also a god of earth and waters – the god at the roots of the World Tree. He was associated with magic and communion with spirits. He was the patron of musicians and poets. He was a guardian of the earth and the underworld beneath it. He was worshipped. Mara was feared."

"Tell me about Mara," Sophia said.

"Mara was once a beautiful goddess, the daughter of Perun and sister of Jarylo. Both she and Jarylo were born on the Great Night of the New Year. When Jarylo returned from the underworld, he brought spring into the realm of the living. He met his sister, Mara, and courted her. Their union brought fertility and abundance to the earth, and peace between Perun and Veles. Their wedding, the sacred union of brother and sister, is still celebrated in the summer on the night of Ivana Kupala. But Jarylo was unfaithful to Mara, and she killed him. Without her husband, the god of fertility, Mara – and all of nature with her – withers and freezes in the winter. She turned into a terrible, old, and dangerous goddess of darkness and death; a goddess of nightmares and end of beginnings."

"So, she appears to us only in dreams?" Sophia asked.

"Your father believed that, 'Reality is such stuff as dreams are made of.'"

"Should I be afraid?"

"She's a vengeful creature with a heart as cold as ice. She'll blame us for taking your father away from her."

"What's the point of the ritual?"

"Our ancestors believed that each year, for spring to return, Mara must be drowned. It's an archetype of death and rebirth that explains the change of seasons."

Yuriy cut the motor. He pointed at the shoreline of Poveglia. A white vog was rising up from the dark trees and climbing up the bell tower. Sophia thought she saw shadows moving among the trees. He dropped the anchor. "We go no farther," he said.

The sun had not yet risen. Father Stephan lifted the crucifix off the tarp. Yuriy pulled back the canvas to reveal a grotesque effigy of Mara. It was a humanoid shape, larger than life, made of branches, twine, and straw. A white cloth with a painted face was wrapped around its head. It was frightening in its primitivity. A necklace of eggshells was strung around its neck. An embroidered white dress covered the torso. The eyes faced the bottom of the boat.

"Hurry, Father. We must drown her before she awakens," Yuriy said.

Father Stephan and Yuriy lifted the effigy from the boat and rolled it over the side. But rather than sink, it floated with its eyes staring up at the moon. The temperature dropped and the wind quickened. Sophia leaned back against the motor, as far away from the effigy as the space in the boat would allow. The effigy bobbed in the rolling waves. Sophia rubbed her eyes. The face on the cloth appeared to be changing as it took on water – wrinkling, grimacing, and taking on human skin. The painted eyes sunk in their sockets and turned their gaze on the occupants of the boat.

"Father! Pray for us," Yuriy cried out.

Father Stephan began reciting the prayer of *Kyrie eleison* but the effigy continued its metamorphosis. The waves pushed it back towards the boat. Its gnarled branches snagged the side.

"Pull up the anchor!" Sophia cried out.

Father Stephan grabbed the anchor rope and pulled. The rope tightened and the boat rolled. Yuriy rushed over to help him. The anchor was snagged on something on the bottom. Together they jerked it free and raised it into the boat. The anchor was coated in black slime. The arm of the anchor was hooked around the remains of a human rib cage. The effigy raised its head above the gunwale. The face cloth was gone. In its place was the sagging skin of a hideous hag.

Sophia bit her lip to wake up from the nightmare. Blood pooled in her mouth. The effigy's branches lengthened into long arms and fingers.

It raised itself up over the gunwale. It eyed Father Stephan. He was clutching his crucifix reciting a prayer of exorcism. It turned its gaze towards Sophia. Sophia felt the gasoline cannister beneath her feet. She disconnected the hose, lifted the cannister, and splashed the effigy's face with gasoline as it was crawling over the gunwale.

"Give me your matches!" Sophia cried out to Yuriy.

Yuriy crossed himself and handed her his book of matches. Sophia struck one after another, but the wind kept snuffing them out. Mara pulled herself up into the boat. Sophia retreated to the stern. The transfiguring effigy of skin, wood, and straw staggered towards her in fits and spasms as its branches turned into bone. Sophia struck another match, shielded it from the wind, and lit the entire book. Mara screamed when the matchbook ignited. Sophia threw the burning book into her gaping mouth. The gasoline-soaked straw burst into flames. Mara thrashed and howled as the fire spread from her head to her torso to the wooden branches of her limbs. The flames threatened to engulf the boat.

Father Stephan came up to Mara with his crucifix and recited the prayer of *Anima Christi*: *Soul of Christ, sanctify me. Body of Christ Save me. . .*With the words, *From the malignant enemy defend me,* he thrust the crucifix into her burning face.

Mara shrieked with the last breath of winter as she fell back into the water. Her effigy flailed and burned as it drifted towards the island. Wraiths lined the shoreline like mourners. Their wails and laments receded with the wind. Father Stephan, Yuriy, and Sophia watched as the dying flames illuminated the water, from red to yellow to black, and Mara turned into ash before sinking into the unholy waters off Poveglia.

No one spoke on the way back to Venice. Sophia hoped that their ordeal had just been a communal nightmare until she saw the burns on Father Stephan's hand. As the sun rose in the east, the wind became warmer. The water turned from black to blue to green. A seagull flew overhead. A dolphin broke the surface. Life returned to the lagoon.

* * *

Andriy was waiting for Sophia at the Kyiv train station. The passengers who got off the overnight train from Lviv were mostly men, young and old, soldiers and volunteers. Sophia emerged from the train with her overnight bag and a knapsack. Andriy hugged her and took her bag. "What's in the knapsack?" he asked.

"My father's ashes. I'm bringing him home."

Andriy didn't question her any further. They returned to his apartment. His bedroom was as she had left it. He'd left her bed untouched while she was away.

"How did you know I'd return?" she asked.

"Bucha," he replied. "We're both searching for the same answers."

"Where is the front now?"

Andriy gave her a guarded smile. "The Russians are abandoning their siege of Kyiv. They withdrew from Bucha two days ago. I received permission to drive there tomorrow. The war crimes investigators are already there. We leave tomorrow morning."

"That's welcome news," she said. "I need to gather my strength, physically and emotionally. I've been living through a nightmare." She returned to the bedroom, placed the green urn on the nightstand, and lay down on the bed. She was exhausted from her journey but afraid to fall asleep. She could not get the image of Mara out of her mind. Father Stephan had told her how Mara had haunted her father for the forty days after he died and how, with their help, he was able to defeat her and seek union with God. Their ordeal off the shores of Poveglia reaffirmed her faith in God and the supernatural. She realized that there were elements of truth in the supernatural tales that her father had written about in his novels. She closed her eyes and clutched the medal of the *Pokrova* that hung around her neck, that portrayed the Mother of God, extending Her Hands and veil to protect her . . ."

"Wake up," Andriy whispered. "It's time to leave."

Sophia rubbed her eyes. She was still in her clothes from the day before.

"How long have I been sleeping?"

"Since you arrived yesterday afternoon."

"No air raid sirens?" she asked.

"Not last night. We have a lull while the Russians are retreating."

"I'll be ready in just a few minutes."

Sophia quickly showered and put on her jeans and a pullover sweater. Andriy had prepared a modest breakfast of rye bread, canned mackerel, and pickled tomatoes. The coffee was hot, black, and bitter. They did not speak over breakfast. They both knew that what awaited them in Bucha was something between hope and horror.

The highway to Bucha was pocked with craters and strewn with the detritus of war: turretless tanks, scorched personnel carriers, and frozen bodies scavenged by crows and wild dogs. Andriy navigated his ZAZ past the obstructions. He had to present his papers at three military checkpoints before his car was allowed into Bucha. He turned off Shevchenko Street and headed south down Vokzalna. When they reached Yablunska Street, the scene was worse than they imagined. It was a bright, sunny day. Bodies were strewn in the street like carrion. Some had lain in the street for weeks. The sickly-sweet stench of death hung in the air. Forensic teams in white protective gear were photographing and tagging corpses and placing them into black plastic bags. The bags were lined in rows that attempted to bring a semblance of order into chaos. They drove towards Irina's house. Andriy knew the route by heart.

The house was as Andriy had remembered it, except the fence was toppled and the ground was scarred with the tracks of military vehicles. The house was dark.

"Wait here," Andriy said.

"No, I'm coming with you. You've helped me deal with my horror. Now let me help you."

The door was open. The interior was cold. The place was in shambles. The television and kitchen appliances had been looted. Human excrement and empty bottles littered the floor. They entered Irina's bedroom and froze. Her body was on the bed, covered with a sheet. Andriy pulled back the sheet. His cousin's body was white and blue, bruised and frozen. The cold had kept it from decomposing. Used prophylactics were scattered throughout the room.

Sophia put her arm around Andriy. At first, he was stoic, but then he began to sob.

"Monsters," he said.

Sophia had seen supernatural evil with her own eyes, but the atrocities committed by humans were far worse.

Andriy began looking through the bedroom drawers for some memento he could bring back to her mother and daughter, something they could remember her by. He found a photograph of the entire family from last Christmas.

"It might be best to not disturb anything," Sophia said. "It's the scene of a war crime. It needs to be documented and prosecuted."

"Yes, of course you're right," he said. "It's hard for me to just leave her like this."

"We'll come back after the investigators have finished," she said. "We'll arrange a proper burial."

Andriy said a prayer and pulled the sheet back over her head. His stoicism returned. "Let's find Alex," he said.

The rest of the house, except for Irina's body, was empty.

"Oksana mentioned a children's camp," Sophia said. "Do you know where it is?"

"Yes, we used to take Oksana there during the summer. It's on the edge of town."

They returned to his ZAZ and drove to the camp in silence. The investigators were already there. The site was cordoned off in yellow tape. Access was restricted.

Andriy took his video camera and approached one of the Ukrainian soldiers who were guarding the perimeter. He showed him his papers.

"I'm a journalist," Andriy said. "I've come to document the investigation."

"They're still exhuming bodies from a mass grave," the soldier replied. "We don't want anyone interfering with the crime scene. You'll have to return later."

Sophia grabbed him by his arm. "Please," she said, "the father of my child may be among them."

An army captain walked up to them. "What's going on?" he asked.

"A journalist and a relative of a victim are requesting to enter."

The captain looked at Sophia. "It's a gruesome scene. Are you sure you're ready to identify a body?"

"Yes, I'm sure," she said. "I need to know if the father of my child is alive or dead."

"I understand," the captain said. "I'm prepared to die for our freedom, but I worry about my family every day."

The Russians had converted the children's camp into a death camp. Fourteen bodies had been exhumed from a shallow grave in the playground. The workers in white were excavating for others. The bodies exhumed so far were laid out in neat rows in the basement of the main building.

"You may want to wear a mask," the captain said.

Sophia and Andriy put on paper masks that did little to mask the smell. The captain unzipped one body bag after another. The first was a woman, naked except for a blood-stained fur coat. The second was a man whose hands had been bound behind his back with tape. The back of his head and forehead were gone. The third was a boy of fourteen. They continued until they reached the last bag. The captain unzipped it to reveal the face of a young man in his thirties. The bullet had exited through the bridge of his nose. The face was covered in dried blood.

"Wait," Sophia said. She scraped away the dried blood with her fingernails. She gasped and collapsed to her knees. "Alex, my love," she sobbed.

Andriy helped her to her feet.

"Is he the man you're looking for?" the captain asked.

Sophia was crying, unable to speak.

Andriy spoke in her place. "His name is Alex Ivanovich. He's from St. Petersburg."

"A Russian? A civilian?"

"He's a Russian filmmaker," Andriy said. "A friend of mine. He came to Bucha to expose the atrocities."

"I'm sorry," the captain said. "He was executed, just like the rest of these poor souls."

Sophia mustered the courage to speak. "Alex, my love. Why oh why did you leave us to come to this hell hole?"

"He came here to confront the devil," Andriy replied. "He came here to protect you and your child."

* * *

Sophia arrived in the foothills of the Carpathians on Holy Saturday. The overnight train from Kyiv to Chernivtsi traveled west to Lviv and then turned south through Ivano-Frankivsk before arriving in the city of Chernivtsi in the late morning. Chernivtsi had been a jewel in the Habsburg crown. The multicultural city at the crossroads of trade routes and state boundaries was once called Little Vienna, Jerusalem upon the Prut, and European Alexandria. So far it had been spared direct missile attacks and was a haven for internally displaced refugees. No one was waiting for her when she got off the train. Andriy had offered to travel with her, but she preferred to discover her roots alone. She was traveling light: an overnight bag and a knapsack with the urn that held her father's ashes.

Sophia planned her itinerary from the notes in her father's KGB files. She was determined to discover who he really was. If she eschewed him during his life, she could at least honor his memory after his death. Her search would begin with his university days, and she would try to reimagine his romance with Lida, his first love. Her search would end in his birthplace where she would scatter his ashes. The village of Dzerelo was about fifty kilometers west of Chernivtsi, high up in the mountains. It was only reachable by single lane roads that were impassable in bad weather. The KGB files contained a map of the village with red circles that marked Lev's childhood home, the village church, and the graveyard where his mother and grandfather were buried. The other places near Dzerelo that she wanted to visit were not on the map. They were described only in his stories, but she was determined to find them. These were his sacred places.

The main campus of Chernivtsi National University was based at the former residence of the Bukovinian and Dalmatian Metropolitans' complex. The elegant terracotta building with its towers and stone carvings was a masterpiece of Habsburg architecture. It was one of the oldest universities in Ukraine and was designated as a UNESCO heritage site. Sophia was familiar with the works of several famous alumni, including the Ukrainian composers Sydir Vorobkevych and Eusebius Mandyczewski. The classrooms were closed for the Easter holidays but the halls were open to shelter homeless refugees. Sophia tried to imagine her father walking through these halls with his books of Ukrainian and French literature. She wondered if he had any friends, other than Lida or his classmates in the Komsomol who had sold their souls to the devil.

Sophia heard a haunting choral melody echoing through the halls. She followed it to a small auditorium, where a student musical and dance group were rehearsing *hahilky* – ritual spring dances – for a performance on Easter Sunday. Sophia had never heard the melody before, but it seemed strangely familiar, as if it were a part of her DNA that had been silenced by the modern world. Girls in Hutsul dress were singing and dancing in a circle around a makeshift maypole. They were accompanied by fellow students playing Hutsul instruments: a violin, drum, cymbals, *sopilka* – wooden flute – and a *dudka* – a small bagpipe. The director of the group was a music professor in her sixties. When she saw Sophia in the doorway, she paused the rehearsal and came over to speak with her.

"What are *you* doing here?" she asked.

Sophia was taken aback by her brusqueness. "I'm . . . I'm just a tourist wandering through the university. I heard the music . . ."

"You're no tourist," the professor retorted. "I *know* who you are. You're Sophia Sergeivna Borodin, the conductor of the St. Petersburg Philharmonic. I idolized you to my students before the war. Why are you here in Ukraine?"

"I'm searching for my roots."

"From what I know, your roots are in Paris and St. Petersburg."

"My parents were Ukrainian."

"Borodin?"

"He was my stepfather. My natural father is Lev Veles."

"The author?"

Sophia nodded. "He studied philology and languages here at Chernivtsi National University before he emigrated to France where he met my mother. While he was here, he had fallen in love with a fellow student, a songwriter by the name of Lida Verbytska."

The music professor took a moment to process the revelation. "I apologize for my rudeness. It's just that my son is fighting on the front lines."

"I understand," Sophia replied. "I share your pain over this war."

"Then there's someone you must meet," the professor said. She called over to one of her students. "Stephania, come here please."

A young woman with green eyes and a long, black braid left the circle and approached them. She offered Sophia her hand.

"Stephania is the great-niece of Lida Verbytska," she said to Sophia. "She's writing her thesis about the musical legacy of her great-aunt."

The professor turned to Stephania. "Maestra Sophia is the conductor of the St. Petersburg Philharmonic Orchestra. She's the daughter of the writer Lev Veles, who was a friend of your great-aunt's. She's come here searching for her roots. I'm thinking, who best to show her that chapter of her father's life than you? If you agree, then you're free to leave rehearsal. I'll need you back here for our performance at noon tomorrow."

Stephania picked up her coat and waved goodbye to her friends. She looked at Sophia suspiciously.

"What do you know of my great-aunt?" she asked.

"I know what really happened to her."

"How? From your father?"

"No, unfortunately not. I wish he could have told me in his own words. I found the truth in the KBG archives."

"I've tried to access my great-aunt's file," Stephania said. "But they can't seem to find it."

"I found what you need to know in my father's KGB file."

"The rumor is that he betrayed her to the KGB and drove her to take her own life."

"That's want what the KGB wanted everyone to believe. He didn't betray her. He loved her. She didn't take her own life. She was a victim of the KGB, just as he was. My friend, Andriy Orishkevich, found my father's file in the KGB archives and took photographs of the documents with his phone. I'll share them with you."

"If you know more than I do," Stephania said, "then how can I help you?"

"I want to see the place where she died."

"I can take you there." Stephania led Sophia to her car, a 1985 Skoda with blankets over the seats and a taped rear window. The short ride up the foothills brought them to an old-growth beech forest. It was as remote and pristine as it was decades ago. Stephania led her through the ancient beeches to a meadow. In the center was a weeping willow that arched over a meandering stream, its yellow catkins dancing in the wind. A bronze plaque with Lida's name and date of death was placed beneath its trunk. Sophia envisioned this place in the late spring, resplendent with wildflowers and teeming with life. She pictured them making love in this sacred meadow. She tried to imagine her father's shock and horror when he found his sweetheart hanging from their lovers' tree. It had driven him to madness. Sophia examined the trunk until she found what was she was looking for: the Cyrillic initials ЛВ + ЛВ.

"They were very much in love," Sophia said. "My father honored her memory by writing about her in his novel, *The Storyteller*. He taught me her songs when I was a little girl."

"Which ones?" Stephania asked.

"All the ones he knew."

"Many of her compositions were destroyed by the KGB and never found."

"Perhaps not all."

Sophia opened her backpack and took out the green urn. She said a prayer beneath her breath and scattered a handful of ashes over the roots of the weeping willow whose branches arched over the rushing stream. A sudden gust stirred the tree and set the pendulant branches in motion. Sunlight streamed through the catkins creating a dance of light and shadow on the floor below. For a moment Sophia thought she glimpsed a young couple frolicking beneath the tree. The girl had green eyes and raven hair. The boy looked familiar. When she rubbed her eyes, they were gone.

"My eyes must be playing tricks on me," Sophia said out loud. "I thought I saw a girl with green eyes and a boy . . ."

Stephania smiled. "There's magic in this place, especially on the night of Ivana Kupala."

Sophia put the urn in the backpack. "I need to get to my father's birthplace, the village of Dzerelo, before dark. Can you can help me find a taxi? From what I see on the map, it's about 50 kilometers west of here."

"I can drive you there," Stephania offered, "if you sing the songs your father taught you on the way. You may know some that I haven't heard before. I'd want to include them in my thesis."

"I'd be delighted. I promised my father that I'd share them with the world."

"I have to return to Chernivtsi this evening for Easter service and for our performance tomorrow. You're welcome to join me."

"Thank you, but I think my visit to Dzerelo will take more than just a few hours. There are a few more places where I want to scatter my father's ashes."

"Do you have a place to stay?"

"No, I'll need to find some lodging once I get there."

"I've not been to Dzerelo, but I've been to some of the Hutsul villages nearby. You'll be lucky if you find a stable to sleep in. If you're not too tired, you can try to stay up all night. The Easter service begins at midnight and continues through tomorrow morning. The whole village will be there. I can return for you tomorrow afternoon after my performance, and we can finish going over my great-aunt's songs."

"We'll not only sing them," Sophia offered. "If you bring me some sheet music paper, I'll transcribe the notes and the lyrics I remember."

The drive to Dzerelo took over two hours. While it was only fifty kilometers away, the road climbed up the mountains in winding circles, over single lane bridges that spanned snow-melt creeks. The road changed from asphalt to gravel to mud as it climbed through the alpine forests. As Stephania drove, Sophia sang the songs that she learned from her father. Some Stephania knew, but others she heard for the first time. Her father had safeguarded them in his heart. They were songs of love, of longing, and of hope. Sophia realized that the Soviet system that silenced Lida was beyond inhuman – her death was not a crime of passion; it was totalitarian, cold-blooded murder meant to extinguish the spirit of a nation.

The final stretch of the road to Dzerelo was little more than thawing mud whose ruts were carved by horse-drawn wagons rather than automobiles. The single road through the village was flanked by Hutsul houses made of wood, each with a bramble fence, piles of firewood, and a dormant garden. Some homes had chicken coops; others a horse, a goat, or a cow. A few had orchards. All had outhouses. The only trapping of modernity was the lone utility wire that brought in electricity. The villagers watched as the Skoda navigated around the ruts and potholes on the way to the church. The onlookers were mostly women, children, and old men. The wooden church was from a bygone era. Its moss-covered shingles sloped over hand-hewn pine walls with intricate wood carvings. A wooden bell tower stood next to the church.

"I'll leave you here," Stephania said. "I suggest you let the village priest know why you've come. The Hutsuls are suspicious of strangers. I'll be back for you this time tomorrow."

The church was open. There were no seats or benches. Painted icons of the stations of the cross hung on the walls. A *plashchenytsia* – a cloth of the crucified Christ in repose – was spread on a long makeshift tomb in front of the wooden iconostasis. His wounds, from the crown of thorns, the spear to His chest, and the nails to His hands and feet, were marked with lipstick kisses.

"Have you brought your Paschal basket to be blessed?" Sophia heard a voice ask behind her. "The blessing service is over, but I can ask my husband, Father Oleh, to come and bless yours."

She turned to see an older woman in an embroidered dress, red coral necklace, woolen *keptar* – jacket – and colorful babushka standing behind her.

"I'm afraid I didn't bring a basket."

"Then you've come to kiss the *plashchenytsia*."

Sophia knelt down, approached the *plashchenytsia* on her knees, and kissed the wounds of Christ. She stood up, crossed herself three times, and bowed. A basket next to the *plashchenytsia* held offerings – coins, bills, bread – whatever the parishioner could afford. Sophia took out a one-thousand hryvnia bill and placed it in the basket.

"God thanks you, my child," the woman said. "My name is Natalia. My husband is the pastor. You're new to our village. How can I help you?"

"My father was born here," Sophia replied. "He died abroad, and I've come here to return his ashes. In my heart I believe that he's always wanted to come home."

"Who was your father?" she asked.

"Lev Veles. He was the grandson of the village priest."

"The author?" Natalia asked. "Veles is an ancient bloodline in our village. Your ancestors rest in the oldest part of the cemetery. Today is Holy Saturday. It might be best to conduct the funeral after Easter service. Those who die during Easter time do not need to suffer through Purgatory. They go straight to heaven. I invite you to join us for the midnight service and for breakfast tomorrow. I'll let my husband know you're here."

"I was hoping to see the house where he lived and perhaps some of the places that he frequented when he was a child."

"Your father was the grandson of the village priest. We now share his home."

"There's a green pool under a waterfall high up the mountain that he describes in his stories. Do you know how I might find it?"

Natalia crossed herself three times. "It's a primeval world up there. Are you sure you want to go?"

"Yes, it's important for me."

Natalia looked up the mountain. "Don't speak to anyone, or anything, that you might encounter along the way. Follow the stream that runs behind the church as it climbs up the mountain. There's an overgrown path that winds from one side of the stream to the other. I don't think anyone's been up ever since I can remember."

"Thank you," Sophia said. "I'll be back for the midnight service."

The stream behind the church was surging from the snow melt. It cascaded down the mountain, and Sophia had to climb over fallen trees and step over slippery boulders to follow it. Spring was returning to the mountains. The conifers were sprouting fresh needles, and the oaks and birches were budding leaves. She spotted an eagle on the highest oak. When the sun hid behind the mountain, the forest, rather than being deadened, became even more alive. Insects were buzzing. Bats streaked overhead. Squirrels and rabbits peaked out of their burrows to see what stranger had entered their world.

Every now and then Sophia thought that she spotted someone watching her. They were tricks of light and shadow, peeking from behind trees and boulders, as the sun set over the mountain. As she climbed the path higher up the mountain, she heard the burbling of a waterfall. She came upon her father's sacred place: a deep green pool nestled under a white-water waterfall, surrounded by primordial ferns, sheared off boulders, and lush blankets of moss. A canopy of old-growth trees protected the pool from whatever lurked above. Sophia opened her knapsack and took out the green urn. She put her hand into the urn and brought out a handful of her father's ashes. She submerged her hand in the water and let her father's ashes disperse through the water of the green pool.

She thought she heard voices in the burbling of the waterfall. As she listened intently, they became more distinct. She heard the voice of a mother telling her child a story. The child was asking questions about a golden egg. She saw them in the moonlight. A young woman was sitting by the edge of the pool with her feet in the water. A boy of five sat on her lap. The mother looked up from her son, met Sophia's gaze, and smiled.

A storm cloud obscured the moon. Lighting flashed in the distance followed seconds later by a clap of thunder. The cloud enveloped the mountain in a bone-chilling mist. Sophia heard a howl higher up the mountain. It was neither a wolf nor a bear, but something half-human. The mother brought her son into her bosom and motioned for Sophia to go. Sophia put the urn back into her knapsack and retraced her steps down the mountain. It was perilous in the mist and dark. She lost her bearings and no longer heard the gurgling of the stream. She tripped over roots and scraped her elbows and knees. The branches snared her clothes. She lost track of time. The howl in the mountain came from the right, then from the left, closer and closer, but always above her. Something seemed to be hunting her. She crawled underneath a fallen fir and listened. Something was cracking the underbrush. It was moving faster than a human. It drew nearer. Every few seconds it would stop to sniff and listen. She wondered whether it could hear her heart pounding. Her breath condensed in the cold. Another flash of lighting would expose her. She felt it step on the fallen trunk above her. She could hear it sniffing. A spindly leg touched the ground in front of her. It began to bend. She clutched her medal of the *Pokrova* and began to pray: *"Hail Mary, full of grace . . ."*

The church bell rang to announce the start of the Easter service. The creature atop her howled and scampered back up the mountain. Sophia saw the lights of dozens of candles in a procession below. She descended towards the lights until she came into the churchyard. The storm clouds vanished behind the mountain. The parishioners led by Father Oleh circled the church with lit candles and stopped at the closed front doors. They sang the Easter hymn that marked the passage from death to life:

> *Your Resurrection, O Christ our Savior,*
> *the angels in heaven praise with hymns.*
> *Make us, on earth, also worthy, with a pure heart,*
> *to extol and give glory to You.*

The procession reentered the church and Sophia followed. She leaned against the hewn-log back wall. Whatever was out there would not dare to enter the church. She tried to make sense of what she had seen or hadn't seen. Her father's novel, *The Storyteller*, was replete with Carpathian folklore – allusions to the supernatural denizens of the mountains, streams, and forest. Each nation has its myths, and these archetypes were deeply rooted in the Ukrainian psyche. When she read his novel, Sophia considered them to be symbols, imbued with archetypal meaning but devoid of reality – until she saw Mara. Now the lines between natural and supernatural were blurred. Within the church, the priest spoke of God, angels, and saints. Outside the church, phantasms still roamed the Carpathian forests.

Father Oleh sang the Paschal Sermon of Saint John Chrysostom and invited all to partake of Christ in Holy Communion. Sophia joined them. Their hearts were filled with the joy of Christ's resurrection and hope for their own salvation. This Easter morning, the congregation of Dzerelo accepted this stranger as one of their own. The service ended with the Easter hymn:

> *Christ is risen from the dead*
> *Trampling down death by death*
> *And to those in the tombs*
> *Bestowing life!*

After Easter service, Father Oleh and his wife invited Sophia to their home for Easter breakfast. This was the home that her father grew up in after he was orphaned. The home had passed from pastor to pastor ever since it was built in the 1800s. It was the largest home in the village with a covered porch and dining room with multiple windows. Bookcases lined the walls with worn tomes in Ukrainian, Polish, German, and English. The shelves also held eight volumes of Compton's Pictured Encyclopedia from 1922. Sophia tried to imagine her father as a little boy playing under the table during Easter breakfast and being scolded by his grandfather. She pictured him paging through the encyclopedia under candlelight, his imagination carrying him to faraway times and places. What he lacked in affection, he found in his books. She wondered what had happened to his own parents.

Father Oleh began breakfast with a blessing. The table was set for six. Three chairs stood empty.

"Are you expecting more guests?" Sophia asked.

"They're set for our children who can't be with us," Natalia replied. "Maksym is on the front line in Luhansk. Luba left for Italy with our granddaughter. We're hoping they'll be able to return once the war is over."

The table was set with the *paska* – traditional Easter bread – and laid out with plates of hard-boiled eggs; butter in the shape of a lamb; sausage; horseradish; and salt that had been blessed on Holy Saturday. A lighted candle was placed in the center of the *paska*. A collection of over a dozen of *pysanky* – Ukrainian Easter eggs – was displayed in a glass bowl next to the *paska*.

"These *pysanky* are beautiful," Sophia said. "May I take closer look?"

"Yes, of course," Natalia replied. "They were painted by the people who had lived in this parish house, going back generations. Some are over one hundred and fifty years old. I believe this one was painted by your grandmother." Natalia handed her a *pysanka* painted in white, green, red, and black.

"How do you make the designs in the different colors?" she asked.

"It's an ancient tradition that began long before the coming of our Savior. You begin with a white egg and use a *kistka* – a wax writing pen – to draw the design you want in white. You then dip the egg in a darker color and cover the added design in wax. You keep going with darker and darker colors. Once our design is finished, you melt off the wax, and you have your finished *pysanka*."

"What do the designs on my grandmother's *pysanka* represent?"

As Sophia held the *pysanka* in the palm of her hand, Natalia pointed to the various drawings. "There are over one hundred different symbols used in painting *pysanky*, each with their own meaning. These symbols date back thousands of years. On your grandmother's *pysanka* the tree with outstretched branches represents the Tree of Life. The line with no beginning and no end is a water symbol; it symbolizes infinity and immortality."

"Do you know what happened to my grandmother?" Sophia asked.

Father Oleh looked at Natalia. She nodded her assent.

"It's a tragic story," he said. "Your grandmother drowned in a pool in a waterfall up the mountain. Your father found her."

"Do you know how she drowned?"

"Some people say she took her own life, but your great-grandfather, Father Ihor, refused to believe it. Otherwise, he could not have buried her in the cemetery."

"What did my great-grandfather believe?"

"He believed it was an accident . . . or worse."

Sophia struggled to make sense of it. "What happened to Lev's father?"

"No one knows. There were rumors . . . that he took his own life, that he was eaten by wolves, or by whatever killed her. Some people claim he emigrated to America and started a new life."

"What happened to my father after my great-grandfather died?"

"He lived through a very difficult time. People were superstitious. They were afraid he had been touched by the *Didko* or at the very least had lost his mind. Your father continued to live in this house and relied on the charity of the villagers to survive. He swept the church, tended to the cemetery, and would assist the itinerant priests as an altar boy during their infrequent visits. He attended school in a village a few kilometers down the mountain. They say that he loved to read. My older parishioners claim that he read every book in the the village. But he had few friends. Most of the children shunned him for being the crazy boy who met the devil up the mountain."

Sophia's heart ached for the trauma that her father had lived through.

"I understand that you've brought his ashes," Father Oleh said. "If I may ask, how did your father die?"

"The pandemic," Sophia replied.

"Years ago, a man came to visit your grandmother's grave. He said he was a writer from Paris, but I don't remember his name. He was a quiet but generous soul. He gave us a donation to repair the bell."

"The bell?" Sophia asked.

"The bell in our belltower has a long and storied history. The legend says that the bell was cast by King Danylo and hung in a church in Halych before the Mongol invasion in the 13th century. It was brought up to Dzerelo for safekeeping during the invasion. The Mongols tried to reach the top of the mountain but were defeated, some say due to the intervention of the Blessed Virgin Mary. Our church in Dzerelo has been built and rebuilt many times over the centuries, but the original bell has always hung in the belltower. On the night that your great-grandfather died, there was a terrible storm, and the belltower was struck by lightning. The bell crashed to the ground and cracked. The Soviets had no interest in repairing the bell. When my wife and I arrived, we heard the local legend that the storm was a fight between Perun and Veles. I had to convince them it was a natural and not a supernatural phenomenon. In any event, I said that God would help us find a way to repair it. Shortly after the Orange Revolution, a writer from France came to Dzerelo and, praise be to God, donated the money we needed. The repair was an expensive and difficult undertaking. We had to obtain permission from the Ministry of Culture to transport the bell to Lviv, where a master welder worked for months to restore it. The Ministry wanted to place it in a museum, but the visitor from France interceded with his embassy to insist that it be returned to its rightful place in Dzerelo. There's something about you that reminds me of him. He had your eyes."

"Daniel Verchant," Sophia said.

"Yes, that was his name."

"It's a pseudonym that my father used to publish his first novels. The man you met was my father, Lev Veles."

Natalia nodded like she already knew. She stood up from the table. "There's something I'd like you to have," she said. She returned with a hand-carved, Hutsul *kasetka* – small wooden box – encrusted with beads and metal and inlaid with a geometric pattern of different colored woods. "It belonged to your great-grandfather, and to his father before him. I don't know how you plan to inter your father's ashes . . ."

"It will be perfect, thank you."

Through the window, Sophia saw young Hutsul girls dancing in a circle and singing *hahilky*. This was no staged performance. It was a ritual that was born in the time before Christianity came to this land, when you could speak to the birds, the trees, and the flowers, and thank the seasons for their bounty. Sophia thanked her hosts for their generosity and went outside to observe the *hahilky*. She watched the dancing and listened to the melodies and lyrics:

O Beautiful Spring, what have you brought us? 'I have brought
you summer, a pink flower, winter wheat, and all sorts of

fragrant things.'

The *hahilky* persuaded the mysterious forces of nature to provide people with a bountiful harvest and a happy life. Some were addressed to birds, trees, and flowers asking them to assist the coming of spring. The dances portrayed ritual plant growth and the behavior of birds and animals. Others celebrated courtship, female charms, and true love. Sophia promised herself that she would compose a symphony of these songs, whose collective melodies and lyrics were more beautiful and complex than any single mind could create.

The village cemetery was located in a meadow above the church. The cemetery had been there for a millennium before the church had been built. A few of the graves were freshly dug and adorned with photos of fallen soldiers and bunches of spring flowers. Others were overgrown with gnarled shrubs and tall grasses. The Veles clan portion of the graveyard was the most ancient of all. The headstones were weathered and covered with lichen. Those that bore the symbol of a cross dated as far back as 1108. The more cryptic stones were odd-shaped and engraved with the symbol of an inverted triangle with two horns. Father Oleh led her to her grandmother's grave. It was placed next to her father and mother. It simply read: Ruslana Veles, 1938-1965. While Sophia was watching the *hahilky*, Natalia had cleared a space next to her grandmother's resting place and dug a shallow grave, deep enough to bury the wooden box with Lev Veles's ashes. Father Oleh had tied together two pieces of birch in the shape of the cross as a grave marker. Sophia placed the Hutsul box with her father's ashes in the shallow grave. Father Oleh said the prayer for the departed:

> *O God of spirits and of all flesh, Who has trampled down death and overthrown the Devil, and given life to Thy world, do Thou, the same Lord, give rest to the souls of Thy departed servant, Lev, in a place of brightness, a place of refreshment, a place of repose, where all sickness, sighing, and sorrow have fled away...*

Father Oleh took a handful of dirt and made the shape of the cross over the small casket. While the traditional final hymn for the departed is "Eternal Memory," during Easter it is replaced with the joyous Easter hymn:

Christ is risen from the dead
Trampling down death by death
And to those in the tombs
Bestowing life!

Natalia handed Sophia a small bouquet of wildflowers. Sophia placed them over the box containing her father's ashes and said: "Father, you will always be with me in my heart. If I have a son, I will name him Lev. If I have a daughter, I will name her Vera. But our family name will always be Veles."

As Father Oleh covered the grave with Carpathian soil, Sophia said: "When I return, I'll place a headstone on your resting place so that my children and their children can visit and know that you were here, that you lived, and loved, and gave of yourself to this world."

* * *

Who am I? Sophia wondered. *Am I my father's daughter, or am I an imposter, a stranger in my own land?* She looked in the mirror to see if she could recognize her true self. The conductor's dressing room at the Odesa National Academic Opera and Ballet Theater was as posh as her dressing room in St. Petersburg. The Odesa theater was considered one of the five most beautiful theaters in the world. Tonight's would be her debut performance as the philharmonic's guest conductor. Andriy, through his connections with the Ministry of Culture, had secured her an invitation to conduct a benefit concert to support victims of the war. Sophia was wearing a black, full-length gown that did not conceal her pregnancy. Her hair was woven in a simple braid. She applied just enough makeup to cover the furrows in her brow. *Only the music can reveal who I truly am.*

When Sophia was appointed as the conductor of the St. Petersburg Philharmonic Orchestra, her mentor, Maestro Nikolai Barsky, told her:

"A conductor is the leader of an orchestra. A Maestra is so much more. To be a Maestra, you must be a medium through which the audience communicates with the spirits of their composers. Through your baton and the orchestral ritual of movements, gestures, and facial expressions you conjure an ecstatic union between the audience, the orchestra and the spirit of the composer. But to achieve this union, you must believe in them and they must believe in you. If not, you will be nothing more than an imposter." Sophia had achieved this pinnacle of ecstatic union while conducting the music of Rachmaninov, Prokofiev, and Shostakovich with the St. Petersburg Philharmonic Orchestra. Achieving this same union with a Ukrainian orchestra, Ukrainian composers, and a Ukrainian audience would require a superhuman effort. She hoped it was in her blood. She accepted the invitation to be a guest conductor of the Odesa Philharmonic Orchestra on the condition that the concert would be a charity fundraiser for children who were orphaned by the war, that she would have complete control over the musical program, and that she be allowed to tell her story in her own words.

Sophia walked up to the podium to muted applause. The majestic orchestra hall was only partly full. Rather than gowns and tuxedos as was the custom in St. Petersburg, the people in the audience wore wartime attire. The front rows, which were reserved for dignitaries, were mostly empty. The rest of the seats were filled with ordinary people – soldiers, widows, volunteers – who were seeking a respite from the war or wanted to know why Sophia Sergeivna Borodin, the conductor of the St. Petersburg Philharmonic Orchestra, would dare to face them in this time of war. As she stepped onto the podium, the musicians readied their instruments. Sophia saw Andriy sitting in the second row. He gave her a reassuring smile. She raised her baton.

She began the concert with Valentyn Silvestrov's *Evening Serenade from Silent Music*. She continued with Dmitry Bortniansky's *Overture to the Opera La Fête du Seigneur*; Reinhold Gi Glière's *Concerto for Harp and Orchestra*; Boris Lyatoshynsky's *Symphony No. 1*; and Maksym Berezovsky's *Symphony in C*. Sophia had conducted the works of individual Ukrainian composers before, but never as an entire program. As the orchestra followed her direction, she felt the music course through her veins. She felt the music resonate with the audience. The compositions spanned centuries and musical styles, yet came from a world that she could connect with and share. She was in her element, as Maestra, uniting the people with their musical heritage.

At the conclusion of Berezovsky's symphony she motioned for the orchestra to stand up for their accolades. She faced the audience and bowed. Before continuing with the finale, she spoke into the microphone.

"I wish to thank the Ministry of Culture, your music director, and the people of Odesa for giving me the honor of guest conducting your world-famous orchestra. I'm sure you're wondering why I, a Russian conductor, would have the audacity to stand before you, here, in the first opera house in Ukraine, when Russian missiles are raining down on your beautiful city.

"As a young girl I grew up in the Soviet embassy in Paris. I moved to St. Petersburg when my mother died, where I lived a life of privilege among the Russian elite. I studied music at the St. Petersburg Conservatory and advanced to first violin in the St. Petersburg Philharmonic Orchestra before being named as its conductor. I was raised believing that the west had lost its way, that the collapse of western civilization was imminent, and that Russia was chosen by God to bring enlightenment to a benighted world. I grew up believing that Russians and Ukrainians are one people, ignoring the facts that Kyiv was founded seven centuries before Moscow, that the Empress Catherine abolished the Cossack hetmanate and annexed Ukraine into the Russian empire, that Ukraine suffered through the "Red Terror" of the Bolsheviks and through Stalin's genocidal 'Holodomor,'" and that over the centuries, Moscow had tried over forty times to ban the Ukrainian language. I was told that Russia is the victim rather the aggressor and that Ukraine's attempts to free itself of this oppression, through the Orange Revolution and the Revolution of Dignity, were sponsored by the west rather than being the awakening of a nation. I know now that in Russia, reality is what the Kremlin wants it to be.

"The truth is that the Soviets robbed me of my identity. They made me believe that I was Russian. They murdered my mother and alienated me from my natural father. The Russians murdered my partner, Alex

Ivanovich, the father of my unborn child, and the bravest man I know. Sergei Borodin, the Soviet Ambassador to France and the man who raised me, was my stepfather. My real name is Sophia Levivna Veles. I am the daughter of the Ukrainian author, Lev Veles."

Murmurs of surprise reverberated through the audience.

"My father's love has opened my eyes. I see that Moscow is not the Third Rome, chosen by God to save Christianity – it is Gehenna, the destroyer and graveyard of nations. The Russians are imperialists who seek to erase our national identity, rewrite our history, and destroy our language and cultural heritage. I have witnessed the horror in Bucha with my own eyes. The human evil that threatens us is far worse than any supernatural evil. Ukraine is where the best in humanity confronts the worst in humanity. The challenge is difficult, and we are facing our own dark night of the soul. But the night is darkest before the dawn." She put her hands on her unborn baby. "I know that thanks to your bravery, my child will be born in an independent, democratic and European Ukraine. I finally know who *I* am, as you know who *you* are, and the world knows who *we* are. We are Ukrainians. Glory to Ukraine!"

"Glory to heroes!" the audience responded in unison.

Sophia raised her baton to command the orchestra. For the finale she chose to fulfill her promise to the Plast scouts and conduct Mykola Lysenko's *Overture to the Opera Taras Bulba*. Nikolai Gogol, the author of the novel *Taras Bulba*, was born in Ukraine, and like herself, had been assimilated into the Russian empire, yet wrote about the glory of his native Ukraine. The Ukrainian Armed Forces had sunk the Russian flagship "Moskva" and had recaptured Snake Island. The rousing Cossack march in *Taras Bulba* captured the jubilant spirit of the nation.

The audience rose to give her a standing ovation. A young girl in an embroidered blouse ran up on the stage to present her with a bouquet of roses. The thunderous applause drowned out the wail of air raid sirens and the shriek of a Kalibr missile as it streaked towards its target – until a Ukrainian S-300 missile intercepted it and sent it crashing into the Black Sea.

Acknowledgments

I want to thank my wife, Christine, for her love and support while I undertook the writing of *The Dark Night of the Soul*, a story about an author who embarks on a spiritual journey to "make it all cohere." Yuval Noah Harari described the spiritual journey as a lonely path that takes you in mysterious ways towards unknown destinations. In addition to the sacred texts, I was guided by the writings of Evelyn Underhill, Ken Wilber, Yuval Noah Harari, and Frank Wilczek among others. Their world views are voiced by the grotesquerie of characters that my protagonist, Lev Veles, encounters at Contessa Rivelli's masquerade ball during the height of the pandemic.

I want to thank Professor John Serio, my friend and colleague, for his editing of my manuscript. John is a Professor Emeritus of Humanities and Social Sciences at Clarkson University and the Honorary Editor of the *Wallace Stevens Journal*. *The Dark Night of the Soul* is my most ambitious, and challenging, novel. John appreciated what I was trying to achieve and helped me bring it to fruition.

Lev's spiritual guide is a Basilian monk, Father Stephan, who acknowledges that there are many paths to the Great Liberation, and the way of Christ works best for him. His character was inspired by my late friend and spiritual mentor, Father Myron Panchuk, who was a Basilian priest and a Jungian scholar. I miss his wisdom and guidance. Lev's spiritual journey follows the path of Christian mysticism. I am grateful to my friends, Father Taras Lonchyna and Father Andriy Onuferko, for helping me faithfully portray the sanctity and beauty of the Ukrainian Byzantine rite.

The Dark Night of the Soul is set in Venice, a dying city that views herself as immortal. I have been captivated by this glorious city in the sea ever since my youth and return to her as often as I can. As I wander through her maze of canals, *calli*, and *campi,* I imagine I encounter the ghosts of her past. Lev's spiritual journey takes place during forty days of Lent, from Carnival to Easter, a time of penitential preparation for resurrection. His journey begins in the enchanted forests of the Carpathians and takes him to the sacred and profane places of Venice, including the Golden Basilica, the haunted island of Poveglia, and the Devil's Bridge in Torcello.

I want to thank my family and friends who read the earlier versions of this novel and offered helpful edits and suggestions. They include Christine Charkewycz Dziuk, Isidre Compta, Tim Erickson, Livia Krzeminski, Vassyl Lonchyna, Pat Mayers, Ihor Poshyvailo, Andriy Ripecky, Damiano Rondelli, and Oleh Skubiak. I especially want to thank my mother, Natalia, who just turned one hundred and continues to read in English, Ukrainian, German, and Polish. She is both my fiercest critic and my greatest supporter.

The artwork of Mara on the front cover was created by Damian Kozbur, a Ukrainian-American artist, with the aim to illustrate the beauty and terror of a betrayed goddess who seeks her revenge on the world by keeping it in perpetual winter. The cover and interior layout were designed by Alan Pranke, who also designed the covers for my previous novels, *Caught in the Current* and *The Dark Night of the Soul.*

As I was writing this novel Russia invaded Ukraine, Americans stormed their capitol, and thousands of innocents were massacred in the Middle East. In my novel, the *Didko* – the devil – tells Lev, "We live in a world of perpetual violence, of eat or be eaten, of kill or be killed.

The things she wanted you to believe in – love, hope, and happiness – are illusions. They are as fleeting as your reflection in the water. The only thing that matters is power." We are sleepwalking into an Orwellian nightmare. Ukrainians are fighting for freedom and a just world order. I pray they will prevail, and we will wake up from our own dark night of the soul.

I dedicate this novel to my first grandchild, Maria Zoriana. You make my world cohere.

Also by Daniel Hryhorczuk

CAUGHT IN THE CURRENT

Caught in the Current takes the reader on a magical mystery tour of Eastern and Western Europe during the summer of 1970, a tumultuous period of free love, equal rights demonstrations, and Vietnam antiwar protests in America, but an equally revolutionary period in Alec's life. Raised in Chicago as Ukrainian, Alec is caught between identities – is he American or Ukrainian? His personal beliefs are pushed to the limit as he undertakes a risky mission to learn about political dissidents in Soviet-dominated Ukraine. Detained, interrogated, and finally deported from the Soviet Union, Alec seeks refuge in earthquake-ravaged Banja Luka where he begins to see the world from a different perspective. Questioning himself and his values, Alec finally finds his anchor in Stefi, his girlfriend from Chicago, who helps him discover his true identity.

MYTH AND MADNESS

During Ukraine's Revolution of Dignity in the winter of 2013-14, Dr. Natalka Slovyanka, a beautiful young psychiatrist from Donbas, tries to cure her mysterious patient of his "philosophical intoxication." Raised by a Molfar, Telesyk is a storyteller who hears voices in the wind. His mind drifts between the immuring reality of the *psikhushka* and an imaginary world inhabited by witches, nymphs and dragons. He engages the other patients in a fairy tale of the quest for a horse that eats burning embers and drinks fire, a myth that parallels Ukraine's search for its identity. Both patient and therapist embark on their own quests – Telesyk, to free himself from the prison of his mind and Natalka, to escape the dark secrets of her past. Natalka struggles to free him of his delusions until she discovers that his world is real, and that dragons are deceivers who disguise themselves in the world of men. As different as East and West, they realize that they must unite to slay the family of dragons that are threatening their existence. My novel blends magical realism with historical events on the Maidan to tell the modern day fairy tale of a nation's quest for its identity. *Myth and Madness* was translated into Ukrainian by Mr. Ihor Poshyvailo, the director of the Museum of the Revolution of Dignity and published by Clio Publishers in Kyiv (*Міф та Божевілля*, 2018, ISBN 978-617-7021-83-7). It was distributed to libraries throughout Ukraine and is part of the book collection of the Museum of the Revolution of Dignity. In 2023 *Міф та Божевілля* was banned in Russia and the occupied territories.

Amerikana

Amerikana is a political thriller about how Russia could influence American politics by infiltrating the religious heart of our country. Mark Rider, a journalism student, is searching for authentic America through his "Americana" blog. He's exploring the traditions, landmarks, and folklore that both unify and divide our multicultural nation. While on the Overseas Highway, a beautiful, Ukrainian runaway jumps into his Trans-Am. She shares an incredible story of being assaulted by an American Senator who is conspiring with a Russian oligarch to infiltrate and subvert American Evangelicalism. In their journey through the back roads of America's political, religious, and cultural landscape, they risk their lives to expose the conspiracy and uphold the rule of law over the rule of power.